Penelope Unbound

Dublin-born Mary Morrissy is the author of three previous novels, *Mother of Pearl*, *The Pretender* and *The Rising of Bella Casey*, and two collections of stories, *A Lazy Eye* and *Prosperity Drive*. Her short fiction has been anthologised widely and two of her novels have been nominated for the Dublin Literary Award. Her debut, *Mother of Pearl*, was shortlisted for the Whitbread Award and she has won a Hennessy Award and a Lannan Foundation Award for her fiction. A member of Aosdána, she is a journalist, a teacher of creative writing and a literary mentor. She blogs on art, fiction and history at marymorrissy.com.

Penelope Unbound

Mary Morrissy

BANSHEE

PRESS

First published 2023 by Banshee Press
www.bansheelit.com

Banshee Press gratefully acknowledges
the financial assistance of the Arts Council.

ISBN 978-1-8383126-8-8

Set in Palatino by Eimear Ryan
Cover design by Anna Morrison
Printed and bound in Great Britain by Clays Ltd, Elcograf S.p.A.

In memoriam:
Ursula Morrissy (1954–2019)
Charlie McCann (1952–2021)

And I thought, as I wiped my eyes on the corner of my apron:
This is an ancient gesture, authentic, antique,
In the very best tradition, classic, Greek;
Ulysses did this too.
But only as a gesture,—a gesture which implied
To the assembled throng that he was much too moved to speak.
He learned it from Penelope ...
Penelope, who really cried.

– 'An Ancient Gesture', Edna St. Vincent Millay

Encore

June 16, 1915

The woman who makes her way painfully to the high pew at one end of the vestibule of the Antient Concert Rooms is only barely in her thirties, but she's uncertain on her feet. She leans on a stick and her gait is staggered like a gondolier poling in a choppy lagoon. She is dressed seriously. A charcoal dress coat and three-quarters skirt with a faint stripe, a silky cowl-necked lilac blouse that seems to fight with the formal suit, a pair of black button boots. Her chestnut hair blooms under a purple cloche set low on her forehead like a cloud. A fabric flower embroiders the rim. She wears pigeon-coloured gloves, one on, one off.

To the side of the high-backed seat there's a marble fireplace with a vast mirror framed elaborately in gold, where she stops to touch her hair distractedly. But she sees only the birds and balls of the encrusted frame and, in the reflection behind her, the blue-badged stewards gathered in tight knots, murmuring among themselves. She folds herself down, inch by inch, onto the upright pew from where she will have an unrestricted view of the circular staircase that sweeps up to the circle.

3

The commissioner presumes she has come out from the performance for a breath of air; it can be stuffy in the theatre when it's a full house. Some of the lady patrons can get overcome – the music, you see, it makes them weak, or certain tenors do. What the liveried gentleman doesn't realize is that the woman hasn't been at the performance. She has only just arrived, and she has timed her arrival for the finale. She is here on a mission. An assignation, if you will, except the other party does not yet know she is here. It will be a surprise to him, although it could be said that he sought the encounter out, in a subterranean manner. Brought it upon himself, the woman in the charcoal suit would say.

When she has settled herself, she reminisces about the last time she was in the Concert Rooms. Eleven years ago. Imagine! For that performance, she was sitting in the front row and the tenor who's on stage tonight sang his heart out. For her, she believed, to her. That was when love was new and everything was just starting and she was proud, even in her green velveteen which had a couple of bald patches in the rear of the premises. Afterwards, they'd gone on to The Crowing Cock and she remembered how delighted he was with himself and how delighted she was in him.

A burst of applause from within brings her back. That's it, she thinks, that's the end, and her stomach does a fluttery heave. But no, there's an encore. She thinks she can make out the strains of 'The Lass of Aughrim', or is it just the memory of it trying to reach her across the years? He sang that very song the last time. She clears her throat of a strange catch. There's more clapping, extended this time, and much hallooing. The bouquets must surely have been thrown by now.

This is it, then.

The stewards scatter and take their positions. At first, it's just a trickle, the single attenders, lonely waders who want to fly off before the throng, then the spreading pool of the stalls ebbs by, all talk and snatched opinions, some lingering here, others congregating on the steps outside. Soldiers in khaki with their dolled-up girls, loud student types from the cheap seats. Then lastly the balcony crowd, they take their time. The woman scans them all. She's afraid she might miss him in this throng. But when the foyer clears, she feels only her singularity. Her nerves are ajangle. She will recognize him, won't she?

Ah Norah, for God's sake, it's like riding a bicycle, sure you couldn't forget. Wasn't he your heart once?

She can see the commissioner eyeing her doubtfully but she avoids his gaze. He probably thinks she has a crush on the tenor and is waiting for an autograph on her programme, though of course she has no programme. But the commissioner is not an observant man. Don't worry, she wants to sing out to him, I'm not setting up headquarters, I just have some unfinished business with the man of the moment.

She hopes there isn't a stage door. That way he could escape without ever having to face her. But no, he'll still be upstairs in the green room lapping up praise. Always did like to be admired.

Imagine that he ended up as a singer! After all his old guff about the writing. She remembers how he scribbled his way across Europe using the lid of their suitcase as a makeshift desk. That's how devoted he was. She smarts now at how often she berated him over it. Throw over that old writing business, she used to say, there's no money in it. Whereas music ... Seems like he finally took her advice and saw sense. But really, she only urged the stage on him because she never really understood what his writing was all about. Nothing happened in those stories of his. Remember the one about the sisters and the old priest who dies in the end and what about it? Or the little boy going to the bazaar who gets nothing because he's left it too late. Or the girl who draws back from going off to Buenos Aires with her beau at the last minute. For no good reason. Unlike herself, who did go off without a second thought. She remembers that he cogged little details from her for that story. The palpitations that girl had were the ones she herself would get after one of her uncle's beatings. She felt sure she recognized that old priest as well, a version of a curate she knew in the Presentation Convent in Galway.

He stole from her all the time, did Jim Joyce. He was a smash-and grab-merchant. Isn't that what he did to her in the heel of the hunt? Took what he wanted and vamoosed. And what's worse, didn't she let him?

Foolish girl that she was.

But not anymore.

She's tormented herself over the years with the thought that if she'd only waited another hour outside that blessed railway station, her life would have been very different. She'd have been living out foreign as he'd always promised. It would be her in the front row tonight throwing kisses in the air at him, her lawfully wedded ... but no, she stems that kind of idle speculation. Particularly here, particularly now. *He* left *her* in the lurch. She could have waited till Kingdom Come, he still wouldn't have appeared because he never meant to return to her.

And yet ... here he is now, eleven years on.

The commissioner is closing over the big double doors to the street, reaching up to shoot the bolts and looking over his shoulder as he does.

Closing up now, ladies and gents, he calls, out of habit probably, but he's looking directly at her. There is no one else. She can almost sense his narrowed eyes and imagine the calculations he's making about her. A streetwalker? An aggrieved wife? A woman with bad news. A woman who's owed. But she's immune to his sort. Jumped-up lockhard. He might be all gussied up in a gold-crusted black suit, but his moustache looks nicotiney and there'll be ochre stains on his fingers underneath those white gloves.

You can glare all you like, she thinks, *but this time I'm staying put till the bitter end.*

Mrs Smith

June 15, 1915

Mrs Smith?

Scrawn-thin Gertie Devenney's voice knifes its way
from the front hall into the well of the stairs, up three
flights to where Mrs Smith is standing at the bow window
on the top landing of Finn's Hotel. Below, the playing
fields of Trinity. The distant cricketers canter over and
back like wind-up soldiers – in this heat! – to little out-
bursts of ragged applause. From here the spectators are
tiny as children. George is among them although she can't
make him out. The porter at the back gate gives him the
nod and lets him pass; our youngest little scholar, he calls
George. She opens the window and leans out. To think that
this morning it was cloudy, even spat a bit. Now it has the
look of thunder. Thunder always reminds her ... Mother
of Moses, it's so blasted close that what she'd like to do is
to wrench open her high-necked blouse, loosen her stays,
let her hair down. But she doesn't. No, she remains stalled
by Gertie's call.

The girl is like a baba woken from a nap who wants to
be picked up immediately, but if you left her for a bit, well,
she might nod off again. Mrs Smith knows the routine. She

stealthily slides the window shut and goes back to dusting the decorative urns perched on flower stands that guard the guest lounge – three curlicued chairs crouched around a low table.

Mrs Smith!

She holds her breath and counts to ten, as if that will do any blessed good. Gertie will pursue her now that the solemn peace of the napping hour – *la penichella*: the word makes her smile secretly – has been disturbed. It is three o'clock on a hot, windless mid-week afternoon. The panes of the bow window, which bellies out over air, divide the view into high blue sky and green coiny leaves. Nine portions of summer.

The dusting is not her job, of course, it's Gertie's, but Mrs Smith has never lost the habit of stowing about her person a spare shammy so she can chase the fine city dust that settles on everything when the front door is thrown open, as it is now, to cool the blessed place down. Gertie hasn't called again and she wonders if her trick of waiting has worked. But even so, it's no earthly good – the peace has been shattered now like the breaking of a vase, the pieces lying there, rebuking you with their ruin. Still, she makes no move and is staring out the windows when Gertie, who's taken the stairs two at a time, arrives on the landing to a sudden halt, hair escaping from her mob cap and her breath coming out in oniony gasps. What did the child have for dinner?

Oh Mrs Smith. Softer now, surprised by her stillness. Beg your pardon, Ma'am.

What is it, Gertie? Cross to be interrupted from her *referee*, that's what Hector used to call it. He liked to use such words, being able to switch from one lingo to another mid-stream.

9

There's a gentleman ... Gertie begins, but being almost out of puff, she stops there. Isn't there always? A gentleman who's lost his key, a gentleman who wants his shoes polished, or wants an early call, or would like the kitchen to rustle something up for him after hours because he's come in from O'Neill's or Davy Byrne's three sheets to the wind and has a mind for a sandwich, white bread if you please, and ham and a dollop of mustard if you have it, to line the bag ...

Yes, Gertie, and it comes out snappish and Mrs Smith realizes it's the mythical gentleman she's irritated with.

There's a gentleman, Gertie repeats.

Yes, you said that. Now it's Gertie she's irritated with. What about him?

There's a gentleman at the desk, Gertie manages to get out and Mrs Smith thinks Lord God, will she go back to the beginning every time she adds a new bit to the story.

Yes ... and?

And he wants to see the maids' quarters.

Well, now, that's a new one. There was once in the past, long before Gertie's time, a gentleman – if you could call him that – who was found in the maids' quarters with a girl from Leitrim who was trying to fend him off while her two companions jittered and screamed, all of a dither at the impropriety of it all. But that was in the wee small hours, not in broad daylight and the girl in question – Martha, Martha, Martha what? Cohen? Conmee? Coleman? Began with a C anyway – had invited the self-same gent upstairs to show him where she slept, she said, I ask your holy pardon. To show him what? The crown jewels, more like. That's what he was expecting, anyway, and sure aren't they all only after the one thing. But no, this is something else. This gent is looking for permission!

There's no one up in the maids' quarters at the moment, Mrs Smith knows. She keeps track. Two on duty and two on their afternoon off, and on a fine sunny day like this, they won't be stretched on their beds. So what exactly would a gentleman be doing up there? Is he some class of inspector?

And did he say why he wanted to see the maids' rooms?

Suddenly, maybe because she's regained her breath, Gertie turns eloquent.

Oh yes, Missus, he says he used to know a maid here long 'go, stepped out with her, I believe, and he wants to see it for old times' sake, she parrots – word for word, it sounds like.

The dirty article! And what would he be doing if he was granted entry, sniffing the sheets, is it?

And where is this gentleman now?

I left him below, Missus.

Below is right.

Very well, Gertie, you go on down and tell him I will be with him presently.

The girl turns away, then back again.

Oh and Missus, Gertie says, he's a foreign gentleman.

Mrs Smith feels a heart-lurch. It couldn't be Hector, could it? Foreign?

But then what would Hector be doing looking for the maids' quarters? Wouldn't he just ask for her direct? The girl has obviously got the wrong end of the stick.

Gertie, fix yourself up there, Mrs Smith says, pointing to the girl's mob cap perched on her flaming hair like a mushroom, and then to her apron. She tries to calm her frizz, tugs at her bodice and apron to get them straight but sure she's crooked herself, one eye smaller than the other, one leg shorter. And still she stands there, mouth open like a codfish, if a codfish had teeth.

Well? What are you waiting for?

Gertie jumps to attention. She turns and scurries downstairs, intent on her mission, muttering to herself the message she's been given so she won't forget it. *Mrs Smith will be with you presently.* She recalls the gossip in the maids' room that once, oh years ago now, Mrs Smith was a chambermaid here before she was married out foreign, or was it England, and made a widow. She must have been fierce young when she was made a widow, the other girls said, as if they doubted the story. They counted up on their fingers. And poor little Georgie, left without a dada! But the story was that's how Missus came to be chief cook and bottle washer in Finn's, because she was left a small fortune when her husband died.

Could he be the gent down below? But if Mrs Smith's a widow, sure Mister Smith has to be dead, unless the man in the hall is a ghost. But he looked real enough with his straw hat and his white suit and spectacles flashing in the sun that made his eyes blind.

A floor above, Mrs Smith is peering into the glass and remembering those evenings in the maids' rooms, the cramped and lonely boredom of girls cooped up together, keyed up with love and the promise of it, pawing letters with *DV*s and *must close*s. Sighing, or turning their faces to the wall for tears. What would a stranger be up to in there? Up to no good, that's what. She will go down now directly, give him a flea in his ear and send him packing.

But the memories of those times hold her, there on the landing, there in the ticking afternoon, and transport her to a time when she was like Gertie Devenney. Never as innocent, mind you, or as useless, and the cut of her! What ails her? Is it love? Could anyone love Gertie Devenney? *Now Norah*, she chastises herself, *don't mock the afflicted*, as she thinks of Gertie's lame leg. Or is she homesick, is that it? Is she pining for her mammy? Thrown out of the nest too soon. What is she, sixteen? When Norah was that age she couldn't wait to be shut of them all, but of her Uncle Tommy in particular with his wagging finger. No, she didn't miss them, well, maybe Pappie, poor banished Pappie. It's half a lifetime since she fled Galway without saying goodbye to any of them and she hasn't darkened their door since. They have no idea where she is, not even that she's back in Dublin a good seven years now, and she's going to keep it that way. Though she wouldn't half mind boasting to Uncle Tommy who used to warn she'd end up on the street the way she was behaving. The wildness in her then, he couldn't be dealing with it. End of his tether, he'd say, spittle flying and reaching for the stick. She wasn't having any more of it, being punished for what came natural. Uncle Tommy who knew nothing about girls but how to beat them. Did he give that poor Bedelia, the creature he married, the same treatment? Probably.

But lookit, she can't have grief for everyone.

She firms her own hair, remembering Gertie's disarray, and fixes herself with the glare that sends the likes of Gertie scurrying. Oh yes, she has sharpened it over the years, whittled it into a weapon; how else would she command respect, with all the tittle-tattle that she was only where she was because she came into money? And it's why, when she halts on the landing, she does so deliberately, not to savour the broken peace, but to keep the gentleman waiting. Mrs Smith has spent so much of her life waiting – on instructions, on tables, on men – that now, as a matter of course, she does it unto others. Let him wait, she thinks, whoever the hell he is.

For whoever it is down there, it's not Hector.

It is seven years since she saw him – imagine! – seven years since she returned from England, broken, broken-hearted, and there has been no word from him. And she hasn't been expecting one. That was the arrangement. When she took over Finn's, the guests used to be sniffing out the possibility of a husband. Himself they'd say, where's Himself? In the early days she would fob them off, saying yes, yes, there was a Mister Smith – an Englishman they'd presume. Who would dream that Mister Smith was a class of Eyetalian? If they persisted, she'd say: I'm a widow. And then they would *oh* and *ah* and *I beg your pardon* and *I'm sorry for your trouble*, while not quite believing. Maybe she didn't look the part? She wasn't tragic enough, not in the habit of weeping or falling down. (Except that once …) Or maybe they expected her to be gamey, scheming to find someone else? And she wasn't that neither. Hector had made a false widow out of her.

Sometimes – even still – she tries to picture the distance between them. First get over the Irish Sea. Rough crossing, was it? Green about the gills. Blur of train windows, string of sooty towns and belching chimneys and then another boat, clickety-clackety of locomotive, prettier now, lakes like mirrors, rocky mountains caped with snow, clock towers and church steeples, miles of fields in drills like hair neatly parted, and rusty houses with wavy roof tiles like a permanent, and finally pulling in to that wretched station in Trieste with the dusty piazza out front, where it all came to an end, and started too. Take the tram next, creaking up the hill, *I think I can I think I can*, towards the villa where Hector is. Out on the verandah, most likely, under the purple glare of the wisteria, smoking like his life depended on it. He's still there. Not dead. She'd know that, she'd sense it, somehow.

Out of the blue she thinks of Cosgrave. So-called pal of Jim Joyce, the other fella in her life, the one she doesn't care to remember if she can possibly avoid it. Cosgrave had been the first one to discover she was back in Dublin. She'd only been home a month when he walked into the bar, by chance, or so he said, though she didn't believe that for one blessed minute. She'd been steaming past the open doorway to the bar, a block of starched sheets resting in the crook of her elbow, when she saw him out of the corner of her eye, waiting to be served, a gentleman, hands thrust into his pockets. All she'd got was an impression, then something niggled at her and she reversed. It *was* him, damn and blast, and just as she was deciding to let on that she hadn't seen him he let a roar out of him.

Nora Barnacle, as I live and breathe!

Shout louder, why don't you, the halfpenny seats didn't hear you.

She squeezed down the narrow passageway between the back hallway and the bar so that she was on the serving side. Hasn't he got stout and look at the ruddy cheeks on him! That's a toper's face. Jim used to say Cosgrave was as vain as Nero, even though they were pals. She didn't understand how his crowd went about like bosom buddies and then sniped about one another behind their backs. Worse than women!

Vinny, she said, resigned.

There was only a smattering of customers, so Peggy Douce on the floor, and Mister Golding behind the bar, were idle – and all ears. When she was beyond in England, where no one knew her from Eve, she used to long to be recognized, to be saluted even. But back home it was vicky-versa. She kept on bracing herself for the day she'd be pointed out, even though no one here knew her secret, sure how could they?

It's Mrs Smith to you, she said sternly, for Mister Golding's benefit more than anything else. He stood watching all of this, his clothy paw stuck in a pint glass. She had to hold her nerve and her authority.

You didn't waste any time! Cosgrave said loudly, gleeful. He rubbed his hands together. A missus, what?

She lifted the serving latch and steered him over to a corner. She could feel the little throb of excitement from him as if he was closing in on his prey. They sat and she set down the sheets between them. Peggy came rushing over with a tray held to her bosom like a trophy.

Missus Smith, she said and dipped a bit. *Let Cosgrave hear that and take notice.*

I'll have a pint with a whisky chaser, and you, Nora?

She shook her head and eyed Peggy meaningfully. Peggy was smart enough to get the message.

Let me look at you.

Cosgrave grabbed her at the top of her arms and wheeled her towards him.

Vincent, she hissed.

He recoiled.

What's eating you? He looked down at the sheets and back at her. And when did I become Vincent?

Vinny, she began, but that sounded wrong too.

And Mister Smith? Cosgrave asked, snide as you like. His eyes were bleary. Was he jarred already? At three in the afternoon?

Dead, she said shortly.

She concentrated on Mister Golding easing the porter out of the tap and letting it settle. Clouds swirling in the glass.

Too bad, Cosgrave said, my condolences. Young to be taken though. What carried him off?

She ignored that, the less said the better. Peggy returned, holding Cosgrave's pint with two hands. She steered it carefully between them on the little marble table. Luckily, she'd retreated when Cosgrave fired his next salvo.

Heard you ran off with a foreign gent when ye got to Trieste, that's the story I heard.

So that's what he told people.

Wouldn't blame you if you did, Cosgrave said, who'd suffer that long string of misery for long?

He lifted the glass and sucked at it. She watched the black tide go down. He smacked his lips together and *aahed* with satisfaction. Then slowly he licked the foamy residue with a cat swipe of his tongue.

She'd thought of telling him how she waited for Jim, ten whole hours outside the railway station in Trieste, like a fool, the darkness falling and she weak from the hunger, and still no sign of him. And not a farthing on her. Abandoned.

And as if she'd broadcast her catalogue of woes out loud, Cosgrave said, Jim deserved all he got.

Another noisy swallow of porter.

I haven't heard from him in years, mind you. Don't know what I did wrong.

I know that feeling.

He fell out with all of us – Gogarty, Byrne. Used always be writing but that stopped too after …

After me, Norah supposed, but she wouldn't inquire.

I'd say he's married by now, Cosgrave said.

She felt the jab, as she was meant to.

Not that I know anything, he said, and raised his hands in surrender. And I don't pay attention to rumours.

What rumours?

He was needling her. She put on her stony face. He took another greedy slug of the porter.

No crime in moving on, isn't that so?

And there was the barb. They were like old biddies, Jim's crowd. All malice and gossip, always trying to best one another. She tried to distract him.

Are you a doctor yet, Vincent?

All those fellas wanted to be doctors. Even Jim tried his hand at it though she couldn't have imagined him as Doctor Joyce. He wasn't good with blood unless it was proof of purity.

Still plugging away, he said, smiling through his porter moustache. Cosgrave, the eternal student, that's what Jim called him. Thinking of heading off to London myself. Sure, all the old crowd have moved on.

She didn't want to hear about the old crowd.

What time do you get off, Nora?

So, she thought, that's what this little visitation was in aid of. If he only knew, the *amadán*. She wouldn't cross the street for one of them now. When she didn't answer, he pressed on.

And tell us, do you still live in?

She couldn't bear his smarmy tone. Tuppence-halfpenny looking down at tuppence.

Yes, she said. I'm the owner.

Get away with you! he said.

It's true.

Well, I'll be damned!

For the first time she heard admiration, from one who'd called her a streetwalker when she'd broken it off with him. Happened right here, but outside on the street.

You're nothing but a tease, he'd said. Rich coming from him. He'd only courted her to have one up on Jim, for he hadn't much interest in the other thing. And she'd made up her mind about Jim by then.

I'm two-timing no one, she'd told him. Because you and me are finished!

And she'd flounced inside and shut the door firmly behind her so that he wouldn't follow.

Heavens, Miss Barnacle, Miss Fitzgerald had said. You nearly took the door off its hinges. Are there no doors where you come from?

Uppity bitch.

She'd lost two nights off over that little episode. Spent them cleaning the brasses. She'd been so furious, she'd spat and rubbed with a fiery passion and Miss Fitzgerald had said wasn't it a pity she didn't bang the door more often for the brasses were certainly the better for it.

But what is she doing going over this ancient history? She's not going to squander a minute more on Vincent Cosgrave, Esquire.

You've landed on your feet here, Nora, he was saying, whistling softly. Nora Barn– he began. Then corrected himself. Nora Smith, I should say, proprietress!

Made her sound like a madam.

Did he leave the place to you in his will? Mister Smith?

Talk of money made her queasy.

That's none of your business, Vincent Cosgrave. She gathered the sheets up again in a bundle in her arms and rose. I should be getting back to work.

Ah don't go, Nora, sure we're just getting started, he said, and when she started to walk away he raised his voice.

I hear Jim went off to the quare place after you broke his heart.

What quare place, she wondered, but she wouldn't turn around. Wouldn't give him the satisfaction. Talk for Cosgrave was like poking a jellyfish with a stick. He wanted something back even if it was only a sting.

Said he searched for you for days, Cosgrave went on, but you'd vanished into thin air.

She couldn't leave that pass.

I went nowhere. He's the one who did the disappearing trick.

That's not what I heard.

So if you already know the story, what do you need to hear it from me for?

Arra, Nora, don't be like that.

She sailed past Mister Golding, wanting to put distance between herself and Cosgrave.

Don't serve that gentleman another, she muttered in passing.

Ah Nora, Cosgrave called after her.

She swept out into the hallway. Lurking dampness greeted her, disguised with strong Gumption, a draught creeping under the footleaf of the front door, cold as the grave. She thought fleetingly of Sonny Bodkin and the graveyard in Rahoon, and she quenched the thought immediately. She hurried to the back office to get a hold of herself. It was only when she shut the door and turned the key that she could breathe and with it came tears. She allowed herself a quick whinge but she couldn't have the staff see her dissolving, if she was going to hold her head up here. Or have the name Barnacle bandied about, as Cosgrave had done.

The day the hotel had changed hands she was terrified that old Mister Finn, the boss in her day, would recognize her even if she was going by a different name. But the old codger hadn't even remembered her. Well, why would he? She'd been just a chambermaid.

Mrs Smith? he'd said, extending his hand.

She hadn't wanted to touch it. Sweaty balls, that's what the girls used to call him, always rearranging himself. That day she'd kept her gloves on deliberate and nodded at him.

Welcome! he'd said, gazing at her with his hand still hanging. Then he'd tugged the tails of his vest instead.

The staff had been lined up behind him like he was the sergeant-at-arms and she was the queen inspecting the troops. He'd led her past them one by one and on instruction they dipped the knee. Until they'd reached the end of the line and there she was, Miss Bloody Fitzgerald.

Shouldn't that be welcome back? her ladyship had said.

Old Mister Finn had got flustered.

You know this lady? She'd loved that, *this lady*.

Oh yes, we do, Miss Fitzgerald had said. Miss Barnacle used to work here as a maid.

Old Mister Finn had peered at her suspiciously as if she'd swindled him.

Mrs Smith …? he queried with a little quaver in his voice.

Too late, she'd thought, you have my money and the deal's done. She turned from him to Miss Fitzgerald. She'd got thinner, sharper, and there were spindles of grey in her hair. *Are there no doors where you come from, Miss Barnacle?*

I'm afraid, Miss Fitzgerald, we won't be needing a
manageress under the new arrangement. I'll be taking
over front of house.

Miss Fitzgerald's chin wobbled. The maids looked on
askance.

Revenge is mine, says the Lord.

She was Mrs Norah Smith now – that's how she'd
signed the contracts of sale, with the H back in her name
that Jim Joyce had made her drop. She was Norah, after
Hanorah, her grand-aunt. And she wasn't going to let
anyone from the past put her down.

After Cosgrave, she was afraid there'd be a parade of
Jim's friends coming to look her over. That was how they
carried on – as if you were only gagging to be taken in
hand by them. But there had only been one more. Gogarty. He'd come on Vinny's bidding, she was pretty sure.
He'd sloped into the dining room a week or two later, thin
lips clamped around a pipe. He had the face of a horse, all
jaw, a widow's peak, a bulby eye. He'd settled himself at
a table and called for her after ordering the roast beef. Her
heart had sunk when Gertie had come with the message –
a gentleman looking for you. Vinny again, she'd thought,
and she'd been relieved when she peered through the
milky glass of the dining room door and saw that no, this
time it was not him. At least she'd never stepped out with
Gogarty. He'd have found her too common. His type went
straight to Monto for their jollies.

Mrs Smith, he'd said, all polite – he'd done his
homework.

That's right, she'd said, who's asking? Though she
knew full well.

Friend of Joyce's.

No friend of mine, then.

Gogarty had a sharp tongue, Jim had always said, and the kind of humour that'd tear strips off you. Jim had liked that sort of thing, word-fencing. Those boys were always at it. This specimen had introduced Jim to the drink. Well, he probably hadn't taken much persuading, wasn't it in his blood with that father of his who'd drink porter from a sore heel?

Owes me money, Gogarty had said then, and laughed and hitched up his pressed trews, revealing a polished tawny brogue.

Don't look at me, she'd said.

Yes, so I heard, you ditched him. Got some letters from him from that wretched place ...

What wretched place?

Fee-um-ay, Gogarty had intoned. Reduced to teaching English to naval cadets. He's worth more than that.

And that's my fault, is it?

While you play the Merry Widow, he'd continued.

Nothing merry about me. She'd glowered at him.

You're looking better than you used to, you've filled out.

She couldn't remember having met him but she'd probably been pointed out.

Suits you, he'd added.

She'd found herself blushing despite herself. Was she showing? How could he have known from just looking?

I don't remember calling for a doctor, she'd said.

You wouldn't have fattened if you'd stayed with Joyce, that's for sure. He's still living off the clippings of tin, last I heard that is. Hope you're satisfied.

He left *me*, she'd said, do none of ye understand that?

Patsy had brushed by her then with a dinner of roast beef and champ and had landed the plate down in front of him unceremoniously. The girl had no finesse, but for once Norah had been glad of it.

None of my concern, my dear woman, Gogarty had said, ignoring the steaming plate, as if he'd come to view a nag and wasn't buying. He'd risen from the table.

Your dinner, Sir, Patsy had begun.

I find I've lost my appetite suddenly, he'd said, fixing Norah with a glare. The way I see it, someone has done very well for herself.

He'd sauntered out then without paying, whacking his cane against the furniture, shouting *tarrah* in his wake. She'd hurried out after him into the hall but he was gone. She'd leaned on the desk, head cradled her arms, and that's where Nellie Longworth found her.

Is everything alright? she'd asked, placing a consoling hand between Norah's shoulder blades. Nellie had guessed her secret but wasn't letting on.

I'm raging, she'd wanted to shout.

Perhaps, Nellie had said, you should lie down. Meant kindly.

But Norah wasn't lying down for anyone.

Gogarty didn't return. Nor did Cosgrave, thank God. If they had, she'd have been ready for them. She wasn't an exhibit in a museum, was she? That's all she was to their likes. The girl who had thrown over Jimmy Joyce. The girl who'd banished him to Fuming, was it? Fuming is right! She'd tried finding it on a map. Borrowed Mister McCarthy's atlas (he'd bore you stiff pointing out every opera house he ever sang in, if you let him) but there was no sign of it. But sure, she didn't even know where to look. What good were maps, anyway? They couldn't find people that were lost to you, could they?

The Joyces hadn't darkened her door either. Probably delighted she hadn't ended up hitched to their precious scholar. She knew for a fact that Stannie, that snotty brother of his, had always been against her even though he'd never even met her.

Where are the Joyces now, she wonders idly. Still moving from pillar to post, one step ahead of the bailiffs. That father was a dead loss, the way he drank … Bad cess to them all. She won't be shedding salt tears over any of them. Especially not Jim. Not after all these years. She shakes off the dander of those days, like a dog with a sneeze. She straightens the doily under the asparagus fern on the low table, swishes her shammy around the urn, then stands back to admire her handiwork. Now she should really go down and deal with this stranger or Gertie will be hollering up at her again …

The sun suddenly goes in and the bright landing melts into gloom around her. Her skirt clinks against her thigh. She always asks the dressmaker to lengthen the pockets. Daughter of a seamstress, she knows all their little tricks, though shame on her, she can barely thread a needle herself. With the long pockets she can keep the master keys about her person as she travels through the house, even though they leave a scrolled imprint on the fabric. On a whim she goes to the street-side of the landing where a small door is built into the wainscot like a kiddies' riddle. Only the small knob gives it away.

When she was a maid here, she used to feel as if she were being walled up when she pulled the door behind her. Maids must learn to fade into the background even when present, she can still hear Miss Fitzgerald say, *Did you ever!* She pulls the door open now, deliberately leaving it ajar and starts climbing the narrow attic stairs. They

creak just as they used to. This part of the house seems
fragile, as if a good wind might blow it away. On the
return, a rectangle of blue skylight throws a twin of light
on the dark wall. She climbs another flight and reaches a
hanky-sized landing, with two doors off it, cheek by jowl.
She raps on the door to her right and when she gets no
reply she fishes out the master key and turns it in the lock.
When she opens the door there's a little squeal of protest
but it's only an unoiled hinge, not a maid in the throes.

She steps into the middle of the room. It's not much
changed since her time – two double beds and a single
pushed under the dormer. Five lives crushed in here. The
view is the same too. A jumble of roof slates, a pair of
cracked chimney pots and the stutter of old leaves in the
lead valleys. The room's half in disarray. One of the big
beds is unmade, sheets thrown back in a hurry to show
the hollow of the mattresses still bowled with the shape of
the girl who has slept there. On the other, which is neatly
made up, sits a straw hat with a ribbon. A pair of abandoned shoes stand splayed in front of the bed under the
window – which will always be Kat Bolger's to her – and
a suitcase has been hurriedly pulled out from underneath,
its almost-closed lid chewing the frill of a pair of bloomers. Is this what the foreign gent was after – a glimpse of a
girl's underthings carelessly on display?

An image of Kat Bolger stands before her in her shift,
stretching and yawning, indolent as a cat. A right strap,
if truth be told, who did the dirty thing on herself under
the covers of this same iron bed, if Norah is not mistaken.
With her and Celia Canty in the room! No shame, that one.
After lights out she would start, like she was rocking a
baba to sleep, the bed springs whining, but it was only
herself she was at. The next morning the first words out

of Kat's mouth were that she couldn't wait until Saturday when she'd see her sweetheart Eddie.

So you didn't bother to wait, Celia said, quick as a flash.

But Kat didn't bat an eyelid. She fixed her cloth tiara, lifted her po and paraded out of the room.

Sweetheart me eye, Norah muttered to Celia as they served breakfast. I hope she has a bath before she sees him else Eddie won't know where those fingers have been.

Norah! Celia said, all shocked, but it wasn't anything she wasn't thinking herself.

Standing here, Norah finds herself smarting at the memory, not of Kat but of herself. How much bolder she was then and gabby with it. She remembers Jim getting a bit het up when she told the story about Kat, but he still took notes. He always loved anything lewd.

She turns to leave the room.

Is that where he is now, she wonders. In the Fuming place? And who's he with? No fear of him being a bachelor. Wouldn't he need a girl's skirts to shield him from the thunder?

He was afraid of the clap, he told her.

Damn right!

She feels guilty but lookit, she isn't betraying him by just thinking it. And didn't he do worse to her? Left her, when he knew that was the very thing she was most afraid of.

When they'd started stepping out together, she hadn't told Celia or Kat about him, for they'd only madden you with the third degree. Where's he from, has he a job, did he drop the hand? Jim always thought that girls talked about that class of thing all the time, even liked the idea that they might. But she'd always been close about love. So she told them nothing about being accosted by Jim at the corner of Kildare Street and Nassau Street and then, bold as brass, him asking her out. Or of how and why she'd said yes. Yes, for the company, yes for a place to go on her night off, yes for the loneliness.

But when his letters started coming, she had to come clean. There was no place to hide anything in that room, and they'd only read it behind your back anyways. She loved to get those letters, the dear Noras. He'd dropped her H from the start. Said that way she was like a heroine in a Swedish play she'd never heard of. Ibsen, was it? He was forever name-dropping.

Suddenly the room feels cramped and small. She doesn't want to revisit those times. No earthly use in that.

Through the attic window the sky rages blue and the trapped sun on the return makes her feel like a prisoner. She steps out of the maids' stairs and closes the door, making sure she can hear the sharp click of the bolt.

The top landing is as she left it. It's the least frequented of the floors. It's where she puts the regulars. Just now there's Mister Grey and Mister Ryder and Mister Duthie. She has a soft spot for Mister Duthie, him being a paint agent and all. They're all off out about their business, as she should be, instead of ghosting around the landings. On summer afternoons like this, the house seems to want to lock her up. That makes her sound dotty. But when she stands in a deserted Finn's with everyone out, the same lonesome feeling creeps over her like the nights alone in Charlton when Hector didn't come home. The same, empty useless feeling, a hollow where her heart once was. But lookit, those days are gone. She has nobody's pleasure to attend to now, except the foreign gent still waiting on her answer, three floors below. She heads for the stairs.

*

The Lakes of Killarney is crooked. Always skew-ways. Did
it get caught in Gertie's tailwind? She fixes the painting,
wrong place for it, too dark here entirely in the well of
the stair, but the sun's out again and catching the silvery
moonpath on the waters so just now it's at its best. Never
been to Killarney herself, they say it's only beautiful but
sure who would she go with? Need a suitor for that sort of
outing and there hasn't been a suitor in a long time.

The last little flutter was for Francesco Novak. Pro-
prietor of the Volta Cinema, Mary Street. The other man
from Trieste, the one who came to her like a consolation
prize for Hector and brought with him the whiff of a city
she was half-homesick for. Frank was keen, she could tell
by the way he looked at her and all they had were looks
and grips. He was the only one who might have popped
the question. She used to imagine making a triumphant
return to Trieste as Mrs Novak, if only to give Hector's
Livia a run for her money, but the little daydream couldn't
hold. She'd have come off second best in any duel with
Livia, and the idea of it would have ruined poor Hector.
And there was the matter of George ... But what was she
getting all wistful about? After Hector, she didn't need to
marry anyone. Not for money, anyway.

Frank had come to the hotel with a snotty Dublin gent,
tricked out in a dicky bow and a frock coat with velvet
lapels. Mister Delacour, he said he was. Looked like he
was hardly out of short trousers, a beanpole, sickly looking, a fella that might have come from the San, he had that
gatch about him. She remembered him introducing Frank
at the reception.

*May I present the manager of our proud new venture, the
Volta Electric Theatre on Mary Street ...*

Before she even knew where he was from, she was back in the Cinema Americano in Trieste on the piazza with the big bank that looked like the GPO. She and Juicy had gone there once or twice but sure it was a dead loss, she couldn't understand a thing.

The first picture house in Dublin, Mister Delacour was declaiming like an MC, hollering about his coming attractions.

Then he'd leaned over the reception desk, coming over all confidential.

He's from abroad, just so youse know.

Is that so? Whereabouts? she'd said as she began to scribe his name in the ledger under Delacour's instruction.

You wouldn't have heard of it, Delacour said, Trieste.

The pen was digging into the page and creating a pooling blot. She took a deep breath.

As a matter of fact, she said – *careful, Norah now, careful, don't get yourself into hot water.* I lived there myself at one time.

Only then did she raise her eyes and what greeted her was Delacour's dumbfounded expression, was he a bit of a *cabóg*? Then Frank's gentle, inquisitive face, and then his smell. It wafted from his person, tobacco plumes, Sweet Aftony. Though it wasn't the lovely Austrian brand with the crown on the box that Hector used to smoke.

Sono una ragazza irlandese, she enunciated carefully.

And before she had it out, Frank had taken her hand and kissed it. He was a dainty man, neat as a small package, a fine head of foxy hair, a pin-striped farting jacket, starched wings. Lovely hands, swear he had the nails manicured.

Behind him, Mister Delacour threw his eyes to heaven as if to say – these foreigners! Just as well he hadn't gone native altogether and kissed her on both cheeks, or else Mister Delacour would have had a fit.

You're very welcome, Mister Novak, she said. *Benvenuto*.

Afterwards, she'd realized how disappointed Frank must have been since hello and goodbye, and a few words for sewing and laundry, was the height of what she knew, especially when they sat in the felty darkness of the Volta – talk about a busman's holiday! – and watched those foreign flicks, the string quartet sawing away, and he thought she'd understand the writing underneath.

If only you had the writing underneath in real life, she'd thought, wouldn't it save a lot of confusion?

She'd put Mister Novak in Room 11 on the second landing. The door is closed now. Unoccupied. She keeps a notion in her head at all times of occupation, a map of the house, or a jigsaw more like. She fishes out her master key and goes in. She'll check the bed and see if it's been properly made. Come the weekend there'll be a new guest in here and it's been vacant for a week or more and it gets stale in those rooms without a window being cracked in between, particularly in the summer. And yes, she was right, there *is* a smell, not of bad breath or old socks, but of vacancy, dead air. Emptiness has its own perfume. She runs her finger along the wainscot for dust. She wasn't trained under Miss Elizabeth Fitzgerald for nothing. Behind her, she imagines Frank Novak standing – oh nothing like that ever happened, no! She had a position to keep up. Nothing much had happened with Frank. How could it with so few words?

Anyway her heart hadn't been in it. She and Frank sat on the hard kitchen chairs of the Volta and held hands in the darkness, very chaste altogether. They saw that film about the Paris orphans and another one about the

Devil Crab. But Frank was always on duty. He would have to leave his seat when the reels broke and go up to the projectionist's box while all around her the audience got restless. He might have had a wife at home for all she knew and she didn't trouble herself to ask. He wouldn't have understood what she was getting at, and it would have ended up a pantomime, pointing at fingers and rings – nothing on his by the way. But that meant nothing. Hector never wore a ring neither, said it strangulated him.

She'd never mentioned George to Frank. In case the word would get back to Trieste. She didn't want Hector to hear of it. The news of a son. It'd break his heart, a son he'd never know. Better to leave him in ignorance. So she'd passed George off as Nellie's.

She smarts at that deception now. She's not ashamed of much but she is of that.

She and Frank didn't amount to much in the end. They strolled together in the Green, him plabbering in his lingo – she liked to hear it for it reminded her of Hector – and she in hers. They had tea and plain bread in the DBC on Dame Street, and took the tram to Howth, but there wasn't much else to be doing if you weren't doing the other thing and Frank's nights were always taken up. And he seemed in no hurry to make a move. Maybe he knew she wasn't that pushed. Or maybe he knew about George all along and wasn't prepared to take on some other fella's son. Whatever the reason, the romance, if you could call it that, petered out. And as it happened, the Volta only lasted kissing time in the end and Frank hightailed it back to Trieste. She could have told him – no one in Dublin will put up with just the pictures, they'll need to know what the people are saying to one another.

She hauls up the window – the *thwock* of the ball on the bat reaches her and the day invades. She hurries out of the room and shuts the door firmly. As she does, the second column of the eleven on the door comes loose, swinging like a pendulum and hangs there upside down. Damn it, she'll need Mister Hull to take a look at that.

Suddenly there's a blast of music. It's 'Marble Halls'. Mister McCarthy, Room 15. The others come and go but Bartle McCarthy's a fixture. There he is now, stuck inside on this glorious day of Our Lord, and he's just dropped the needle on his gramophone. Awful dust-catcher, that yoke, particularly the horn like an elephant's ear. Often he has to be asked to turn it down, he has trouble sleeping, even with the cup of Fry's he wheedles out of Bridgie when he comes in with a few jars. That's when the trouble starts. Thinks he's back in the opera, standing in front of the gramophone singing along to the music and conducting the air while he's at it. Poor cratur, she thinks, he's only lonesome, that's all, only his memories to keep him going now that his voice is gone to a froggy croak.

Why don't you listen with Bartle, he's always saying to the chambermaids, patting the candlewick bed cover, this is the great McCormack! He makes a small hen-hole of his mouth and he screws up his face, all tortured with expression and mimes his way through whole operas until the needle hits the rim of the shellac and makes the sounds of the sea.

The girls just want to get in and out of the room as quick as they can and some of them are afraid he'll get fresh but sure he's no interest in that direction at all. He's harmless, she tells them, he wouldn't lay a hand, but these young ones think everyone's after them. Or else they're milk-fed

and afraid of every man's shadow. In her day, you'd give
a fella a puck if you didn't want his attentions. 'Marble
Halls' makes her think of Jim. Now he wasn't half-bad
as a singer. Something light and boyish about his voice,
but sweet too and he could hit the high notes. Lyric, he
called it himself. Bel Canto. Always sounded like another
woman to her. He could have made something of himself
if he'd stuck to the singing. The great McCormack said
so, recommended a teacher and all to him. He was pals
with McCormack in those days, imagine, and it was him
who'd said you're good enough for the Feis Ceoil. Gogarty and Byrne had lent him the money for the lessons,
seven bob a go, with a singing master whose name was
like palm trees. He even got a piano on the never-never
from Pigott's, a baby grand, and managed to get it trans-
ported up the stairs to the two-pair front on Shelbourne
Road where he was staying at the time. Temporary like,
he was always temporary. He didn't have the entrance fee
for the tenor contest – surprise, surprise – but he cadged
it off someone, never told her who. Not Cosgrave or Gogarty, else he would have said, probably some doxy from
Mecklenburgh Street. She'd often wondered was he clean.
She didn't want to be picking up any old pox off him but
while they were courting, he'd stuck with her. At least, she
thinks he did. But what did she know of him, really? Anyways, she couldn't exactly point the finger, what with her
little dally with Cosgrave.

Mister McCarthy's music, the awful sweetness of it,
makes her homesick and what ails her, isn't she already
at home? Anyways, where was she? Oh yes. Jim and the
singing. He got a bronze medal at the Feis but missed gold
because he wouldn't do the sight-reading test. All swelled
up with pride in his refusal. Cutting off his nose to spite

his face, she called it. Eyes weren't up to it, probably, and too proud to wear glasses. Or too poor. Though in ways he was well got. Not only was he pals with McCormack, but he shared a stage with him – what would Bartle McCarthy make of that? He got her a seat in a reserved row of the Concert Rooms during Horse Show Week. Oh it was a grand affair and she had to think long and hard over what to wear – her green velveteen with the covered buttons. Jim was a warmer-upper for McCormack, and she was all of a dither on his account because Miss Reidy, the accompanist, had upped and left in a snot over some slight and there was another lady who took over just before his set. He swaggered on expecting Miss Reidy and handed this new one his sheets, gave her shoulder a squeeze. Norah noticed that – funny the things that'll make you jealous. She was a prim one, years older, but still … And then a quick gargly cough, he pulled on his jacket tails, and jutted out his chin. Assumed the position. He always kept his eyes tight shut, wasn't that a strange thing now, preferred to sing blind … But your woman couldn't find her place on the sheet and he had to go back to the beginning twice over, and the crowd was beginning with the slow hand-clap and the boots on the boards, and the accompanist had fled off the stage in tears and Jim had had to sit down at the keys and play for himself. 'Down by the Salley Gardens', was it? Isn't it a fright she can't remember! And he got not one encore but two.

Oh please, enough of him now!

She could knock on Mister McCarthy's door now and say *is that the great tenor himself* and sit down beside him and *ooh* and *ah* at the great voice, for wouldn't the old gent get a kick out of that, but something stops her. It'd be too hard to get away. Loneliness makes you greedy. Mister

McCarthy would look at her with those moist eyes that old men have, and he'd snuffle and take out a large hand-kerchief none too clean, and then he'd be embarrassed so no, she won't. She'll keep her distance, better that way. It'd only bring her back and isn't she worn out telling herself she doesn't want to go back, thank you very much. She grips the bannisters and goes on down.

Time seems to have galloped. As she reaches the first floor, the sun is back, blazing a golden path across the landing. The cricket must be over. She can no longer hear ripples of applause. Are they in the pavilion for tea? Never under-stood that game, what took them so long, hours and hours of it, thwacking the ball and then all that running up and down on a narrow little runner of turf when you could have the whole field. And the scoring! Vinny Cosgrave had once tried to explain it to her but everything he said sounded like a lewd joke about hosiery – leg before garter, declaring your runs.

She checks her watch. Great God, it's coming up for half four, how did that happen? George should be back by now; he's probably in the kitchen, Bridgie feeding him morsels that'll ruin his tea.

They all have a little claim on George – Bridgie, Nellie, even Peggy Douce who's a bit of a glamour puss and more interested in fellas than babas. When George was a little lad, Peggy used to sit him up on the high stools at the bar and serve him cordial. She'd play beggar-my-neighbour with him and always let him win. Even Gertie Devenney forgets she's a child herself with him. Saves him a gob-stopper or a bonbon when she goes to the sweet shop. He's winning that way. A small tawny boy with big brown eyes he got from his dearly departed Dada. Norah feels a little shiver, someone walking over her grave. She should get Gertie to shut the windows because the street-side of the house will be plunged into shade now, and even though it's high summer, it'll move from fresh to just plain draughty with the sun on the move. Then she remembers, Gertie is already on a mission. So she goes herself to the sash window facing out front and peers up into the sky that has begun to pale from its earlier blue. Now it looks all washed out. On days like these, she's glad not to be out foreign, you'd be destroyed in Trieste with the skeeters and midges that'd descend at this time of the day. Oh how they had loved her pale flesh, new, juicy. She laughs to herself. Juicy! Where is she now? Still in the Villa Veneziani, or has she moved on?

She shuts the window. The pulleys are worn out behind the sash and it closes with a crash. That, she thinks would wake the dead. Sometimes she expects Lizzie Fitzgerald to come storming up the stairs with knitted brows looking for a culprit, until she reminds herself she is the Miss Fitzgerald now. Nothing stirs in the thrumming silence except the call of these old stories. Where do they all come from?

She used to ask Jim the same thing, where do the stories come from and he made it out to be pure mystery but sure she already knew the answer. Didn't he plunder other people's lives for them, hers especially. She told him about a girl, Adelaide Cuffe, who used to work with her here in Finn's when she was a maid. He'd called her Eveline, but it was the same girl. Adelaide was all set to go to New York with a gent who worked for a shipping broker, only she lost her bottle and dropped out at the last minute. She'd trailed back to Finn's looking for her job back but Miss Fitzgerald had been merciless. You left, my girl, she told Adelaide, your goose is cooked.

I wouldn't have come back with my tail between my legs, she'd said to Jim when she told him the story, I'd have too much pride.

The waft of fried sausages reaches her on the first floor. Bridgie has started early teas. She thinks of the stink of congealed lard running up through the house. Odours rise like heat, lodging in the runners and the drapes. How often has she warned Bridgie to keep the blessed kitchen door shut! Normally she likes it, finds the smell homely, thinks of salt and smoke and sizzle, and it brings her back to a Sunday afternoon in Galway, a spring long 'go when she was only a girleen and just home from a visit to her mother, and she was all puffed out from a game of skipping, the first game of the season, and she'd shown Dilly how to run in and Mamo was busy in the scullery frying up and Uncle Michael was standing with his back to the range, puffing on his pipe, and he raised his eyes when she came in and seeing her flushed cheeks he sang an entire verse of 'Red is the Rose'. He'd meant it as a bit of funning but it came out like a lament. That's music for you, no telling what way it'll turn you, and make you sad for no reason. What is it about today and remembering old God's time!

She's about to roar Bridgie's name, or stick her head over the bannisters and yell at whoever might be on the desk, but she thinks better of it. If the strange gentleman is still waiting down there, it'll only lower the tone or make her sound fishwifey, though why she should worry about some dirty old pervert who wants to see the maids' rooms, she doesn't know. She can hear hectic birdsong outside. They're lodged in the college trees, hidden in the foliage, and though she doesn't recognize which one is which – Hector knew all the birds, all the better to shoot them he

38

used to say, for the Eyetalians are hoors for bang-bang and the birds – they make her melancholy.

There's not much straightening to be done on the first landing, her least favourite of the three, though the most used. Maybe that's why, too many others traipsing through for her to have a claim on it. She puts her short-termers here, and tries to keep the ladies together. At the moment there's just the one, Miss Julia Rea, elderly, musical type, she's here for a recital in the Concert Rooms, a tenor from abroad with a lyric voice, she said at the desk this morning – light, you know. And Nellie Longworth, bless her – who wouldn't know a light tenor from a hole in the wall – said is that so, how interesting.

Very horsey Protestant, Miss Rea, smells of elderflower soap, but isn't she great all the same, a woman of her age, must be well into her seventies and that sprightly! Maybe there's something in that horse-riding … the gripping with your thighs, *ah Norah, stop it now.*

Here's the residents' lounge, straight opposite the stairwell, and far enough away from the ground-floor bar to discourage casual callers. She's sometimes caught a gentleman guest exchanging reluctant kisses with a lady friend right here on this spot, despite the severe warnings posted up behind reception. No ladies past the first landing unless the lady is your wife or a guest here. There's a little bald patch on the carpet at the top of the stairs to mark the spot, the threads loosened and gapped like a comb-over. She peers into the residents' lounge. There's no one there, she goes in anyway and straightens the cushions and plumps them up for good measure. She opens the windows a crack. There's a fine view of the playing fields though they're deserted now. Everyone in the world has something better to do, somewhere else to go.

She squints over the bannisters, while keeping out of sight for fear whoever's down in the hall might suddenly look up and catch her spying. The bloody step creaks noisily as she puts her weight on it and she can feel a little give. Is it rotting? She'll have to get Mister Hull to lift the stair rods and investigate – there's another job for him and what was that other thing? It's gone. She'll have to write a list. She imagines the pep talk she'll give Mister Hull – *we can't have the guests breaking their necks on the stairs or we'd have the law after us.*

Mister Hull will think her a nag, like his own wife at home. Isn't that what he comes to work for, to get away from all of that palaver? Except Mrs Smith has no one to get on to – is that what happened to the poor dead husband, do you think, nagged him to death? This is Mister Hull's firm belief.

She goes down. Oh yes, she goes down with an almighty wallop. It must have been the heel of her boot catching in the loose stitching of her hem, though she's adjusted her hemlines like everyone else. This blessed war, it's not just the tea and sugar in short supply, but we have to skimp on our skirts as well. She read in the *Daily Mail* about a barber in Surbiton who had to take up clock repairs because all of his patrons have signed up and his business is almost ruined. She has her share of students, medicals at the college mostly, who board for the term, but if they were to dry up, she might well be out on the street herself – and what would she do instead? Take in laundry, God forbid, do sewing and alterations like her mother? But come here to me Norah, there's a war on, it isn't costumes they'll want but socks for the men at the Front. And she couldn't turn a heel in a sock to save her life. Maybe it was the thinking of the sock heels that did it, but one minute she's upright and the next she's tumbling ...

She lands in a heap at the bottom of the stairs just short of the half-moon table and the welcome mat. Welcome, how are you. Her leg is trapped under her and her heel is still caught in the fold of her hem and she can't work it free. The blooming front door is still open and as she lies there spreadeagled, she can see a pair of putteed legs pass, a khaki trouser leg, the click of army boots going by on the pavement outside. Will she call out? Not what our boys are for, no! So she lies there and hopes someone inside will happen upon her, preferably not a guest. And she thinks, yes, this is what the end will be like. Sudden and foolish.

Eventually, Gertie appears, poor crippled Gertie comes at her, oh Missus, oh Missus, she laments and she hovers, afraid to come near.

Here, help me up, Norah says.

But still the girl dithers, afraid to do the wrong thing.

Fetch Miss Longworth, so.

Gertie heads for the office on the little passageway behind the bar.

There's no sign of the foreign gent. But sure that must be an hour ago, and as she thinks it the grandmother clock in the hall strikes five. No wonder, what man is going to hang about that long?

What's keeping Gertie? Minutes pass.

She'd better try to haul herself up, see if she can. Still that sausagey smell. She gets up on all fours and eases her boot off. The size of her ankle, like a balloon. Is it broken? And look, there's the rip. Not only has her heel sheared away a good yard of the stitching but it's made a H-shaped tear in the magenta poplin. And there she was setting herself up as a seamstress, that'll put the tin hat on your daydreaming, Norah Barnacle!

Pride before a fall.

She heaves herself up, staggering to standing, leaning her arm against the maroon flock. Oh the marrowfat feel of it! She tries to put weight on her right ankle, but no, it won't bear it, but at least she's upright now.

Gertie, she calls weakly – the pain is something terrible – but nobody comes.

She leans on the edge of the half-moon table and catches a sight of herself in the round brass mirror, a big O as if it's got a fright as well.

Still no sign of anyone. God above, how long will she have to wait? And then she sees it on the silver platter for the post.

A gentleman's card. She picks it up idly.

Signor Giacomo Joyce …

No! It can't be. But it is.

Signor Giacomo Joyce.

It's him but in disguise. But she'd know him anywhere.

Irish-Italian Tenor, Music Professor, Via Alice 16, Trieste.

A calling card! After all these years without a word? The bloody brass neck of him! As if he were some stage-door Johnny and she … what does it make her? A piece of left luggage, as if he could drop her off and pick her up again when the mood took him. And what was all that about viewing the servants' quarters? Was that just to get a foot in the door? Or was that another gentleman? But the card is his, no mistaking him though she can see he's trying to pass himself off as an Eyetie.

She forgets herself and puts her foot down. The pain almost fells her.

Just then Nellie comes to her rescue.

Oh Norah, Norah, what is it? she cries. There's a funny edge of panic in her voice. She surveys Norah's stockinged foot, her overturned boot, the white edges of her knuckles still gripping the table for dear life.

It's nothing, Nellie, just took a fall. Can't bear my own weight.

With that, Nellie clasps her under the oxters and half carries her to the back office. They're like a pantomime horse: three good legs and a hoppity one. Nellie settles her on the couch and gets her to roll down her stocking to take a look. She presses her fingers against the puffed-up skin of the ankle. God, the pain is only ferocious. That's when George arrives.

Mama, he wails, seeing her stretched out. What's wrong?

Shush, shush, my dear it's nothing.

You run along, Sonny, Nellie says, I'll look after your mama.

But, but …

Do as Nellie says, she tells him. She knows how rickety the world is for him without the ballast of a father. He doesn't need the other pillar in his life falling down.

Go on now, Bridgie will have your tea ready.

He backs out of the office, hands clutching the door frame as if he was holding up the whole house.

Go on, she says again. Everything's going to be all right.

Nellie waits for him to go.

Broken, I'd say, she says. We'll have to get the doctor.

A couple of minutes later a breathless Gertie appears in the doorway.

Where were you? Nellie demands.

Looking for you, Ma'am, Gertie says.

How is it possible that they missed one another? As if the hotel were the size of the Fifteen Acres. My God, the girl's a painful case.

Speaking of … Norah's ankle feels big as a turnip, a globe of pain. She cries out with it, now that George isn't there to hear her.

Go and fetch Doctor Neville, Nellie orders Gertie.

The girl looks from one to the other as if she's waiting for Norah to offer a second opinion.

Go! Nellie shouts.

When the girl is gone, Nellie plumps a cushion to prop Norah up on the sofa. Wait there, she says, as if Norah's likely to go anywhere in this state. I'm getting you a brandy. The only thing for a shock.

She doesn't know the half of it.

While she's gone, Norah unclenches her fist which has been balled up in pain and finds the card mangled in her hand. She smooths it out but the creases are permanent and the raised gold lettering is all cracked. Her gilty secret.

Via Alice 16, Trieste.

He's in Trieste? No, that couldn't be, could it? Didn't Gogarty say he was in Fuming? But what if Gogarty was wrong? Or maybe he'd set her wrong deliberately. Always had a malicious streak, that yoke. What if …

Her fury in the hall has been overtaken by something else. A queer kind of delight. A relief that allows her to exhale. He's come back from that far-off unknown world he's been lost in. Not only that, he's come back for her. Sought her out. Didn't he leave his card? He'd only do that if …

Take that, Nellie orders, thrusting a glass tumbler at her and eyeing her suspiciously. Whatever happened?

I tripped on the stairs, the low sun. Any old excuse, she thinks, but not the real one.

Irish-Italian Tenor?

Tell me, she says to Nellie as she downs the snifter in one go. (It stings as much as her ankle.) Do you know anything about this concert?

Nellie looks at her oddly.

The one Miss Rea was talking about this morning?

Was that only this morning? Before the world turned.

Nellie humours her; must be the shock taking hold. A fall can do that.

The fella with the Irish name, is that it? she says. Joyce, I think.

That's it, Norah says, when is that on?

Tomorrow night, I believe, Nellie says. What in heaven's name has that got to do with the …

She cuts Nellie off. Maybe Bartle McCarthy would know?

The *Freeman's* is lying on the desk. Nellie shakes it open.

Homecoming concert, Nellie reads.

Homecoming, is it? Is it the fatted calf he's expecting?

I'll have to go, she says, so murmured that Nellie almost misses it.

Raving Norah may be, but Nellie cannot abide waywardness – in the maids' attire, in the gentlemen's conversation. Not even in a good friend, as Norah is when she's not being Mrs Smith for the staff. They have forged a friendship, a reliance on one another. Two women alone with a small empire to run. A child between them and a fondness for one another though it's unspoken.

Not on that foot you won't!

When he comes, Doctor Neville says just a sprain but a bad one. No break.

Are you sure? Norah asks, for her ankle looks like a club now. Will she ever get a boot on that by tomorrow?

Nothing broken, he declares. That's what he thinks.

But bed rest, he says, wagging a finger.

See! says Nellie triumphantly, even though her diagnosis has been contradicted. Gertie is still hovering.

By the time Doctor Neville leaves, she's hatched a plan.

Here's what I'm going to do, she instructs Nellie. You'll order a cab to take me to the concert tomorrow night.

I beg your pardon ...?

You heard. Send Gertie here to the stand on Brunswick Street. I'll go for the finale.

But ...

Miss Longworth, she says firmly when she sees Nellie's face pinched with disapproval and Gertie's open mouth. Nellie knows she means business with the Miss Longworth.

I insist, she says.

Just about eleven years too late.

Nora With an H

October 20, 1904

How could he, how *could* he? After she warning him, don't
leave me on my tod, for I can't bear it. And yet here she is
stuck outside the station in Tree-estay like a total *gam*. She's
boiling. Dressed for winter and goodbye forever so what's
not in the valeeze is on her back in a mixum-gatherum of
seasons. Jim's left her with his overcoat, too bulky for the
case, so the only way to carry it is to wear it, and she has her
straw hat on that'd be crushed anywhere but on her head,
so she's like winter and summer having a row. *Where is he?*

It's three hours, three whole hours, since he left. You
won't even know I'm gone, he said when he left, and look,
you can keep track by the station clock, which she can
just about make out through the trees. He'd just go and
find the Beryl-its school, where there's a job waiting, and
hope he'd catch the manager, Mister Artie Foney, before he
shut up shop. Norah'd only slow him up, he said, and he
wouldn't drag her through the streets in this heat with the
luggage and all.

So far nobody's bothered her. But if they did, sure what
could she say for herself, since she hasn't two words of
their lingo to rub together?

And what'll she do when the dark comes?
She's not going to think about that.

This is the third time he's left her in as many days. First time was in London, at Euston Station where he put her sitting on a park bench near a huge arch like a stage set in the Tivoli. There were plaques with statues high up on it. They're allegories, he said, whatever they are when they're at home. Ireland was up there, apparently, though how he knew she couldn't fathom since he couldn't see straight in front of him let alone a mile over his head. His excuse in London was that he was going off to see a Mister Symons about his book, and to try and touch him up for some money. But no sooner was he gone than a fella had come up, wearing a suit, all shiny with wear and a sagging arse. He bowed and doffed his hat, a little bowler. Old as her Uncle Tommy and twice as ugly.

Good day to you, he said.

Toffee-mouth or else he was putting it on.

Took in their luggage in a glance. Her cardboard valeeze from Bowling Green Street, the top caved in from being squeezed under the bed at Finn's and held closed with a belt because the right catch had been damaged and wouldn't click on its own. Jim's was a Gladstone, large and soft like a doctor's – maybe that's what he got it for, when he was trying for the medicals. He had books in there and scads of paper and not much in the way of a wardrobe. He'd traipsed across the Continent with only a pair of canvas shoes held together by white caulk.

Waiting for someone, is you? yer man asked.

My husband, she said magisterially while smirking inside her cheek. The day Jim will be her husband there'll be a blue moon, but if it puts this fella off, she could live with the lie. Wasn't she lying down with a lie as it was, with a curtain ring on her finger?

Gone far, 'as he?

Now if she could answer that ...

What does she really know about him? And what is there to keep them together? A couple of months of clinches and the dodge, a joult on the mail boat, not even a berth but sitting stiffly on chairs with the reek of drink coming from the bar, a stench of wood rot in the air, and a gale blowing in from the deck every time someone stepped outside. And Jim sulking, looking like she felt, as if he'd made a terrible *botún*. He'd turned away from her to sleep, as if she was a stranger who'd just happened to plank herself down beside him. Neither of them had slept a wink on the boat. It was dawn when they docked in Holyhead, a godforsaken place, wind howling along the platform. Jim dozed beside her, looking perished, and for the first time she felt afraid. Afraid of the silence that might grow between them. Most of the time he could talk for Ireland but when he clammed up, she worried. For that was when his thoughts came and then his mind might turn to doubt. And in his silence, she'd get the haunts herself, for fear of having nothing to say to him. Would he tire of her because she couldn't do the chit-chat about the books? And when he was done asking her about her habits, and the habits of her people, or, narrow-eyed, quizzing her about this fella or that who she might have stepped out with, what then?

The Holyhead sky was like clay and the boat they'd just left was groaning against the quay. A crowd had gathered going in the opposite direction. Men in coats, breaths hanging in the air as if they'd eaten clouds, women with high-built bonnets and drums of luggage. And it took all that was within her not to rise up and join this throng and go back. But Jim woke then with a start and looked at her and smiled – the sun came up in his smile – and he said, all pent up, we've done it! And she was with him then without question.

Or for another while at least.

While they sat there waiting for the mail boat train, she wondered if they were up in Finn's Hotel yet. Had they found her note? She'd made sure to pick up her wages Friday but hadn't given them any warning of her plans because old Mister Finn would dock her for not giving notice. Her name would be muck there now but sure what did she care? She was well and truly finished with that place now. Never again would she wear a maid's cap and dip the knee, thank you very much. No more pot-walloping and mattress-turning, or rainwater only for the asparagus fern, or the fumes of Cardinal polish from the boot-blacking on a Saturday night. And then, *call this clean, Miss Barnacle? A bit more elbow grease, if you please.* Well, here's the news, this goose has flown, no more fire irons or piss pots for me.

But then she remembered the early morning routine at Finn's and she softened. The scrape and clamour of the coal shovel as Harry the Boots bent to his job, head in the mouth of the bin in the yard, as he filled the scuttles. Bridgie Kenny in the kitchen singing softly as she buttered the bread, then scraped the top layer off again, as she'd been told. Miss Fitzgerald wouldn't allow pats on the table for the gentleman would eat you out of house and home that way. She'd be hollering at the maids, as they fixed their caps like upturned bloomers on their heads, frills and all. They'd be standing to attention as Major Tweedy – up with the lark and always first to the trough – passed them with a rolled-up newspaper under his oxter like a parade ground baton. He'd twirl his moustache and march through the door marked DINING on the milky glass. Celia and Kat would scurry after him, upturning cups and settling cloths – envelope corners, if you please, says Miss Fitzgerald. God spare us from a spinster. Finicky as all get out. The rest of the guests would be trickling in. Quiet of a morning, newspaper confetti on their chins. No high argument unlike the evening meal, day's work done and fresh disappointments to rail and moan about. Fussy about their tea then – milk first, three sugars, did no one let this draw and this sausage is cremated, but in the mornings it's would you mind, speak softly now and a tap to the beating brain.

Gone far, 'as he? yer man with the hat tried again and she was back in London.

Go on outa that, she muttered at him.

But the memories kept coming. Mister Holohan, the traveller, pressing his greasy lapel in her face one night on the stairs thinking she was there for the taking. The uniform gave them licence, as if they thought it was part of the service. Well, not for Norah Barnacle, not anymore, thank you very much.

My husband'll thrash you if he finds you here, she said sharpish.

Major Tweedy used to say that – come here girl, snap of the fingers, or I'll thrash you – but the girls had to humour him all the same. But this fella was just a corner boy, trying his luck. Trying it on.

Look lively, she said, another one of the Major's expressions, here's my husband now, pointing to a chap in a hat who was not Jim.

Any port in a storm. Made her think of Celia Canty whom she'd shared a bed with in Finn's and that's a way of knowing somebody, isn't it? Celia believed she'd snare a better class of fella, or any fella at all, if she showed willing. But Celia was a girl as hadn't known love. Probably hadn't ever been kissed, let alone been broken into. Poor Celia.

Skedaddle, she said, whooshing at yer man with her gloves like he was a dirty pigeon. Shoo!

At least in London she could bark at them. But here? She's afraid to budge from the seat. There's a couple of men at the next bench carrying on a loud conversation in that infernal chatter of theirs. Would they snatch our bags? Let them thieve Jim's bag, see if I care.

From where she sits, she can see the portico of the station on one side with that ruddy clock she's gone blind looking at.

Twenty to two now.

Place looks important with those pillars but it's painted the colour of mustard powder. On her left is a statue, a black queen with ELISABETTA in big letters underneath.

An empress, Jim said with some satisfaction, like you!

For when he's in the throes that's what he calls her.

Around the black queen, there's a clutch of lady statues with not a stitch on. She spies at least one bare *bundún*. The trees have strange, dry barks, and clouds of leaves high up. She's glad of the shelter of them for she's still sweating, and when she looks up the sky is high and blue. There's sea nearby, she can smell it, and now she could really do with spending a penny.

Hold it in, Norah, hold it in.

It's not the first time she's done a runner. Left Galway the same way – was that only six months ago? She might have stayed if Uncle Tommy hadn't taken to interfering. She'd a good job in the Presentation Convent, had risen from the laundry to be a porteress. She sat in the convent auntie room. That's what the professed sisters called it, but it was a glorified cubby hole, dark as night unless you left the inner door ajar. The inside light of the convent came flooding in, the green of the cloister, the grey of the stone. It was soothing to be there until the bell jangled, operated by a rope out on the street. You always shut the inner door before opening the outer one. You asked them, politely, what their business was and who they were looking for. Curates, doctors, ladies of all descriptions, Salthill matrons and fishwives, and girls in trouble. Always girls in trouble. That's where she learned.

Never be a girl in trouble.

You always knew them even if they weren't showing. They were mad to get in off the street, casting an eye over their shoulders and pushing inside as soon as you'd opened the door a crack. You didn't have to ask their business and who they were looking for – an audience in the public parlour with the Reverend Mother. But you only got that if you were respectable.

The lay sister who guarded the inner door would have none of it. No beggars, there's alms day for that and they should know that, no commercial travellers and no tradesmen. We have Mister Morrigan to clean the windows and do the slops, tell them that. No, no, not in so many words. Tell them we have made alternative arrangements.

She kept an ear out for the poor box too. A funny contraption like a letter slot. There was a hatch set into the street wall outside with a matching mouth. You'd hear the creak and whinge as the person pulled on the handle of the door and a bucket opened out like an accordion for them to make a contribution. Silently if it was paper money, noisily for coin. She'd listen to it sliding down the chute and landing in the padlocked compartment on the inside down near the skirting. Her job was to record the number of donations, but only Mother Bursar had the key to the padlock.

No one had ever put the shift on her in the convent. Though once there was a priest who'd got a bit fresh. Laid his hand on her cheek to bless her, *mar dhea*. Sweet creature, he breathed, let me put my tongue in your mouth, imagine the host. Whispered it into her ear as if that meant he hadn't said it at all.

I'll show you out now, Father, she said as the bell rope jangled and came to her rescue.

Mostly the visitors didn't bother with her, too busy with troubles of their own. Sinners and drinkers who'd been ordered by the assizes to give to the poor. She entered their contributions into a big ledger. The court clerk would want a chit for proof, and anyways the nuns were mad for the record-keeping, every last penny accounted for. These fellas came with their caps crushed in their hands with their *yes sisters* and *no sisters*. Even to her. Must have been the black duster coat she wore over her street clothes that confused them for if she met those same fellas out on the street they'd be hallooing after her, is that you Norah Barnacle, is you free? She took no notice of them. She had Sonny Bodkin, and the thought of him kept them away, like the scent of a bar of lemony soap that would dispel flies.

When she wasn't watching the door, she'd be sent on messages – to the candlemakers, the stationers, the cobblers. The nuns were fierce hard on their boots and they couldn't be dealing with men, even men who would shoe them. Weren't they dead to all of that when they entered? And dead to their families too.

She wouldn't have minded that herself. To be out of reach of Uncle Tommy's long arm. Took it upon himself. No one asked him. Didn't she already have a father, thank you very much. But poor Pappie, God help us, was useless, a useless collop her mother called him, and what he earned went down his throat. The ovens, the heat, he'd say, gives you a shocking thirst. But still, she'd a soft spot for him. *Cratur.* When she was twelve, her mother had sent him packing. The first she knew was his shoes, dandruffed with flour, gone. He was banished to Oughterard – he can do the loaves and fishes trick out there, her mother had said, then she took out the separation papers. That was her mother's way, good at dispatching people.

Norah had already been farmed out to her Granny Healy by then to make room for the twins. It wasn't all bad at Mamo's. Quieter than Bowling Green Street with the new babbies caterwauling, and Mary, Dilly and her, heads and tails in the one bed. In Mamo's she had her own room – well, an alcove off the kitchen with a settle bed – though she'd have liked, sometimes, to have crawled in beside Mamo. But Mamo wasn't that sort. It wasn't that she wasn't kind, remember those button boots she gave you, and a polka pinny, but Lord, she was strict. Don't put a knife in your mouth unless you want to cut yourself, a napkin – if you please – is not for the nostrils. When she moved into Mamo's she'd been lonesome for her mother but she'd never let on. And after the twins, there were two more buns in the oven, Thomas and Kathleen, and then she knew she'd never be going back. What she got instead was Mamo with her notions, Uncle Michael who minded his own business, and Uncle Tommy who minded hers.

*

Holy Moses! Three on the dot. Is Jim getting his revenge? Is that what this is? Is he punishing her for standing him up that first time? Does he know about that? But he couldn't, could he?

They'd arranged to meet outside the Surgeon Wilde's house, but she hadn't showed. Told him a fib about having to work overtime, how Miss Fitzgerald came up to her on her way out the door, as she was trying to spear her hat with a pin in the hall mirror, and said that Molly Fowler was sick and couldn't do her shift.

Sure what could I do?

It *could* have happened like that. Only it didn't. Instead, she'd said, But Miss Fitzgerald, I have a date with my young man. As if they were an item when they'd only just met. He'd picked her up on Nassau Street a couple of days before with a saucy smile and a sailor's suit. A boy with jam-jar specs, not her type at all.

I see that, Miss Barnacle, Miss Fitzgerald had said, looking into the glass behind her with her eyebrow up.

And before she had time to cajole, for she had a way of getting on the sweet side of you when she wanted something, Norah pulled open the heavy front door of Finn's and out with her into the dusty sunlit lozenge of the street.

But as she hurried, hand on hat, towards Merrion Square, a strange desolate feeling overtook her, a pang of misgiving. She slowed her tripping step to a heavy-footed stroll, and then to a halt. What had possessed her, to say yes? Yes to a college boy with a boater. Though he wasn't the first college boy she'd had. Hadn't Sonny Bodkin been at the university, even if he didn't finish – no, she wouldn't think of him, not now. She darted around by Sweny's

Chemists and scurried across to the pillars of the Gospel Hall. She could hear singing from inside. *Funny, I thought those Prods didn't hold with that.* From here she could spy on yer man without him seeing her. And sure enough, there he was, a stick of worry, standing at the corner, hands on hips. Then pacing a little this way and back. He had on the same get-up as the day he'd chatted her up. Not bad looking up close, a bit skinny, pull through for a rifle, when did he last have a square meal, I wonder, and his clothes have seen better days. Then she remembered she'd told him where she worked. If he had a titter of wit, he could duck down and ask after her in Finn's and then her fib would be exposed. He'd *know* then she'd stood him up. Deliberate like. And it wasn't that she wanted to say no, she just wasn't sure about saying yes. Outright.

And if he had come to Finn's looking for her, would that have decided her about him? She just wasn't sure, not like with Sonny Bodkin. Poor Sonny who had stood in the Pres garden and called out to her in the flogging rain, while she half-delighted, half-mortified, hid in the darkness letting on she wasn't there. Afraid of his keenness. But this fella was no Sonny Bodkin, she could tell that even from afar. Sure, no one could be. No one could be the first after the first.

He was dithering now, she could tell. But so was she and the longer she waited the stranger he became. Was he a foreigner, was that what made her hesitate? A Swedish sailor, maybe, with that naval cap he has? Reasons not to approach. Now that she was here, she could find a dozen. The minutes passed, five, nearly ten, and her delaying was like a jelly left to set. If she'd got a penny for every time he changed his mind she'd have made a fortune. There he'd go, gathering himself up then doubling back like a dog at a post sniffing, then trying and sniffing again. The hum and the haw of him.

Hello, hello, she could have rushed up all breathless and false and full of sorrys and old excuses he wouldn't even listen to because he'd be so relieved. She'd almost moved then but she didn't. She was stuck to the spot as if she was the one being stood up. And as she stood there debating, didn't he make her mind up for her. Fixed his cap on his crown and strode away up the west side of Merrion Square. In a temper, she'd have said, by the look of him.

And then she felt the let-down.

What did she go and do that for? What was all the mirror-gazing in Finn's for, and wondering will I do?

She remembered the lightness of her step as she had set off and now she was morose and cursing herself for being so perverse.

What ails you, girl? That's what Mamo used to say. What ails you?

No, she told herself shaking her head, I did the right thing, a fella who'd pick you up on the street like that, what kind of fella would he be? Not a patch on Sonny Bodkin, that's what.

She turned to go, checking one last time to see had he changed his mind. But he hadn't – he was a cross white speck in the summer sunlight now.

She'd trailed back the way she came, her hat in her hand, her hair dejected. She hadn't the heart to do anything else with her precious night off. If she knew where Vinny Cosgrave was she might have sought him out, but no, if he saw she was keen, he'd only get a swelled head.

Miss Fitzgerald was at the desk when she got back to Finn's.

Back so soon, Miss Barnacle? She was a prissy one.

Lucky for you, Norah said as she donned her apron, he stood me up.

Like he's done to her now. Only last night she told him don't ever leave me waiting. Not after Sonny Bodkin. For I'll imagine the worst. I'll imagine you dead and buried and no one has told me.

Sonny had been the picture of health, a false bloom it was, tricking her with his ruddy cheeks. One minute there, the next gone. His family said he was infectious so they wouldn't let her see him in the San. She'd met his mother on the street.

Tell him I'll wait for him.

But his mother was so beside herself she probably didn't pass the message on and Sonny must have wondered why she'd never come.

But you got over him, Jim said, didn't you?

Always a barb with him, jealous as a girl. As if he were as pure as the driven snow himself. The things he'd asked her to do, he must have spent a fair few nights on Railway Street. He's convinced she has experience, even likes the idea, and puts it down to Sonny Bodkin. But what Jim didn't understand was that she'd known Sonny with a girleen's heart and he'd died chaste, no hand on him, not hers, not even his own.

When he was hardly cold in the grave she was haunted by dreams in which Sonny would turn up at the convent. He'd lift the knocker, bold as brass, and demand entry. Her heart would thump, she'd want to run to the door, quick, quick, but her head would counsel – no, hang on a minute, make him wait – and then she'd remind herself, this is Sonny Bodkin, catch him before he's gone. She would throw open the door and find, not Sonny, but that same drill-haired curate, fingering the rim of his hat, and whispering sweet creature, let me put my tongue in your mouth, imagine the host.

She'd wake with a start, head teeming with calculations. If it were Sonny at the other side of the door, come back to life, risen from the grave in Rahoon, wouldn't that be worse? For he'd have to go back and wouldn't he be wanting her to go with him?

And would she?

No, she would not.

She'd prefer life, even this fix she's in now, abandoned in Tree-estay by the man she thought she'd spend her whole life with. Who's only turned out to be a barefaced liar. But even so, she'd take this over being like Sonny. Six feet under and it all over.

Six hours now. She feels a niggle from her bladder. Oh God, how's she going to manage if she has to go? She can't understand it. A drop hasn't passed her lips since the blooming wine last night and she's sweated half a pint out in this sun. *Don't think about it, Norah, that only makes it worse.*

What is she going to do if he really *has* left her? But if he *was* going to leave her, wouldn't he have made up a reason to take his stuff with him? Not that there's much. The soft bag with books and papers, full of his scribbling. Threadbare clothes that have seen better days. Limp pants, grime on his shirt collars, so ground in that no amount of starch could shift it; she knew that much from the laundry. If he doesn't come back, he'll have to parade around in his skin for she has no intention of lugging his bag around as well as her own.

Serve him right!

No, he has to come back, doesn't he?

He came back in London, didn't he? He came back in Paree.

Oh yes, he left her again in Paree in a park near the Saint Lazarus station. A queer name for a station, never knew Lazarus was a saint, sure all he ever did was die and wasn't it Jesus who brought him back? Maun-so this place was called. Very highfalutin with a rotunda inside the decorated gate and a little bridge like Stephen's Green, but sure she couldn't stir for fear of the luggage. He'd turned her into a cloakroom girl. This time he'd gone off to scare up a loan from some doctor fella he'd known during his studies and true to his word, he'd come back with enough for a room in the Hotel Cor Nail and a slap-up feed.

When they'd got themselves settled in the hotel, he was all for the business, had it all planned. But her monthly visitor was in, and he'd got all worked up. I could do the other, she said, but he would have none of it. Treated her like she was some kind of touch-me-not. Is he carrying a grudge on account of that? Or is it something else she's supposed to have done agin him? She racks her brain but can't think. Listen to yourself, Norah. Why should you be examining your conscience? Didn't you make it up to him in Zoorick? Didn't you go all the way?

But maybe that's why he's left her. Because he's got his way now and that's all he wanted. But isn't it a long way to come to get what she would have given him earlier, only she wanted it proper, in a bed and not on the kerb, thank you very much. Anyways, she'd wanted to be well away from Ireland before she let him in, so as no one could accuse her of having done a bunk on account of being in a peculiar condition.

Did her mother know she was gone, she wondered. Would old Mister Finn telegraph her to say she'd gone absent without leave? Would they put a notice in the papers? MISSING: *£5 reward for information leading to the discovery of Miss Norah Barnacle, late of Bowling Green Street and the Presentation Convent, long auburn hair, trim figure, regal bearing, turn in her eye* ... ah but no, she wouldn't mention that now, would she, you'd hardly notice the thing in her eye.

Believed to be travelling in the company of a young gentleman.

But sure nobody even knew that much. She'd had to board the mail boat in Dublin on her own because his blessed father couldn't be told about her. A maid at Finn's! She'd watched the Joyces from the deck. What a rigmarole! That father of his, a holy terror, his brother Stannie, and that must be Auntie Josephine, and was that his sister, Poppie? All huddled around him – wasn't it a wonder they didn't carry him shoulder-high up the gangway?

She'd turned away. Disheartened, lonesome.

The mail boat's hooter sounded. A tug nosed along the prow of the ship like a calf nuzzling. She'd watched as it steamed out on its own ahead of the mother ship. She'd been watching these manoeuvres, leaning out over the rail on the far deck away from the pier so she wouldn't have to be watching his nibs and the fond farewells. She had nobody mourning her going. Not that she'd want her lot here. She'd shed them all and good riddance. Except for Mary O.

She smiles as she remembers. That time when they'd put on Mary's uncle's clothes and paraded around the house in them. Her Uncle Pat had been killed in the Boer

War and Mary's ma hadn't the heart to get rid of his civ-
vies. When they'd donned them, baggy pants and galluses
and hobnail boots, and painted moustaches under their
noses with soot, Mary said I dare you, Norah, I dare you
to wear them out on the street.

Well, she couldn't pass by a dare. Set a fire in her. (Isn't
that how she's fetched up in this fix? A dare from James
Joyce to Norah Barnacle, will we run away, will we elope?)

So she and Mary stepped out at nightfall with the
uncle's suits on. They prowled around Eyre Square, gay
and giddy with the freedom of it. The best of it was to be
invisible, no country gougers coming up to bother you,
digging you in the ribs and saying the usual rude things,
no they just let you be, and you had nothing to worry
about. Able to saunter about after dark where you wanted,
down the docks and through the square and even into a
public house. She, being taller and able to put on a deep
voice, went up to the bar and ordered a big black pint but
sure they'd no money on them and had to flee before the
barman came back with the seething glass with the white
head on it. The funniest thing ever was they passed by
Uncle Tommy on Shop Street and he didn't even recognize
her.

But then she had this queer thought, that in this get-up
she could be Sonny Bodkin ghosting around the city, and
it sent a shiver down her spine.

Let's get out of these yokes, she said to Mary O who
was still swaggering and hallooing and nearly giving
them away with her high shrill voice.

Mary's face fell.

What's up?

What if we're found out, Norah said, walking around
town in a dead man's clothes?

Ah Norah, you're only an old spoilsport, Mary said, but the good was gone out of it and they'd become suddenly sober.

Norah had always been the wilder of the two. Wild with grief for Sonny if truth were told but she'd kept that to herself. Even from Mary O.

When she made the trip out to visit Sonny's grave she went on her own. Sometimes she'd get the feeling that he was still there in the plot in Rahoon and not ascended into Heaven at all. For he was that good, where else was he bound? She'd think of him below ground still holding his breath, his poor precious breath, waiting for her to come. Then she'd feel the terrible tug of the grave, the yawning blackness under her feet and she'd want to be there in the cold earth in the box beside him. But how could she say that to anyone? They'd think she had a screw loose.

Has Jim picked up with someone else? Could that be it? He has a bit of a glad eye, she knows that, and with his Eyetalian, wouldn't he be able to flirt at will, while she sits here tongue-tied, racked with the hunger? Did he plan it this way all along? But no, with the crooked tacking they've been doing – London, Zoorick, Paree – going from Billy to Jack in search of a teacher's job as was promised to him, he couldn't have organized that amount of happenstance, now, could he? No, this will be a fling with some gladneck he's stopped on the street, just as he stopped her.

If it's punishing her he is, it's only out of jealousy. He's always at it, poking and prodding for tidbits on who she's been with and then when you tell him, he carries on as if you'd stabbed him in the heart. She hadn't wanted to confide about Sonny. It might have been a full four years ago but she was still heartsore and there were secrets a girl should keep for they belong to no one but herself. But no, he'd wanted all the gen and more and it didn't take him long to worm it out of her.

When she didn't show up for their first date, he'd written her a letter straight away, must have been directly when he got home because it came second post on Wednesday. *I may be blind*, he wrote. *I looked for a long time at a head of reddish-brown hair* – oh God, she thought, had he seen her after all skulking in the doorway of the Brethren, but no, it must have been another girl he was ogling – *and decided it was not yours. I went home quite dejected*. When she read that she all but melted. She didn't understand what had made her baulk. The rest of his note was all polite and gentlemanly and asking for another appointment, if you don't mind, as if she were a lady doctor – *if you have not forgotten me!* And without thinking she wrote back straight away – *Same time, same place, Thursday* – and she signed it but still she did not say yes.

And now look at her.

Wasn't she right to have her doubts?

Twenty-five to five now she sees from the station clock. She wishes she had something to occupy her hands. If she was a knitter she could be clacking up the rows. But who's she codding? She never had the patience for the needles, and she'd only be drawing attention to herself out here in the open like this, like whatshername in the French Revolution.

Where the dickens is he?

After giving her the third degree on Sonny, he'd wanted the low down on Willie Mulvey. He blamed Willie for

65

what she knew, not that he was complaining when she practised what she preached. No moaning then, except the other kind. Bet he can't write like me, Jim used to say, but sure what's so great about writing, she'd think, but she didn't say it for that would only rile him. And what's more, she liked getting his letters. So she told him about meeting Willie Mulvey.

It was on O'Brien's Bridge one evening with Mary O. They often went there, it was something to do, a reason to be out and about – a good excuse for Uncle Tommy who was always hounding her with questions as to where she'd been and who she'd been with. When the spring weather came, it was only gorgeous there, river bubbling underneath, and you could follow the waters to the weir and see the sparky salmon fighting their way upstream.

Willie had sidled up beside her and asked her straight would she step out with him. And she said to him she'd have to talk it over with her friend first and she pulled Mary aside and they had a confab.

What'll I do, she asked Mary and Mary said you should say yes.

So she did, out of divilment. It was the first time in a long time that she'd put Sonny Bodkin to the back of her mind and sure she couldn't hide away forever now, could she? A bit of fun is all it was. Willie had a job in the soda factory and a bit of money to throw about, sure what harm? She didn't love him but do you have to love every fella who asks you out, and if so, who says?

Mary O used to cover for her when she met up with Willie, for it had to be a bit of a secret because Willie kicked with the other foot. They'd say they were going for a ramble or to a Sodality meeting to throw Uncle Tommy off the scent. He was always on the warpath, scouring town for her with his stick whistling the same old tune 'My Mountain Maid Arise'. She'd always hated that old song. So Mary O would dip into the Abbey Church and wait while she stepped out with Willie so at least one of them wouldn't be found out in a lie. Mary must have worked up a plenary indulgence the amount of time she spent in the Abbey on her knees.

Willie nearly always brought a box of Clarendon's soft centres. Share those with Mary, won't you, he'd say. He was a big strapping fella with a centre-part and he knew all the dodges. Here, he'd say, show us your hanky, then he'd take her hand and guide it while they leaned against the parapet of the bridge, all innocent like, taking in the scenery. No wonder he was always saying he loved her. And who's to say she wouldn't have married Willie Mulvey? Once he'd converted, that is.

Uncle Tommy had set a curfew for her, ten o'clock on a weeknight, and it was the one rule she tried to keep. But sure with the hanky-panky they'd forgotten the time and Mary O was long gone, so Willie offered to walk her home.

Leave me here at the bottom of the street, she told him, for she knew she'd be in hot water but he, being a gent, insisted on bringing her to the door. She waited till he was out of sight before she put her hand in the letter-box and fished out the key on a string. She shut the hall door quietly behind her and the darkness fooled her for she thought Uncle Tommy might be waiting up, but no, she stopped and listened and there wasn't a murmur, they were all abed. All the same she tiptoed down the passage to the scullery and that's when he pounced from behind.

And what time do you call this?

When she turned, she saw his eyes aglitter in the dark, the cut of him! He raised his stick and brought it down on her beam end.

Well, well my girl, out with your Protestant again is you!

He caught her by the hair and forced her over and he thrashed her good and proper. It was a wonder he didn't pull her bloomers down, he was that worked up, and he muttered and spat all the way through – what a disgrace she was and how it went beyond all decency and hadn't he warned her often enough? When he was done, he climbed the stairs still maundering away to himself, while she lay fully clothed on her bed. That's when it came to her. She couldn't go on seeing Willie Mulvey. She couldn't go on trying to skirt around Tommy, trying to divine his moods. And she couldn't show up to the Pres in this state, bruises on her arms and an eye that would turn black by morning. He'd even ruined that for her. If Mamo had still been alive, she wouldn't have stood for it. But she'd been dead these six years. There was no going home to her mother. Sure there'd never been room for her there. No, the only way out was the road to Dublin.

She heaved the cardboard valeeze out and packed her belongings, twelve years in this house would you believe, and this was how it would end, sneaking away like a thief in the night. She sat up till first light. At six she let herself out into the grey and washed-out dawn, the Mountain Maid Arising.

A quarter to five! She's standing now hopping from foot to foot doing that jig that smallies do when they need to go. Don't, Norah. She thinks of her first evening with Jim instead. He suggested a walk to Ringsend, probably because he didn't have the spondulicks to do anything else. If it was Vinny Cosgrave, he'd have taken her into town, to Bewley's Oriental or Jammet's but this fella was better looking than Vinny. By then she knew he wasn't a Johnny Foreigner and she was a bit disappointed to tell the truth for she'd always fancied a foreign husband who'd whisk her off to Paree with a lady's maid in tow. Working in Finn's had made her yearn to be the bidder not the biddy.

It was a grim old walk past the Grand Canal Dock where she'd felt sorry for the water all scummy and trapped, not like Salthill where it's let out into the open. And that made her lonely again. Lonely for home. Past the idle chimneys and the mill with its windows, bars like gnashers, and there was no one else about and himself rattled on but she liked his voice. It had a kind of tune to it. He'd hesitated outside Tunney's but he didn't go in, a shortage of funds he said, and anyways there's no ladies' snug in there, and they walked on. He'd been to the Royal College, he told her. That's three, she said to herself, three of her fellas who'd been to college. His mother was dead. Only died a few months previous, didn't he come home from Paree, interrupted his medical studies, when he heard she was poorly. His poor put-upon mother, that's what he said. He had no proper job and that was a bit of a let-down but better than a sailor, she supposed. And he hadn't got fresh with her. Not then.

They went as far as the strand and they sat on a rock, side by side. The tide was gone to England so it was hard to see where the sand and the sea met. All blue out there like the glaze on the Indian Tree dinner set in Mamo's cabinet. That'll go to you, she used to say, it's Staffordshire, but Norah didn't give a fig for crockery, let her sisters squabble over it. Jim purred in her ear and clamped a hand on her waist and she knew what he wanted – there was a mist rising on his glasses – and where else was this heading? It wasn't a burden to unbutton him and slip her hand in.

It's a small thing to relieve a man, that's what Willie Mulvey taught her. Though when he'd suggested she plant her hand in there the first time she hadn't wanted to and only did as she was bid because he said all sweetly, Norah, Norah, don't leave me this way when you've got me all hot and bothered. Willie guided her that first time. Is this a terrible thing I've done, she'd said to him afterwards, but he said kinder far than teasing a man, to finish him off. Think of it as relief, he'd said, you're providing relief. And she thought of Black '47 that her long dead Nana Barnacle remembered, we'd a died but for the relief work, she used to say.

There weren't too many preliminaries with Jim. He'd only grazed her cheek with his lips and tried his hand around her breast and she'd felt it straight away and saw in his eyes that stallion look and she knew she'd have to move quick or it'd be all over. He was a bit taken aback when she took the law into her own hands but he was all aquiver at that stage and it was a mercy to put him out of his misery.

Hold your horses, she'd said to him.

It was the first time for him, first time a girl put the hand in without getting paid for it. Afterwards they had to go back straight away, for half past ten was the limit at Finn's, and he was awful quiet and she wondered had she shocked him by being so forward. When they'd got to Finn's he'd kissed her hand and she'd brought no gloves, it being so warm, and she thought it must be the smell of himself he's after, but she didn't dwell on that, and he said all gentle like, can I see you again and she realized his silence was gratitude. So she said yes again, for a man that's grateful will keep on coming back.

God isn't the sun fierce low! She's wall-falling with the hunger. She'd take the scraps the birds are pecking at. Funny-looking birds, magpies are they? One for sorrow, oh but there's a pair. But still no joy. There is some class of midgies buzzing around her. Like flies on dung. She swats them off. It's gone awful quiet, hasn't been a train in an age. The ground rumbles with the sound of them and then she can see little knots of passengers coming out into the circus in front of the station. Some get greeted, all the kissing they do here, even the men with one another. Is it natural? But it's a distraction, takes her mind off. Earlier there were a couple of old men playing cards at the bench next door, jawing away and slapping down their cards and taking sly looks at her, but she only glared at them and they lost interest and went back to their business. And then they went off. She nearly misses them now. She's got a few odd looks, but sure mostly they couldn't give a tup- penny damn.

Here's someone now, just when she thought she was safe. Bunty fella. Well turned out, though, frock coat, wing collar and satin lapels. He bows in front of her. They're demons for the bowing.

See Norah, he says.

Makes her jump.

How do you know my name? she says. Maybe Jim has sent him?

He doffs his hat, one of those hard little bowlers with a lip for a rim.

Has my husband sent you? Mister Joyce?

He looks at her blankly.

See Norah, he repeats, and gestures to her luggage. A storm of words issues from his mouth. She looks at his shoes, you could almost see your face in them. And the pressed pants, the striped waistcoat, the bloom in his lapel, there's a woman behind that. Or a servant. Or maybe he's finicky, don't like a finicky man, not in that way. Though she likes them to have more than one pair of ruddy plimsolls to their name, unlike some other parties she could mention.

See Norah, he says for the third time and smiles at her. Wet lips, he has. Big brown eyes under cliffy eyebrows.

He hasn't been sent, she realizes.

She waves a gloveless hand at him so as he'll see the pretend ring on her finger. I'm nearly a married woman she wants to say, but nearly never killed a man. But he takes no notice. He goes to bow again, or is he trying to whip her valeeze? She snatches at the handle and collides with him on the way up. He stumbles sideways. Oh God, is he going to fall over? Will she be had up for being drunk and disorderly, wouldn't that be a laugh and she as sober as a judge and as hungry as famine grass. He rubs his crown and straightens up. He has a kind face, fleshy, big-nosed though it is, maybe he means no harm.

I don't speak your language, Sir, she says to him very slowly.

He watches her intently. Then he points to his own chest extravagantly.

Kind English, he says and steps back.

She softens.

Now she doesn't want him to go, better a polite nuisance than no one at all and so she launches forth, how she's been abandoned by a blackguard that she loves but doesn't love her, and he's left her now for good and why couldn't he just have said he was going to dump her instead of dragging her halfway across the Continent, mortifying her like this, how she's as good as destitute, doesn't have a bed for the night and doesn't know a living soul here. And that he's left her without two coppers to rub together and what's more she really needs the lav now. The grievances flow, her eyes fill up.

The dapper man takes another step backwards, looking around in case they're being overheard. But she's not shouting, is she? This is what Jim Joyce has reduced her to, snivelling at strangers.

Me dis-pee-atchy, See Norah.

Glory be, what does that mean?

What am I going to do? she says to him, her voice rising as she does. She reaches out her hand to him. Maybe he'll take pity and give her a coin. She'd murder a cup of tea if such a thing could be had around here.

He retreats a few steps then turns on his heel. She's frightened him off.

Come back, she shouts after Mister Dispatchee and she doesn't care if she's making a holy show of herself. Come back!

But he beetles away, head down.

She sits down slowly. Is there no one who understands? She looks around and gets her answer. No, no one.

No one has seen her squabble with Mister Dispatchee. Even if someone had, who'd get in between a lady and a gentleman having a tiff? That is, if anyone is presuming she's a lady in the first place. More likely they'll think she's a floozy shooing away an awkward customer. Up close, she wouldn't pass for a lady, that's for sure. There's a ghost thread from her skirt that would unravel the entire hem if it was pulled so she has let it be, her boots are scuffed and dusty from all the traipsing, her hat is dinged, the coat she has is his, a dowdy old gaberdine. Glad of it now, though, with the sun gone, it's got a bit nippy.

Clock says ten past six. Jalopy goes by, the driver hooting madly.

It's almost black dark now and she doesn't like it. The glimmer man comes and climbs his ladder and flames the lamps and that helps. But not for long because now, now she's really dying to go. And she can think of nothing else. She is sitting again, with her legs crossed firm. If she stood up, there might be an accident. O sweet divine, she's bursting, she has to get to a WC and she can't do that out here on the street. If she were home maybe … she remembers getting short-taken with Jim once and she put him on guard in the mouth of Tangier Lane. Turn your back, she told him, but he kept on taking sneaky looks of her doing it in the gutter.

She's desperate now. But she can't do it here, can she? Could she go behind the statue? But sure the little park is an island stuck in the middle of the street. Anyway, she'd be had up surely, carted off, arrested. So the station is her only hope. But how is she going to manage with the two bags? She'll need two hands for the valeeze, it's that heavy. This is like the old riddle with the fox, the goose and the stook of corn. If she's going to do this it'll have to be two trips and which bag would she leave behind?

His, she thinks spitefully.

It wouldn't last kissing time out on the street in Dublin – sure the porter in Finn's once got the boot for leaving a ladies' hat box embroidering the pavement. He was only gone a minute or two but someone had whipped it. Is it the same here, she wonders, then all of a sudden there's no time for debate, she just has to go so she gets up, catching the handle of the valeeze. Holy Divine, what's in this? Boulders?

She holds on to her hat and lumbers across the street. An omnibus brake screeches and she almost gets herself mown down but she doesn't look behind her, she doesn't care. She has the valeeze with one hand, so she's all canted over, then she has to change to the other, then she has to use both. She lands outside the station portico, up the steps, the valeeze hitting them in spots, making gravelly noises. Here comes the revolving door, will she and the case fit in there together, yes, and the merry-go-round turns. Oh God, she swears there's leakage now as if her bladder knows how close the lav is … She falls into a vast booking hall she remembers from earlier, dumps the valeeze just inside the door, and gallops down the corridor ahead of her shouting *toilet toilet*, she doesn't care now, and she almost crashes into a lady with a feathered hat who takes one good look at her and says *Ban-Yo*? And she nods because she thinks any woman, lady or not, would recognize the signs and your wan points to a door at the far end, not much longer she says to herself, hold on, hold on for God's sake and she ploughs on throwing herself against the door with a picture of a lady on it, and in, and there, at last, a privy … she launches herself at the bowl though it's not a bowl, it's a strange little plinth with a hole in the middle and two shoe-shaped platforms either side but she doesn't care now, down with the drawers and ooh, the relief.

Yes! Oh yes!

It is only when she is done, she looks up and realizes she has done her business in full view of the attendant, a prim-looking yoke as old as Mamo, hair the colour of

75

straw, who's sitting at a little table, folding sheets of paper into squares. There are little towers of coins in front of her, and Norah realizes she hasn't paid. Spent a penny, though and my God, was it good. Coming up from crouching all she can think of is to say *sorry, sorry* and *excuse me, pardon* though she knows it's no use. Sure this woman thinks she's some hollering wild creature so she pulls up her drawers without even bothering to wipe, just a quick shake, and it's only then she thinks to pull the door closed but what odds, hasn't the horse bolted? The chain grazes her cheek like a hangman's noose and she yanks it down and is glad of the clattery noise of it as the pipes rumble and the water whooshes and she thinks she could stay in here for good. But she's going to have to go out there again sometime and lookit, the main thing is she's got here in time. She couldn't face the misery of wet bloomers on top of every-thing else. She straightens up and fixes herself as well as she can, spatters on the dusty boots, she sees, oh well. She gingerly opens the door.

The attendant is standing directly outside. Norah makes for one of the gleaming basins – the taps look like they've just been scoured and polished. She catches sight of her-self in the glass and thinks what a fright, regal bearing my eye. She takes her hat off, the inside rim of it is dark with sweat, God, she even peed with her hat on! Her hair is like a bird's nest and she wouldn't be surprised to find a slew of those blessed midges that were flying around under the trees had taken up lodgings in it. She should try to draw a comb through it, but the attendant is prowling around behind her, so she'll dispense with the niceties. There's no sign of a towel, though she can see one folded over the attendant's arm, but sure she's hardly going to offer it since no money has changed hands. She shakes the wet off her hands like a drenched dog and the attendant retreats from the flying drops.

She plays with the brim of her sad hat. When she's rich she'll have a rake of hats, one for every day of the week and a fancy one for Sunday. She tilts the hat so the grapes are round the back, then she remembers – blessed Saint Joseph, the valeeze!

She hares out the door leaving the attendant gawping after her.

She heads back towards the main door of the station. She can get a whiff of sweat from herself, salty, stale, but she's not going back inside to douse her armpits. And there, just where she left it, is the wretched yoke. She plonks herself down on it.

The relief of the bursting bladder is short-lived. She feels now like someone has let the air out of her tyres. Only this morning wasn't this their destination and a job for sure? Soon she'd be the wife of a schoolteacher, no he corrected her, a *professore-ay*. That's what he kept on promising. He'd sent a guinea through the post to a Miss Gilford who was supposed to fix him up with a position in Paree. She turned out to be a total fraud. No job in Paree, why not try Zoorick, they said. Nothing there, but what about Tree-es-tay? And that was supposed to be the end of it. But by that stage she'd got so used to the rumble and shoosh-shoosh of the train, the heeling over and back of it, that she began to think she'd never done anything else. That this was her job for life. To wander and never arrive.

The next *botún* was Jim's alone. That was yesterday, imagine, only yesterday! They were on the train from Zoorick and taking it easy – feet up if you don't mind, these blessed boots were pinching her – when it slowed coming into some big place and Jim leapt up and stuck his head out the window. Against all the rules. Hadn't he pointed out the warning to her written on a brass plate under the window. *Aye Vee-aytato Spor Jersey.* He'd made her repeat it, you'll have to learn some time, he said, but what good was that to her? It is forbidden to hang out, just the thing for small talk. And suddenly he's shouting at her, this is it, this is it! They bundled up their belongings, the coats they'd thrown off, the blooming hat, and fell out of the carriage and landed in a heap on the platform as the train shuddered off, the door swinging open, almost braining Jim.

They'd stood beside their upended baggage and drew breath. She dusted down her skirts and fetched her hat that had rolled away as if it wanted to escape from them and it was only then that Jim looked up and saw the station sign.

Shite and onions. He stamped up and down and threw his cap to the ground.

What ...?

We're in the wrong bloody place. He pointed to the station name in big bold letters – LAIBACH.

This is Lie Back, he said.

Lie Back is right. *Lie back and think of ...* Isn't he supposed to be the smart alec with the languages, the little bit of parlay vu in Paree, the Eyetalian? Even tried his hand at German in Zoorick.

What?

Trieste is the next stop, we alighted too soon.

Alighted, would you listen to him.

And who decided that?

Don't start, he hissed.

Sour puss.

Now what?

He shrugged.

At the far end of the platform there was a railway guard who'd flagged the train off. *Our train.*

Ask yer man, she said, when we can get the next train.

They picked up their bags and tramped towards him. There was a gabble then of scoozies and doevays and kwandos and the guard took out his logbook and ran his fingers down the columns and shook his head. He pointed to the big station clock overhead and said:

Doe-man-ee.

And even though she hadn't a clue what he was saying she knew the way Jim turned to her that it was bad news.

Next one isn't till tomorrow, he said.

She felt like bawling but she stopped herself. She might have given him her all two nights ago in Zoorick but she didn't know him well enough yet to be giving in to the waterworks in front of him. Fellas didn't like that. And in the mood he was in, he might walk off on her and then where would she be?

He'd been surly on the train. Was he having second thoughts, she'd wondered. Well, he wasn't the only one.

Lie Back, she said, where's that?

He didn't answer her but picked up his own bag and left her to struggle with the dented valeeze. She trailed after him into the station hall. He found the Ladies' Waiting, a huge hall of a place with high windows.

I'll go and find us a room, he said.

With what?

She took out her little notebook to do her sums.

Five pound from Lady Gregory – gone. Tenner from Mister Russell. Gone. Do we still have the seven quid from

79

your da? And what about the doctor's guinea you got for the story in the *Homestead*? Where's that got to?

The queen is in her counting house, he said.

She ignored that.

I might wire the Beryl-its, maybe they'd stump up for a night somewhere on tick.

On tick, how often had she heard that! Was this how their life was going to be, touching strangers for funds, forever with their hands out?

She sighed. Am I going to be left again?

Jesus falls for the third time, he said and smiled at her.

She hated when he reached for God in his mocking voice, especially since he's a pure heathen himself. If there was a joke in it, she didn't get it.

I don't know about Jesus, but if I'm on bag-watching duty again, you'd better not come back with your hands hanging ...

Jesus accosts his blessed Mother, he said.

Will you stop taking the Lord's name in vain and talk to me. I'm fed up with all this palaver. On trains, off trains ... I've sat in more public parks than a stray dog.

Well, that's quite a speech, Missy!

Don't Missy me!

Ah but, he said and smiled again. I will missy thee.

And then he kissed away the last of her bad temper. But he left her again, just the same.

The Ladies' Waiting in Lie Back was empty, thanks be to God, a frowning room with a varnished seat running all the way round. High and brown as a Protestant pew. The window sills were so high you couldn't see out. She'd spent an age staring at the speckled floor. It had little shiny bits in it like buried treasure. She'd tried to work out if there was a pattern to it, but she couldn't see one. She wandered over to the black fireplace at the far end of the room. Green veins ran through the marble-like rivers on a map, but there was no fire lit and the empty grate looked desolate.

The station was silent, echoey like a church after Benediction and then when she'd got used to the feeling of being the last person in the world alive, there was a *tatar-rattat* on the glass of the waiting room door and the Station Master entered and brandished his fob watch before her, tapping on it. Then he pointed showily to the door. She didn't need the lingo to understand what he meant.

My husband … she began.

But the Station Master wagged his finger in her face.

Know in-glazey.

She gestured to the bags.

Please Sir, she began again, but he stopped her with the self-same finger.

Know in-glazey.

She felt her temper rising, not at this gent, hadn't he got a station to run and a home to go to, but with Jim. That no good *bostún*, who couldn't even read a ruddy timetable. If he were here, she'd wrap the laces of his tennis shoes tight around his neck …

Pear Mess-oh, she heard from behind the Station Master and there was Jim and she'd never been so glad to see anyone. She rushed to him and he said, there, there, Wifey, and launched a new spurt at the Station Master who seemed to relent. Well, he smiled, which is more than she'd got out of him. Things were looking up.

But not for long.

There's no wire office open at this hour, Jim muttered to her, and no way to get a room.

He lugged up the valeeze. It looked like it'd been through the wars. No wonder. Sure, it had been practically flung from the train. There was the sleeve of a shirt hanging out of it. She felt exactly the same way, like a ragged remnant. They made their way out through the station hall followed by the Station Master and stepped outside. Behind them, they could hear the sound of the doors being bolted.

The gods are against us, he said.

As if there was more than one God. One was enough for her, thank you very much.

It'll have to be the park.

No! I won't, Jim, no!

The last time, I promise!

Stay out all night? Like a pair of tramps?

At least there's two of us, he said.

They were standing forlorn on a large square outside the station. A few people scurried home bent against the wind. It wasn't exactly cold but there was a niggling breeze, and because they were outcasts it felt colder.

Got us some grub, Jim said and produced from the pocket of his gaberdine a baton of bread broken in two with the heel gnawed off at one end.

You didn't waste any time, I see!

And cheese!

Like a magician, he produced from the other pocket a lump of hard-looking stuff wrapped in butter paper. He held it up to her nose. Smelled like buttermilk.

We'll have a picnic in the park, he said, sounding silly bright.

Another ruddy park, she thought.

We'll sleep under the stars.

And what if it rains, she asked looking up at the sky, what then?

If it rains the trees will shelter us. We'll survive, Mrs Joyce, never fear!

Mrs Joyce, indeed! He walked on jauntily ahead of her, carrying the luggage. She couldn't abide him when he was being cheerful like this. Particularly when he was the one who'd made a bags of everything!

She looked up at the inky sky and the arching trees with their piney umbrellas overhead. You'll see the Continent, he'd promised, the cities of Europe. But all she'd seen so far was a string of scruffy waiting rooms and the arse end of public parks. She followed him and threw herself down on one of the wooden seats under the halo of a street lamp. Jim sat down beside her and clasped her knee as if he owned her. She tucked the valeeze in safe under her feet.

No one's going to steal it, he said.

And what if we fall asleep? Though she had no intention of it.

Fat chance, he said gloomily.

And then she wanted his brightness back.

Come on, he said, let's eat.

The bread was hard. Stale probably – end of the day's leavings from the bakery and he'd probably paid full price for it. It wasn't like the honest-to-god bread of home, Mamo's soda loaf, or even her Pappie's spongy batch. But it was food and she could have eaten a horse. The cheese, Lord save us, the colour of meal, hard too and peppered with holes. From a sheep, he said. Whoever heard the like? But it filled a hole. And then out of those deep pockets of his overcoat, he produced a bottle of red wine.

The piece of resistance, he said.

Did the last of our money go on that? she demanded.

The barkeep opened it for me, he said. Like the bread, it had been broken into. He went at the cork with his teeth. It'll be a long night, we'll need it.

He threw back his head and took a good slug. Then wiped his mouth along his sleeve.

Here, he said.

Holy God, she said as she drank a bit, it's like knocking back the Communion wine. But it tasted good, warmed her inside.

Snuggle in here, Wifey, he said to her and with a half-full stomach and the wine singing in her head, she thought, maybe this isn't the worst.

But now is. She sits in the station vestibule directly under the big station clock. It wheezes and inches forward. Nine hours waiting. Nine! That's it now. He's definitely left her.

When the wine was all gone, Jim had produced the tobacco and he rolled for two though it was nasty stuff, Hungarian he said, but it did the trick. Inhaling was like comfort, something familiar, the smoke of memory, she and Mary O learning how to do it with plug tobacco pilfered from Mary's da, all the coughing and spluttering and spitting out the curly hairs of it like from down below, before they got the hang of it.

The wind started to shiver through the trees. Then came the first rumble, a long way off.

Do you hear that? she asked him.

She saw a look come over his face. A storm, you think?

She cocked a weather ear. Thunder by the sounds of it, I'd say.

She looked at him and there it was again.

Thunder? I hate the thunder, it scares me half to death, he said in a low voice, as if the thunder might hear him.

It was far off then, like clattery gunfire, and she said sure maybe it'll pass us by but then the trees were taitering and flailing like they were pleading with the sky and it wasn't long before the first big roll came overhead, a grumble, then a rumble, then a roar and Jim grabbed her hand and dug his fingernails into her palm. He trembled with every wave of it and he ejaculated Holy God and Glory Be and Sweet Divine and Jesus, Mary and Tom, staring up at the drifting sky and clapping his hands over his ears as if that could block it out. And in between he said, and dogs, I don't like dogs either, and what's more they don't like me.

What a mixture he was, all bold swagger one minute and like a scaredy cat the next. Wonder did a dog have a go at him at some stage? Though he'd never said so, but sure what else had he not told her? And no wonder dogs didn't like him, they'd smell his fear a mile off. But thunder?

Then the lightning came and it was her turn to be afraid. This was like nothing from home. The forks cracked the sky open and in the midst of the howling tantrum, the heavens opened, first with fat teardrops so large they peppered holes in the leaves, just like the old cheese, then came the torrents. Her hat was flat as a pancake and the straw would rot surely. He unpeeled his gaberdine and threw it over both of them, but in that downpour it was like the wet weight of the world. Her hair was dripping in rats' tails, her boots were letting in but himself was only happy that the thunder had passed.

A pray mwa, lay dell huge, he said and looked her in the eye for the first time that night and laughed.

She didn't understand but she was relieved to see his smile, his great opening-up smile.

He surveyed the ruin of their wardrobe. His shoes were almost a goner – made for tennis not the ark. He shook them off and wrung out his socks. His hair all slicked down on his crown, his jacket sodden.

By midnight, the rain had let up but there was no possibility of sleeping now since they were cold and wet through. They huddled and shivered together. She'd seen him at his lowest, whimpering like a whipped dog as the sky roared over them. And she thought, maybe this is how people are really wed. Not like in Zoorick, where they'd shared a feather bed and a bolster and a bit of rumpy-pumpy. Now weren't they joined by their fears? His and hers.

And that was when she plucked up the courage to tell him. The never-ever-keep-me-waiting rule, and the why of it. Sonny Bodkin.

Now here she is in the right station, sitting on her valeeze, but no Jim. The other bag is probably took by now and what'll he say when he comes back and finds it gone? But she's not going back out into the night for it. What's in it but all his scribbling. In Zoorick, after they'd done the deed and she'd lain there all snoozy and content, he leapt up without a stitch on and fished out the scads of paper from his bag. He'd pulled on his long johns for he wouldn't do his writing in his figure and sat himself down at the little writing desk in the corner of the room. No sweet nothings afterward with this fella. Or even a fag, and God, she'd been dying for one. She'd asked but he'd run out.

Are you writing about me, she asked as she smoothed down the hem of the sheet with her fingers and played with a loose thread. The bed sheets had been starched stiff, like tablecloths nearly, and it had taken a while to put manners on them. But at least they'd been fresh, weren't they her honeymoon sheets after all? But he didn't answer. As he scribbled away, she thought of the laundresses at the other end of those sheets, and their poor red hands, just like her own had been when she'd done that kind of work, and she thought, haven't I moved on, all the same. I'm in Zoorick on my honeymoon and I'm never going back.

Over her head, the clock strikes the half hour. Is this what Mamo meant when she'd read Norah's tea leaves and told her – *you'll end up in a Crown building.*

Are you sure this is the right train, she pestered him when they presented themselves at Lie Back station at cockcrow this morning. Run up the platform and check for we don't want a repeat of yesterday's fiasco.

She was milking it a bit, but she had a right. She'd spent the night on the streets, she'd been soaked through and frozen stiff, and it'd be a miracle if she didn't come down with double pneumonia. He went off with a puss on him for he didn't like to be bossed around.

This is it, he said when he came back.

They tumbled into the same compartment as yesterday, the exact same spot Jim said, for he took notice of the numbers, and it was pure heaven, so warm that their clothes gave off more gouts of steam than the engine, and probably odours too, but she didn't give two hoots. All she wanted was a soft seat and a place to doze off. And she thought well, they'd been through a bit of a nightmare, but it was over now, wasn't it? Surely, now everything'll come good. But had he already been plotting his escape, even then? Was it the night in Lie Back that decided him? Or the row on the train?

It was one of those arguments she couldn't for the life of her remember what had started it, some passed remark, probably. It was often like that with them, a silly *cipín* of a thing would cause a blaze. There was just one other gentleman in the carriage, who watched their words fly back and forth like a tennis match, though he didn't understand a word. And you, and you, she said, and Jim rolling his eyes in yer man's direction as if to say hush now, but a fat lot she cared, and what about you, he batted back, who does nothing but complain.

Complain? Me complain?

As if she had no reason to, dumped in parks, sleeping in the open air, and ignored when better company came along.

Like the gent in the carriage. Jim struck up a conversation with him rather than finish the row with her. He was so happy in his confab with his new friend, it was a wonder he didn't touch him for a loan.

She sat and fumed and looked out the window and thought, what in God's holy name have I done? And Jim went on talking to yer man. He even moved across the aisle so he wouldn't have to sit with her. The gent kept on giving her the eye. She knew his type from Finn's, gents who thought they were entitled because they had a club collar and you had an apron. He was looking her up and down like that, while Jim was playing the man of the world. She recognized the words *Earland Daisies* and *Squalid Beryl-its* being bandied about even though Jim kept on telling her she was fierce slow cottoning on to the lingo.

She sensed them unite against her, and she became convinced that Jim was talking about her, disparaging her with a stranger. She glared at him daggers, and finally he deigned to sit with her again.

Are you talking about me behind my back? she hissed at him.

Your name wasn't even mentioned and how would you know, anyhow?

You've changed your tune from last night, she said.

And what do you mean by that? He leaned in, the words like stabbing breaths in her ear.

I was good enough then when you needed someone to cling to in the thunder, wasn't I?

Keep your voice down now, he said, shooting glances at the gent opposite who was studiously looking out the window. He can hear.

I don't care if he can hear or not. I have just one thing to say to you sunny Jim. That's the last time I'll sleep on the streets for you. I'm warning you here and now. If it happens again, I'll be gone!

Well, hark at her!

She knew when he started with that hark business that he was losing the argument. Just then the conductor passed by on the corridor outside calling *Tree-e-stay, Tree-estay, Stats-eeony Tree-estay* and this time she jumped up.

Hark at the conductor, you! she said. Unless you want to spend another night under the stars.

Didn't like that one bit. Didn't like his old romantic guff being thrown back at him. He lifted down his own bag from the overhead rack and pushed past her, leaving her to struggle with the valeeze, too heavy to heave up there in the first place.

The Eyetalian gent came to her rescue, holding back the door, doffing his hat and taking the case from her as Jim stomped off in a huff. The gent followed them and handed out the valeeze to her on the platform.

Gratsee, she managed to remember and he doffed his hat at her and smiled. See that, sunny Jim, but he didn't because he was busy marching off in high dudgeon.

Pray go, the gent said and she thought, yes, she'd better hurry after Jim or she'd lose him.

So that's how they arrived, at loggerheads, she fit to be tied and him in a snot, in the midst of their first matrimonial.

Why is it always me that's left, she said to him when he deposited her on the green outside the station. She was sulking, she knew it, but she wasn't going to let it go.

Oh well, said he, please yourself. I'll sit here so and you go off and see how far you'll get.

He gave the valeeze a kick for good measure. As if it hadn't suffered enough.

She could feel her ire rise again. She nearly shouted at him that if Vinny Cosgrave were here he'd have hailed a cab and gone direct to a hotel, and they'd have travelled in style, no tumbling in and out of third class, if you please. And she was going to add for good measure – I could just as well have chosen Vinny. It might as well be him as another, and he'd have made an honest woman of me by now, having had his way with me in his mother's house one evening when the maid was off. But she said none of that and Jim sloped off.

I won't be long, he said.

Famous last words.

And now they might be his last words ever!

Now what?

She wonders again where the Ladies' Waiting is, but what's the point, she'll only get shown the door at a certain hour of the night, same as in Lie Back, and she's tired now of trying to explain that her husband will be back any minute now.

He's not her husband and he isn't coming back.

She's a woman with a curtain ring on her finger, no papers to say who she is, didn't Jim carry those off with him, and not a penny to her name. But no matter what, she's not spending a second night under the stars and that's just that.

With or without him.

She gets up. She can't sit here any longer. She goes to heave the valeeze up but she seems to have lost all of her strength for she can't get a budge out of it. Oh well. When she straightens up she feels dizzy. She remembers the feeling from childhood, her and Dilly playing duck, duck, goose, wheeling around with their eyes closed so they could unharness from the world, escape. She staggers as the station reels around her and next thing she's danced herself out of it.

Signorah

See Norah, See Norah, a voice calls and she feels her face
being tapped, ever so politely. She opens her eyes and
finds herself in a sweet-smelling cloud, she thinks of Benediction, and wonders if she's airborne or heaven-bound,
but when she puts out her hand to steady herself, she
finds cold tile and little pieces of grit on the palps of her
fingers and she realizes she's on the station floor, so not
dead or ascended into heaven. The incense cloud clears
and she's looking up into the twin portholes of a man's
nostrils, sitting in the tidy bed of a moustache. Her head is
on something white, the snowy square of a handkerchief,
which is draped over this fella's lap and she's lying there
practically on his crown jewels. Heavenly God!

What has she done, or agreed to do? O my God, I am
heartily sorry …

She tries to raise herself up.

See Norah, the voice insists quietly. *Calma, Calma.*

The nostrils disappear and she sees a pair of brown
eyes peer at her from under a bowler hat. His right hand
is supporting her neck, like he's nursing a baby, his left
is holding a cigarette that's burning low because he's too
busy holding her head. When she puts a hand up to her
head, she realizes her own hat is gone and she looks to

one side and sees it like an abandoned spinning top some way off, still rolling from side to side, taunting her. So she can't have been out that long. But does every blessed thing want to get away from her, even her ruddy hat? No gloves neither, then it comes back to her that she'd recently come from the lav, but where's the valeeze?

She tries to stir again – she's already lost one piece of luggage, Jim'll kill her if two pieces are gone. Jim, Jim, it all comes rushing back. A new head appears. A halo of dry brassy hair, the quivery double chin with little specks of white downy hair where she can see, so close, the lady has plucked. Or failed to. She's in some kind of uniform – the privy attendant! – now she remembers, the one gathering in the sheaves in the lav. Behind her she sees the striped legs of the Station Master – another one! She can see the puckered hem of his serge coat, his bulging waistcoat, how odd everything looks from down here. He leans over now and takes off his peaked hat and hands it to the lav lady and she begins to wave it back and forth over Norah trying to create a breeze.

Mister Gentleman leans over her face and says: Layee, come ay see key amah?

The dirty article! Amo, Jim has told her, is the verb to love. *A mo, a mass, a mat ...* that's as far as he'd got. Or was that Latin, sounded like the Mass to her or that bit in confession, *day in, day echo.*

Mister Gentleman hands the smoking fag to the Station Master and he hurries off with it. Pity, she'd die for one.

Lady Lav mimes at her. Norah sees a china cup and saucer in her hands and almost faints again. That's what's happened. Nothing to eat or drink since yesterday, no wonder. But she crimsons with shame, she never was that weak wilty type. Strong as a horse, her. The Station Master comes back.

Ackwa, ackwa, Lady Lav says, sounding like a peeved duck, swatting him away again as she continues making a breeze with his gold-braided cap. He scurries off. At the beck and call of them all.

Now Mister Gentleman shrugs off his coat, a smart black one with tails and a velvet collar and while Lady Lav holds her head, he slides out from under her and inserts the bundled roll of his coat instead. Thanks be to God for that. It'll get ruined she thinks, on this grimy floor, but she's not going to object. The Station Master is back with a tall glass of water, which he hands to Lady Lav. She motions to Norah to open her lips and the water slips down her throat and suddenly she's so thirsty she raises herself up on her elbows and whips the glass and downs it all in one loud slurping guzzle and she doesn't care how undignified it looks. Dignified, there's a laugh, when she's stretched out on a train station floor. And then she sees the valeeze, Lady Lav is sitting on it and she can see the sleeve of Jim's shirts still escaping, same one, and the lid pressing down on it with Lady Lav's weight, and she thinks that's how we are now, cut off from one another, and I'd better start trying to get on without him.

She's half up now so she struggles to sitting so at least she won't be looking up their noses or have them looking down theirs at her. Lady Lav catches her around the waist as she stands up. She's still feeling strange, not dizzy or faint but at a remove, as if she's watching this and herself from the next room. Mister Gentleman peers at her – what kind eyes he has and his brow wrinkles.

Maylee-oh?

Sounds like a cat with a fiddle. It's a question, that's all she knows. She shakes her head. He and the Station

Master exchange a flurry of talk while Lady Lav still holds on to her in a constable's clinch and throws in her half-penny's worth when the gents stop talking, and all of them keep looking at her intently. *I must get away now*, she thinks, this has the look of something official, as if polis might be called. She tries to unharness herself from Lady Lav but to no avail.

Me, Mister Gentleman finally says, Meester Schmitz.

Mister Smith, sounds like. That old chestnut!

You? he queries, pointing.

She'd better say nothing, particularly if this fella speaks English, so she clamps her lips together. But he just stands there and waits. Looks fierce respectable, hat off now, pol-ished shoes, older than her Jim. *My Jim, what a laugh, no my about it.* And still he waits and it's like those card games with Uncle Tommy where Mamo would take so long to throw down, she'd force someone else to declare. She can't bear it, all eyes on her, Mister Gentleman, Lady Lav and the Station Master craning in.

Norah, she says slowly.

You are *da sola*? he asks, sweeping his hand around magisterially, taking in her battered hat, the dejected valeeze, herself canted to one side.

Layee ay con kwal coono?

Heavens above, what's that?

Your marry toe? he persists. Husband?

She shakes her head.

He's gone, she says and once she says that she's in floods like she's set off the tears of years. Pappie, Mamo, Sonny, Willie Mulvey like the roll call of the holy souls read from the altar and she can't stop, fat blubbery tears and hiccoughy sobs like a child after a tantrum, she just can't stop.

The three of them stand around her, the Station Master mouth agape, a wrinkle of distress growing on Mister Gentleman's globey forehead. They're at a loss. She doesn't know what to do with herself but sob and carry on. Even if they spoke English, she wouldn't be able to explain. Lady Lav keeps a firm grip around her waist.

See Norah Norah, Mister Smith begins – and suddenly she gets it, it's Missus, it means Missus, but Lady Lav interrupts him. She holds her liver-spotty hands in a bunch to her mouth and says, Fam-ay?

It's another question.

Lady Lav scrabbles in her pocket and produces an apple. Lurid green and shiny as an ornament. Norah practically grabs it and sinks her teeth into it. The flesh inside is almost white but it fills her stale mouth with a wash of green and she wolfs it down to its core. And, like a child, she hands the core back when she's finished.

Mister Smith begins again: See Norah Norah?

She nods. Norah twice. This is who she is now, for better or worse.

Non pray-occupar-chee, we will found Meester Norah! he says loudly as if that will make her understand better.

It's a fool's errand, she wants to say, that fella's gone for good and glory and good riddance to him. The only surprise is that he left his bag behind him, with all the scribblings inside. But that's not her concern now.

Mister Smith holds another confab with the Station Master, who bows and retreats after being given another errand to perform. On instruction, Lady Lav lets go of her, and scurries off, first to retrieve Norah's hat, and then with a small baby wave and an *add-io*, *See Norah* – must be the Eyetalian for cheerio – she retreats to her privy kingdom and Norah is left alone with Mister Smith.

He clicks his finger and a porter appears and picks up the valeeze. She's about to protest but Mister Smith shakes his head.

See Norah, please to come with me.

He points towards the portico where between the pillars she can see a carriage. The porter is hefting her valeeze into a drum on the back. It's black dark out there and she doesn't want to be out in it again, alone.

Please, he says again, pleasant enough.

Lookit, she's had her head in his lap, hasn't she? And what choice does she have? It's now or never, Jim, and she calls on God or whoever is in charge of arrivals and departures, to make him appear, even now, and save the day.

I'll go with you so, she says, but no funny business, do you hear?

She's sure he doesn't know what she said but Mister Smith begins to move towards the carriage and she follows him. He waits on her to catch up, and they walk, like man and wife, but he keeps his distance. His hand hovers in the air near the small of her back but he doesn't touch her, not until they get to the station steps, where he catches her elbow as they descend. He helps her into the carriage. She gets a whiff of armpit as she does. When was the last time she had a wash, was it Zoorick, she couldn't smell of the other thing still, could she? Well, so what if she does. She flops down on the cushioned inside, deep red and buttony, and keeps her arms close to her sides to keep the whiff to herself. The door closes. No escape then.

She watches as Mister Smith presses a coin in the porter's palm and suddenly she panics, are they in cahoots, the pair of them, con men who prey upon … The far door of the cab opens and Mister Smith, who has lit another cigarette on the journey, climbs in.

Oh well, too late.

See Norah. He smiles, lovely teeth. Can you tell me, Da dovay veiny?

Veiny? What's he on about? Every time he tries the English he lapses into his own lingo and it sounds like singing to her, like do-ray-me.

Where, he tries again, do you in-habit?

Live, does he mean?

Nowhere, she's tempted to say. Haven't I been on the road for months, that's what it feels like, though it's only been what – four days, five?

Dublin, she says.

Dublin-oh? he asks. Why do they put an *oh* on everything? As if everything is a surprise.

Ireland, she adds.

Ear-landa?

She nods.

And your husband?

She's torn between accusing Jim of every crime he's committed over the past few days or hoping against hope that he might still show up, though the carriage is rocking now and the horses are wheeling around and they're leaving the circus in front of the station and lumbering out onto the street.

Beryl-its School, she offers, half-heartedly, wanting to find Jim and wanting to show him, all in the same breath.

Squalid Beryl-its, Mister Smith repeats and he smiles and seems excited.

He raps on the roof of the carriage and rolls down the window, shouting at the driver. Squalid Beryl-its!

He seems relieved, he's probably thinking what'll he do with this mad woman who had her head in his lap and she gets all indignant thinking about that. *I didn't put it there.*

They pass the grove of trees and the bench she sat on and she almost expects to see herself still sitting there. But there's no one in the park now and it's as if she was never there herself. Then she sees it, Jim's soft bag, sitting in plain sight exactly where she left it at the kerb. She's about to touch Mister Smith on the arm and ask him to stop. To step down from the rocking carriage and fetch it in.

It's a decision of a moment. Will she, won't she?

She doesn't.

What earthly good is his blooming bag to her? She watches it through the window as they pass, and she winds her head back, pressing her nose against the glass until she can see it no longer.

There, she thinks firmly, that's it now.

Over.

She turns to look at Mister Smith, oozy brown eyes regarding her. Hat off now and his hair showing, retreating from his smooth forehead. He has a worried look. Has she ever seen that look in Jim's eye? No, she can say, never. Not through all the scrapes he's led her into.

Two-toe bane-ay? Mister Smith says, like a question and then again like a lullaby. Two-toe bane-ay. She thinks of a two-step. The beginning of a new dance.

Even so, she keeps an eye out for Jim as they clop along a sea promenade and she sees what she's been sensing all this time – choppy, silvery water and a low moon making a boreen across it, nothing now between her and it, and then some grand buildings come into view on her side, and still she keeps her eyes peeled for he could still turn up, couldn't he, and save the day? Rushing along with his coat-tails flying behind him and the broken-down plimsolls. Funny word that. That's what he called the tattered shoes, said it had something to do with boats. A plimsoll line – a plimsoll liar, more like.

The carriage veers away from the sea and as it does, she begins to worry about herself.

Where is this fella taking her? Is this the last time she'll be seen? This can't be the end of her story, can it? Done in in Tree-estay. No, no, stop it, this very minute, Norah! Look at him, hasn't he been the perfect gent and with those kind eyes, squinting in the smoke he's made. *Hasn't stopped puffing since we started. Do I make him nervous, is that it?* Is he married, she wonders, probably, aren't they all? Hasn't he the cut of a man that a woman has turned out? But then there was all that luggage the porter was loading up on the roof. Must have been away on a trip. A long trip by the look of it, and maybe no time to be courting. *Would you stop it this very minute, Norah Barnacle? He's getting you out of a jam is all, not marching you down the aisle.* She would ask him, but he won't understand her, so she just smiles at him foolishly because it's all she can do. *Enjoy the journey, Norah girl, but remember the way you've come for you might need to go back.*

Back to the station? *Don't be mad! Let Jim do the waiting for a change and see how he likes it!*

They judder across a huge, cobbled square and she can hear the urgings of the driver. The *rub-a-dub-dub* of the carriage sets her teeth chattering and throws their shoulders together, her and Mister Smith, and he glances at her sidelong, comradely, tentacles of kindness reaching out to her. No, this one won't hurt her. They pass through streets tight as alleys with buildings you can't see the end of, balconies jutting out, held up by stony slaves, faces craggy and arms bulging with the effort, and then they swing out into the open again, passing over a bridge and there's a sort of a lagoon, a calm glistening bath of water, mantled with moon again, ships moored on it making clinking sounds. There's a breeze building up, does that mean another storm and she remembers last night again, oh and look, a big gold dome. They come to a halt.

Squalid Berly-its, Mister Smith says to her by way of explanation. He raises one finger of an ungloved hand. Oon atty-mo.

He steps outside and leaves the door open and she sees him rapping on the wood of a grand entrance, a set of double doors with shining brasses – some poor slavey has been busy on them – and presently a man with a shock of blond hair answers, is that Mister Foney, she wonders. There's an avid conversation between them, all hands flying – Mister Smith can't open his mouth but his hands are dancing, that is if he's not lighting up. Lights one cig-arette off another, asked permission with his eyes, mind you, at least that, and they smell good ... It's sweet, his tobacco, sweet, spicy. She sees Mister Foney shaking his head and Mister Smith pointing to the carriage and then further back in the direction of the station wherever that is now, and even without the lingo she can see what the answer is.

For the first time she feels desolate.

Now what?

Mister Smith must be thinking the same thing. He climbs back in the carriage, this time sitting across from her and when the driver shouts out, he doesn't answer, doesn't know what to answer, it looks like. Except that he's thinking, he's stuck with her.

Nun chay, he says sorrowfully. No nuns here, just as well for Jim would cross the street if he saw a nun coming.

So the answer is no. But Mister Smith's no comes with a sorry in his voice. Not like Mister Foney who was cross at being disturbed so late.

A rinse of loneliness comes over her, *now this is bloody ridiculous, don't let yer man see you. Oh no, that wouldn't do at all, at all, not when you've only been sprawled over his knees for God knows how long.* Anyway, it's not crying, more like the leaking as happens at the start of your monthlies. A silent tear rolls down her cheek, followed by another and they can't be stopped so she doesn't even try. She wipes them away with her hand until Mister Smith leans across and offers her a hanky – the same one. She mops herself up while he says again, *calma*, but she feels he's talking to himself.

After a few minutes he takes out his fob watch, looks at it, then sighs and slips it back in his pocket again. He raps on the roof with his fist once more and says loudly for the benefit of the driver – Villa Venet-see-annie, Serve-ol-ah – and the driver takes a whip to the horses and they jolt into rumbling movement.

La mia cas-ah, he says to her, she is my house.

Did her tears do that?

Where is his house? Sure Jim'll never find me now.

She rattles back and forth between the two of them like a shuttlecock. This man is kind and here, Jim is useless and not. It's Hobson's choice. She'll have to take her chances with this fella who's the better bet, if only to give her a roof over her head for a night.

She can't remember the last time she slept proper. She leans back against the velvety upholstery and she's so exhausted that it's all she can do to keep her eyes open. But she fights it. Even though there's not much point keeping her eyes peeled now, she's lost all sense of direction.

They seem to be climbing and she's sure she can see the sea again but much further away now. Mister Smith is still watching her, though surreptitiously. But he's given up on trying to talk to her and she's relieved. The carriage rattles on but the silence between them is soothing.

Maybe he thinks I'm a chancer? It's the first time she's thought of herself like that. As someone who needs watching. She braves a smile at him but he's miles away, looking out the window at the moon-spattered sea far below, glimpsed in between the sentries of trees. Finally, the carriage slows. She hears the driver call *woe, wo-oh-woe* and Mister Smith looks at her and smiles.

See-amo kwee, he announces. She hears love in the middle of his words.

He gets out and runs around to her side of the carriage and opens it wide, although there's a boots of some sort standing by bowing and scraping, who looks at her askance. *If it's a place with servants, they'll be on my side, won't they?*

She steps out into the night and feels the crunch of gravel underfoot. It's black dark – *where has the moon gone?* – but the sky is pepper and salted with stars, and she can see columns of tall narrow trees like you'd see in a graveyard, what are they called now, she's heard the name but it won't come to her. If Jim were here he'd know the answer in two lingos and be quick to tell her. Always parading words in front of her – did you know, he'd begin, and she'd know for sure that whatever it was, she didn't.

There's a big house, standing on its own, white masonry looming out of the night, with steps leading to a thrown-open front door. Two big stone lions stare at her. There's a verandah all wrapped in greenery. When she looks up there are bow-shaped balconies on the second floor with barley twist pillars. Very grand. She glances across the courtyard. To her right she can see the twin gables of a big building that looks for all the world like a workhouse. Oh God, is that where he's taking her? That's where she was born and as sure as God made little apples she's not going back there.

A small woman with a gigantic nest of fair hair piled high on her head rushes down the steps and Mister Smith surges forward calling Livia, Livia, and they embrace. *She's the wife, so. There had to be a wife, didn't there?* She crushes him to her, only has eyes for him so she doesn't notice Norah standing there, two hands hanging. Himself must have been sorely missed. While they're having their court, a footman is heaving down the bags. He rescues her old battered valeeze and she thinks how poor and mean it looks beside Mister Smith's cases with the capped corners and riveted edges. She's seen luggage like that at Finn's belonging to ship's brokers from Liverpool or Guernsey, or the music hall artistes who stay for a run at the Tivoli, though they're never in mint condition like these.

A little girl appears shouting Papa, Papa, a dark little thing with a big bow in her hair and a white dress with a sailor collar and she fastens herself around Mister Smith's waist.

Eventually, the little girl disentangles herself and it is she who turns a pair of dark eyes on Norah. She taps her mother's arm.

Mama, Mama!

Mama takes Norah in with one long cool look. Then the torrent begins. Norah doesn't know what's being said but she knows there's questions, lots of them from Mama, and explanations too from the way Mister is gesticulating. He speaks with his fingers, waving them about, then rubbing his palps together as if he was feeding the birds, then shaking the birdy hands up and down, then opening them wide again like an opera singer. He's saying hush and not to worry, Norah knows that much, for she's used to the tone fellas use when they're making excuses. He keeps on gesturing at her, then shaking his head, then appealing to his wife. She can see from Mama's expression that she's not convinced. She doesn't know the Eyetalian for *but*, but it's written all over the woman's broad face with the pert nose. Look at the fine dress she has, is that organza? Hard to tell in this light, it's not serge anyway, and impossible to know the colour, is it black or plum? Empire line, lovely work on the neck and lace trim on the sleeves. All she needs is a pair of gloves and a hat and she could be going to a ball. These people must have money to burn, but that means nothing. She could still be turned away. Have mercy, Mama, please, she finds herself pleading silently.

The little girl is watching Norah avidly and then looking at her parents, deep in discussion, back and forth, and Norah tries smiling at her. Silly isn't it, it's what you do with a baba, but she's never been much good with babas, can't be doing with them when they can't tell you what ails them. It'd scald you trying to work out their woe from their wails. And just at the moment, she feels too like a baba herself, no words to say what she's feeling and too big and ugly to start shrieking about it. Anyways, this girl must be seven or eight – she's reached the age of reason, if they observe such things here, but aren't they all Catholics, isn't that where they all come from, Rome? The girl smiles back shyly as if Norah were a new playmate.

Bwona Sara, See Norah, she says and does a little curtsy.

Lay-teats-iyah, Mama says sharply.

Lay what?

The girl backs away. Spindly little thing, but no mistaking who her father is, she has those same eyes, black as coals. Like a little gypsy.

She wishes that Mama would make her mind up for there's a breeze with an edge stirring now. It's making her eyes tear up. Suddenly the matrimonial comes to a halt. Mister has noticed the glisten on her cheeks and makes for her, saying, See Norah, no, no no, and Mama stays put, makes a clucking noise that could be a tut-tut or could mean you poor thing. But the tear trap works. They are standing yards apart now, no more lovey-dovey. *I knows the feeling, Missus, if sunny Jim were to turn up now, I'd be keeping my distance too.*

Mama steps forward, drawing level with Mister like it's some complicated dance, and holds out her hand.

Can I present Madame Schmitz, Mister says. He draws the madam word out at the end like they did in Paree.

Looks like she's in, for the night, anyway.

Her hand is tiny when Norah takes it, wondering if she's supposed to kiss it. From what she's seen the Eyetalians will kiss one another at the drop of a hat. *She don't like me, I can tell straight off.* But there's nothing she can do about that so she takes Madame's hand and shakes it decorously, not too hearty, mind, not like a man in other words.

See Norah, she says and smiles tightly, welcome to Villa Venet-Sea-Annie.

So a villa, not the workhouse, after all.

Welcome, indeed. But it's the first thing Norah's understood clearly since she set foot in this bloody country, and she's so relieved she could weep in earnest. The flunkey lifts her valeeze onto the trolley and she sees Jim's shirt

106

trailing from it, thin and wrinkled and dragged through the mud, and she feels as if it's his corpse she's carrying around. But if she has his remains, where in the name of all that's good and holy is he?

They make a procession two by two into the house. Mister and the little girl first, then the Madame. Norah takes up the rear. Up the white steps – who was it said, Jim of course, that these are for the gentry's horses, that's why they're so shallow, but why would you bring a horse into the house? Isn't there a stable? Is that where they'll put her up? At the front door there's a maid who dips the knee though she has a hoity-toity look on her face that says *who's this the cat's dragged in*. Insolent is what Miss Fitzgerald would call it. The maid shuts the door behind them. It has a heavy sound, thundery, final like a jailer's lock-up, and she thinks, that's it now, that's the end of Jim Joyce.

Madame takes the lead and shows her through a large doorway on the left into a dining room. It has coloured glass windows like in a cathedral. Over the fireplace there's the head of a huge deer with a pair of horns, big as an oak tree, and two dead, beady eyes. The grate, like the mouth of a railway tunnel, is set but not lit. Madame travels around the dining table which is all laid out with stacks of plates and rows of cutlery. She clicks her fingers and a butler runs off and is back within minutes with a new setting, bowl and dinner plate. Madame gestures to this new place – *oh it's straight into dinner, even at this hour, must be ten o'clock*. She must have been keeping it hot for hours.

Pray go, See Norah, see a comedy, she says.

It's a comedy alright and she's so weary of the joke always being on her.

Then Madame remembers herself. Sit, please sit.

A woman in a fluster enters, as small as she is wide, with a red-hot face as if she's come straight from the kitchen in a temper, armed with tureens with silver hats and sets them down. She hears Madame call her Maria. The child has disappeared, must have been sent to bed. Madame is at the top of a very long dining table and she and Mister are at either side of her like the Holy Trinity.

The butler returns with two crofts of wine, like the cruets at Mass, only bigger. He halts by her side and bows a little. He's old and white-haired with a whiskery, lined face, and looks permanently bent over, as if he's spent so long tugging the forelock he can't straighten up. She looks across at Mister.

Veeno, Mister says, then carefully, there is red and white.

She doesn't know much about either. They had red last night so she plumps for that and Old Man Whiskers sets down the tray and pours it into the chalice glass, one of three glasses that sit before her. Around the rim small bubbles dance. Maria, meanwhile, lifts the plates and sets down in front of her what looks like porridge. My God what time is it, is it breakfast already? But no, there's a red sauce poured over it.

Pick Aunty, Maria says, offering her a little bowl shaped like an opened petal, filled with what looks like pale wood chippings. Go on, say the granny eyes, leading Norah to the tiny spoon inside. She takes the spoon and scatters the shavings on the top. Maria nods in approval, then bustles away and she's left alone with the pair.

Mister Smith sitting opposite lifts up his glass and she follows his lead, and she slugs back a good mouthful of it. It tastes sharp but it makes her feel warmed. Not like that paint stripper they had in the park last night – was that only last night? She can't believe how quickly they've moved. Or is it that time has stalled? She takes another gulp before turning her attention to the food.

She knows from Finn's that you work from the outside in with the silverware. The plates are pure white with a gold rim and a family crest on them. There are large doughy pieces in the dinner shaped like pen nibs, wouldn't Jim fancy that now, covered in a pungent red sauce. She recognizes a sausage here and there. The wood shavings taste of nothing at all, but she's so hungry it doesn't matter, it's food and she falls on it. Jim used to say – is that how she'll have to talk from now on about him, how he *used* to? – that he loved her appetite. For everything, he'd add smuttily. She smarts at the memory. She feels as foolish as Celia Canty, taken in by *plámás*. She's concentrating so hard now that she doesn't know if she's spoken out loud or just thought this, but there's silence around the table, punctuated by the scrape of forks on the china.

She's the first to finish. She's eaten that fast her stomach doesn't know it's been fed yet.

When she looks up Mister is only halfway through and Madame is looking at her scraped bowl as if Norah's a wild dog that has been put up to the table with a napkin around her neck.

A look passes between Mister and Madame she can't decipher. They're thinking she's vulgar, common, she's sure, or else they've never been faced with hunger.

Madame steeples her fingers.

My husband says you have lost your marry-toe.

My marry toe, indeed.

She nods, what else can she do.

Madame starts to talk to Mister then, a babble of Eyetal-ian, a normal conversation as much as she can judge, not tetchy anyway. Not about her, she's guessing. And thank God for that. She can drift and not have to pay attention. But as it goes on, she feels her eyelids drooping and since dinner is over – though what are all these other flat plates for, to catch the droppings or for show? – she knows she can't stay awake another minute. She yawns and that's fatal for one yawn leads to another. Her head will be in the soup, shortly. If there was soup. There's nothing for it, she thinks, here goes.

It's way past my bedtime, she announces and goes to rise from the table. Mister shoots up immediately.

They both look at her, then at one another, and she knows they haven't a clue so she does the little signal, her head over sideways underneath her prayerful hands. Have to go bye-byes. She hates this ruddy dumbshow, makes her feel like a thick.

Madame's face breaks into a pretty smile, Mister lets out a honking laugh, the kind you'd expect from a donkey. But they're triumphant with understanding.

See, see, see, he says and rings a little bell, a copper yoke in the shape of a lady with a stiff skirt.

The stuck-up maid comes in and Madame points to Norah. The maid nods and murmurs. She has a halo of hair escaping from her cap that looks golden in this light, but a puss on her that would stop a clock. The whiskery butler pulls back Norah's chair and she finds herself bowing her way out of the room, remembering gratsy, gratsy, as she does, and almost colliding with Maria the cook who has come in with a trayful of more plates. So there *is* more. Is that chicken she sees? Too late, she's made her excuses now.

She follows the snooty maid out into the hall and they climb a wide wooden staircase with scrolled bannisters, up to the return, and up again. The maid sashays like she was parading on a prom and her black button boots make a clack on the polished wood. Norah trails behind her swishing skirts. In spite of it all, she's enjoying this. Being shown rather than the one showing.

Up on the first landing the maid opens a pair of double doors and leads her into a large chamber. So dark is it that she can barely see the end of it, and she has to depend on the maid's lamp. It seems like a ghostly parlour, the bulky furniture draped with dust sheets. The maid halts to set down a lamp on the mantel and for the first time Norah steals a march on her. There are doors thrown open at the end of the room and she wonders is that where she's supposed to go. But when she turns to say something – though what could she say, well she could ask about her case, that's what – she finds that the maid has melted away into the shadows, without a by-your-leave. Norah turns back and sees the answer to her question. Just inside the next doorway, her valeeze has been deposited on a small side table, with Jim's arm still hanging out of it. She's so relieved to see it there, bruised, familiar, she feels like crying again. Though if Madame knew how this yoke has been dragged through the muck and mud of the parks of the Continent, she'd have had it fumigated. Norah opens it despondently and fishes out her night shift with the scalloped neck and a worked hem. Jim got a kick out of hearing that the lay nuns had stitched it in the convent. That was when he was about to whip it off her in Zoorick, but she won't dwell on that memory, thank you very much. Isn't it because of that very jape that she's in this pickle now? Had his fun, didn't he? If she'd only known what was going to happen, she could have cut him down to size. Could have told him it wasn't her first time, just to spite him.

She presses her nose to the nightie now and inhales Galway, starch and sea salt and the briney tide. It's the only thing she's brought from there. She dips out and fetches the maid's lamp from the other room to examine her new quarters. The room has four windows, casement jobs, but when she goes to look out she finds there are shutters on the outside, bar one. It has bleached muslin nets that shiver slightly. She pushes the curtains aside and finds she's looking out over a garden, full of dark trees, a cloud of leaves at the glass and below a smooth lawn with markings that looks like a tennis court. Beyond that there's the sea, further away now, but it consoles her. She doesn't know why but it places her, even though she doesn't have a bull's notion where she is. Somewhere in Tree-estay – in an empire, isn't it, just like the British Empire but dou-ble-barrelled? She remembers the classroom map in sixth class and Sister Consilio saying with a smirk, sure why would Norah Barnacle need to know where Prussia is, because sure as eggs she's not going to be going there any time soon. Well, aha, Sister C, you were wrong there, weren't you! London, Paree, Zoorick and now – *ta dah!* – Tree-estay. Bate that!

After days and nights of journeying and the fearful tedium of waiting, she has arrived.

Somewhere.

From the other room she hears the golden chimes of a clock, singing into the dark. She begins to count …

Light fingers in between the slits of the shutters, it could be dawn or mid-day. For a minute, she forgets where she is and what's after happening. Then she hears the birds going nineteen to the dozen and she remembers. She looks down and realizes she's lying fully clothed on the bed, the linen shift still pressed to her breast. She has this wild thought that she'll shove the nightie back in the valeeze, tiptoe down that staircase she came up last night and out through the front door before the rest of the house wakes and try to make her way back to the station and maybe Jim'd be there … when there's a little knock on the door of the outer room and someone comes in with a tray and she hears it being set down.

See Norah, a voice calls out but Norah doesn't want her to see that she's slept in her clothes.

Just a minute, she calls. That's what the ladies in Finn's always said to an unexpected knock. But sure this girl won't understand that.

I am leaving your breakfast here, the voice says.

Did she dream that up? The only one around here as speaks English is the Madame and she's sure as eggs not delivering Norah her breakfast. She runs to the doorway between the two rooms in time to see a dark-haired girl disappearing out the door. The air feels unsettled, little dusty things winging around. There's a cup of steaming something and a plate with a little pastry on it set down on a small table. She'd murder a cup of tea but she knows by the smell of it, it's coffee. Ah well, beggars can't be choosers.

But first, she has to wash. She goes back into the bedroom. In the corner there's a washstand with a jug and basin. Did someone come in earlier to fill it? If so, she heard nothing. Dead to the world. Must have been much earlier, the water's tepid. She pours the water into the bowl and strips down, leaving her clothes in a pile on the floor. She'd kill for a bath but a lick and a promise will have to do. There's a lovely soft flannel, and a bar of rose-scented soap, and when she's lathered it all over and doused herself off and wiped herself down with the towel hanging from the washstand, she feels like a new woman. She can't bear to look at the cowpat of clothes on the floor. She's barely been out of them since she left Finn's. God above, they must stink to high heaven but she doesn't put her nose to them just in case. She'd like to burn them, if truth be told.

She opens the valeeze, it lets out a belch of stale air. She has to be seen wearing something different. As she rustles through the valeeze she comes across something hard, what's this? A book, a monstrous doorstop with hard green leather covers and a decorated spine and gold borders. She opens it up – *The Dramatic Works of William Shakespeare: With Remarks On His Life and Writings* by Thomas Campbell. How long has she been lugging that around unbeknownst? No wonder the case nearly tore her arm from its socket yesterday. She feels like picking it up and flinging it across the room but it's too heavy. Isn't this just the giddy limit?

She retrieves her cream blouse with the high collar, and her brown cheviot skirt with the buttons down the hip. They're more rumpled than the clothes she slept in, but a change is as good as a rest said Mamie Rahilly when she turned her hat inside out. She dumps yesterday's clothes in on top of Jim's shirt – when did he smuggle that in here? *Well, I suppose we're mixed up with one another every which way.* And now it's all she has of him, his blooming shirt and his ruddy Shakespeare.

A memory of him in Zoorick comes to her, hollering out when the deed was done. Like the charge of the light brigade. She'd had to shush him, though she was pleased to see the train arrive in the station, for without the sound effects how would you know? Willie Mulvey used to be

114

like that, quiet till you rubbed him up the right way. Lord God, she wouldn't be, would she? No! Not after the one go! No, it was soon enough after her visitor. She's not even going to think of that now.

She goes back to the outer room where the tray was left. She lifts the little tumbler of coffee to her lips, and sips. God, it's only brutal. Thick as treacle, bitter as all get-out. And have they never heard of milk? If this were Finn's, you'd be sent back to the kitchens with this. Muck, she can hear Major Tweedy shouting. She lifts the pastry to get rid of the taste. It looks like an exploded scone as if someone left it in the oven too long but when she bites into it, a scented cloud of just-baked flour escapes. It's only heavenly. Brings her back to Bowling Green Street, Pappie bent over the range and whipping out an apple tart, like a magician. Wasn't she the luckiest girl with a daddy a baker, he said, and he set the tart on the table and standing in the middle of the four fields of pastry was a little roll of dough and he broke it off. That's the *cáicín páiste*, he said, the bit for the child, and he handed it to her. And her mother coming in, face on her like thunder – ah Tommy sure that'll only give her colic, straight from the oven like that.

There's another knock and a maid comes in and from the doorway does a little *ahem* and catches Norah with her mouth full and flakes of the little pudding all over her bosom. This is a different maid, not the frosty, frizzy-haired wan from last night. She points out into the landing and Norah reads the signs. Knows them from Finn's, from silent summonses to Miss Fitzgerald's office. Once a maid …

They head out into the hallway. Through an open window somewhere in the house she can hear a church

bell pealing. She counts in her head. One, two three ...
eleven?

Eleven in the day! Jesus wept! No wonder the maid
was sent in with the breakfast, it was a way of getting her
up, the unwanted guest still sprawling abed at practically
mid-day. Talk about the dead arose and appeared to many.

They reach the hallway of last night and the maid ducks
into the shadow of the stairwell and opens the door on a
new room. Gingerly, she steps inside.

There's a crowd in the room. Mister and Madame stand
like bookends at either side of the fireplace. Green-leaf light
comes through the shutters. There's a grand piano, very
black and shiny, with the lid up so wide it looks like it's
howling. This must be the good room but there's no carpet
in here all the same, just the parkay like in the nuns' parlour
in the Pres. There are two other gents standing around. One
of them is tall, with a shock of sandy hair, and a monocle
he's holding on with a frown. The other is smaller, dark-
eyed, tricked out in a fancy suit. The tall one has a weak
little chin and a pinched nose, as if he's caught a bad smell.

This Mister Monocle steps forward. Harry L. Churchill,
His Majesty's consul for Dalmatia, Carniola and the Austrian Littoral, he announces.

Sweet Divine, how many handles does he have?

Bachelor of Arts, Royal University of Ireland.

At last a native speaker! He'll get it all sorted out.

At your service, he finishes. Sounds like a bishop, does
he expect her to kiss his hand? Well, he'll be waiting.

Mister Monocle clicks his heels and bows deeply.

And may I ask whom I have the pleasure of meeting?
Miss ...?

Barnacle, she says. Should she add – of the great Galway
family, the Barnacles, daughter of Tommy, Itinerant

Baker, and Honoraria Healy, Seamstress and Dressmaker, esteemed niece of Mister Michael Healy, Collector of Customs, Receiver of Wrecks ...

And it's Mrs, she adds, for she's stuck with that lie now.

Ah, he says, you're Ahrish. He sounds like he has a spatula in his mouth and is saying *ah* for the doctor.

Well, Mrs Barnacle, he says, hesitating over her name as if it's sticking in his throat. These good people here – he shifts his gaze from Mister to Madame, who nod and smile like trained dogs – seem to think you have lost your husband.

He smirks at her like it was a handbag she'd mislaid.

Perhaps we can sort out the trouble you're in. He trains his goggle eye on her.

Now hold your horses, I'm in no trouble, she begins, for she sees what this old fogey is doing. Trying to paint her as some kind of a renegade by just looking at her, and what has she done? Sweet Fanny Adams, that's what.

Pardon me, Ma'am, we are only trying to help.

Call this help? she mutters.

Mister Monocle continues as if she hasn't spoken.

It appears that you have no papers, nor any visible means of support, and in this country, Madame, that is very serious trouble indeed.

I've done nothing wrong, Sir, I was left to mind the cases while my husband went off to find the Beryl-its School and he never came back, and that's the God's honest truth.

That may very well be the case, Mrs Barnacle, but we have made enquiries at the Scuole Berlitz and no man answering the description of your husband ever appeared so we only have your word for it. Signor Artifoni informs us that there is no position open at the Scuole for a teacher at the present.

So, no job for Jim here either. Was there ever one, or was that more of him spinning yarns?

Are you calling me a liar, is that it?

Her dander is up now and she's beginning to think she'd have been better off dealing with the Eyetalians who are mannerly, instead of this counter-jumper.

Furthermore, we have no idea what it is you, or Mister Barnacle, might be fleeing from.

Mister Barnacle, that's a good one, now. But she can't go back on what she's told them for that'll make it look like she's changing her story mid-stream. The devil mend you, Jimmy Joyce, you're a married man now with my name.

Excuse me, but we're not on the run from anything. My husband has a degree from the Royal College and is a professoray – she remembers the word, it just comes to her – and what's more he's a writer, a published writer.

Never thought I'd be boasting about that.

Is that so? says Mister Monocle and Mister Smith looks at her curious.

It is, she says.

And you, Mrs Barnacle?

What do you mean?

Perhaps you're not telling us everything …

She hates the way he lets his sentences tail off like that. Suggesting things he's not prepared to say out loud.

I'm hiding nothing. I'm a respectable girl with six years in service and a reference from Finn's Hotel of Leinster Street, Dublin … then she stops.

A chambermaid on the run doesn't sound too hot. Is she handing him ammunition?

Mister Monocle doesn't seem to notice, but Madame does. Norah can see the penny dropping. Suddenly the second man jumps in.

Excuse me, perhaps if I may be allowed to intervene? he says and steps in front of Mister Monocle with the fifteen handles, as if he's about to take over the dance.

Mister Monocle says a bit sniffily: This is Mister Roberto Prezioso, the editor of *Il Piccolo della Sera*, the evening newspaper.

Oh, like the pink *Telegraph* at home. She loves the ads in it, and those court cases with the drawings, the breach of promises. *Miss Maggie Delaney plaintiff; Mister Burke the defendant conducting his own defence* ... why is her mind running on like this?

Mister Precious is a beauty with a moustache twirled to a point and his sharp little goatee, and those fine eyebrows as look like they've been gardened. He plants his lips on her knuckles. His moustache tickles her fingers but she's not complaining, the only gent in the company, not like that other stuffed shirt Monocle, with his Ma'am this and his Ma'am that.

Madame comes to life suddenly as the maid backs in with a shivering tray.

A little tea?

At last, a brew.

Perhaps, says Mister Precious from the tin whistle paper, we can place an advertisement to find the lost couple?

There's only one of this couple lost, she wants to say. All the times she imagined her name in the paper, but it was more an engagement notice in the *Advertiser* she had in mind. Now it looks like she'll be appearing in the Lost and Found.

The maid, the dark-haired one, bends over and pours the tea from a very fancy pot, more like an urn with a little tap at the side, and it hasn't been drawn, she can see even from this distance. It's piss-weak when it lands in a stream in the china cups.

When the maid is through pouring, Madame says, Sit.

Like we're poodles.

All at once the men part their swallow tails. She makes for the nearest chair and nearly crashes into Mister Precious who's about to back into the same one.

Please, he says, and bows again.

What's with all the bowing? She hopes he isn't going to make another grab at her hand. They're fierce for this pawing, but at least it's not the sly groping like in Finn's where there were Roman hands and Russian fingers the whole day long but pretending it was something else. Oh Miss and a tug at your sleeve, there's no sugar, as the hand drops.

She sits into the chair. Just as she expected. Hard as the hob of hell. Not for sitting on, only admiring.

The maid places a cup and saucer in her hand. Lovely fine china with a rose pattern, is it a wedding set, she wonders. The maid's going around now with milk and sugar and a slice of lemon, did you ever, and all for naught. No *fal-de-dals* is going to rescue this brew, sure the tea leaves have only met the water in passing and did they even think to scald the pot? Oh and here come the sandwiches, little white soldiers with the crusts cut off, like you'd give to a baba. Sure the crusts are the best bit. Wonder what they do with them here? In Finn's they used them for Tuesday's egg pudding. What has her thinking of that, now? God knows what the filling is but it's very thin anyway, just like the upholstery. Watery and green.

She takes one out of politeness and sure who knows when the next bite'll come, then she has to do a juggling act, the cup and saucer in her hand, the plate on her lap, and then there's the napkin to contend with. They'd charge for this at the circus. Just as well she doesn't have to talk as well.

Mister Precious and Madame are at it now in Eyetalian. Is something being decided? Across the little table on which all the tea things are spread she catches Mister's eye. He smiles and wiggles his eyebrows at her as if to say *what do you make of this comedy?* Normally, she'd ignore such face gymnastics but as she looks around her, she wonders, who else here will stand up for her?

Not Mister Monocle, nor Mister Precious, why should they care? Not Madame. Only Mister Smith has shown his good faith. So she smiles back.

Of course, Mister Monocle drawls, speaking for His Majesty again, we must also consider the possibility that some harm has befallen Mister Barnacle.

It stands out in the middle of all the foreign hugger-mugger as if he'd shouted it. O jumping Jupiter, she'd never even thought of that.

Some misfortune, ill met by moonlight, that sort of thing, he goes on.

What ...? The tea goes down the wrong way. What if all this time he's been lying in a pool somewhere?

She starts to splutter and cough. She has a grip of the cup but the saucer and plate go flying. The saucer smashes, but the plate wavers like a spinning top and they all watch it – Mister, Madame, Monocle and Precious – like it was a performance on the stage until it winds up face down on the bare floor, all in one piece.

Mister Smith rushes over and kneels beside her and gently claps her back between her shoulder blades. The coughing stops but the tears are rolling down her cheeks and she's not sure if it's the choking or the fright that has brought them on.

Or there's the canal ... Mister Monocle ploughs on.

Can he even swim? She thinks of Jim's long pale legs jellied by water turned fishy and green, his slender hands lifeless, his bony ardour stilled. *Stop it, stop it now.*

That in fact he could be ...

Dead! No, not dead, please God, not that.

She thinks of all her mean thoughts about him and she's ashamed. But if he's dead, she'll kill him so she will, and if he isn't, she'll kill him as well.

The resolve makes her hiccough and Mister Smith kneels down once more and lifts her chin with his hand and says those magic words again – *calma, calma* – and she clutches his hand, grateful to have someone to hang on to. Mister Monocle has stopped mid-stream. Madame is sitting with eyes lowered as if Mister is making a show of her.

The maid comes rushing in with a cloth and starts mopping – the floor first, Norah notices – then the trim of her skirt, God the only clean stitch she has, ruined, and a damp patch in her lap.

Of course, we don't know this, Mister Monocle resumes, and perhaps it's all a false alarm.

He fixes a stare on her.

I'm sure between us, Signor Prezioso and myself, we'll find your Mister Barnacle and discover it's all been a little domestic misunderstanding.

Professor Bareknuckle, Mister Smith corrects.

A domestic misunderstanding, is that what he said? Smarmy so-and-so.

Excuse me, now, she says hotly.

They all look at her.

There was no misunderstanding, one minute he was there and the next gone, although I waited all day and half the night.

We will arrange a little notice, Mister Precious says and she thinks immediately of a mortuary card and everyone is talking at once while Mister Smith, who's still bending over her, says softly: He is not aband-owning a lady as sim-pat-a-cake as you, See Norah Bareknuckle.

The maid's on her knees with a dustpan and brush sweeping up the remains of the shattered saucer. Norah sees her napkin has landed under the table. The men are all sticking their oars in, Mister Monocle talking over Mister Precious. Suddenly Madame issues a command.

Bastard cosy!

Everyone stops. Is that as bad as it sounds? The scene is frozen for a moment.

Then Madame says very quietly, we need to decide how is best to help See Norah Barna-culla.

God, how many ways can they mangle her name?

Mister resumes his seat. The maid straightens and bears away the shattered shards of the saucer. The breakages could have been avoided, Norah wants to say, if you'd thrown a rug on the floor.

Signor Prezioso will place a noteez-ia in the *giornale* and we will await. Signor Cherch-eel will make enquiries …

Yes, Madame, police cells et cetera, Mister Monocle says.

Etcetera indeed.

My Jim is not a criminal … she starts, but no one's listening to her.

Mister Smith rises and says: And we will take care of See Norah Bareknuckle until such time …

Madame says nothing. She rings the bell and the maid who swept up the broken bits reappears. Next thing Norah's being steered from the room. Before the door closes, she catches Madame's eye, who looks at her as if she's left a silvery trail behind her, like a slug would make.

La Ragazza Irlandese

When the visiting Signora is marched into the kitchen a week after her arrival, Pina Malfenti is on all fours by the newly scrubbed table, breathing in the acrid fumes and remembering the bleach man with the cart who would stop at the top of their street in Providence, Rhode Island, crying *biangolin, biangolin*. And how her mama would send her out to collect a jug of it and hand over a nickel because though they might be poor, they were always clean. And she was so busy scouring the tabletop trying to scrub those memories away that she sent a cup flying.

'*Madonna!*' Pina mutters as she heaves herself up to standing, shards of cup in her hand, startling the Signora.

'*Madonna!*' the Signora echoes her. Then she composes herself. 'Fetch this lady's things if you please, Pina.'

This, Pina knows for certain, is no lady. She knew it from the moment this creature appeared upstairs that she didn't belong. Not up there. The way she said *just a minute* the first morning when Pina had brought in the breakfast tray – she learned that, it doesn't come natural. You're lucky if you get a *va beh* out of them upstairs most of the time. They only see you when you put a foot wrong. She remembered Signora Francini telling her that when Madame and the Signore were newly-weds, they'd be so busy *ooh*ing and *aah*ing over one another they'd forget their dinners, and then they'd complain the food had gone cold, and what was the meaning of it? Well, Madame did, at any rate; he has a kinder heart, the Signore. What Pina couldn't figure out was how this woman had managed to get herself installed in the *appartamento di sopra*. That must have been the Signore's doing. Wasn't he the one who found her, wherever that was? Out on the street, by the look of her. She'd stayed in the *appartamento* for three nights, though once the Signore was off on his travels again, Madame ordered that her meals be brought on a tray to her room. No more dining with the family.

'She'll be moving in with you,' Signora Francini says.

Now she doesn't even get a name. But Pina knows her name. She's heard them calling her Signora Norah like an echo of herself. Pretty enough, but only a girl, a fleshy *figura* with a face that's blunt looking. Foreigner.

Then Signora Francini sees the broken pieces in Pina's hand. She doesn't even need to say it. Breakages will be deducted from your wages.

'Off with you,' Signora Francini barks.

Pina hurries upstairs. The visitor hasn't spread herself about, but then, there isn't much to spread about. When Pina looks in the carved armoire, it's empty. Everything the girl owns seems to be in the cardboard case. When Pina opens it, it lets out a bad breath. Inside is a jumble of clothes and boots. Balled up in a man's shirt is a brown linen skirt and a creased blouse. There's a drab-looking navy dress and a long grey cardigan, a man's waistcoat, a shawl, a frock coat. There are bloomers and vests. And socks with holes. On the wingback chair is a ragged topcoat and the hat, well, the less said. She bundles them into the case and slams the lid shut.

When she reaches the servants' quarters at the top of the house, Signora Francini and Signora Norah are already in the room waiting for her. The visitor is sitting on the spare bed looking browned off. Pina sneaks a good look at her. Not even a married lady, she thinks, and that ring on her finger isn't fooling anyone. And her big hands, they've known work, no disguising that. When she looks up, there's a funny turn in her eye. A lady would have had that seen to.

'Look after her,' Signora Francini commands.

She marches off and still no introductions.

Pina feels a wave of pity for the visitor who's come down in the world; she can't help it. It isn't in her nature to gloat, too many mishaps of her own. And if she's going to have to share with this girl, then she might as well get along with her. She drops the girl's suitcase at her feet.

'*Sono Giuseppina*,' she says, thumping her little breasts that don't fill the bib she's wearing. Like a boy, they used to say to her in Providence.

'*E tu?*' She points. No *lei* for her, not anymore.

The visitor looks at Pina blankly.

'What's your name?' Pina asks.

Norah.

Well, that's easy. She's met other Norahs but she doesn't mention that now for it's a source of regret. She's an Italian girl who has come back from America with neither a fortune nor a husband.

And who are you? Norah asks, as if she hadn't heard the first time.

'Giuse ...' Pina repeats, saying it slowly, '... pina.'

Juicy? The girl makes it a question.

The name sticks.

127

*

Juicy marks her cards for her. Explains the household. There's the old man Veneziani, harmless old *chooch*, thatch of white hair, big and loud, or at least he used to be, but he's ailing now and spends his time in bed instructing anyone who comes near on the three laws of business. Even if you're only there to clear the chamber pots, Juicy says. There's Madame's mother, Olga. *Una stronza*, she's the boss of everyone, runs the factory, oh yes, the factory, see across the courtyard in the front, where the chimney is, they make the paint here, war paint, paints for boats and Signor Schmitz owns this factory and another one in Inghilterra and that's where he was coming back from when he met you, married to the daughter, that's Madame to you, and Letizia, that's their little girl, we see her in the kitchen sometimes, she likes to lick the bowl.

Once this house was full with Madame's sisters, Nella, Fausta and Dora, but they're all gone now, married with families of their own, and Master Bruno is off at boarding school. Manly men are not made at home, according to Olga. Now without them, Juicy says, only the animals are left, a right menagerie – a Great Dane the size of a small donkey, and two other ratty specimens that the maids are always tripping over.

That's Antonia's bed you're sitting on, she says. She was let go.

What did she do to deserve that?

Well, she let Letizia out in the sun without her hat. And when Letizia refused to drink her warm milk last thing, Antonia slugged it down herself so as to keep Madame off her back but that's another story.

On Sundays, Juicy says, wait till you see it. They have their big parties and *la tutta Trieste* comes – you'd be run

128

off your feet, literally. Oh they drink and they sing in the big *salotto* – sounds dirty to Norah – that's where you were today. And Signor Schmitz plays the violin and Letizia runs from the room with her hands over her ears! And I wouldn't mind but he spends hours practising in his *studiolo* off the verandah, oh you haven't seen the verandah, well, I'll show you. I go out there for a smoke.

Smoke? Norah says. I'd murder a fag. Does Maria let you?

You mean Signora Francini? Juicy asks. Maria indeed – there'll be no more Maria now you're below stairs. No, no, she don't approve so you have to do it in secret. But the Signore is always at it, smokes like a chimney. Puffs away in his studiolo. Ash everywhere. It's the devil to clean because you're not allowed to touch anything because he writes in there.

Writes what?

Juicy shrugs.

He used to be a *scrittore*. She mimes writing.

Norah throws her eyes to heaven.

God above, not another one, she says.

Must be a story there, Juicy thinks.

And where did you learn to speak English, Juicy?

America, Juicy says, but isn't any more give-ish.

Must be a story there, Norah thinks.

Mister Precious comes every day for a week.

What's he after? Juicy demands. It don't take a week of visits to put an ad in the paper, she says.

Juicy is probably right but Norah likes the attention, getting called upstairs. The bell jangles in the kitchen and she always knows when it's Madame because it's sharper and longer than anyone else's. The meetings with Mr

Precious all take place in the same room, the one they call the salowny in the shadows of the stairs. It's an escape from the tedium of waiting particularly when she doesn't know what or who she's waiting for. But then it's back down to the kitchen where she feels like a piece of left luggage that's getting in everyone's way. She looks forward to mealtimes but even eating here is something new to learn. Juicy has to tell her how to use the fork. Gives her a spoon to begin with like you do with children, so you've something to twirl the noodles in. Takes her an age to get the hang of it. You have to eat that before you get your meat and veg. They've wolfed down their dinner and their afters and she's still curling and twisting, and she doesn't much like the taste of it anyway. Oh for a pork chop! Maria, Mrs Francheeny to her, doesn't approve of her, she can tell. Acts like she's been foisted with Norah. When she goes upstairs, Madame is just as bad. No sign of Mister for days now. Is he off on his travels again? Funny, but Norah misses him.

She learns her way around. From the narrow bed in Juicy's room and the cold feel of the tile underfoot to the hubbub of the kitchen. The screeching of brakes outside the villa, that's the first tram. Same wheeze and *clank-clank* as at home, but different advertisements. No more Wallace's Coal, Donnelly's Bacon, Fry's Cocoa. And with that she thinks of Finn's, seems like another world now, all of it does. Even thinking about Jim seems like a dream. And despite Mister Monocle's prognostications and Mister Precious's daily visits, there's still no sign of him, dead or alive.

She won't believe he's dead. She'd sooner believe he's just left her, or found someone else, or had it arranged all along. But how can someone just go up in smoke like that?

He *must* have had somewhere to go to. But who does he know here that might put him up? It was different in Paree where he had studied. He knew plenty of people there, enough to tap them for sixty francs. Anyway, if he's left her on purpose, then he won't want to be found and no amount of appeals in the newspaper is going to raise him.

All the same, Mister Precious keeps on coming with his questions and his notebook.

Your husband, what do he look like?

Ah Mister Precious, he's tall and slender with the face of a saint, refined you know, those cornflower eyes that look right through you, a smile that'd melt you though you don't see much of it, and words to beat the band. I'd listen to him all day. He has a queer way of dressing but could be quite natty if he had the spondulicks. And if he'd become a teacher as was the plan, he could have afforded to splash out a bit. I always fancied us in Paree, don't know where the notion came from. Once we had a French lady stop at Finn's, oh she was the bee's knees, furs with eyes, gloves to her elbows, brooches for buttons. A hat of crimson velvet, high-built with a netting flower on the brim, and shingled hair as if every strand had been polished by hand. And I imagined myself got up like that, until Miss Fitzgerald barked – Miss Barnacle, could we have your attention please. Always one to spoil a mood.

See Norah? Mister Precious presses.

Or should she say, he's a wastrel, a schemer, a cad, who only wanted the one thing and now he's got it, he's dropped me like a hot potato and was there ever a teaching job at all? Is that why we had to traipse from pillar to post all over Europe? Sure everywhere he's tried, there hasn't been a place for him and didn't Mister Monocle say no one had turned up at the school and they weren't looking for a teacher in the first place. Maybe the school and the teaching were all a pigment of his imagination.

He's led me on a proper goose chase, she says out loud, not meaning to.

Mister Precious is sitting, pen poised, eyeballs out on sticks as if he's straining at stool. Why is he still jotting down everything she says, sure the notice must be in the paper days ago?

Quay?

And she's thinking of Burgh Quay where she and Jim went strolling one evening in August, sweltering it was, the gulls wheeling and pealing around them, they're a guttersnipey bird all the same, take the eye out of your head given half a chance, and not clean, and he was *ullagón*ing about Dublin, a kip he said, an awful kip. The pong off the river was something desperate that day, it'd choke you in the good weather. Smelt like death, he said. He'd a good mind to go off again.

So why don't you so, go off?

I'd go to Paree, he said, and get a job teaching.

I could see myself there, she said.

And he said all excited will you come and she said yes, of course I'll come for she was so bored with Finn's, she could have fought with her nails.

And while she's lost in that thought and Madame is out of the room, Mister Precious makes his move.

My little flower, he says, kissing her hand with his moustache, the sun rises for you, you are my little Earlanda.

Ah cut it out now, she thinks, for this is a bit much. *Juicy was right, Mister Precious don't give two hoots about finding Jim.*

His brushy tache is rough against her cheek when Madame sweeps back in. He springs back. She doesn't know if Madame has spotted his dropped hand.

Signor Prezioso, she cries out, but says no more. She rings for tea.

Mister Precious coughs, smiles, showing his nice teeth, and settles himself. Tugs at his vest, fiddles with his tache.

He starts in with Madame with the Eyetalian and the little flower sits silent, ignored.

It turns out to be his last visit.

Was it then they gave up the ghost? Or stopped believing in her story? Was it then that Jim was lost for good?

Downstairs, she's neither flesh nor fowl. Not grand enough to be waited on anymore – do they hate her because once they had to dip the knee to her? If she slooches around the kitchen, she's only getting in the way so she sits at the table while the kitchen maid, Mary Kirn, chops vegetables, or teems potatoes, or rolls dough under Mrs Francheeny's strict instruction. After a week or two of being glowered at, they begin to ignore her, which is a blessed relief.

Norah talks to Mary even though she hasn't a word of English. But Norah chats away to her anyway, about household things, how hard it is to dry clothes at home, how much better the tea is and would she like to learn how to brew it proper, how they made bread and butter pudding in Finn's, and how lonely she is. Mary not understanding is a help; she can say whatever she likes. She tries things out for size.

Being left is more lonesome than just plain being on your own.

Is he dead, do you think?

Will he ever come back?

Did he ever love me?

*

From the windows of the villa, she can see high trees tormented by the wind and the sea. The horizon is so wide and high, and so far away, it makes her feel dizzy and light-headed. But too open, she tells Mary, without the bent arm of Howth Head to keep you safe. Although she *is* safe and isn't she better off here than being destitute on the street? Even if the villa is like a cage. A beautiful cage. And she's beholden now, since they've taken her in.

The other maid, Luzia, is a stuck-up article. A slyboots, who lives out. She notices how Luzia salts away food when she thinks no one else is looking. Meat especially. But when Norah says this to Juicy, glad to have gossip to deliver, Juicy puts her fingers to her lips.

Luzia steals for her little girl who's very sick.

Makes Norah feel like a snitch but it doesn't make her like Luzia any better.

She gets to know them from their footsteps. Mrs Francheeny, soft-soled but heavy-footed, Luzia's *clickety-click*. Juicy favours her left foot, Mary Kirn's is light and trippy, she almost runs. She's always running, running late, running amok with her high shrill laughter, she's the only girl among them. Not so Juicy. Norah watches her. Her inward face, her springy dark hair, hard to manage, she says sorrowfully, as if it's an affliction. She has to bundle it up under her cap and hold it down with grips and yet it defies her. Moss-brown gaze, a bony nose. There's a little mole under her lip like a spot of her dinner she's forgotten to wipe away.

As for upstairs, who knows?

Norah isn't let up there anymore.

*

And did you love him, Juicy asks.

Well, did she? Of course, she did, isn't that why she feels so scalded now? Or is that only her pride talking?

Yes, she nods, oh yes.

When she tells Juicy the whole story, a fat tear rolls down Juicy's cheek and Norah thinks what an old softie she must be. They've been getting on like a house on fire and Norah sees Mary O in Juicy, a true friend. On Juicy's next day off she offers to bring Norah back to the railway station.

For say, he will be there?

How strange it is to step out into the daylit street, feel the blow of the wind and the blue of the sky. To step onto a tram – Juicy pays for her – and career down past red roofs and church spires and out into the big square Juicy calls the Peeatsa Grand Day. And it is a grand day. Wide open to the sea, white horsey waves, ships bellowing out there like beasts waiting to be fed, foghorn, though this day there's no fog. Arrive in a heap at the seafront, then change trams and follow the harbour with a stiff wind behind you. The smell of garlic would nearly knock you out. How do they eat that stuff? She sees how many cloves of it Mrs Francheeny puts in the dinner sometimes and it makes her eyes water.

When they get to the park opposite the station, she points it out to Juicy. Here, here's where I waited for ten whole hours. Juicy sut-suts. They walk into the station and she mimes falling down in front of Mister. And this time it is she who tears up, remembering all those little plans she and Jim had made. Hot chocolate in the morning, Jim said, hot chocolate you divil, you'll like that, keep you sweet so it will, then you'll run along while I see my private students, maybe we'll even have a maid to open the door.

She could just see it, their flat high up with a balcony and a sea view, a breeze blowing through her hair when she's out and about in the morning to do her messages. And all she'd have to worry about was what she'd cook for dinner. Jim'd be done by lunch-time and then back home for a nap like the Eyetalians do, he said, but not you and me, my love, we'll do the other thing, throwing the sheets off because it'll be too hot for that business even without a stitch on ... Stop it, she says to herself. But she can't. The students will be good payers, professional men, brokers and bankers or men with their own firms. In the evening, we'll eat out in a trat-oh-ree-a, or maybe go to the opera, for crying out loud, and then on to a bar for the newspapers for Jim will have to catch up on world affairs, as well as the news from home, and to practise his Eyetalian and he'll teach her too, the words for ... She stops.

Ay amoray, Juicy says and holds her hands in a prayer to her heart. It is love, *cara* Norah.

Then she folds Norah in a hug while the station clatters all around them and Norah thinks isn't she good, but where in the name of all that's good and holy is Jim?

She starts to help Juicy with her chores. Just to be doing. Mondays, Juicy is in the scullery squaring up to the mangle and rubbing her forehead with the back of her wrist. Hair all awry with the heat and the damp. Can I help, she asks, and she doesn't wait for an answer, but elbows her way in and starts to turn the handle. Flavio has to do the silver service on Wednesdays, buffing and polishing so it doesn't go tarnished, so she offers wordlessly to give him a hand. He's awful slow, she has hers done in jig time. Sees herself in the blades, tongue stuck out in concentration. She's pleased to do it, to do anything to pass the time.

Spud peeling for Mary Kirn, sweeping the servants' corridor. She's the tall one, called upon to reach up into the high shelves in the hot press, or the little-used pans on the roof of the dresser. Mrs Francheeny is less peppery with her when she shows willing. Even smiles at her the odd time, though when she sits down to eat, she swears her portions are being eyed up as if the housekeeping were coming straight out of Mrs F's own pocket.

Work is the great leveller, her Uncle Michael used to say that. Even saying his name drives a stake through her heart and she never thought she would say that. But not Uncle Tommy – that blackguard. Isn't he really the source of her trouble? If he hadn't beaten her, she'd be in Galway now, minding her own business, maybe with Willie Mulvey, or maybe with someone else altogether. But lookit, she can't be thinking about that now.

Despite herself, she grows to love that kitchen, engine of the house, the copper pans hanging like hams over the stove, and the blue and white tiles over the stone sinks with their pictures of farm girls in clogs. There's always some drama with six of them around the table, Mrs Francheeny, Mary Kirn, Luzia, Juicy, the doddery Flavio, and Joosto the coachman who drove her here. The men don't say much but the maids chatter among themselves and Norah sits witness. Sometimes Juicy translates, sometimes not. Must be a scourge having to say everything twice but Juicy doesn't seem to mind. She begins to pick up a few words. *Prima colazione* is breakfast, just like one full meal and two collations during Lent. Lunch is *pranzo* and tea is really dinner. *Cena*, they call it, the dinner of an evening. And after the dishes are done there's smokes. Cigarette is the same but with an *ah* at the end. She and Juicy creep out and share a fag in the lee of the back verandah. They can hear the sound of Madame and the little girl, and also Madame's parents above them as she and Juicy draw on their rollies. She feels bad taking Juicy's tobacco but what can she do? I'll pay you back, she keeps on promising, but how? Everyone has forgotten about her. Not just Jim, but Mister Monocle, Mister Precious and even Mister Smith. Without Juicy, she'd be invisible entirely.

Juicy is the first person Norah has ever met who came back from America, making a liar out of Mamo. It's one-way traffic there, Mamo used to say, once you go that's it, isn't that why we have the American wake? She often thinks about that in her situation. Her *situazione*. She might as well be in America, for all her family know. Good as dead. And Jim, where in heaven's name does he think she is? Does he even wonder? Does he give a tinker's curse? Well, curses on him.

She concentrates on Juicy's story. How she emigrated, the whole family of them off to Providence, Rhode Island. Never heard of the place, Norah thought, is she making it up? When Pina was thirteen, they travelled on a big ship, oh how her brothers loved that ship, scrambling from deck to deck, and its big horn sounding when they arrived in Boston. Then on to Providence on the railroad, a rackety train full to the roof with a whole slew of Eyeties all bound for the one place.

Five years Juicy stayed.

Is that how long I'll be here?

Juicy's mother was a seamstress and Juicy helped her out with piecework from the factories. Poring over scraps, doing seaming in the dark slum room on Federal Hill.

Schifozz! Juicy says, bright new world, my foot!

The plan was never to stay, but like all the others, her papa was going to save to buy land and go back to where he was from. But Papa soon forgot about that once they'd settled in and said sure they wouldn't bother now. Nothing for us back there. That was when her mama started hankering after home, Juicy says. Never picked up the lingo like the men who were out and about all day. She depended on Juicy to do the messages and deal with the rent man. They all lived at close quarters on the hill. Stacked up like packing cases one on top of the other, caught between lines of washing, sheets that'd slap you in the face and never be clean. Consumption ran through the landings like wildfire. Norah thinks of those lanes near Fitzgibbon Street where people were so hemmed in it'd be enough to breathe for the TB to travel, and afterwards they'd have to burn the furniture, beds and mattresses and all. And still you couldn't be sure. And look at poor Sonny Bodkin, from a good clean home and still he succumbed. Oh Sonny! She feels a stab of remorse, or is it pity? With Sonny she never knows. Did she do the first wrong by making him wait out in the rain like that?

The first sign, Juicy says, was when Mama coughed up a gout of blood all over the buttons. Like red phlegm it was. Juicy took over her work doing twice the daily quota to cover, but she couldn't save her. Last thing her mama said to her, her hand a claw on Juicy's breast, was *torna, torna, torna.*

And weren't there fellas, Norah asks, for though Juicy is homely looking, and she has a bit of a squint, she must have been exotic over beyond. Even to those smart-alec Yanks. But Eyeties were ten a penny in Providence, Juicy tells her.

When she announced she was going back home, her papa forbade it. Who'll keep house he demanded, but

Juicy said can't you pay a slavey to do it with all your money saved up from the railroad? As if I was only there to make *giambott*. Norah can't credit that kind of back-chat from Juicy of all people who seems so mousy.

He deserved it, Juicy says, gave her mama a dog's life, even before America. She has no time for him anymore with all his applesauce.

What?

Juicy has the strangest expressions and sometimes Norah doesn't know which one she is using: English, Eyetalian, or something in between?

Through the open windows above they hear Madame ringing the bell.

Madonna! Juicy says exhaling impatiently and it sounds like she's swearing.

The call from upstairs is for Norah. Madame wants to see her. Her heart leaps.

Is it Jim? Is it Mister Precious with news?

There's no sign of Mister when she gets shown in and she feels let down.

We hear, Madame says, you've been helping Maria in the kitchen.

For a minute Norah doesn't know if this is a good or a bad thing. In this house she doesn't know the difference.

We must pay you for your labour, Madame says. It will give you dignity.

I have that already, thank you very much, she thinks. But whatever about dignity, it'll give her a few pennies to rub together.

So, it's official, she thinks with a heavy heart, *I'm back in service*.

*

She's fitted with a uniform. Black serge with a white apron and a mob cap. She hates those bloody things. But it saves the clothes she has. The dress she travelled in is in flitters, and everything else she owns seems held together with the grace of God and two policemen.

She's put on laundry duty. Well, she knows about that from the time at the Pres, the sluicing of sheets, the hanging out to dry – she knows about that too – the starching and ironing. She could do it in her sleep. There are trousers, pinafores and petticoats to be washed and pressed, socks and rags to be boiled. She's forever making lists in case any item would go astray and she'd be accused. Juicy writes her words down beside them – *sottovesti*, chemises is the same, *fazzoletti*, hankies, *pantaloni*, she can guess that, *intimi* is bloomers.

They get through a lot upstairs, Mister especially. New shirt every day, collars and cuffs to be stiffened with *amido*. Right Little Lord Fauntleroy! But she takes special care with his cravats – *le cravatte* – pressing down the heavy iron, weighs a ton, would give you muscles lifting it, and making creases so sharp you could cut yourself on them. She wants to leave an impression.

She's not a fool. She knows her place even though she doesn't like it, not when she was supposed to have something different, but she has to quench those thoughts now, put them away.

That's over, Norah.

It's great, all the same, to have her own money again, though she'll never get the hang of these crowns. With a wage coming in, she can begin salting a bit away, for what she doesn't know just yet. Would it pay the fare home? How long would she have to save for that?

In the meantime, she could do with a new hat – *il cappello*.

*

One night there's a terrible storm, trees whining against the eaves, and when Juicy opens the tiny window like a square porthole up high in their room, she can hear the sea boiling, oh the whiplash of it when it's all riled up. All through the night there's a kind of a roar. There's lightning too, spitting fire on the walls of the room. Juicy sleeps through it but Norah is wide awake. Thinking of Jim. Where in the world is he? Is he suffering through this? She feels sorry for him if he is. She knows how secret fears can prey on you. She's afraid of heights herself but she never got around to telling Jim. She wasn't afeared of climbing but of the pull you might feel at the top. That's why she wouldn't go up the Pillar with him, told him she didn't like the inside, like being buried before your time. But it was the outside she didn't want, the awful freedom at the top and the ground beckoning to you, *step off, step off* into the nothing. A queer thing. And now he'll never know that about her, will he?

Juicy asks does she want to go to church in Servola. Is it a special church for servants like the Three Patrons in Rathgar, she wonders, but it turns out to be for everyone. She and Juicy pick their way across the tramlines, skeetering on the cobbles slimy with rain, or was it sea spray after the storm? Past the twin gables of the factory with a metal bridge running between them, a forbidding-looking place, five storeys high. Is that where Mister disappears to for days on end? There's no sign of life there on a Sunday, though on weekdays the chimney coughs out gouts of smoke and pungent smells, and she gets glimpses of the men dressed in white coats smoking in the cobbled yard between the factory and the villa.

Can't smoke inside, Juicy tells her, the place would go up.

A remnant wind blows up from the sea, perishing it is, kind of bad-tempered. She wears Jim's gaberdine to church because her own one is in the trunk Jim sent on ahead and where the blazes is that now? The coat smells of him, hair oil and tobacco, but it's adulterated now with her own smells of dread and stale fear. They sit squeezed into the tiny church. She expected a cathedral, like they saw in Paree. When she gets over her disappointment, she likes the church in Servola. Tightly packed in pews, the comradely feel of Juicy's shoulder up against hers, heads bowed in unison. Isn't that the beauty of the Mass, you'd know it anywhere, *et cum spiritu tuo*, Juicy by her side. Sometimes, she wants to reach across and grab Juicy's hand, so grateful is she for her, but she's not sure Juicy would like it.

One good thing is that she doesn't have to put up with sarcastic comments about the priests from Mister James Joyce who believed in nothing and worse, didn't want anyone else to believe neither. Silly, isn't it, she prays for him to be safe but if he walked into the church this bloody minute she'd read him the riot act. She'd kick up such a stink he would never forget it, and then she'd fall upon him and forgive him everything. Or kiss him first then give out to him? But no, not that way round for she'd never get to the reprimand that way.

There's no sense to her feelings.

After Mass, it's back to the villa where there's dinner to cook and then the Sunday shindig upstairs. There are drinks to be poured and little plates of fancies to be handed out. Juicy and Luzia do those. Madame doesn't allow Norah up top. Well, she couldn't understand what

143

they'd be wanting, she supposes. And anyway, Mister Precious sometimes attends those Sunday swarries. Madame must have seen him putting the feelers on her, for he hasn't visited since. Not allowed to, she suspects. Does Madame think it's her fault that he can't keep his hands to himself? Anyways, she wants Norah out of sight, that's plain as a pikestaff. She'd only be a spectacle up there, the girl Mister picked up out of the gutter, the charity case. They'd be talking behind their hands even if she couldn't understand them and the uniform would be no disguise, she'd still be *la ragazza irlandese*.

That's what she is in Italian, Juicy has told her.

The raggedy-ass girl from Ireland.

Mrs Svevo

Ettore Schmitz stands on the verandah of his *studiolo* in the Villa Veneziani and lights a cigarette. The flame quivers theatrically and as the tip glows in the darkness, he inhales. Aaaaah. The sweet draw, filling the mouth, like a *puttana*'s kiss, plumes of smoke snaking through the body's tunnels, the throat, the head, the chest, the lungs. Intake complete, he holds the feeling for as long as he can, like preparing himself for a leap from a great height, and then … exhalation. A lifetime of rumination can occur between those two breaths.

He looks forward to every single cigarette, as if it was his last, and it is often meant to be. Until the next one, that is. But of all the smokes of the day, the *aperitivo* smoke is the most precious. A draught of freedom.

There is a niggle at the base of his stomach, something unpleasant that has to be done that slightly sours the moment, but he ignores it to savour the feeling of release from the day's work, from the interminable boat journey from Murano, and the bumpy ride in the brougham from the station.

WORK and SCHMITZ.

An unholy alliance. Yet, he has been a salary man for nearly twenty years now. How many cigarettes is that?

He has counted out his life in stamped-out fag ends. More butts than ifs.

Tobacco had seen him through his apprenticeship at the Unionbank, under that high-liver Vivante. He can picture him now: fat, self-satisfied, lazy, peering over his pince-nez, stroking his niggardly beard. Ettore had never encountered a character so portentously protective of his own incompetence. Vivante didn't smoke, another black mark against him. Never trust a man who has not inhaled. He'll be immune to the world, while the smoker breathes it in. When he was under Vivante's yoke, Ettore would often step out onto one of the many balconies leading off the banking hall and look down on the scurrying creatures on the piazza far below, imagining himself as a man of leisure and not a mere correspondence clerk, transcribing other people's words and going home in the dark.

Smoking had propelled him through writing as well, his other work. Through the two lost novels of his youth, the numerous half-finished plays, a betrothal diary for Livia. All created in self-made clouds of nicotine. There were those comradely smokes at the *Indipendente* with the young subs Ullmann and Zampieri after the paper was put to bed. Or later when those poor chaps were put behind bars and he and Benco were bringing the paper out on their own, there were the chain-smoking early mornings as he sweated over his political column before heading off to his day job at the bank. He never regretted those cigarettes, at least not while he was having them. It was only afterwards remorse set in, or when Livia raised an inquisitive eyebrow as he lit up. It helps me think, he'd say in answer to her silent acrobatic rebuke. You don't need to think to run a paint factory, she told him, you just need to do. Now, even though he's his own boss, he's running out of places where he can smoke legally and undisturbed. He risks frostbite if he tries it in his office. His secretary, under orders from Livia no doubt, raises all the windows and runs about the place like a dervish with a fly swat if he lights up at his desk. He can't do it anywhere near the factory floor, obviously. *Boom!* He's often reduced to hovering on the iron walkways that link the two wings of the Veneziani-Moravia Corrosive and Anti-Fouling Composition Works, the unedifying title of the paint plant that has made his wife's family fortune. Despite having married in and worked for the business for years, Ettore is not family, not really. It was only last year that he was made privy to the components that make up the marine paint that is their trademark product. It's the one family secret he and his mother-in-law, Olga Veneziani, share.

It is often Olga's moods that drive him out to smoke. She's a constant thorn in his side. *Conscience*, his pal Veruda used to say, wagging his finger, *is like a mother-in-law whose visits never end.* He can hear Veruda's hollow laughter. *You've gone the whole hog, Ettore, you've moved in with your tyrannical boss.*

Olga Veneziani is a little woman – little in stature, that is. Her stout pragmatic face, those falsely candid eyes, hide a neurotic nature addicted to chaos. It isn't that she is incapable of making a good decision, it's that she could make and remake it several times over, each time with the certainty of finality. How often had he been on his way to the Murano factory, rattling across country on the infernal Bummelzug or being tossed on the open sea on the night packet to Venice, when she would change her mind. He made thirteen trips this year to Murano and each time she telegrammed ahead of him, countermanding the instructions she had given him in person. He arrived like

147

a cuckolded general, reduced to the status of a messenger boy with outdated dispatches. Made an utter fool of in front of the workers, men whom he had carefully cultivated to trust him.

And that isn't the end of her capriciousness. The company books are a nightmare. The woman is so mean, she would make a florin screech. Viewing the accounts is like going to a bad operetta, Olga playing the outraged dame pointing lavishly at his travelling expenses and shrieking *what's this?* then clutching her head in dramatic exasperation. Behind her back she is known as the dragon. Sometimes, when she's in the midst of her fulminations, he catches something fleeting in Olga's expression – the impatient crease of her forehead, the same agile eyebrow, the thin lips of pained disappointment – and he sees an image of his own dear Livia, as if staring into his own future.

The little pith of dread returns. Now he remembers. He has a crow to pluck with Livia.

About Signora Barnacle.

He lights the second cigarette from the first and inhales. Hold it there, hold the pleasure. Pleasure brings Giuseppina Zergol to mind. It may be a twenty-year-old memory – those coal-black eyes, her sleek mane, her puckered mouth like that of a spoilt child – but the pleasure it evokes is mint-new every time. He met her at the Metro Cubo, but she wasn't one of the girls there, he is sure of that. He was twenty-four and she was younger, but she acted like his tutor. It was first love for him, or first lesson in love, but the undoubted erotic pleasure was twinned with the most delectable pain. He was crazy about her, literally, driven mad by her on-again, off-again antics. Not to speak of his own waxing and waning emotions, full of vehemence one minute, abject and chastising the next. A folly of his youth, Giuseppina had scalded his heart and turned him into a panther, prowling the streets in all weathers seeking her out, or standing sentry by her door in the depths of winter, snow powdering his shoulders, his feet turned to ice, waiting for her return. He hadn't always wanted to see her, he'd wanted to see whom she was seeing. The perversity of it.

Beware of working girls, Veruda said to him.

'Working-class,' he insisted to Veruda. 'Giuseppina can sing, dance, she has performed on the stage.'

Veruda scoffed. *Exactly!*

Ettore releases the trapped-in smoke in a rush, exploding in a paroxysm of coughing.

'You're home, *Knospe*,' Livia says, sweeping into the room. She still uses their courtship language. 'Your lungs betray you.'

He ploughs his face into his pocket square. He will not let her turn this into a debate about his smoking.

'Yes, Giusto picked me up from the quay,' he says through an acre of cotton.

'And how is everything in Murano?'

When he lowers the kerchief, she brushes her lips against his cheek.

'Everything is fine there,' he says, 'but the same cannot be said for here.'

'Whatever do you mean?'

He knows this sweet tone; it's the one she adopts when she's caught out in dissembling.

'You know exactly what I mean,' he says.

How he hates these disputes. Isn't it enough that he has to deal with the flaring rows with Olga without having to endure the same with his wife?

'Pumpkin,' she croons. She comes up behind him and ticklingly kisses him on the neck. Now she's being coquettish to distract him from his say. His justifiable say. 'What is it?'

He lights another cigarette, the good having gone out of the last one.

'It's Signora Barnacle.'

She didn't consult him. No, she waited till he was safely out of the way for five whole days in Murano and then she pounced. (Is she her mother's daughter?) In one arrogant manoeuvre, she turned a house guest, the wife of a *professore*, and a writer, into a *Dienstmädchen*.

'What about her?'

Livia sighs extravagantly as if indifferently bored.

'You know perfectly well!'

What gives her the right to act as God? Blessed be the paintmakers for they shall inherit the earth? Is that it?

'Maria tells me you have moved her in with the servants.'

Thank heavens for Maria Francini, his spy below stairs. Otherwise he wouldn't know what's happening in his own household. Though he can't rightly call it his own; isn't that the trouble? It's Gioachino and Olga Veneziani's home, and Livia's. He comes in a poor fourth. His parents-in-law defer to him as if he's the head of the household, particularly with old Gioachino failing, but it's lip service. Remember that time he forbade Livia to buy gas heaters for the *appartamento di sopra* because of the cost? She acquiesced without a word, played the dutiful wife. But as soon as he was out of the house – it was the first time he'd gone to London, to set up the new factory there – she'd ordered those damned heaters anyway and presented him with a *fait accompli*. Isn't it cosy here all the same, she'd purred at him, as if the heaters had never been a bone of contention.

Livia and her mother rule the roost, just as Veruda had warned him they would.

A bourgeois marriage, he said, *is a tender trap*.

Poor Veruda, he feels a stab of remorse. His marriage to Livia drove a wedge between them. Now Veruda was dead and there was no opportunity to heal the rift.

'And if I have?' Livia says.

There is a tinge of colour in her cheek, what might be an attractive blush in other circumstances.

'It is outrageous!' he blurts out and takes a last draw of his cigarette, then stubs it out viciously. He counts the butts – five! Look what you've driven me to, he thinks.

'The Signora is a guest in our home …' he begins.

'She is *your* guest, Ettore.'

With a flounce, Giuseppina Zergol is back in his head, doing a pirouette, hands on her hips. With her, it was Ettore who was the guest. He thinks of her little boudoir, a nest of tossed fabric, soft down pillows, ruched drapes, lace shawls dripping over the chairs. He loved going there, being shown in. Less so, being shown out.

Why is he even thinking of her now?

'It was an act of Christian charity,' he counters.

She thinks he gained nothing from his Catholic instruction bar the splash of water at San Giacomo in Monte. But it hadn't all gone over his head.

Livia is having none of it.

'You are not in a position to lecture me on Christian charity, Ettore.'

No pumpkin now, no *Knospe*.

'She's a married woman, her husband is a professor …'

'So she says … but where is he? This mythical husband?'

'Why would she lie?'

'Oh Ettore, she's a chamber maid, they are born lying. By her own admission, she belongs with the servants. And her husband, if there is one, is a lowly teacher at the Berlitz, not a distinguished man of letters as you would have him. If he were ever to be found, we wouldn't even invite *him* to be a guest here.'

That's Livia. Everything in its place. And everyone.

'Can you really see her at one of our Sunday soireés?'

'That's not the point,' he begins but Livia interrupts.

'No, Ettore, it is precisely the point. If we would not consider her a suitable house-party guest, why would we invite her to stay in our home? Mother and I ...'

'I might have known your dear mama would be mixed up in this.'

'No, Ettore, it was I who decided.'

'That you would turn our house guest into a servant?'

'Your charity is misplaced, Ettore. This young woman is lucky that she has a roof over her head.'

'And what do you have her doing?'

'Maria started her in the laundry. She seems to have some experience in that area.'

'I won't hear of it. When Professor Barnacle turns up, what is he going to think, that we put his wife to work a few days after we took her in?'

'I will wager, Ettore, that the so-called husband will never turn up. It's a ruse – the woman is a trickster, a gold digger, trying to worm her way into the affections of strangers.'

Ah! His turn to pounce. 'Livia, you're jealous, I do believe!'

So good to turn the tables at last.

Jealousy has always been *his* failing. He learned it first with Giuseppina whom he couldn't bear to share. It made him bilious when men, gentlemen at that, eyed her up on the street. That's why he liked her little parlour. There he could have her all to himself, though he knew how deluded this was.

Finish it with the Zergol woman, Veruda advised. *If you can't stand the thought of others, because there will always be others. Have you ever heard of a doctor with only one patient?*

'Have I something to be jealous of?' Livia's turn to parry.

Trapped.

'Now, *you're* the one being ridiculous!'

He didn't say that when he saw Signora Barnacle's coppery hair, and that broad fresh face, he thought it was Giuseppina Zergol come back after ten years, to forgive him.

He'd broken the association to prove Veruda wrong, But not seeing Giuseppina only made his jealousy ten times worse. She had a parade of gentlemen friends about whom he now couldn't remonstrate because he'd abdicated his rights to her. But still he persisted, calling at her door, demanding the maid produce her.

The maid would instead produce Giuseppina's simpleton mother.

Oh no, Veruda interrupted, *she may be an old crone but there's nothing wrong with her upstairs. She's the brains of the operation.*

Lord, he'd thought when he first saw her, what a life the woman must have lived. Her face as craterous as the Karst, her cheeks stoved in – did the woman have any teeth?

'No Sir, Giuseppina is not at home.' Gormlessly smiling.

'But I saw her coming in not five minutes ago.'

'She is not receiving.'

'Is she alone?'

'Now, Sir, with respect, that is no longer your business.'

If it ever had been, Veruda interjected.

Then the day came when the answer to his doorstep enquiries was: 'She is gone, Sir, she has left the city.'

He didn't believe it. He pushed past Madame Zergol and searched their little house, storming into the cushiony boudoir, but there was no sign of her. Her perfume bottles, her powder puffs. The little wicker screen, over which there was always a snowy petticoat or a fringed stole thrown, was bare, forlorn.

'Where has she gone?' he demanded.

'She has joined the circus, Sir,' her mother said with a straight face.

He thought this a ridiculous joke, some euphemism, some triestino patois, but Madame Zergol was insistent.

'Giuseppina is travelling as a bareback rider with the Casartelli Circus!'

Madame Zergol said it with such inordinate pride that he couldn't doubt it. It was an explanation so outlandish it couldn't be fictional. It filled him with a foolish sense of admiration – the girl sang and danced, now she was an equestrienne. Despite the circumstances, the thought excited him.

'Perhaps you would like to meet her sister?' Madame Zergol suggested.

'Sister?'

See, he heard Veruda's voice in his head. *What did I tell you?*

He doubts that Livia knows about Giuseppina, the specifics of her, that is. She was long before Livia's time. Not relevant, he ruled. But once, when his own jealousy flared and he demanded to know the company Livia was

keeping while on her summer spa treatment in Salsomag-
giore, she said sweetly: 'You must not judge me by the
standards of those beautiful women of pleasure you knew
before your marriage.'

He saw the steel in her then. 'Signora Barnacle was a
lady in distress. I did what any gentleman would do.'

'She's no lady, Ettore, that's the point.'

'Nevertheless, I cannot have her treated with such
disrespect.'

'Well, it's either this way, or we put her out on the
street.'

'Livia!'

'And what would your solution be?'

At that moment, the door of the *studiolo* bursts open
and Letizia appears, a small dark bullet coming straight
at his heart.

'Papa, papa, you're home!'

'Titina, my sweet!'

She throws her arms around his waist. He raises his cigarette hand so her hair won't get singed; he is a danger to
himself and others. Then, looking down at the crown of
his little daughter's head, he has an idea.

'Lessons?' Livia says, incredulous.

'Yes, dear, English lessons.'

*Proceed with care, Ettore. A single ill-chosen word could be
the end of everything.*

'Signora Barnacle is a native speaker, is she not? She
could teach Titina, you'd like that wouldn't you, Titina?'

The child stands between them, looking from one
to the other, her dark inquisitive eyes clouded with
uncertainty.

'But Ettore ...' Livia objects.

'But what?' he says. 'It is the perfect solution, she can be like a governess. Your mother would like that idea, wouldn't she?'

Better to get the dragon in early on in the piece, since all decisions would have to go through her, anyway. He could imagine how a governess might become the talking point at the Sunday salons.

And who is the plain creature in the dowdy clothes, hanging about in the shadows?

Though plain is not the word to use for the Signora. Plain suggests meek and there is nothing obsequious in the Signora's character, even in her present straitened circumstances.

That is Letizia's English governess.

You don't say!

My, my!

'And when Professore Barnacle turns up, at least we won't have to show him into the laundry to meet his wife.'

'Lessons?' Livia repeats like a stuck gramophone needle. 'But what kind of English would she teach her? The girl is clearly not educated. Can she even read?'

'It is her native tongue, Livia, that is the best qualification in the world.'

'I don't know,' Livia says. Wisps are escaping from her chignon in sympathy. He thinks of her magnificent hair down, the blonde tumble of it, and wishes he could just take her in his arms right now and be done with these tiresome arguments. What exactly is she afraid of?

'Well,' she concedes, 'I suppose I could supervise the classes and see if she's a suitable companion ...'

It is Ettore's turn to pounce.

'Why don't I take the classes with Titina? My spoken English leaves much to be desired. Remember how badly I fared on my trip to London? None of the men could understand me. I lost face with them. And Olga would want me to be proficient, for carrying out the family business, no?'

Calling on Olga's approbation is a master stroke. Everyone in this household needs her approval. Even Livia. Particularly Livia.

'A governess?' Titina chimes in gleefully. 'My own English governess? Oh can I, Mama, please, oh please ...'

The matter is settled. The gong sounds for dinner. Ettore stubs out another cigarette.

Mister is back. Norah senses it without knowing, a different air in the house. She is summoned to the salowny where she finds Mister pacing up and down. It is the first time she has been upstairs in a month, since Mister Precious was banished. When she enters Mister halts in his worrying of the parkay and smiles. No sign of Madame. Since she's been sent below, Norah hasn't had any dealings with her, and when she's passed her in the house – hefting the ironed sheets up to the airing cupboard on the landing near the nursery, funny, they call it the nursery though the little girl is gone well beyond nursing – Madame has even managed a smile. A tight little smile.

Well, she's put me in my place, hasn't she, why wouldn't she be pleased with herself?

Mister lights a cigarette and gets lost in his cloud. Jim used to get into the same kind of fug when he was writing, chewing up the fags, and his own brain power adding to it. But no, no thoughts of Jim now. Is Mister going to put her out, is that it, she wonders. Is he going to do Madame's dirty work for her? He draws on the cigarette and smiles at her, a creeping shy kind of smile.

Signorah Bareknuckle, he begins.

Lord, how many ways to make mincemeat of her name.

Maybe he has news of Jim, is that it? Her spirits rise despite herself. Spit it out, she wants to shout.

He comes and stands in front of her. He reaches for her mob cap and takes it from her head. He crumples it in his hand. He walks around behind her and she thinks what next, what's next to come off and her mind wanders back to Finn's and Mister Holohan getting fresh with her on the stairs, his thing sticking up at her like a hat rack. But no, surely not, Mister Smith's a gent, isn't he? The kind of man who'd leave the room to blow his nose. And didn't he have chances all this time back and he didn't? He unties her apron and lets it fall to the ground. These people never pick up after themselves. Then he circles around her to face her again.

You will have a new situ-atzee-oney, he announces.

Aren't they divils for dragging the arse out of words?

She watches his face intently, the kindly eyes, his olive skin. What's coming? The poor house. A polis cell? Or has he something bedroomy in mind?

You will teech the Eeenglish.

A full sentence, he must have been practising for hours. What?

What would Jim Joyce say about that! Norah Barnacle as the teacher in the family! She wants to laugh out loud but she can see that Mister is serious.

Who will I teach?

Our little Tit-eeena, he says beaming.

Is he making a laugh out of her?

Layteetsia, he says. Our daughter.

Lord God!

You are a governess, Mister says as if he's waved a wand over her.

Her – a governess? What a hoot! Well, it's better than ruining her hands with blue. And it'll pay more, won't it? Jim told her he was going to get ten pence an hour. But maybe he was making that up; sure, she can't rely on a word that fella said anymore.

Mister explains. She'll sit in his study every morning with little Letty – she can't manage the full name and she is not going to call her the other which sounds too much like titties to her – and teach her how to talk in English. Norah will still live with the servants, well isn't that a mercy! The cook's room is free – Mrs Francheeny lives out, hoofs it in at cockshout to do the breakfast, and bustles off after supper. Norah will be moved in there. To make the distinction. Oh, they're wild keen on their distinctions! Or Madame is, at least.

And when do I start? she asks.

Monday.

Won't I need books?

The only book she has is the wretched Shakespeare, which just at the moment is acting as the fourth leg of the tallboy in Juicy's room. She could do with one of those primers Jim had stashed away in the trunk. The blessed trunk! They sent it ahead when they left Dublin, God knows where it is now; sure, the trunk must be like a headless chicken trying to follow them about. She imagines some bored railway porters in a baggage hall somewhere rifling through all her good clothes, her fancy drawers and Sunday best. Stuff she could do with having with her now.

No, says Mister, you are making the converse-atzioney.

Madonna! Juicy exclaims when Nora tells her.

Madonna is right if it means Holy Mother Divine.

*

She is up at cockcrow on Monday morning. Nervous, despite herself. Sure, Letty is only – what? – seven years of age, and obedient as far as she can tell. And it's not as if she's a novice. Hasn't she got sisters? She feels a little pang when she thinks of them. But she won't treat Letty the same way. She'll be like a strict visitor. Will she be able to keep her temper? Well, she'll just have to for no one has ever looked crooked at that child, she can tell. Let alone raised a hand to her.

She has breakfast as usual round the kitchen table, those half-moon buns with the cross name that she likes, the kind Jim talked about when he was spinning her that dream of the two of them in a French love nest, well ahem to all that, she has a job to do now. The kitchen staff have only started their morning chores when the bell in the study goes and Mrs Francheeny gives her the nod – *that'll be for you* – and Norah rises, feeling all their eyes – Juicy's, Luzia's, Mary Kirn's – on her. She goes upstairs and makes her way gingerly to Mister's little office. She hesitates at the door, knocks, then thinks what is she doing knocking at the door for a seven-year-old and she marches right in, bold as brass.

Signorina Barna-calais!

It's bloody Madame – *pardon my French* – standing behind the desk. No one mentioned *she* was going to be here.

And why is she suddenly Noreenah, not Norah?

Letty chimes in with a bon jorno. The child is sitting on one of those hard chairs with her legs swinging and her hair up in the two biggest bows Norah has ever seen. A foam of frills in her skirt, lace trim on her pinny straps.

The door opens behind her. She looks around, it's only himself. My God does she have to teach them all – can she charge triple?

Signora, Mister says and goes to kiss her hand before Livia looks at him and he drops the notion.

Mister joins Letty at the desk, like they're posing for one of those studio photographs. Look how carefully he hitches up his *pantaloni* before he sits. She's pretty sure she ironed those last week.

Let us begin, he says and Madame sweeps out letting them at it.

My name is – she beats her chest – Norah.

She spells it out with chalk on the blackboard Mister has set up in the study.

N-O-R-A-H.

Decides it there and then, to put the H back. *I'm taking it back, Jim.*

H at the terminoose? Mister queries. He has brought a big notebook and writes everything down.

Termi-noose?

At the end?

The penny drops.

Yes, she says, the H is silent. Now you! My name is Letizia.

Lay-teats-iyah, the child parrots.

She points at Mister.

My name is Ettore – but in English, Ector, he helpfully offers.

Hector. Hector Smith.

He's become a new man with a new name.

She loses track of time. That's what work does, eats up days. Letty is twitchy and restless in class, can't sit still, always wandering off to look out the window or go out onto the verandah and Norah feels like giving her a clip across the ear sometimes, she's that skittish. But sure, she was like this at school herself except she wasn't allowed to move from her desk without a rap of the cane from Sister Benedict. She smiles at Mister but no help there. He smiles indulgently back. Letty has him wrapped around her little finger. And isn't that the way it's meant to be with little girls and their fathers? Her own Pappie, God love him, he could have been like that if he'd had the ease of money Mister has. Money'll cure most ills, won't it? She keeps that in mind as she struggles to fill up the time during the classes. Lookit, it's not exactly hard labour. Two hours in the morning and sometimes she takes Letty for a stroll around the garden in the afternoons, and Letty does all the talking then, and Norah lets her rattle on. The child wants only a listening ear.

Madame has ordered her another uniform. This time it's a prim skirt in plum serge and a nice white blouse – *la camicia* – with a high neck with brothery-and-glaze down the front. It's Juicy who runs them up. She's a wizard with a needle – *l'ago* – never saw the likes. She whips the tape measure – *il metro* – around Norah's bust and hips and measures, she holds the fabric up and talks with pins – *gli spilli* – in her mouth. She's glad it's Juicy who's doing it, it'll be made with love, that's what she thinks. It makes a welcome change from her own awful duds and when the first pay comes, she can go into town with Juicy and get a Sunday rig-out and burn these yokes she's been wearing for months. Make a bonfire of them and that'll be the last of Jim. Even using his name now sounds strange. That fella is how she thinks of him now. That Other Fella, who broke my heart – *il cuore*. Every word in Eyetalian is a mister or a miss. The heart, Juicy says, is a man.

*

Her new room is a couple of steps away from Juicy's with a little landing all its own. There's the same pink distemper as in Juicy's room, and windows set high up so she can see the water from one and the roof of the factory from the other, then the timber yards and the shops and houses of Servola beyond. She has it all to herself, the first time that's ever happened. And Juicy only down the passage for company. Best of both worlds. Mary Kirn and Mrs F treat her just the same and Luzia is cranky with everyone. She still gives Juicy a dig-out with the ironing – *stirare* – but she draws the line at sewing. She keeps Juicy company as she darns – *rammendare* – and hems and button-holes – *le asole.* You could make your own, Juicy says to her, I could teach you, but Norah shakes her head. Her mother always said her hem-stitches looked like they were made with a shovel, *and don't get me started on the bockety seaming.* When she was at school, the nuns tried to teach them embroidery, chalice cloths for the altar. But Norah had worked on the same ragged piece of work all year and she'd lost track of the number of times she was made to rip the blessed thing back and start again. We'll never make a lacemaker out of you, Mother Annunciation announced as she held up the grubby doily to the class. Would you have the gall to offer this to Father Devlin, let alone to the Lord! No, needlework was for those who had time on their hands, those who were waiting for something to happen. And Norah Barnacle wasn't waiting any longer.

Ettore is consumed with trying to work out when, exactly, it began. Was it when Signora Barnacle fainted in front of him at the station? Was it the competitive pantomime with Prezioso who was sniffing about her from the start?

Offering his services to find her husband; a fictional pretext, if ever he heard one. Maybe Livia was right about Norah and her story was all a fiction. Maybe there was no husband. Should he bow to his wife's womanly intuition? But no, he can't believe it. There is something about Norah that speaks of loss. He sees it in her doleful expression. But it's a face that has known sensual pleasure. She has a rounded wifely look, yet she's quick with her tongue and merry, if her smile is anything to go by. She's not coquettish, doesn't have the language so how could she be? And yet, she has a quality, an earthiness, a vibrancy ... *Steady, Ettore, steady.*

He compares her with Livia. Of course, he does. Places them side by side. Livia's composure. Norah's wildness.

His mother had engineered the match with Livia, he was sure, even though at the time she was on her deathbed. A long, slow death. Sometimes she would rear awake, sit upright in bed, and stare around, wild-eyed, as if she didn't know where she was and who anyone was. She seemed to be looking through them or beyond them, at something frightful but irresistible. When these fits of sudden vigour occurred, she would have to be cajoled into lying down again. His sister Paolina was the only one who could calm her. If Paolina were not close, Ettore would try but he always felt he was manhandling his poor mother. He would call to her, *Mama, Mama, Mama,* manacling her wrist with his hand to make her stay, while she too cried out but for something beyond him that he couldn't understand.

Livia had witnessed one of these episodes. She had been visiting the house for months, sitting mutely by his mama's bedside and smiling at him. Little more than a schoolgirl, really, his little cousin. He got used to her being there, the constancy of it, so his mama dying and Livia's presence seemed connected, one depending on the other. He even wondered if Livia's being there was keeping her alive, a silly superstition, he knew, but it comforted him.

On that occasion, she quietly placed her hand over Mama's fingers, still saying nothing. Something in her touch must have soothed because Mama instantly fell back on the pillows and slipped back into rest. Then Livia rose and disappeared, and when she came back it was as Epione, bearing him a thimbleful of Marsala. It was a simple gesture but it stayed with him. Was it a trick of the light, or some falling of the scales from his own eyes that effected the transformation? To this day he doesn't know.

From the day of the Marsala, he found himself longing to bury himself in Livia's magnificent, flumey hair and drown in those eau-de-Nil eyes. The Giuseppina business was well over by then, and there hadn't been anyone else, bar a few flirtations. He was too old for flirtations by then – he was forty-one. If his mama were in her right mind she would say, It is time, Ettore. So he decided – that was what you did with love.

It wasn't a case of falling.

You decided.

Un'attimo, a voice interrupts. *Did you decide? A matter of will, was it?*

He's about to round on Veruda, until he realizes this is not Veruda, but his own inner voice. Remember your courtship? How you'd take the tram out from the bank on a Friday evening, or sometimes you'd pedal out on your bicycle, heart in your mouth, couldn't wait to see her? Arriving breathless at the Villa Veneziani, flinging

your bicycle down in front of the house like an impetu-
ous child, the spokes still whirring, bounding up the steps
and hoping you'd get a moment alone with Livia without
those sisters of hers, Fausta or Dora, buzzing around you,
acting as chaperones. (And didn't you sometimes wonder
if you'd chosen the right sister?)

Decide.

Who decided?

Was it you?

Remember the kiss in the brougham after your engagement was announced? Alone at last, if you didn't count
old Giusto sitting in splendour up front driving the horses
on, and your lips met Livia's and there were fireworks!
Did you decide that too? Afterwards, you were sitting in
the drawing room when Giusto came rushing in, gesticulating wildly.

'The carriage is on fire,' he was shouting, 'gone up in
flames.'

'See what our passion has done,' you murmured to
Livia. 'It's a sign!'

'Oh Ettore,' she'd sighed, 'don't be silly. You must have
left one of your cigarettes burning in the upholstery.'

The brougham was destroyed, pushed out onto the fore-
court like evidence, a black lacquered shell still smoking.

Good work, Veruda says and cackles.

Despite the fiery start, his life with Livia was a bath of
warm domesticity. She saved him from his worst instincts,
his tendency towards gloom and introspection. But not his
smoking; Livia had never managed to control that. Theirs
was a civilized existence, a house full of Venezianis coming
and going, and the business, which it turned out, he had
an aptitude for. Who would have thought? Ettore Schmitz,

Industrialist. And there was Titina. Livia had given him Titina, at great peril to her health, and had turned him into a family man, an unexpected father.

But what about your writing, Veruda interrupts, *see how marriage kills the promise of art.*

But his writing, such as it was, was probably no great loss. Would the universe feel the loss of the great unknown author Italo Svevo? (He hadn't even the courage to write under his own name.) It was a half-and-half name, neither one thing nor the other, much like his writing. He stubs his half-smoked cigarette out, grinding it into the ashtray.

'I am a man of business; I have no time to write.'

And what about transgression, have you time for that?

Veruda again.

He sits and watches Norah across the *studiolo* desk, holding up his daughter's fingers and counting – one, two, three. Then Giuseppina, now Norah. Norah with an h. Two sides of the one coin. He warms to Norah's antics. There's something clownish about the way she treats the child, as if she's a child herself. Next week Norah has promised to take her to the kitchens to bake in English. But soon, he suspects, Titina will lose interest, used as she is to more sophisticated company.

But he won't.

He listens intently to the songful chatter that emanates from Norah's lips, full of hushes and shushes. It has always been his ambition to speak English exactly like this, the silly nothings, the small talk of the street. He'd gone to an old duffer in the Berlitz school for months – what was his name, Cautley, that's it! – who insisted he must learn to decline all of the irregular verbs. But what good was that to him who had to deal with workers in England, plain fellows who smoked pipes and drank bitter. He'd learn more watching this pantomime with his daughter than from all the primers in the Berlitz school.

One morning, Mister arrives for the class with a speech prepared.

'I have been to Irlanda. Queen's Town. Do you know it?'

Queenstown, Queenstown? She racks her brain. Is that in Cork? Imagine, him having been there, why didn't he say before? Pity, she's never been. Now Kingstown she could talk about, the salty air, the view of the Hill of Howth like the curve of a woman's beam end dipped in the water, and what you might do up there, or the wind-blown piers jutting out into the water trying to reach one another across the harbour, she could tell him tales about that with sunny J. But no, she's not going to give that fella lodging in her mind. Particularly now when days go by and she forgets, forgets all about him and why she's here.

Haltingly Mister tells his story. His business took him to Ireland, something to do with Lord Muskerry's yacht, whoever he is when he's at home. They were painting it. Is that what Mister Smith does, a painter decorator? Not with those hands. She can't imagine him up a ladder in spattered overalls, whistling. Must be some mistake, she's not picking up the right end of the stick. She looks across at him now and he's smiling at her, kindly again. They stayed in a hotel called the Commodore that had a balcony looking out onto the sea and when they went to view the lord's yacht, Livia stayed behind on the shore. Wouldn't go out on the launch, water too rough.

Oh, she feels a draught of disappointment, Madame was there too.

There was a cottage on the jetty with flowers around the door, and a little girl came out of it with a lamb in her arms – was it a lamb, or a puppy? Norah can't be sure, it was a little animal, anyway, the way Mister describes it – and the girl went paddling in the small waves and gave the creature a wash.

Charmingeh, Mister says, it was charmingeh.

The picture makes Norah homesick for a place she's never been.

Afterwards, following the child's example, he went swimming in the tide himself, threw off his clothes and plunged right in. He loves to swim, he tells her, or at least that's what she thinks he's saying.

She's nearly dead from concentrating on the story, her ear sprouting to twice its size like a gramophone horn. But he's so keen to tell her that she wills him to keep going. She likes the curlicues of his pronunciation and while they're locked like this, eyes to eyes, as she strains to catch his meaning, it's like there's nothing else. She forgets herself; she forgets Jim.

Love is made with words, Jim used to say, but she pooh-poohed that because he had an answer for everything.

Love is tits and cocks and tongues, she told him.

Now she's not so sure.

Finally, Mister gets to the end of his tale. The pair of them wake as if from a long sleep and find themselves alone. Titina is gone, grown bored with the adult talk.

It's the last class the child comes to. The following week she's struck down, a cough at first, a burning throat. The house is in a state, the kitchen in an uproar of cures, Mrs Francheeny concocting mixes of ginger and lemon juice, trays are ferried up and down, soft treats are invented for poor Letty because her throat is aflame. She's shut away in the nursery, behind a mosquito net veil, and Juicy tells Norah she has to be lifted out of the bed because all her joints ache. A hush falls when the doctor arrives, hairy old dundrearies on him that would frighten a full-grown man, let alone a child. Ancient as his soft Gladstone.

That's put the kibosh on the classes, that's the end of my cushy job. Now I'm definitely for the chop.

But no.

The morning after the doctor comes, the bell jangles and Mrs Francheeny gestures to her to go up. Mister is in the study, as usual, sitting behind the desk, head in his hands. A pall of smoke hangs over his head and he's pulling on a fag as if engaged in a tug o' war.

Sit, sit, Norah, he says, and for the first time he calls her Norah. Just plain Norah.

Titina, she is very sick.

What's wrong? she asks, for she thought it just one of those childhood lurgies, something with spots.

The doctor says a fever, he says.

Is it scarlet fever, Norah wonders. She remembers Thomas coming down with that – a rash and a raging temperature, a bad old dose, but he got over it.

Febbray roomatica, he says.

Is that the same thing?

He takes out a handkerchief and she thinks for a moment he's going to cry and then what'll she do. She can't just sit there and watch him. But he only mops his forehead, and she sees beads of sweat there. He's in a lather, poor man.

It's not catching, is it? she asks, worried for him.

No, no …

So no more classes? she says.

For Titina, no.

He lights a cigarette, then offers one to her.

How did he know? She picks the slim cigarette from his elegant silver case with his initials on the cover. He strikes a match and holds the flame out to her. They smoke in conspiratorial unison.

But we continue, he says eventually.

He can't do the future tense, she notices.

Madame is sleeping in the nursery with Letty and has ordered everyone else to keep their distance, including Mister. Their classes happen now during the napping hour and not in the study anymore, but in Mister's office in the factory. Although Mister hasn't said so, Norah knows to keep it a secret. It isn't that hard for it's like leaving a dead house, slipping out at two o'clock in the day when all of them are asleep or dozing. She remembers what Jim promised they'd be doing in the *penichella* but she shakes it off like a dog shucking off water.

She throws on her coat for the journey to Mister's office. It's February now, the bloody wind cuts through the worn thin tails of Jim's coat, and she hasn't saved enough to buy a new one, with one eye on saving. For the fare home, she tells herself. What else is there for her to do? Jim isn't coming for her, that's for sure. Lately, though, she's been thinking, maybe she could make a life for herself here. It's not so bad, is it? She has Juicy as a friend and she's already made her way up the ladder. Not a servant, but a teacher, a governess, no less. Couldn't she teach English elsewhere now that she has experience and a few words of the lingo?

She hurries across the large expanse of cobbles between the house and the factory. She dips into a pathway overshadowed by a parade of small stunted-looking trees whose gnarled arms have been cut off at the elbows. At the end there's a wicket gate that leads to the two-faced factory. One looking at the villa, the other looking away to the timber yards. She pushes open the heavy door and practically falls inside with the effort as if a huge wind was working against her. The smell is overpowering. She's heard Olga and Livia give out stink about it. What do they know of bad pongs – they've never been in Galway on fair day, smell of cowshit on the wind. This is clean, bitter as lemon, oily as paraffin, fumey as boot black. The hallway of the factory is lined with pillars with decoration at the ceilings and the floor is made of tiny tiles that make up a picture in the middle. There's a woman on some kind of settle bed and a boy with a palm frond but that's all she can make out. The place is deserted. She pushes through the double doors at the end of the hall and goes left down the panelled corridor as instructed. Mister's door has a gold plaque outside with his name on it, she presumes. Ettore Schmitz it reads. Doesn't look a bit like Hector Smith, but there you go.

She knocks and waits.

He hasn't been unfaithful, has he? The worst he has done is to scheme, to carve out this little piece of territory for himself and Norah. He has kept his vows.

Vows! The voice of Veruda scoffs from beyond the grave. Spitting like a conscience. *Is this what you've been reduced to? The same man who wanted a marriage of equals with your sensible, cousinly wife?*

The knocking is so faint he barely hears it.

And now you're creeping around like an adulterer in a bad play!

A second knock comes, a little louder.

Spare me from the bourgeoisie. Bah!

'Come in!'
And to Veruda. 'Enough!'

Here is the strange deal he makes with her. You talk, just talk, he says, and I will listen.

When has a fella ever offered that, you talk and I'll be all ears?

So that I may understand, he says, so I may be educated in the spontaneous conversation.

It's fierce hard, at first, to clear your throat and start off cold. To gab about yourself. Even though for months Norah has longed for such a conversation, now that it's being offered she's unexpectedly shy about it. She'll have to go way back if she has to keep going for an hour three times a week, as the classes demand. Hard to be listened to so hard, would you credit that? But she persists and it gets easier. She finds herself telling him about Sonny and Willie and even Jim. She finds herself telling him things she never told them.

He is true to his promise. He hangs on her every word. Often, she sees a little crease of worry appear between his eyebrows and she knows then he hasn't a clue what she's on about. Even while he nods fiercely at her, his brow contradicts him. The rest of his face is smooth. A comfortable life don't give you a lined forehead. But it's not a hanging offence, is it, to be comfortable? And didn't he save her in her hour of need? And it isn't too much to ask for, is it?

To talk to him.

To talk at him.

It's the German of his schooldays that comes into Ettore's head as Norah talks. There is something about a *Kloster*, has she been a *Nonne*? How so? But I thought she was a *Hausfrau*, but now she seems to be lying down with her

Mann somewhere on a *Berg* – and there's a *Strand*, yes? Hard to say, and what's this about a *Schiff*, and the family waving goodbye, and yet she seems to be alone. And who is this Jim?

The stream of Norah's thoughts coming at him at full tilt makes him want to confide, or is it confess? *A confession in Italian is always a lie*, Veruda used to say. But what about in English? He wants to trade. He could tell her about his two published novels, ignored, or worse, damned with faint praise – 'influences of Zola and de Kock', 'not the work of a tyro', 'promise of full achievement'. Full achievement? Ha! Look at him now. A paint manufacturer taking language lessons from a working girl.

No, a working-class girl.

She is unstoppable, a river in flood. He feels an urge, well yes, but no, not that. It's the urge to write again. It was something he put aside after marriage. A nice hobby, Livia said, but not a career for a family man with commercial responsibilities. He agreed with her. Time to put away childish things. Take up the violin, she said. He did. After much practice, he put together a little quartet for their Sunday evening salons. He's no Fritz Kreisler, but it was enough, wasn't it? He'd thought so. But something about Norah's voice, the lilting words, the sheer, unadulterated flow of it, makes him wonder if he's found his Muse at last.

Stop it now, Ettore, concentrate!

Here's another part of the deal they've made. Without words. It'd be too complicated to say, with Mister's English and her with only the bare necessities in Eyetalian. So it just happens. Some deals need no words. Afterwards she thinks, they both knew, right from the very start that it would turn out this way. When they meet in the villa, say, on the stairs when she's going up to bed and he's coming down from Letty's sickroom now that he's let in, he greets her but there is no talking.

Miss Barnacle, he says and bows his head.

She's taught him that much. How to say her name.

Barnacle, she'd said, like the goose. She flapped her arms outstretched and barked, got up and hoofed about, as if she had companions.

She sells sea shells, she said, by the seashore.

In the end she had to draw a picture. A little stick bird.

Die Nonnegans! he said, jubilant. *L'oca facciabianco!*

She wasn't sure he'd got her drift.

A little goose, he said.

It seemed he had.

And you must call me Hector.

Be careful, Juicy warns. She's cottoned on to the secret lessons.

It's harmless, Norah reassures her.

And for months it is.

Christmas comes, her second at the villa. It's festive enough sitting with the maids in the kitchen and once Mrs F has gone, there's wine and Flavio has them all in stitches letting on he's Santy with a false beard. The wind howls through the house. Up in the servants' eyrie the shutters bang and the eaves creak. It's like being on a ship with the sails slapping and sometimes Norah worries the roof will fly off. Have I turned into the Other Fella, she wonders, a scaredy cat afraid of the thunder? It's at times like these she wishes she was still sharing with Juicy. She thinks of tip-toeing down the corridor and slipping into the spare bed next to her friend. But something stops her. She chastises herself. What are you afraid of? A bit of a gale? Hasn't the worst already happened? Abandoned by the man you thought would keep you and love you, for better or worse? So what's a roaring wind and a loose roof slate in comparison to that, I ask your pardon! But she doesn't seek comfort from Juicy for she feels the weight of her caution.

Be careful.

The child is out of bed now but pushed around in a kind of bath chair. She's hollow-eyed, poor pet, and listless, not the little sprite that greeted Norah a year and a half ago. She's more cossetted now – no running, no outdoor activities, no more English lessons, too taxing. She must build up her strength. Fresh air! She must watch her heart.

Madame is the whisper of a wife disappearing into the nursery, still keeping the hours of vigil, missing from the heart of the house. Then Hector announces she's going away and Norah's heart skips a treacherous beat.

For a cure, Hector says, at Salzo-madge-oray. She'll take Titina with her.

A cure for what? she asks Juicy.

Her nerves, Juicy says. She's not been right since Letizia was born, woman's troubles.

And what's better about that place?

They have public baths there, Juicy explains, sulphurous green water that's warm and bubbles and spits and you lower yourself in and it fixes your skin and your hair and whatever else ails you.

I'd prefer a week in bed myself, Norah says.

Juicy gives her a funny look.

The house exhales without Madame. The *salone* bell falls silent and the maids have no fear of meeting her on the landings and being reprimanded. It should be like a holi-day for all of them, but Hector is in a bad mood. Was there a matrimonial, she wonders, before Madame left? Then he cancels his lessons without warning. Mrs Francheeny informs her she won't be needed for the foreseeable. So everybody knows now about the hush-hush classes. She finds herself mooning around the coppery kitchen, getting under Mrs Francheeny's feet. Makes her feel useless and disappointed, both. Don't he still have to go to London and speak English at the factory, she argues to herself. It should be business as usual, even without Madame.

Oh well.

Her thoughts turn to home. Would she ever make it back? And what would she do there? It wouldn't be the same with-out Jim. But who's to say he's not there now? What if he'd gone directly home in the hope of finding her there? Was he wandering around Dublin thinking she'd do the same thing? But sure, how could she have, with not a red cent to her name? He'd seen to that. No, he meant to leave her and that's a fact. And even if she managed to scrape up the fare, would he still be in Dublin after all this time?

Waiting for her?

Would he, my eye!

Why had they never had the presence of mind to make plans for being separated? When she and Mamo used to go to the church bazaar in the meeting hall on Shop Street, she'd always say if we get parted, I'll meet you at the front door, do you hear? But she and Jim didn't bother with that; sure, they thought they'd always be together. She'd got so used to being left, she hadn't worried when he'd disappeared. Maybe if she had kicked up more of a fuss, she wouldn't be where she is now. She'd made it too easy for him.

All these running thoughts scald her heart. Make her mutinous and reckless.

Is he missing Madame? she asks Juicy.

Are you? Juicy snaps back.

What's got her goat?

What ails him? she persists, though she knows she's talking to the wrong person.

Oh, the Master, is it? Juicy says all airy as if she didn't know. He's given the smokes up. Offering it up for Titina's recovery. He's always like a bear when he does that.

The month of April passes wicked slow. Feels like donkey's years. No classes, Juicy being short with her, and Hector not even greeting her on the stairs when there's no need for them to be careful.

Careful of what, anyway, sure nothing's happened.

Nothing, Juicy prods, are you sure? It don't have to be kissing and cuddling, you know.

She doesn't want to contradict Juicy, but it's always been more than kissing and cuddling with her, it's been the feel of a breast and the little help down below, that's what she calls something happening. Now she's in a desert, ignored by Hector and disappointing Juicy. What is she doing here, anyway? She's only here by a series of mishaps. Weren't she and Jim bound for Paree. Paree! Her lost life.

Can you pine for something you never had?

Was it all just talk with Jim, so?

Was that all it ever was?

Everything ends in a question.

And then after months of it, the becalming is over. Madame is back and Letty is running through the halls.

She can hear Hector's hee-haw laugh, and the awful fiddle playing starts up again. Juicy says the two go together, the violin and the fags, as skeins of smoke snake through the rooms, even rising as far as the servants' quarters. It is like his smell, sweet and spicy. That's the brand he favours. Reeks of the East, harems and dancing girls. Though Hector seems too well-behaved for that sort of caper. He isn't even a toper. She knows all is well when the classes start up again and now there's an urgency for he's told her he must travel to England before the end of the year and his English has to be tip-top by then. Tip-top – he's proud of the phrase, learnt it from one of the workers in the Charlton factory.

Hector comes up with the idea of the walking lessons. She's not imagining it, is she, that he's scheming to get her out of the house, to be alone with her, but lookit, he's never laid a hand on her so what's all the scheming in aid of? They walk first around the grounds of the villa, up and down the bowling green and around the tennis courts like prisoners out on exercise. The weather is warming and the cherry trees are in blossom and the petals fly about and get in her hair. They ramble past the timber yards, smelling of pine and giving off sawdusty vapours. The shipyard is in the distance. She can see the ribs of an enormous ship appealing to the sky and the tiny figures of men clambering all over the skeleton like ants. They can hear the clangour from the foundry. Thunderous, like the plates of the earth moving. Everywhere they turn there are men at work.

He suggests taking the tram to the city. They do the esplanade. The Marie they call it here, out on the quays. Fierce windy, she says and puckers up her lips and blows. The bora they say and sure enough it does bore into you. That first day she nearly loses her hat to it. Yes, Juicy took her to a milliner's, she has a harlequin toque but no pin to hold it down and off it sails. They both go scrabbling after it, bend over at the same time, heads colliding.

Ow!

What do the Eyetalians say for that?

Ahi!

She teaches him the words for weather, awful important in England where it's so changeable. No more than here, she says, for the sea is always changing its mind, flinty in sun, placid and yellow in winter.

Before thunder, Hector says, he stretches so far you can't see where sea and sky kiss.

This makes her anxious, as if a curtain has dropped and she's inside the suffocating drapes and can't find the parting to get out. She doesn't understand this restlessness – isn't she safe here? Isn't she? Is it so bad? It's not, but it's not what was promised. This is Jim's life she's living, just without him.

Is he living hers elsewhere?

Sometimes they just walk in silence. It's a balm not to be constantly trying to follow and decipher. Anyway, when she talks too much, Hector doesn't understand and she longs to take him in hand, yes, yes literally, is that so bad to admit? Wouldn't it unravel the odd scratchiness between them, choked up by all the things that can't be said for neither of them have the words for it. When she was with Jim, she used to have to silence him sometimes, put a finger to his lips, anything to get him to stop for he used words like a boy skimming stones. Firing them across the water till he got the bounce right. Or else he'd be examining hers, inspecting her turn of phrase like a medic checking her tonsils. Say *aah*. Very interesting. Say it again. Then scribbling it down. Often, she had to distract him, put her breasts or her hair in the way. She'd want his touch and the games of love, the slap of flesh, the rough tomboyish play of it to work off all those lonesome feelings that'd come over her when she wasn't with him, when she feared he would leave her.

And now he has, so what is she waiting for?

Permission?

Maybe courtship is different here, she thinks, and she can't ask the person who'd be able to answer. Juicy would twig straight away. When a fella asks you out for a walk, is that the sign, or is it when he takes you to a pastry shop? Hector has taken her to this very tony café where the cakes come on trays carried by waiters tricked up in dicky bows, more like afternoon tea in the Shelbourne, not that she's been but she's heard tell of it. This place is equally fancy, with linen napkins and a little boy to replenish the pot. The first time Hector seemed very pleased with himself, sitting in state, introducing her as his English instructress to his cronies. They're business types, with frock coats and roundy hats, bowing and scraping and asking, is she strict? Or so she imagines. She sits back and lets them gossip and thinks, well, if a fella brought you to such a place at home, you'd be in no doubt that he meant business.

But she's not sure the same rules apply here and Hector's being such a gent, she wonders if this is all just in her mind. That first day in the Vunch café, she felt like stretching her hand across the table and saying something smutty to him, using one of those words Jim used to say to her – cockspit, fuckbird – then she thought better of it. What would be the use, Hector wouldn't understand it, but he'd get the message, wouldn't he? He's not *that* much of a gent.

Ettore is exhilarated by her and appalled at himself. Taking a servant, no a governess, a teacher of English, to

181

Wunsch's. Livia would have a fit. But Livia doesn't know about the walking lessons and he doesn't tell her. He's told her, in retrospect, about the lessons in his office in the factory, a place she never ventures. The smell of turpentine sends her into fits, always did, even as a child. She merely shrugged. She is a tiger now about Titina, it consumes her to the exclusion of all else. Now that Norah is part of the household – the under-household, he corrects himself – Livia has put her out of her mind. So, all is in order.

Meanwhile, it gives him such pleasure to sit here and receive compliments from his friends who are curious about the strange young woman who's in his company, a woman not his wife. Who's the lady with Schmitz, they'll say. What lady? That's no lady! Like a music hall turn. He's taking a chance, he knows. Trieste is a small city, word will get back. But his impending trip to Inghilterra makes him reckless. Anyway, the acquaintances from the café are not the type Livia would invite to the villa for Sunday salon. Small-time merchants, bankers' clerks, scriveners? Ah the lowly scriveners of the world, of which he was one once. Livia saved him from that.

Bought you off, Veruda says.

Dammit Veruda, get out of my head.

He tries to remonstrate with Veruda. Don't you see that I'm back at my writing?

Scribbling a bit, jottings, says Veruda.

It could become a novel ...

But you're keeping it a secret, I see, no grand announcements.

That would only kill it.

So what's it about?

A man trying to give up cigarettes.

And this girl has prompted it? Veruda says sneerily. *Your Muse!*

She doesn't even know.

He looks across the table at Norah, thinking – wouldn't Giuseppina have loved this? Tea at the Wunsch. If I'd done this with her, would I still have her?

Hardly!

Bloody Veruda again!

This one will go the same way, Ettore. She's no stay-at-home Penelope, faithful and fixed. For now, she's yours. That is all.

They go to the Stella Polare and sit in the window. Hector orders something clear in a small glass and urges it on her – here, taste. But no, she can't be doing with wine, though sometimes in the kitchen they offer it to her with her dinner. Tastes sharp as medicine to her. The alternative is these rough spirits, white and lethal. She opts for tea and one of their buns. She likes the clatter of the place, the men and the smoke and the long batons on which the newspapers are pegged like laundry, though they're no use to her because she can't read a word. *The Freeman's Journal* doesn't get this far. Anyway, she'd only be looking at the ads and the funnies.

The waters of the canal outside are lapping and busy with boats, tall-masted ones, and others piled high with fish that are unloaded in writhing creels, fellas with caps that wouldn't look out of place on the Claddagh, while the empty ones couple together clunkily. Every time she sees the canal she thinks of Jim, of how she was sure this was his watery grave, but if it was, wouldn't he have been found by now?

No, she chastises herself, I am here now with Hector; this is it, until it changes.

He takes her to the studio of the Maestro Giordano. He tells her he wants to learn how to use musical terms in English,

183

but he's thinking of the little inner showroom lined with display cases filled with Alberto's showpiece instruments. A magnificent bowl-backed mandolin, or the spruce scroll of a Genovese viola. The maestro will lay these treasures out on plump red velvet cushions and withdraw, leaving them alone in a room intimate as a bed-chamber, hushed as a church and no prying eyes.

He brings his own violin for restringing, but the maestro leads him through to the workshop while Norah is left alone with the instruments. *Cazzo!* He stands among the shavings while Alberto fiddles and twangs and Norah waits in the inner room with her new hat on, a dinged solemn affair with a clutch of little balls on the brim trying to imitate fruit.

Loo-what?

Liutaio. Our word for the maker of violins, Hector says.

Sounds more like a flute than a fiddle to Norah.

It's a repair shop. The fiddle-maker is a tall man with showy grey whiskers and a slight stoop like the curve of a cello. But his fingers in hers are slender and womanly; his nails have perfect half-moons. She notices these things now, how refined these foreigners are, no nicotine stains on their fingers, no gapped teeth. She clamps her own lips shut when he greets her, remembering her own bockety mouthful.

She wanders around the back room while Hector goes to the workshop to get new strings for his bow. It's full of glass cases with instruments inside, set up on stands like models posing in vitrines. There's one that looks like a guitar at the bottom and a harp at the top and a row of mandolins with saucy bottoms and ivory around their portholes. Their necks are carved into lions' heads. Just like the ones that guard the villa – they do love their lions.

From the dim workshop she can hear Hector and the fiddle-maker talking. Over their heads, suspended from the ceiling she can see pale pieces of wood strung up, the fronts and backs of fiddles like the scenery flats at the Tivoli. She gets the whiff of varnish and sees there's a little boot boy polishing them till they turn as dark as the floorboards. She inhales it, smells of home, linseed, eucalypt, that Gumption in the green and white tin Miss Fitzgerald had on special order from Lenehans ... the tell-tale smell of Finn's.

Afterwards they go to the market.

These are oranges, those are grapefruit. These are – merciful hour, what are they?

Carciofi, Hector says.

Car-cho-fee, she repeats. Sounds like a train going uphill to her, and gives her no clue. These yokes are green and globey, scaly as fish, or like cabbage with a grass skirt. Never seen anything like it. They agree to call them by their Eyetalian name – another useless word for her.

Car-cho-fee – *never off the table at home.*

Here come onions, mushrooms, but then there are other onions with a green, ferny top. Hector picks it up.

Fin-okey-oh. He makes a comical teapot shape, one hand on his hip, the other like a spout. He hams it up; she wishes she understood.

Fin-okey-oh, he repeats.

He thinks if he says it often enough she will understand, or come up with an English word.

But she's thinking of Finn's again.

There is the trip to the House of Tombas, as Hector calls it, which catches her by surprise when it turns out to be a cemetery. She hasn't been in a graveyard since poor Sonny died. His dates on the headstone were like an accusation.

Aren't you the reason he got caught out in the downpour and the pleurisy set in? Aren't you? She doesn't want to think about that, but the cemetery brings up a close, morbid kind of feeling. As if we're all to blame for something. Like original sin, that is, and she doesn't believe in that, so she shakes the thought off. If it's original, someone, somewhere, is responsible, just not her.

Hector leads the way, taking her down a long stone arcade with a high, arching ceiling like a church aisle outside. They keep their dead in urns here, or in high-up altars, or in tombs – *tombas*, now she gets it – that look like doorways to the other world. Whereas we, she wants to say to Hector, we leave ours out to suffer in all weathers like they did in life. If they didn't die of the rain and cold before, they will now.

They pass all sorts of memorials, one made of black marble that looks like the body of a young girl laid out, only the point of her nose and the dimples of her toes visible under her stone shroud. Another shows a small boy in a sailor suit clambering up a steep bank that is his father's death bed, with three stone women crying over him. You'd swear they were about to move so life-like are they.

She and Hector leave the arcade behind and step out into the sunlight, taking a winding route between the headstones, along damp boreens. It's been raining. A watery sun is glancing through the clouds and everything is sprouting, ferns and grasses and brambles and the overhanging trees, whose leaves are laden with rain. Everything drips. She wishes they could get to wherever it is they are going. Finally, he halts in front of a tree. There's a memorial stone that looks like a piece of parchment rolled at the top. The tablet is attached to the tree with a metal band that goes all around the bark. Hector stands, hat in hands, head bowed and she wonders should she kneel, is that what Jewboys do? Madame is Catholic, she's seen her at the church in Servola, but Hector doesn't seem to bother with worship.

That's because he's really a Jew, Juicy has whispered to her.

ELIO SCHMITZ, she reads, the rest she can't make out.

Welcome to my brother, Hector says.

All she can think of is Jim's brother, Georgie, the one who died and Jim couldn't save him despite his doctoring experience. His mother had fed the boy solid food too soon after a fever, that's what Jim said, and that's what finished him off. Only fifteen, he was, a bright boy, Jim said, a boy like me.

How could there be another like you? she'd said. Was she daft or what, for betrayers like him are ten a penny.

If ever I have a son, I'll call him George, Jim had said, he was that fond of him.

All the dead boys, she thinks, as Hector puts a small stone on his brother's headstone. Sonny, George, Elio … Jim?

Pain stabs at her heart and she tamps it down. Enough to weep for the dead, but not that fella who's just unfaithfully departed.

Hector produces his cigarettes. He's less of a man without his smokes. Half-man, half-cigarette, he says, at least she thinks that's what he says and if they weren't in a graveyard, she'd ask him for one. Plumes of blue escape from Hector's mouth. She can't see his eyes for they are narrowed by the inhale, but she thinks there may be tears there. For his brother, she supposes.

He feels a fool and a fraud, using poor Elio as grief bait to wring out some sympathy for himself, to look wounded and tortured, to excite her … what? Pity? *Shame on you, Ettore!* And too good for you that it mattered not a jot to her, your snivelling show of sentiment. Did you expect she would embrace you, shower your face with kisses, declare undying love? Undying love in a graveyard? *Really, Ettore!*

Her limbo has lasted well over a year. She must be paying off some kind of penance but what has she done, only be left? She feels restless, impatient. Like she's still in the Ladies' Waiting at the station, hanging around, hanging on. What is the point of Trieste? It was a sanctuary at first, and she was glad to have it, but now? She no longer believes, not even in the deepest part of her heart, that Jim will come back, so what is she only a glorified maid with a jumped-up position as an English teacher? If things with Juicy were as they used to be, the gaiety and laughs of the shared room, she'd be content, but even that has dwindled away. Juicy has grown cold and distant as the lessons with Hector become more frequent.

They are done with Madame's blessing, she tells Juicy, but Juicy is still being prissy about it.

Titina's illness has cast a shadow over Madame, Juicy says, while you … She never goes any further.

If you were a mother, you'd understand, Juicy says,

Isn't that rich from her who has neither chick nor child?

I told you, nothing has happened, she hisses. They are at the kitchen table with all the others, who have no doubt been gossiping about her too. Has Juicy painted her as some kind of Jezebel? Well, she doesn't care a pin. But even as she says it, she knows it's a fib.

Because something *has* happened, even though she can't put a name on it – in either language.

*

The trip to London is announced quite sudden and she knows then what she's suffering from. Hector will spend at least two months in the factory in Charlton. What in the name of all that's good and holy is she going to do? Left alone with Madame and slavey work with Juicy, who treats her now like she's a Monto girl.

I will be lost without your lessons, Signora, Hector says to her and she's on the alert. Why is she back to being Signora all of a sudden?

They're sitting in his office, the green baize desk between them. Hector's unattended cigarette in a large glass ashtray sends a question mark signal upwards.

Won't you be speaking like a native on account of all my good teaching?

Can he tell how false her voice is? Surely, he can tell. She can feel him pulling away already, and she has that empty feeling like when a train disappears out of the station and leaves you behind waving at nothing. That's her now.

Two whole months! She's already totting on her fingers – that means it'll be mid-summer before he's back. She feels a rush of panic rising in her throat like sour bile. She'll never manage. What if he never comes back? Like the Other Fella?

Hector's the only one who understands her, the only one who knows her story. She still has only bits and pieces of the lingo so she can't talk to anyone below stairs, bar Juicy, who's giving her the cold shoulder. Madame has never cared for her. Is she waiting for when Hector's back is turned like the last time, to send her away? And then what would she do? Here she is with the same old questions as if she was still waiting outside the station. She hasn't moved a blessed inch. Does she have enough saved to get home? She doesn't even know how much a ticket costs; Jim did all of that. And where is home anyway? Couldn't go back to Galway with her tail between her legs. Dublin, maybe? But what if that's where Jim is? She couldn't bear the thought of running into him with some new girl and making small talk, letting on it was all a joke and she didn't give a toss.

But if she stays …

Hector leans forward and clasps her hand.

I have an idea, he says.

She's wary now. Hector's ideas always involve her.

I am thinking you can come with me, Norah.

What?

As a housekeeper in London, and to help me with my English. Translate and et cetera.

Et cetera, I wonder what he has in mind. He still has hold of her hand.

Make those English understand me!

She thinks of him in that moment like a conjurer, who can wave a wand and change her from a destitute foreigner to a ladies' maid, then an English teacher and now a housekeeper just by thinking. Does he know about her cooking? He'd better like chicken. She can do a decent roast and a rhubarb pudding with a meringue top, but that's about the height of it.

To London?

Her heart swells with relief at the thought of being nearer home. Not home, but close. Somewhere she can talk and be understood by more than one person. She hadn't thought it mattered, but she feels suddenly like she's been let out of prison.

Yes, I will need the help and the house in London … Hector pulls a sad, clownish face. Madame would come, but she won't leave Titina.

The sickly child sits there protecting them.

And what does Madame make of your idea? she asks.

I can talk to Madame, but what do *you* say?

She doesn't know if that means Madame doesn't know yet, or whether he has already persuaded her. Either way, Norah thinks, Madame may be the boss but she has no idea what's going on under her nose. No idea at all.

Hector smiles and it's contagious. They're like children on a spree, and in a moment she's forgotten all her doubts and worries.

I say yes, yes I will.

Hector lights up.

Madame summons her to the *salone* the day before the journey. Norah stands before her just like at the start, and Madame brings out her perfect English for the occasion.

Signor Schmitz needs a great deal of looking after, she says sternly.

Yes, Ma'am.

Regular meals, no offal and no eggs.

Do you think I've noticed nothing, Norah thinks.

And watch out for burning cigarettes. He forgets he has one lit before starting another. Madame looks at her squarely then. As you may know.

As a smoker, did she mean?

He likes his tea weak and his coffee strong.

What else does he like, she is itching to say, can you tell me that? Does he like it rough or tender?

Just remember, Madame says, that you are still part of this household even though you will be in England. Standards must be maintained.

Was that a warning?

Fresh collar every day, she says.

Yes Ma'am.

And then out of the blue, Madame asks: Tell me, was there ever a Signor Barnacle?

Cheek of her! So, she was never believed. Norah points to the curtain ring on her finger. She's kept it, like a little charm of the life she and Jim might have had.

Yes, Norah says simply, for it's that simple in the end.

Madame has her poker face on.

You will want to spend your last night with the servants, she says, and with that Norah is dismissed.

Mrs Francheeny and Mary Kirn have been cooking up a storm all day, a big dinner, baby cow and fin-okey-oh. She does the teapot mime that Hector showed her and they all laugh. Her first joke in Eyetalian! It makes her lonesome to be leaving them just when she was getting the hang of the house and its workings. Even Flavio and Guisto join the toast to her, raising their little buckety glasses filled with sparkling wine the colour of straw. Only Juicy is missing. They all notice but no one says anything, as if she and Juicy are sweethearts who've had a tiff. It's Juicy's day off and she's been gone from early morning, making herself scarce on purpose so she wouldn't be seen to give her blessing. When they are all in bed, she hears Juicy coming in, her footsteps halting outside Norah's door, but she passes on without even knocking.

It is still dark when Guisto drives them to the station, all in the villa fast asleep. As they draw up by the little park outside the station, she half expects to see Jim there, or even herself in some strange way, as if a little piece of her is still there waiting for an ending that isn't going to come now. Everything else is the same as when she arrived. The

same station hall. Same station master, even the lav attendant though she doesn't remember Norah, or if she does
she doesn't let on.

Have I changed so much, she wants to ask. Or is it the
company I'm keeping? Hector catches her hand when
they pass the spot where she dropped in a heap.

In case you fall again, he says. And winks.

The first time his hand is openly in hers.

They board the train. First Class carriage, very grand.
Red-buttoned plush and a man to serve them tea. The
journey's the same. The man is different is all.

Hector cups his hand over hers like he's the shell and
she's the pearl, and keeps it there all the way to Paree –
yes, Paree!

For a night she has a glorified version of the life Jim
promised. They stay in a grand hotel, so grand that's what
it's called. They eat in a dining room ablaze with chande-
liers, mirrors all around that make the two of them look
like a crowd, waiters bowing low and reversing out of
their way. When the Mayter Dee comes to the table, Hector
orders for her because it's all in French.

Mrs Svevo, he begins in his best English, for her benefit.

Mrs Svevo, that's her.

Signora Italo Svevo, he writes in the register. He can't,
or won't pass her off as Livia, so he uses his pen name, the
one he used when he was a writer. Gave that up, thanks
be to God, got sense! He'd never be able to afford all this if
he was a writer still.

So for one night only, she becomes his missus. It is
Signora Svevo he takes up to their room, a vast chamber
with painted ceilings and a matrimonial bed, though they
don't go near it. Once he has turned the key in the door, he
lifts her hat off and pads around her. She tries to wriggle

out of her coat but he wags his finger admonishingly – no.
He peels it from her shoulders and lets it drop. Then he
travels down the row of covered buttons of her duck-egg
blouse, unfurls her vest over her head like a flag. Wordlessly, he unpicks the eyelets of her corset. She leans on his
shoulder as she steps out of her skirt; he rolls down her
hose as she unshoes herself. Last to go are her bloomers
and still he hasn't touched her. Her skin pebbles – is it cold
in here? And still he circles around her as if she were one
of those buck-naked marbles in the park outside the station in Trieste. Like she's something to behold. Then she
feels the ache, that hollowy ache between her legs, where
she wants him to cup his hand. She almost cries out for
him to do it, but the wanting of it is so delicious a pain,
and so new to her, that she says nothing. She waits and
waits and just when she thinks she can't wait a moment
longer, he drops to his knees and she feels his lips on hers.
Oh sweet suffering Signora Svevo!

She loves the foreign sound of it. She loves the sound
of it full stop.

Mrs Svevo will have the Foy Grass.

Look at that now, Hector's got the hang of the future,
she thinks.

And what's that, she asks.

A goose spread, he says.

Mrs Barnacle

April 28, 1906

There's a mushroomy smell when Hector pushes open the front door of number 67 Church Lane, Charlton, on the dank night of their arrival. It's a grim-looking fortress outside and inside it's perishing and even though it's night-time and she's exhausted, Norah sets to, getting the boiler in the kitchen lit and rummaging in the linen press on the return which has been left in a complete heap for something to dress the bed. The cupboards are bare. She's afraid they'll get pneumonia from the unaired sheets and it's a far cry from the Grand Hotel in Paree with its scented pillows and the dinners that came under domes of gold.

She's a poor excuse for a housekeeper, though better than no one. Hector is useless. Couldn't make a bed and that's something she knows about, and how to lie in it too. She can boil spuds, fry an egg, or roast a chicken, but that doesn't mean she has to like it, does it? For Hector's sake, she tries to make a fist of it, joining the other women on Church Lane with their cane baskets, weighing the heft of spuds, the ripeness of apples, but all the time there are sly enquiries – the Eyetalian gentleman in number 67 you're with, a strange lot, aren't they? That's Mrs Percival, the

195

most beady-eyed of them, lives three doors up, thin and mean and dangerous with it for she has a son, Archie, on the line in Hector's paint factory. Not the brightest tool in the box, given the amount spattered on his overalls at the end of the shift.

That boy's wearing my profits, Hector would say. Or words to that effect.

Young isn't you, Mrs Pee says, for a housekeeper. Were you in service before? Dying to get the low-down on her.

Norah doesn't give her the soot of a reply, for if she were to say yes, Mrs Pee would want the gory details and if she were to tell a fib and promote herself, a teacher, she could say – for hadn't she been a class of a teacher? – or a governess, she'd only be landing herself in more hot water for one lie would borrow another.

Say nothing, *cara*, Hector commands. *Niente!*

And Mister Barnacle, Mrs Pee wheedles.

I lost him, Norah says, in Trieste. Out foreign, she adds helpfully.

She has started to play the widow but there is no lie in what she says. She did lose Jim there.

With Mrs Pee, she is often tempted to brazen it out and tell her all. I'm the fancy woman, if you must know. Just to see her jaw drop. If she stops at the gate for a gossip, Norah is tempted to say, Welcome to our love nest! Isn't that what the *Daily Mail* would call it? She imagines Mrs Pee reading all about it in the court pages, always the juiciest bits there.

CHURCH LANE'S HOUSE OF SHAME!

GRASPING IRISH MISTRESS PASSED HERSELF OFF AS HOUSEKEEPER.

WRONGED WIFE HAD NO INKLING OF PAIR'S SECRET TRYSTS IN LONDON.

Thoughts of Livia curb Norah's tongue. Instead, she tries to thwart Mrs Pee by waiting for her to make the first housewifely move – clothes on the line on a Monday morning, slops out on a Wednesday – then she shifts her own chores one hour later so she won't bump into her. But Mrs Pee is wily. She must be in league with the butcher for that is where they most often coincide.

And that funny food they have, long strings of flour like rats' tails. Do you have to serve that up to him?

Two lamb chops if you please, Mister Cavendish, *and let me out of here before I lose my temper.*

In the beginning she can't settle, though there's plenty work to do. She misses the crowd at the villa, she's used to clatter and chatter, even if she didn't always understand what was being said. It was company. Now Hector is gone from early morning and the house is still. She feels the wash of loneliness when she shuts the door on him, envying him his easy passage down the steps and out onto the thronged street, past those huxter shops opposite, where the noisy cobbler and the beefy butcher and the mutton-chop barber are as likely to be hogging their doorways as going about their business, sucking on a pipe or loading up snuff, or just plain flirting with the women doing their messages early. Whereas when Norah goes out, she is always on her guard.

All Hector worries about is keeping warm. It is a wet, windy spring.

He is a different kind of cold here, he would say, a damp cold.

Goes through you, she agrees. So she has to light the boiler early and keep it stoked throughout the day so the place is toasty when he gets back from the factory. Meggie used to, Hector would say, talking about the girl who did for him before, and she's sick to the back teeth hearing tales of Meggie, Meggie who did a lunch of meat and two veg with spuds and a mean *estra*, whatever that was when it was home. But Norah says sure couldn't he eat at the factory with the men in the middle of the day and then they could have the dinner in the evening like in Trieste? Instead she'd pack him a lunch of salt beef sandwiches and mustard like the English fellas have.

Excellente, he says when she suggests it. When in Rome!

He's so biddable, she feels a bit of a harridan, but lookit, it saves her the palaver of cooking in the morning and isn't there plenty to keep her busy besides. She cleans the grate and sets the fire in the front parlour, then there's the shopping to do and appearances to be kept up – that's a job in itself. Daily she cleans the house, from stem to stern, starting with Hector's room and finishing with her own kingdom, the back scullery.

Hector's room is the big one in the front, and she tackles it daily, for he's a man and not used to picking up after himself. The po could be left to fester under the bed for days. One day he goes out to buy fags and comes back with a tin whistle. He might plough upstairs in search of a book and come down empty-handed. She often hears him muttering the item to himself as he travels so that he'll be sure to remember.

It's living in too many languages, he says, makes you forget in all of them.

He has Italian, and the funny version they speak in Trieste, as well as German and – when he and Livia wanted to hide something from the child, or the servants – French. Now he's adding English to the stew. He spreads out his primers on the drop-leaf table in the back parlour, the butts gathering in the ashtray as he fumes about words that sound the same but mean something different.

Take a bow, he would say, and all the things it can be. To lean over, a cravat, a ribbon for your hair, a string for your fiddle, the front of a boat. *Madonna!*

That makes her think of Juicy.

By the time Hector comes home in the evening she has all her chores done and is waiting for him. Often just inside the door, counting the rust tiles versus the blue and cream and checking herself in the hall mirror, nervous in case she doesn't measure up. *To whom, you ninny,* she chides herself. *Livia? The young women at the factory?*

They are some right doxees, Hector says.

He says the word carefully because, she suspects, he doesn't believe it exists outside of her mouth. She knows he hasn't put it in his little black notebook for his new words. Only when he can insert a word into the general run of a sentence does he commit it to the notebook. And some of Norah's words aren't easy to find a home for. Or else he is afraid that when he goes back to Livia, he will open his mouth and Norah will come out.

So there are some words that become part of their secret language. *Doxy* and *ruffian* and *skiver* and *toper*. Her words.

But God Almighty, sometimes it drives her pure mad, this carefulness. His little notebook, and her own self turned into a scaredy cat. Timid and lonely from the closeted hours in the house, it makes her mad for his attention. She clutches at him once the door is closed and the world shut out. He steers her down the passageway, down the three steps into the kitchen, where there's no chance they can be overlooked.

And how's my fiery girl? he says, but in his arms she feels like a small explosive, a firecracker that might go off. Unstable. Isn't that what they say about dynamite?

After the dinner, he pours her a thimbleful of sherry and they smoke together either side of the parlour fire. It calms her. She thinks of all the others she's shared fags with – Mary O, Celia Canty, Juicy, even Jim – and the thread of smoke she exhales makes her feel connected to them, wherever they might be now.

Hector, she discovers, is a creature of habit. Always goes to Mister Wickett for his hair. The man who dresses hair, he calls him. He worries about his receding hairline, though there is sweet Fanny Adams Mister Wickett can do about that, she wants to say. Wickett is a flighty article with a shop down the village near the railway station. He does ladies too and she can imagine the fuss they make of the foreign gent to his face, and how afterwards behind his back they'd say was the cut-throat and the basin at home too plain for him? Wickett would keep up a stream of cockney chatter that didn't require an answer and Hector liked the surrender of that – he wasn't required to say anything and Wickett, not used to not being interrupted, became a fast friend. When he moved to Richmond, Hector was beside himself.

Sure, I can work a razor, Norah told him, if you trust me with a cut-throat.

So she took Wickett's place, turning Hector's face into a sea of soap in front of the mirror. This is what he'll be like when he's old, she thought. A grandfather with a snowy beard, but will she be there to see it? One thing's for sure, she won't believe in forever again.

On Sundays they go to church separately. Hector is a fair-weather Catholic. He was born a Jewboy but he changed for Livia and she would check in her letters to see if he was attending. As if it made much difference. When he went to Mass, he wasn't keeping faith with God, he was keeping faith with Livia. He'd only taken instruction to please her. Or to get past his mother-in-law, the Dragon Olga. Norah has never seen him as much as bless himself. He's like a class of souper, except he did the switch for love not money.

For Livia. For Livia always gets her way.

The Mass, she is difficult, on your knees, Hector says after one of his rare forays.

Is it the arthritis? she asks, for he's a martyr to the damp. He looks at her strangely.

In your knees?

Sometimes even the simplest thing between them gets knotted up.

No, no, no, he says, but Jews don't kneel.

Is that so, on principle is it?

And he says yes. He can't explain it, he says.

So a genuflection would be out of the question so?

She doesn't know why but she finds her temper flaring. These men and their principles. With the Other Fella, it was marriage and how he couldn't put a ring on her finger because of Mother Church, for crying out loud. But it was less of the church and more of the mother, if you asked Norah. His own poor ma was afflicted by that wastrel she married, and Jim said he had the same streak in him, and he'd only do the same to her. And why couldn't you just stop yourself, she asked him, but she got no reply.

It would be nice, once in a blue moon, if she and Hector could worship together, respectable, like. But that would set tongues wagging. And maybe it's just as well. She knows she can't quite trust herself out in the world. Can't guarantee she won't forget herself and link Hector's arm, act as if she owns him.

As for herself, going to Mass makes her doleful because it reminds her of the lost companionship of Juicy.

The back room beside the kitchen is hers and all made up, *mar dhea*, as if she were the housekeeper. She fills the wardrobe with her clothes, she turns the sheet down every night and uses the dresser mirror to comb her hair in front of, but she doesn't live there. It's like a stranger's place, belonging to some primmer version of herself who would disapprove of this set-up they have. But once she climbs the stairs to Hector's room, it's another story. With him she is wanton and saucy for that is what Hector wants from her; that's what they all want in the end, the danger, the boldness. In Hector's room she sheds. Every stitch and all her sorrows. But when they are done she has to gather herself up, pluck the discarded clothes from the floor and carry them in a faint over her arm back downstairs, for there can't be any trace of her there, in case, Hector is always saying.

In case what?

In case Livia should turn up – as if she would, out of the blue like that with no warning? Not Lady Livia! Oh no, there would be trumpets blaring for that particular royal visit.

But they live as if she might.

They are always under Livia's cosh even though she's beyond in Trieste.

If only Livia would … Hector sometimes says, agitated, as if he is practising his conditional tense.

And she stops him right there and then.

If only Livia would what, she demands. Die?

It was all my eye.

What difference does a ring on your finger make, she says to him. And I should know!

*

Every couple of weeks, Hector goes to London on business. Forty minutes on a rattling train if there's no trouble with the signals or work on the tracks. He has to see shipping agents or the Admiralty in Whitehall. Same name, imagine, as Mamo's place on Augustine Street, and it makes her smile to imagine Hector meeting Admiralty chaps in her granny's kitchen. Chaps, that's what he calls them. In her mind's eye she sees Major Tweedy's monocle. Hector meets them in a club in London, a chandeliered place with shuffling waiters wearing white gloves for fear they'd smudge the glasses.

Stahfee, he says. A word he hasn't learned from her. His English turns the plainest word fanciful.

Stuffy, do you mean? she says to him. I think you enjoy it.

Cara, they're my *pane* and *vino*, he says when she pouts. Are you jealous?

And though he'd like her to say yes, she isn't.

She doesn't speculate on what he gets up to in London. She doesn't rightly know what Hector's smutty tastes might run to. Dancing girls? Dirty postcards? Bare titties? Or would he be like the Other Fella running round with hoors? But doesn't Hector already have a dirty little secret? Her.

The other place he goes on his own is the football. He supports Athletic, local boys scrapping about after a ball on Saturday afternoons. From the house she can hear the chants and roars from the grounds, rising and falling in waves, like a crowd in the throes of you know what.

The workers should see me, is good for relations, he explains, but she knows that's not the only reason.

He likes the shouldery jostle of men and the shuffled march to the pitch, all that shouting in unison and the back-slapping beers in the pub afterwards. At first, he didn't understand the rules but of course he did his homework. She comes across a pamphlet sitting in the back parlour along with his English lesson books.

LAWS OF THE GAME
Alterations made by the International Football Association
Board at Ayr on
June 15, 1903
Number of Players …

Three, she thinks sourly.

He comes back from the games merry and gassy with more new words. *Off-side. Penalty.*

He is a simple pleasure, Hector would say, turning football into his best friend.

Unlike Norah. There was nothing simple about her pleasure at all.

Vai, vai, Hector says, impatient-sounding, meaning go out, enjoy yourself, when she complains of being lonely. Take the train into London, see the museums, he's a divil for museums himself, but she's never been one for collections of things. Give her a café, or the pictures or a turn on the stage. Jim took her once to the Dead Zoo in Dublin, a desperate place, all those vitrines filled with dead birds, stuffed to the gills to make them look alive, but fooling no one. Hector waves money at her, as if that's the problem. But she has money, her own money, for he pays a wage.

He is strict about those things, keeps his accounts. He has the Dragon Olga squabbling over every penny, so Norah appears in Trieste every month as an entry in the books. A foot in both camps.

Or visit the parks, Hector says, the lovely parks.

But he doesn't understand, how could he, that she never wants to see a blooming ornamental bed or a park bench ever again. No one wants reminding of how they were thrown away like a rotten old parsnip.

Truth is, apart from doing the messages and going to Mass of a Sunday, she finds it hard to leave the house at all. Makes her uneasy. Always has this little dread that when she'd get back to number 67, she'd find her key didn't slide into the lock, and that when she knocked some stranger housekeeper would answer, guarding the threshold, looking her up and down and saying we're not buying.

In her darker moods, she wonders what would happen if she upped and left, would Hector even miss her? Hasn't he his factory, his paper in the morning, his beer after the football on a Saturday in the Rose of Denmark, his Admiralty chaps. He even has his own lady friend, Miss Streeter, the postmistress, whom he plays the violin with on a Sunday afternoon.

Hector says he learns more of real conversation from Miss Streeter than all the lessons he's ever taken.

Does that include hers? Norah feels a twinge.

Proper English, he means, not her kind.

Sometimes, she takes a saunter past the factory just to reassure herself that Hector is actually there. She can't go in, Hector wouldn't like it. How could he explain it? The boss's housekeeper acting like a nagging wife, is what he means. Only in an *emergenzia*, he would warn. But there isn't a law against taking a constitutional down Anchor and Hope Lane, now is there? It's a free country, isn't it?

The factory is a squat, low building in red brick with four gables, and rows of secretive windows that dazzle like a man with spectacles in the sun so you can't see into his eyes. Even here Livia is the boss. Her name is there. Well, not hers, but her father's. Gioachino Veneziani's Works. There's a mouthful. It's a busy place, men out front rolling barrels into pyramids, and carts coming and going with deliveries. The gates are locked every night and the windows of the works are shuttered in case anyone would steal the formula. The ruddy formula they are all obsessed by. Livia, Olga, even Hector.

And what makes the paint so special, she asks him one Saturday in the kitchen. She is baking bread – she'd got a fit to have the smell of baking in the house, something else to bring back home. That and a kettle always on the boil. And tea in the making, and not that old coffee that was like tar. She has rolled the dough out on the table and brushed a lock of her hair off her forehead with a floury paw.

It's for the ships, he says, and it sounds like sheeps the way he says it. Protects them from … and then he stops.

From what, she asks, thinking he doesn't have the word.

From the sea creatures, he says.

What sea creatures?

Hector looks shifty.

Spit it out, she says.

Shirapayday, he says. He doesn't *want* to say it. She always knows when he's being pig-headed. I don't know her in English.

There's that she again! A constant reminder of the three in this arrangement, this mysterious she who creeps into every conversation.

Get out your dictionary, so, and show me, she says.

He hefts out the well-thumbed book with the little cleats in its pages and opens up at C. He shows her *cirrapedi*.

Barnacles. The shells that cling to rocks. The paint, she repels them, he says.

And do you have the same for me? she asks. A magic paint that'll protect you? So that I won't cling?

Cara, he says, and reaches out to caress her cheek. There is nothing between us.

Not realizing his mistake, he crushes her to him. She inhales him, the smell of cologne and smoke and maybe something turpentiney from the paint – is she imagining that? – and they do it there and then in the kitchen which is against his principles. And he whispers *cirrapedi* in her ear as they thrash about on the floured table, and other foreign words she doesn't recognize, that's how he always is, talkative when they're doing it. Aren't they a pair with barely one decent language between, both of them useless at the other's talk? How have they ever managed it, at all?

When she finally gets the loaf in the oven, she's so distracted it comes out wrong for she's overdone the raising agent. And it tastes of nothing but bickerbonnet. Salty, rank. Smell of home is right.

Love, Hector says all rueful, she makes bad bread.

Who is this she?

Her?

Love?

Is it just a mistake or is he being a slyboots and getting a dig in? How can you ever know with men, what they're thinking, even the ones with words, like the Other Fella? Trouble is, he had too many and Hector has too few.

Then she chastises herself. Lookit, things could be worse. She doesn't have to have her hand out like her mother used to. And isn't Hector generosity itself when it comes to the housekeeping, if that's what you'd call it. Hush money more like. What is she only a glorified skivvy, but one liquidy look from Hector and she forgets all that.

The worst times, though, are when Hector isn't there at all, when he's gone back to Trieste to play happy families with Livia. She spends two summers alone in Charlton, and one Christmas. The summer is the worst, the desolation of a dusty house closed for the season in which she ghosts around, no performance to put on. It's in that first summer alone she first thinks of escape and feels a pang for even thinking it, for it makes Hector her jailer and that isn't fair.

But she finds herself stacking up objections to him. He isn't always a piece of cake, God knows. He's fierce jealous. He can work himself up into a lather about her, when she's up to absolutely nothing, only keeping his dinner warm. He's worst when Livia's letters come, sometimes two or three together. They are forever writing to one another. Once she stole a look, but Livia, cute out, writes in French so she couldn't make head nor tail of it. When the post comes, Hector shuts himself away in his room to read her letters, poring over them like accounts. He's guilty as sin about Livia, but if he starts his *ullagón*ing about her, Norah puts her hand up like a constable.

No, no, I can't be having that. I'm the one who's got the raw end of the stick here. Only here on sufferance, letting on I amn't here at all.

Sure as eggs she isn't going to be mopping his brow over frigging Livia. She does enough of that playing Florence Nightingale to his colds and his chills.

He's always coming down with something; if it isn't his chest, it's his vitals. He's like an organ recital, his kidneys, his liver! Forever afraid of catching something. But bad and all as he is, he'd never abandon her like the Other Fella, would he?

No, never, unless …

Every morning he takes his pulse, fingers on the blue veiny part and counting.

Take *my* hand, she thinks, measure my pulse and see how weak it's getting, why don't you?

He finds the English winter hard on his bronicals.

Try a wet week in Galway, she says.

She toils all day long, to keep the fires lit, and yet a chill persists. When they were setting up the paint factory the year before, Hector and Nico Bravin, the young foreman, tried camping out in the house, but it was too perishing so they moved into the office close to the boilers. Even there, they had to pile on all their clothes in layers to keep warm.

We were like *trogloditi*, Hector says. Grrr, grrr, he mimes, with his arms raised in fists.

Stop it, she says, trying not to laugh, but he likes to make fun of himself and then to laugh uproariously at his own joke.

Caveman, she guesses.

Which is what you looked like in the station in Trieste when I first see you, he says, all tender and reminiscing.

But she doesn't want to be reminded of that, no matter how tenderly. Although maybe the reason Hector stopped to help was that he knew what her trouble was from being a cold emigrant in Charlton.

She longs to throw the doors open to air the place, but you couldn't do that either. Winter or summer, the smut from the factories and the trains would land on the nets and drapes – not to talk of washing, there was no way you could put a line out so everything was done inside – and then there's the smog that'd choke you good and proper if you got it in your lungs. On winter evenings, Hector brings home the yellowish fog and it settles on the house like a gloom.

They begin to receive visitors. Nico is the most frequent of them. He's begun stepping out with Nell Francis next door. Nell is a beautiful russet-haired girl, a slip of a thing, and Norah's kitchen is a place the lovebirds can meet up. While they wait for Nell, Nico sits in the kitchen and tries out his English on Norah – he needs practice. He can talk about barrels and machines and the consistency of paint, but he needs help with the sweet *nientes*. He seems a boy to Norah, though she only has a few years on him. Great mop of curly dark hair, and cheerful as the day is long, as if he's never known bad luck.

Hector isn't pleased about the match. A spy in the house of love, he says. It gives Nell's mother licence to invite herself in. She's a thin, reedy woman, everything about her a bit faded. Peppery hair, pinched face.

Be careful, Hector warns her.

Reminds her of Juicy.

She's always on tenterhooks for fear Mrs Francis will sniff out something awry in their arrangement. But now that Nell is stepping out with Nico, Mrs Francis is more interested in pumping Norah for information about

Eyetalians in general, taking her to be an expert. Hadn't she lived out there? As soon as the pot is scalded and the tea drawn, she gets started and Norah lets her ramble for the less she says the better.

They're a rum lot, aren't they? Always coming and going. Not like us, Norah, and I mean it's not just they speak different. Not that I'm complaining, no, they're good payers, on the dot. You should have seen the state of this place before they took Meggie on. A right pigsty. She earned her thirty bob, I can tell you!

Is that all she got, Norah thinks. She's getting twice that, but then she's offering more …

You know what gentlemen on their own is like, oh I don't have to tell you, fag ends everywhere, newspapers piling up, and never heard of laundry. I swear in the beginning Mister Smith was bringing all his laundry home in his trunk for his poor wife to do!

His poor wife! Livia? Who'd never seen the business end of a mangle.

My own Stanley, he's the very same. We've lived in that house twenty year together – she wags her finger in the direction of next door – and he couldn't find the sugar bowl, if you paid him. They takes no notice of these things, now do they? Ooh, I don't know how he'll take it, our Nell fetching up with a dago.

Mister Francis is a barge master on the river, a grumpy specimen. Norah often passes him on the street but he doesn't salute her even when he sees her mounting the steps to number 67. Fly rink for a head, a pair of parboiled eyes. Sitting on a fortune, Hector tells her, owns properties up and down Church Lane, including ours. That was a surprise, for Norah thinks he looks like someone you'd give a penny to.

Haven't you told him about Nico? she asks Mrs Francis.

Why do you think they meet in your kitchen, dear? Nell Francis asks back. And what if she decides to take up with Nico permanent, then what? Oh perish the thought, for she's awful young, Norah, only sixteen, and he's turned her head, and if he takes her away, how would she manage over there without her mother? A girl needs her mother, Norah, and I have only the one girl. Is your mother still living?

Norah doesn't answer for she feels Mrs Francis is only fishing now.

Isn't it terrible that Mister Smith is all on his own, away from his poor wife, and the little girl, I was …

Norah rises at that stage. Must be getting along, Mrs Francis.

Oh call me Nell, everyone does.

Another caller is Miss Streeter, Hector's precious postmistress, though she never crosses the threshold. Thinks herself a step above. But what is Miss Streeter except a glugger, the wrong side of forty, selling stamps behind a counter? She hand-delivers notes for Hector with barely a word for Norah. Oh no, she's just there to pass the message along. Bring your Brahms sheet music next time and such like.

Another billy-do from Miss Streeter, she'd say.

Are you jealous? he would ask.

Don't cod yourself. Miss Streeter?

A spindly yoke with dark rings under her eyes and hands so thin they look like you could crush them in a firm handshake.

What do you want me to say? I forbid you to visit her, is that it?

But if she does that, she'll have to suffer the Charlton string quartet in Church Lane every Sunday afternoon.

God forbid! If they play anything like Hector, she'll have to make herself scarce.

Mister Richards, the smith, now he will come inside and wait for Hector if he isn't at home. He's a big man with huge, nicked hands but so nervous with a cup in his hand, you'd fear for the china. He is Hector's age, his fleshy face aflame as if the fire of the forge has printed itself on his features. He talks politics while Hector takes notes, because he wants to understand the English. What is there to understand, she wants to ask? They are people, like the Irish and the Eyetalians and she has known both and can't see a whit of difference.

Mister Richards talks weather with Norah. He points to the birds wheeling about in the evening sky and says – there, that's a bad sign, rain on the way – or he sniffs at the sky and predicts sleet. Or he reads the waves on the river, the chop and the change of it, the glinty grey of it, and knows a storm is on the way. And storms always bring her back to the Other Fella.

When the rapping of the knocker comes that night in October, her second year in, Norah sits bolt upright in bed and immediately clutches the sheets to her bosom as if for modesty although she is completely kitted out in a nightie and all. Sometimes, though, she falls asleep in Hector's room, and this is one of those nights. She sits stalled on her side of the bed, feeling about on the cold floor for a pair of slippers and finding instead the curlicued handle of the po. All is silent in the house. She must have imagined it. Hector claims to be a light sleeper. That's as may be but he's a noisy one, and he is making little blubbery sounds now and hasn't stirred.

She fishes Hector's yellow silk dressing gown from the knob of the bed-post. Superstitiously, she feels it best she go back to her own bed, even though it's a false alarm. Then the unknown hand raps again, this time accompanied by shouting – Mister Smith, Mister Smith! – and she knows, knows it in her waters, that this is the knock that she's been dreading.

She patters downstairs, shrugging on her street coat over Hector's dressing gown and gathering her hair up in a pair of combs on the back of her head, so that when she opens the door she looks respectable and composed. A man she's never met is hovering on the steps outside, cap crushed in his hand, coat collar up around his neck, a muffler too, and his breath sending smoke signals into the air.

What is it? she asks a mite impatiently. There's frost on the grass, she can see now. Early for that.

Mister Bravin sent me, the boss must come immediate, the place is in flames.

Will you wait, she asks.

Yes, he says, please hurry.

She rushes back upstairs to rouse Hector, shaking him awake.

Mister Smith, Mister Smith, she calls out loudly as much for the benefit of the man below in the hall. You've got to get up.

Che, che? He always wakes up in Italian.

It's a fire, she says and mimes an explosion, though the man below didn't say how it had started. But sure paint would go up in a flash, even she knows that.

Fuoco? Fuoco? Hector mumbles then he puts two and two together. *O Dio, O Dio.*

She throws open the wardrobe and fetches out a clean shirt. He piles it on over his pajamas, stiff collar over prison blues, as if he's keeping their love still close to his chest. What she wants to say is don't go for you'll come

214

back changed, but she can't say that. Instead, she bundles him into his jacket and then his overcoat and practically leads him downstairs to where the man is still waiting.

Mister Penrose, Hector says by way of greeting.

So that's Willie Penrose, she thinks, Hector was always giving out about him, one of the paint mixers. He has those quick eyes that dart about the place as if he's taking everything in.

Andiamo, Hector says, and it's all she can do to stop herself pecking him on the cheek as she does every morning. With a despairing glance backwards at her, he and Penrose hurry off into the fireglow dawn.

Four hours later when there's still no sign of him, she puts on her street clothes and goes to Anchor and Hope Lane. It's seven in the morning and she joins the normal throng of workmen off to Greenwich and the Woolwich Arsenal. All the talk among them is about the fire, the Moravia paint place, they say, up like a tinder box. Someone had laid the fire, another says, a disgruntled employee. How do such stories happen, Norah wonders, for most of these people must have been still in their beds when the fire began. There's a knot of people in front of the factory, at the very spot she often halted and mooned over Hector, but now there's a constable patrolling who won't let anyone get close.

Stand back, stand back, he keeps on hollering, nothing to see.

Did you ever hear such tripe! Women whose husbands will be out of a job, plenty for them to see, as the charred roof timbers fall ever so softly.

Everything wood in the building has gone up and the stone outside is black-faced. The smell is poisonous from the paint, it stings her eyes and makes them smart, but it isn't just the chemicals. It's tears for her whole life going up in smoke. She turns away and hurries back to Church Lane.

When Hector eventually returns he looks as if he's been dragged through a hedge backwards and left for dead.

We are destroyed, he says.

They're sitting in the little green scullery where she has set the kettle on the hob. Since she's come home, it must have boiled twenty times over.

But isn't it a mercy no one is dead, she says.

No, he says meaning yes, but the business ... she is finished.

He sits in his rag-bag collection of clothes, his hair askew and soot smudges on his cheeks and that charred smell coming off him, looking like a martyr who's been burned at the stake. In Trieste, she thought he had a gentleman's job, that he sat in an office and clerked. But here he's come home with cut hands and holes burned in his shoes from acid. Now there's oil on his shirt that'll never come out, and scorch marks on his waistcoat. She finds her heart bruised with a kind of pity for him.

How did it start?

No one know, it is one of the furnaces, *forse*. She is giving trouble last week, heating over ...

Does the Dragon know?

Normally, Hector gives out to her for calling his mother-in-law names – it isn't the worst of the names they called her, Norah would have liked to say, from her time below stairs. Battleaxe, bitch, *putana*. Olga is going to be on the warpath about this, Norah is sure. She will find a way to blame Hector for it because she doesn't trust him.

Not really. All the below stairs said so. Doesn't think he's good enough for her precious Livia, and too dreamy to run her business, that's what Juicy used to tell her.

We will send the cable, Hector is saying.

Is Olga going to come?

Hector shakes his head miserably and says, *non so*.

He's in one of his so-so moods. She knows better than to continue with the third degree. He'll only shut her out, clam up on her, as if he is the barnacle with the scissor-edged shell.

Come to bed, she says, sure you've hardly slept.

He seems touched by her nursey noises and allows her to lead him upstairs and into the big front bedroom, where she strips him as if he's a child.

What about a bath? she says. Wouldn't that make you feel better?

Usually he's so finicky, and insists on her lighting the geyser in the scullery and taking the cover off the bath before he goes down, for it's the coldest part of the house, that blessed scullery, and she should know, she's spent enough time there. But now he just shakes his head even though every stitch on him is destroyed and he smells of tar and cinders. She fetches a clean nightshirt.

You can wash later, she says, cooing at him like a nanny.

She climbs into the unmade bed after him and they cling to one another, with neither saying the words. It's a relief, to tell the truth, to lie there.

Let's fuck, she says to him. And let there be no words, she thinks to herself, to be misunderstood in.

At first, he's alarmed when she throws off her blouse and skirts and sits on him in her shift and rides him like he's a bareback pony. This is how it used to be with the Other Fella. Spitting and dirty words, that's how he wanted it. Whereas Hector is more gentlemanly, and she more ladylike with him. And that's not really her, now is it? She remembers the girl Hector told her about, the one he had stepped out with as a young man before he went respectable for Livia's sake.

I'm Josephina Seagull, she cries out, as she lassoes the air with one arm, and for the first time, she comes good and proper. *Take that, Jim Joyce!*

She doesn't care if Nell Francis next door can hear her. Let her, for she's tired of whispers, it's no way to live.

Che? Hector asks, breathless.

The girl who ran off to a circus after you dumped her, she says.

He lets it go till afterwards when they're splayed out on the sheets, spent.

Who did you mean? Guiseppina Zergol?

Always the corrector. No more than the Other Fella.

What are you driving at? he asks.

There's something I taught you, Mister, she thinks.

Because I'd like to do the same now, run off and join the blooming circus and take you with me.

For the first time in this whole bloody rigmarole, Hector laughs. That laugh, all loud and honky, she'll miss that. Then he reaches for a cigarette and lights up. She holds out her fingers, and he lodges the lit cigarette in the V, and starts again with his own. They puff away and it's contented, really, an odd feeling when your heart is about to be broken.

Remember that day in the station when I have found you?

Well, she's not likely to forget.

I think for a moment you are Giuseppina … but when I get close I know it is a mistake, he says.

Is that what I am, a mistake? she asks.

But he doesn't answer.

Some hours later when they've fallen into a drowse, the door knocker is rapped three times. It's Norah who rises, dresses hurriedly, dispensing with undergarments – who's going to look under her skirts? – and rakes her fingers through her hair in the absence of a comb, before answering. This time it's the telegram boy. She knows then that it's not the fire that's the clincher, but this message in the young fella's paw. She takes it from him, pays him, and brings it to Hector.

He reaches for a nightshirt as if he can't face the Dragon in his pelt. His tousled head appears through the shirt he puts on inside out. He tears the cable open. Something stricken crosses his face.

What, what is it? she asks, for Hector's life has been full of griefs. His brother, Elio – she thinks of a slippery fish – dead at twenty-three, and his two sisters with names she can't get her mouth around, also gone while only young. Funny how she feels less for them because she cannot fix their names in her head. But Elio, whose grave she's seen, she feels for him like she does for Sonny Bodkin, both of them young men who don't belong in the cemetery. The Other Fella never understood that. You're a bit of a man-killer, he would jeer.

Is bad news, Hector says.

What, what? she repeats. What's happening now?

It is not Olga who comes, it is Livia.

The jig is up.

They lie back to back on the unmade bed, he in his nightshirt, and she with her housekeeper's garb and no knickers.

She won't play the slavey for Livia and that's final.

I'll look after you, he says finally, after an age steeped in silence, just at the moment she has chosen to say: I'll have to go, so.

A penny for them? he asks. Another one she's taught him.

They are half sitting with the pillows and the bolster banked up behind them, all decorum lost now, sure what's the point, who is there to put on a show for? She is staring out the window on to the roof slates of Church Lane, the chimneys beginning to cough up their plumes, and the noise of the shopkeepers opening up below, whining doors on unoiled hinges, the clunk of Mister Cavendish's sandwich board being set out on the pavement, the squeal of the chalk as his apprentice scribes the day's deal on it, *Lamb chops 1/6 a* ... the wheeling out of the awnings over Orr's, the fishmongers, Miss Peggy in her rubber gauntlets cranking on the lever for all she's worth.

Where will you go?

There, it is said, but it's taken a night of abandon, the sort that goes with endings. The sort she never had with the Other Fella for she never knew it was the end.

She wants Hector now to reach for her hand so the gap between them won't be so wide, but he doesn't. He's already on the retreat, she can see the mark of Livia's outstretched fingers already on him, leaving a dent in the cloth of his arm.

Dublin, she says, without realizing she has an answer.

Home, he says, and she can sense his smile though she isn't looking at him.

Not home, she contradicts.

Home is Mamo's house on Augustine Street now in the hands of Uncle Tommy and Bedelia. Or Bowling Green

Street with her mother and whoever of the crew is left there. No, not there, either. And then she thinks of Finn's, Finn's of all places! Isn't that the giddy limit? Finn's.

Home.

Even with the factory gone, Hector rises every morning, dresses and walks to Anchor and Hope Lane. Within days he has arranged for workmen to come in to start the rebuilding, though he has nowhere to shelter himself since the office was the first place to go. Nico is operating out of the back of Mister Richards' smithy, sitting among the barrels the draymen managed to salvage. In the far north end of the factory some of the mixing vats remain intact and with a skeleton staff, Nico is supervising the outstanding orders. Hector spends his days writing to reassure the Navies of the world that their orders will be honoured. It's hard to imagine that the power of the Admiralty depends on this fire-blackened factory in Charlton, that all the great ships would rust and fall apart without Hector's paint. That the barnacles would run rampant.

What was the cause of the conflagration, she wonders. She thinks of Hector and his fags, he was forever leaving one lit behind him and going into the next room and starting another. Or could it have been Nico, who had a brazier in the office along with his little camp bed. Who knows but he might have had young Nell in there? But no, no use setting the cat among the pigeons asking about that. What good would it do to know what caused the fire? Would she feel better if she knew why the Other Fella took it into his head to desert her in Trieste? Would the knowing be better than the not-knowing?

Then as if to support her niggling doubts, a constable comes to interview Hector. Norah shows him into the front parlour and stays to help with the questions. The when-did-yous, the how-longs, the whys and wherefores of the factory. When the constable takes his helmet off in the house, Norah sees that he's still wet behind the ears. He's a strapper, six foot at least, but he's barely able to sprout a growth.

No, Constable, nothing untoward.

Yes, Constable, in all night.

They suspect Hector set the fire himself, Norah thinks, for the insurance.

The young man scribbles in his notebook and refuses to sit down, so she and Hector sit gazing up at him. But the way he asks the questions makes her feel that she and Hector are telling fibs.

Are you accusing Mister Smith of something, she asks the constable, the first time she's spoken. The copper notices her accent.

You from Ireland, then, Miss? and when she nods, he says with a foolish grin: My mum's Irish.

After that, she fields his answers easily. Once you have a blessed Irish mother in common it's plain sailing.

Will I ask him about the cat? Hector mutters to her as they show the young policeman out.

There had been a fat tabby that he and Nico befriended last year when the two of them were camping out in the office. The creature moved in when it saw the rich pickings from the scraps of two homesick foreigners. He'd have got a toe up the you-know-where from an English fella, but Hector and Nico had practically invited the creature in to dine and put a napkin around its neck.

Will you hush? she hisses, or he'll think all you're worried about is a blessed cat.

Hector looks wounded.

Goodbye so, Constable, she says and shuts the door on him.

If the cat's dead, it's dead, and if it's not, it'll come back, simple as that, she says.

He's a he, Hector says, all upset with her. The cat is a boy.

They refuse to talk about the future during this limbo. It is only when Livia cables her intention to leave Trieste that they have to face the music.

You can stay here, Hector says. You don't have to go.

And play the skivvy for Livia?

No, I mean … not here.

What do you mean, stay?

I mean, wait, wait for me, in London.

Wait? Has he understood nothing about her? Wait, my foot.

And what would I be doing with myself? Skulking around waiting for Livia to leave?

He looks a bit glum.

I can set you up, he says.

Isn't he well up now on all those terms, the keeping of the fancy woman words?

Set me up?

He's desperate now, like throwing a last hand at cards. He used to be a betting man, he's told her, but a bad betting man, a poor gambler, and it shows.

She shakes her head.

Norah Barnacle knows when she's bet. She'd be a mistress then, isn't that what the continentals call it? A mistress. And he'd drop by when he had the time.

No, Hector, she says. It's not defiant, it's resigned.

No.

*

The week after the fire is condemned time. They count the days, and then the hours, punctuated by the arrival of Livia's cables – depart Trieste this a.m., arrive Milano, overnight Paris – like the funeral bell tolling. Norah fetches down her battered valeeze from the attic.

No, Hector says, you can't go home with that and he crushes a note into her hand.

What's this? she asks, though she knows full well.

For you, *Knospe*, he says. Blossom, he means. She can't stand it.

Why don't you just call me by my name?

She's cross with him now. Stop it, stop it, she tells herself, don't let the past curdle the present when there's so little of it.

Get a proper trunk and a lady's valeeze, not this, he says tipping the cardboard yoke with the toe of his boot. Buy yourself clothes for the journey.

She wishes he wouldn't mention the journey for she has deliberately put it out of her mind as each day ticks away. She has stopped playing housekeeper and has given up on cooking. They eat meat-paste sandwiches for every meal washed down by pots of tea in the back scullery. As for cleaning house, let Livia take care of that when she comes.

Despite her misgivings about the money she goes to London on the train and she has a field day. First to Drews in Piccadilly where she orders a brown canvas trunk with brass corners, bentwood bands and twin locks, and a leather vanity case with patterned green silk lining, the stitching so tiny it must have been done by a small child. Not to mention the rig-outs, three new ones, off the peg in Bon Marché. An elephant-grey pinstripe dress with kimono sleeves and a lacey chemisette, a travelling suit in red twill with gimp trim and matching deep black cuffs and a full pleated peplum, a skirt in tan pique and white linen blouse with sleeve puffs, a black velour hat with spider veil, a pair of lace-up boots with a two-inch heel ... She has never felt richer and more bereft.

You're leaving? Mrs Francis demands, her eyes narrowed. In Mister Smith's hour of need? What will he do without you?

His wife is on her way, she can look after him, Norah says, and it comes out more surly than she intended. Anyway, I have troubles of my own.

Is that so? Mrs Francis is still thin-lipped. Always a whiff of distrust from her.

Norah invents a mother with a weak heart, and before she can stop herself she kills her off, there on Mrs Francis's doorstep.

Oh, says Mrs Francis, her mouth drawn up in a little pucker. I'm very sorry to hear that. Was it sudden?

Very, Norah says, but doesn't give any more details in case she'll be struck down or that somewhere her mother might feel a dart of something in her heart, the sharp point of her fibs.

We'll be sad to see you go, Mrs Francis says. Oh the liar, the hypocrite! But uttered sweet as pie.

I was wondering if you could find someone local to do for Mister Smith? *I wonder*, she thinks, *does Mrs Francis have any notion of all I do?* She rushes on. I mean someone who could rustle up a breakfast and a simple supper and clean and change the beds.

Well, I suppose we could get Meggie back, though she was in a right temper being let go on your account and will demand 35 bob even when Mister Smith isn't here, Mrs Francis says warningly.

Let Hector decide on the rate, she thinks.

Will you ask her? Norah asks through gritted teeth, not wanting to be beholden to this woman.

It is like arranging her own wake.

She relents on the cleaning when Meggie agrees to come back. Can't be letting the side down, she tells herself. She's doing this for Hector, not for Livia. She sets to, hosing, scrubbing and polishing, removing all trace of herself. And then she has to think about her own departure. Makes her feel like a stage magician, one minute here, the next gone. There will be the boat train to Holyhead, the mail boat to the North Wall, how flat the names seem now. After Trieste, Servola, Paris.

One good thing, she won't be the ragamuffin she was when she left. And that's important if she's to hold her head high in Dublin for Jim's pals will all still be there, still holding court. And maybe he'll be there too.

Do we all come back in the end?

She has no plan except for one. To stay in Finn's. She promised herself that if she ever returned she'd march right into that place as a guest and have Mister Finn and Miss Fitzgerald kowtow to her. That's for her own satisfaction, no one else's.

The parting is terrible.

I want you to have this, Hector says thrusting an envelope into her gloved hand for she's been sitting in the hallway since dawn, trunk at her feet, ready to go but not able. Oncoming Livia will plough directly into the hall if she waits much longer. Hector is going to London to meet her train. A cab is waiting outside.

Is this for my services? she snaps.

Three years ago she followed the Other Fella halfway across the world without a second thought on the promise of nothing. Now she's being paid to shut up and go away.

Hector's face has that pained look as if he feels her words in his teeth. Has she spent her time wounding him because she can't get at the Other Fella?

This will make a new life, he says patiently.

No, she said, I don't want your money.

Please, Norah, please …

Anyways, how can you afford it with the state things are in? The fire and all?

This, he says slowly, is money lost in the fire.

What? She feels slow as if she's back at the beginning, two different lingos, everything muddled and strange.

This is money lost in the fire, he repeats. Signora Veneziana, she believes it all went up … He mimes the explosion.

No, she says again, feeling chastened.

He says nothing but puts the envelope on the hall table, puts his hat on.

You must know how I feel, he says.

But does she, really, since he would never say it, not in so many words? Just like the Other Fella who could bleed onto the page but couldn't stand directly in front of you and declare himself.

Norah, Hector pleads.

He goes to kiss her on the lips but she turns her head and he gets her cheek instead. She cannot look at him. He puts his hat on, firms it in place and still she will not look, then he opens the door and leaves, shutting it behind him as if it was an ordinary day. She could run after him and slather him with kisses, even if it is out on the street. Who cares, all is lost now. But she doesn't. Maybe he'll come back, try one more time to reach her? But he doesn't. She could go out onto the top step and wave him off, that wouldn't hurt anyone, now would it? But she does nothing. She hears the wheels of the cab rumbling, bearing him away, its sound melding with the traffic of the street while she stands, stubborn.

She eyes the package still sitting untouched on the shelf of the hall stand as if it's alive and watching her. Still she does nothing but stand and wait.

Finally, having stood numb for an age, she reaches for it, tears it open and begins to count. It is a bunch of treasury notes, more than she has ever seen in her life before. She counts again, sure she's made a mistake. She's never seen notes this colour, never knew they even existed. Oh Hector, Hector, she feels a rush of gratitude. But that's not love, she chastises herself. But he has given all he can, and she thinks of how they parted with all her quibbling and her foolish pride, spoiling their last precious moments together, squandering them on vehemence and protest.

She sees her own face speckled like a quail's egg in the glass, all dressed up and nowhere to go, with her wide-brimmed hat with the bunch of grapes, the tawny coat with the mink collar, a brooch on her breast showing a galleon in full sail, a gift Hector brought from one of his trips.

Is this you, Norah Barnacle, is it really you?

Mrs Joyce

June 15, 1915

'*Aspetta, Signor, aspetta!*'

Amalia tumbles out of the Gresham Hotel and rushes across the wide pavement towards the cab, which sits at the kerb, a brooding black egg on polished wheels. The horse is jostling, looking ready to bolt at any moment. The cab driver, back turned, hands in pockets, ears sticking out under his bowler, ignores her. Then she remembers, English, English! *You're in Dublino, Mali.*

Come se dice aspetta?

She knows this, she *knows* it, but the word won't come. All those years poring over her English primers and she's stuck for something as simple as …

'WAIT!'

It works. The cabman turns. His face is a whiskery walnut, teeth a mahogany brown. He shoves his bowler off his forehead in a gesture of impatience. He's wearing a heavy overcoat buttoned almost to the neck, as if he's ready for a polar expedition, but she tells herself he must spend a lot of his time standing on the street just waiting, or in her case almost giving up waiting, and perhaps his circulation is poor. And there is the matter of the doubtful summer. She eyes the watery sky. That was what had delayed her. Trying to decide what to wear in this moody weather. The *portiere* in a high hat, scarlet silks and a caped greatcoat, who guards the door of the Gresham, stalks up behind her and reaching for the silvery door handle, opens the door of the hansom and says something that ends with Missus Joyce.

Is that her? She can scarcely believe it. Eight weeks ago, she was Amalia Popper, university scholar, laurel wreath in her hair. Now she's Signora Joyce, a war wife married to her English *professore* and about to start a new life in Zurigo. She climbs aboard. The *portiere* retreats.

'Where to?' roars the cab driver.

In answer she proffers her list, glad of her gloved hand. He nabs it and frowns as he peruses it. Perhaps he can't make out her writing, even though she has carefully inscribed each destination in capitals, rather than relying on her own cobwebby script. The names are still strange to her and she doesn't trust herself to pronounce them.

The list trembles in his warty hands, more ruined than his face. Perhaps he can't read at all.

'North Richmond Street?' he says, loud as a *direttore di circo*. 'What brings you there?'

What strange locutions they have, not like anything she has seen written down. Meaning *perché*?

Why? The eternal cry. She wailed it often at G when he was still Professor Zois to her and coming to the house twice a week to give her lessons. The difficulty of English, the perfect tense, the paradoxical pronunciations. Why? Why is it alldough but I thawt? Because, G would sigh, because it just is. And now that she's here, where the language is spoken, it doesn't even sound like English to her. It's as if the cabbie is speaking in riddles.

'Is it the Brothers?'

Fratelli?

She thought this was going to be straightforward. Order a carriage. Hand the driver the list. Follow the instructions.

The *portiere* has retreated. A couple of passing clerks in crumpled suits slow down, sensing a scene in the making. There's nothing we like better than a good show, G is always saying, but she doesn't want to be part of a spectacle, not out on the street in full view, playing the stupid *straniera*.

'No,' she says, 'not the brothers, the street.'

'And what's this?' The cabbie's voice rises querulously.

Drive on, she wants to say, drive on. She is the paying customer and the customer is always right no matter that she's an Eyetie (that's what they'll call you, G has warned, no harm meant). G is her name for him, makes him sound like an Everyman, Citizen of the World. Only in company does she call him Giacomo. Never James, or Jim – these are the names he left behind.

The cabman moves on down the list.

'Henrietta Street? Ah now this won't do at all. What business would you have there, full of rough types, crawling with street Arabs ...'

Arabs?

'The ceremonial arch,' she says from memory. 'King's Inns.'

'Ah,' he replies, more concessionary. 'Legal business is it?' He taps his nose with his finger. 'Say no more.'

'No,' she begins and then stops. Why is she explaining herself to a mere cabman, whose business it is not? The nag hoofs the ground and whinnies. She's with the beast, *let me start my journey*. She climbs aboard, unaided, since the cabman clearly isn't going to help her. She hopes this will signal an end to the interrogation.

But he leans in conspiratorially. A buckled tooth protrudes, digging into his fat lip.

'You're not from these parts, are you Miss?'

These parts?

'You're a stranger, I'm thinking,' he persists, 'by your accent?'

What is he asking, is he a *sempliciotto*?

'You'll be wanting to see the sights. The Pillar, now, the Castle, the Fifteen Acres, that sort of thing ...'

'No,' she interrupts, not wanting to sound rude but she might drown in his gabble if she doesn't get him to stop. 'No,' she repeats and points to the list, now trembling in his gnarled paw. 'These places, I wish to go to these places.'

Teddy Coombs sighs deeply. God above. A high-class lady, clearly. Hat shaped like a Chinaman's but with a yard of material wrapped around it, umbrella with a frill for the changeable weather, well that's sensible now. All kitted out for this? A tour of the tenements of Dublin, if the list is to be believed.

'And Usher's Island?'

The last destination on her billy-do. What's her business at all, at all, a cruelty woman, a lady magistrate? He tries one last time.

'Are you sure now, I can do a nice loop now, round by Trinity College and ...'

'No thank you,' she says levelly.

The nag softly defecates.

Knows her own mind. Ah well, it's her own look-out so.

'Please to drive on,' she says sharpish this time and she looks away. A bit of a hump on now and sure he's only trying to help. Very well so.

'Where to first?' he asks.

'As on the list,' she says.

He reads down. Not an eye nor an ear to it. Still, if that's what the lady wants. He heaves himself up and turns to Flora, clicks his tongue.

'Gee-up there,' he hollers.

Horse language, she thinks, the same the world over.

Disgruntled, he wheels the carriage around, glass rattling in the windows. They travel north. She settles herself on the mildewed leather. Her mission is illicit; perhaps it's her deception the cabman has detected. G cannot know what she is doing, and she mustn't tell anyone else either. She believes that somehow it would get back to him. Everyone knows everyone else's business, he has warned her. This city, too damned small. Eyes everywhere. Already she feels spied upon, by the *portiere*, the passing clerks, even the maid who kept on scuttling into the room loading coal onto the already high-built blazing fire, even when Amalia announced in her best English – 'I am going out presently.' The girl halted and Amalia asked her name, and she said something that sounded like jasmine then carried on with her task as if she had never spoken. Amalia inhales the memory of jasmine on Via Alice and feels a crack of grief in her breastbone. Trieste. Home.

A trolley careening past, gonging urgently, startles her. Trams she is used to but at a stately uphill pace; here, they seem to be driven by *i banditi*. She has only two hours to complete her trip while G has stepped out to pay a visit to his old friend, Dottor St John Gogarty. All those Gs! She told him she was tired and would stay in the hotel to rest. Her second lie. The first she's already incubating.

She had planned her secret itinerary from the moment it was decided they would travel to Dublino. But the seeds of it were sown on that awful day three years ago when she scorched the palps of her fingers trying to rescue G's precious manuscript from the fire in the drawing room on Via Alice. Roberts, the publisher, had returned the proofs of the stories G called *Dubliners*. They'd come in the afternoon mail with a note saying the firm had changed its mind about publication. She'd been out with Mother, being fitted for a coat for the winter in Firenze. She was about to start her first year at university and she and G were going to be apart for several months, so her mind was not on the relative qualities of mulberry wool serge versus the grey worsted. With the fitting done, she left Mother in town and hurried back to the house where she knew G would be waiting impatiently. After years of unrequited love, it was his impatience she most treasured now, his hunger for her; she even secretly thrilled to his jealousy. She rushed down the chequered hallway and into the drawing room and came upon him bent before the hearth, the unbound manuscript in his hands. He was in the process of ripping each page in two and feeding the sheets one by one into the roaring grate. She ran at him from behind and tried to wrestle the pages from him. Between them they dropped the manuscript, and the pages fanned out and scattered. He fell to his knees scrabbling for the fallen leaves and balling them up to make firebombs of them.

She was on all fours trying to snatch the burning ones from the grate. The tips of her fingers felt as if they were on fire. Behind her, he was crying as he attacked the manuscript. She had never seen him cry. She had never seen any man cry and it was a shock.

'This book is like a child to me. I've carried it for years and years in the womb of my imagination ...'

She turned and grabbed his wrist. 'And this is what you would do with a treasured child?'

Such was the scene of primitive disorder that when Papa burst into the room and saw the pair of them, he thought something else entirely was going on. No wonder! G with hair and spectacles askew and her all hot-faced and awry paddling on the Persian rug, the fireplace aflame with paper, the carpet covered with singed pages and the smell of burning in the room as though a portal to Hades had been opened up. G stood up, pushed past Papa and stormed out.

'What on earth …?' Papa began. 'My darling, are you all right?'

She could see the terrible doubt in his eye – how could he have agreed to let this madman court his daughter? Just when she'd won him around.

'Yes, Papa, I'm fine,' she said, settling her hair as she bent to gather up the tussled-over pages on the floor.

'Has he hurt you?'

Yes, she wanted to answer, but Papa would not understand.

'No, no, nothing like that. I haven't excited this passion,' she began. A dry sob escaped. What was she doing with this man who was so volatile, so strangely absolute in his emotions? 'It's his work.'

Papa held out his hands and raised her up, folding her in an embrace. He tried to comfort her.

'There now.'

'I'm not weeping for me,' she murmured into his shoulder, 'but for the lost masterpiece the world will never know.'

Papa eyed her ruefully.

'Amalia,' was all he said.

It was both lament and rebuke.

*

She managed to save five complete stories – 'Araby', 'Counterparts', 'A Little Cloud', 'Eveline' and 'The Dead' from the flames. There were a few odd pages from the others, but being incomplete, they were useless. After the maid had swept up the remains from the grate – imagine this is all that's left of great art, soot and ashes – Amalia uncrumpled the pages and had the maid iron them. When she got them back, their blackened corners crackled at her touch. Her fingertips were still smarting as if in sympathy. She pressed the sheets between the pages of her Liceo atlas as if they were flowers, closing the world on them. G would never find them here. And she made a vow. She would take care of them, even if he wouldn't. She would translate these unloved stories in secret, arrange for their publication and then … and then she would present them to him. His work in her language. It would give her three years of study at the University of Firenze a purpose. When she was done, she was certain the world would recognize him as the great writer she knew him to be.

But her certainty had been misplaced.

I have a surprise for you, he'd written during Epiphany term, *you'll see when you return*.

A new work, she thought. A novel, she was sure.

Frankly, she hadn't believed him when he'd insisted he was abandoning his writing.

'I'm finished with all that,' he told her after he'd calmed down. 'It's a nightmare I've woken up from. Forging the uncreated conscience of my race in the smithy of my soul? Who was I codding? My race, or its publishers, couldn't give a tuppenny damn.'

Making a bonfire of his stories was a gesture, a passionate gesture, that was all, she'd told herself. He'd done so much work on those stories, pored over them for years, straining his eyesight in the process. He'd made changes he didn't want to, and then just when it should have been his moment of glory, Roberts, that *spreguidicato*, had crushed him underfoot. No wonder he was bitter, but it was a passing despair, Amalia was sure.

The surprise he promised was not a new novel, nothing of the sort.

'I'm training to become an opera singer,' he announced at the station. He had come hot-foot from rehearsals at the Teatro Verdi. He was playing one of Wagner's *Meistersingers*. 'The grocer!' he added.

She had never seen him so animated as he described his secret apprenticeship. For months he'd been taking lessons at the Conservatorio with the great Professore Bartoli, no less! (How had he afforded it, she wondered; not from what he earned teaching English, certainly. Had Papa helped him out? *Would* he?) G had always tinkered with music, but that was all it was, tinkering. He pounded the piano, fancied himself as a drawing room *divo* and he loved the opera, particularly the expensive view from the Popper box after years of craning his neck in the cheap seats. And he didn't half mind the showy services of the bewigged Master Beadle who summoned the carriages by name after the performance.

'Not something the patrons of the gods enjoy,' he said wryly, the first time he and Amalia had gone to the opera together. His total immersion in the music had fascinated her; sometimes she would spend more time casting sidelong glances at him watching the opera than watching it herself.

Opera has always left her cold. All those antics, those overblown emotions attached to puny stories.

'A singer?' She felt sick, as if he'd been unfaithful to her. She had left a great writer and returned to a light tenor, her prince turned into a performing frog. But what could she say? She didn't want to puncture his triumph, but it was as if, behind her back, her beloved G had been spirited away and replaced by a stranger whose main boast was he could reach B natural with ease. What had happened to the man she'd fallen in love with? Or was it the writer she had loved, and not the man?

The question made her queasy, so she said nothing. Instead, she quietly determined that once they were properly together again, she would make him drop all this budding *tenorino* nonsense and return to his true vocation.

From the cab, she stares up at the dove-grey sky. So much for their honeymoon trip! That's what she's been calling this detour, though G sees it as a kind of vengeful homecoming. Payback for all the mortifications his native city has imposed on him. An hour or two upon the stage, will that reverse the humiliations of years? But she holds her counsel. Dublino has provided respite, disguised the fact that she and her new husband are going into exile.

Little did she think when the caskets of the Archduke Ferdinand and the Duchess Sophie were borne on gun carriages through the black-shrouded streets of Trieste last summer, that it would have any bearing on her life, beyond an extravaganza of mourning. A terrible act by a political hothead, she'd thought. Her head was full of love then, not war. Now this wretched war has driven her from her home. She cannot bear to think of it, her beloved Trieste. Will she ever see Via Alice again, or walk in the Piazza

Grande, or take a picnic basket to the Revoltella Gardens? Although even before she and G had left, most of these simple pleasures had already been denied to them. Once the war came, lawlessness had ruled. Gangs of looters on the streets, the *Piccolo* offices set alight, Verdi's statue on the Piazza San Giovanni defaced. Anything Italian was set upon. Suddenly home seemed the most dangerous place to be.

She had only been back in Trieste for a couple of weeks – after three long years away at university – when Papa decreed she must leave. It isn't safe for Giacomo here, Papa said, and therefore not safe for you, my darling. As a foreign alien, G had already lost his teaching job and was regarded as an enemy subject. Hence their unseemly parade down the aisle two calendar months ago.

'Anyone would think I'd got you in the family way,' G said, but he'd agreed to marry her nonetheless.

But being wed to a citizen wouldn't spare him from a call-up, or worse. Look at his brother, Stanislaus, locked up since January in the Schloss Kirchberg! Sweet and sober Stanino (at one time Amalia suspected he might be – *come si dice* – sweet on her). But the Trieste authorities cast him as an irredentist, a radical. Preposterous! Stanino hasn't a violent bone in his body. But that's what this war has done, turning friends into enemies overnight. Which is why she and G must build a new life in Zurigo. Or bide their time until they can go back. Exiles, together.

The cab careens through a square of gaunt grey houses baring their toothed windows at her. She could never live here. The truth is she doesn't know how to *be* here, and it's not just the language. There's the problem of G's family. What a strange assortment they are. And their circumstances, so diminished. G hadn't prepared her for that.

It wasn't evident from the welcoming party at the station. She was still mildly nauseous from the sea journey. The First Class lounge had been stuffy and noisy – was it that the Irish talked more or was it that she couldn't understand a word, despite her studies? Whether it was the noise or the heat, she couldn't bear it. It was better up on deck, though the temperature was the other extreme. Her hands were blue by journey's end despite the muff – yes, *that* muff! – which she had rescued from her luggage. G had snickered when he saw it going into their trunk. For the Swiss winter, she'd said, though it was for sentimental reasons, but she kept those to herself. She didn't care how ridiculous the muff looked on a boat in high summer on the Irish Sea – she needed it.

She was determined to be above board with G, is that how they say it? On the open deck. The last time he had made this journey was outbound with *her* – Signorina Barnacle – and Amalia wasn't going to allow him to wallow in any kind of nostalgia. She was going to be beside him all the way even if she died of frostbite in the process. She had grown up with the bora, she could withstand a choppy wind on the Irish Sea, couldn't she? But by the time they berthed, she was chilled to the marrow.

'It's a different kind of cold here,' G said to her. 'A damp cold.'

She felt her spirits plummet.

As they made their way through the covered arcade to the waiting train, she wondered was this where Eveline had broken away from Frank in the *Dubliners* story, but she didn't ask. He'd wonder why and it might alert him to her secret translation work.

'My first steps on Irish soil,' she said.

What he was feeling she couldn't guess. They settled into the train and sat in silence for the short journey to the city. That was where they were met by the greeting party. She didn't know whether G had been warned and had said nothing or whether it was a surprise to him too, but as the train came to a screeching halt, he had rolled down the window in their compartment in expectation of something. And there they were, the family, ranged in a group as if posing for a photograph. All in their Sunday best. Pappie, wine-faced and beady-eyed, stood magisterial with an arm apiece around G's sisters, Eileen and Eva. Eva with G's weak eyes, dark circles of worry underneath, Eileen, tilting a frail neck curiously. His brother Charles, bare-headed, sandy-haired, stood tall and to attention while his little wife, Mary, a thin creature without her hat, bent over trying to hold on to three small children with two hands. Another sister, Florrie, stood to one side, resplendent in white, holding an extra hat – Mary's? – crushed in her hands.

So many of them!

Amalia almost expected the dead ones, Georgie and little Mabel, to appear.

The money, such as there was, must have gone on the millinery – a harlequin for Eva, a cloche for Florrie, a toque for Eileen. She would probably have found signs of wear on their Sunday best – at cuffs and collars – if she'd examined them closely. G stepped out first, gingerly, and handed her down onto the platform. The father rushed forward to embrace his son robustly, knocking G's spectacles askew. There was some kerfuffle after that, a bending over, a shuffling, then Pappie turned his operatic attention on her.

'Welcome, welcome,' he purred and grabbed her by both arms heartily. 'And what do you make of us here, Miss Popper?'

'It's Signora Joyce,' she said, eyeing G who was brushing down his jacket. He has told them, hasn't he? That we are married.

'Of course, of course,' he boomed. 'Keep forgetting. Hurried nuptials soon forgotten. Aha!'

He followed many of his declarations with this declarative bark. *Aha.*

'Come, come, my girl, you must meet the family,' he said, shunting her towards the tableau as if she was a visiting dignitary. The sisters had small, cool hands. Even after the introductions, they eyed her, taking in her cream linen travelling suit – an unfortunate choice, her lap was scored with creases, the sleeves looked grubby already – her taupe hat with chiffon veil, and the silly muff. She was a mix of all seasons.

'Our family is your family,' Pappie announced, slowing up his speech for her benefit and beaming, as he led the procession out of the station and onto the street. Overhead, the rounded arch of a railway bridge shook with the bellowing of a train lumbering over it. There were so many Joyces crowded in a knot that she nearly lost sight of G.

'I thought Finn's for a bite to eat,' Pappie said loudly. 'You must be famished.'

Finn's? No, not there. Why would he suggest that? She sought out G's face in the family crowd, hoping he'd heard. He wouldn't want that either, another place tied up with the memory of Nora.

'Ah now, Pappie, we can do better than that. What about the Shelbourne?' G said.

242

'Used to know a fella did the billiard markings there,' Charlie offered but no one paid much notice.

Because she couldn't always understand, Amalia had time to see the little patterns among them, the voices who were heard, the voices who weren't.

'Let's push the boat out,' G said.

He was heard.

They all laughed but she didn't see the joke.

'After all, *we'll* be paying for it,' he muttered to her sotto voce.

They moved in a phalanx. She saw something of G in all of them, the same lean face in Eileen, the haunting eyes in Eva, the nerviness of Charlie. Thankfully, G took her arm, and with Pappie, led the procession and the chat. 'You're looking well, son, and a great tan, you must be out in all weathers, sharp suit, and a homecoming concert, isn't that the way to do it, first time home ...'

She thought of her own father, careful, refined, and compared him to this ... *buffone*. How on earth did G come from this?

'Miss Popper, I can't tell you how proud we are of this fella – why, when in good form, his voice is second only to McCormack, rich and pure, goes through your bosom like a strong wine ...'

Eileen sidled up to her as Pappie rattled on.

'Is that chiffon in your hat,' she asked and touched the brim.

They settled at the table almost like a wedding party. Starched linen, cut glassware, sisters on her side, father of the bride between her and G and his brother.

'Giacomo tells me ...' she began. She'd rehearsed a few entreés.

'Who's this Jackamo when he's at home, girl? Jim, is it?'
Jovial Pappie was keen to set her right. 'Sure that's just a
name for the concert posters, isn't it, Jim, aha!'

Jim sounded all wrong to her, too clipped, too ordinary.
Her G has never been ordinary.

'Makes you sound like a half-caste, but good for business, I'd say, what Jim?'

'Well, isn't it half true?' G said, 'now that I have an
Italian wife.' He peered at her from his father's side and
she felt, for one single moment, he only had eyes for
her.

Pappie looked from one to the other, mystified. Then
he moved swiftly on. 'So tell us, Jim, what is it you'll be
singing at this concert of yours?'

'Well, the programme is not quite decided yet,' G said.
'"Where e'er you Walk", for openers.'

'Aha! A belt of old Handel, nothing like it to open up
the voice.'

'"Una Furtiva Lagrima", certainly.'

'Ah lovely, what!'

'And "Tombe Degli Avi Miei" ...'

'Remind me again,' Pappie said.

'Lucia,' G said, like the name of a beloved. 'Tombs of
my fathers, last son of an unhappy race.' He hummed a
few notes.

'Now you're talking!'

'"Let Me Like a Soldier Fall"?'

Pappie beamed. 'I have to tell you Miss –'

'Amalia,' she prompted, 'you must call me Amalia.'

Pappie struggled with it.

'Ama-leeeee-a.'

Wrong emphasis.

'Am-aah-lee-ah,' she repeated.

244

'Do you know what I'm going to tell you now, Amelia, we used to have Eyetalian companies coming here, two a penny, in the old days. I remember one tenor, saw it myself with my own two eyes, who did five encores of "Let Me Like a" at the Royal. Would you credit that?'

'What about "When Other Lips"?' Eileen piped up.

An awkward silence fell on the company. No one would say it, but they were all thinking the same thing. The other lips of Nora Barnacle.

For an instant, Amalia felt part of the family.

The one name that won't come up is *hers*, G had insisted. But she was a ghost at this feast.

He'd never introduced Nora to his sisters although of course, they knew her by reputation, as the deserter of their darling 'Jim'. Amalia had always wondered about this secrecy. Could it be G was ashamed of Nora? Then again, when they left Dublino, they were eloping. Although as G kept on insisting to her, he and Nora had never married.

'And never would.' Said with some pride.

And he has married *her*, after all.

She comforts herself with this thought: Nora would never have been a fit companion for a man of letters.

As G was then.

But still she gets pangs of envy. Nora knew him only as a wholehearted writer. Will I ever know him as a writer again, she wondered, instead of the song and dance man he has decided to become?

'"It's a Long Way to Tipperary",' G said and she quailed. 'For the encore.'

She'd been trying to dissuade him from this. It's a marching song, no more, a rabble-rousing anthem for the troops.

'And what of it?' he'd said, sounding wounded. 'Hasn't McCormack recorded it, and what's good enough for him is good enough for me. I know my crowd.'

His crowd will be his downfall. If he'd stay with the opera, at least, but this concert is the next best thing to the circus. She noticed he didn't mention the Smareglia to the family, Lorenzo's 'Sebbene Io Passi' from *Nozze Istriane* – oh no, he'll trade marches and parlour songs with them but not the work of note. They would know nothing of Smareglia, anyway, not in this backward place ... no, she must stop this.

'Our Jim didn't lick it up off the stones,' Pappie was saying.

What on earth was he talking about?

'Did he tell you, Amelia, I sang in the Concert Rooms myself with the famous Bartle McCarthy. Ah yes, in the eighties. He went off to London after that, did *The Castle of Como*.'

Como?

'... and then with the D'Oyly Carte in New York.'

She was lost.

'Or "The Lass of Aughrim"?' Eileen persisted. 'I do love that one. I remember you singing that when Mam was alive.'

A little cloud hovered over the company. But it passed.

Soon they were all chiming in, trading titles like it was a game. 'I Dreamt I Dwelt', 'The Bohemian Girl', 'I'll Sing Thee Songs of Araby' ...

'North Richmond Street,' the cabman hollers.

Teddy hushes Flora down to a walk. Poor nag, she's glad of the break, getting old now and where would he get another? Half the horses in this town have been snaffled by the army. He waits for instructions but none come so he keeps going. Past the Christian Brothers where the windows are open and some chanting can be heard – times table, is it, or a poem? Don't know what they'd be learning poems for when there's a war going on, not to speak of the other thing. Two of his sons have been up the mountains drilling without a gun between them. Denis brought a hoe. That's right, son, we'll take the empire down with garden rakes.

Is this it? The street in 'Araby'? It's shorter than she thought. And poorer. G had called it a cul-de-sac and he was right; it was the bottom of the bag. She feels the leaded windows eyeing her, the vertigo of the shabby brown houses leaning in. There's a deserted feel to the place as if everybody has already left it, bar the droning boys. So this must be where he went to school.

'Number 13, if you please,' she calls out.

'Which side?' he yells, as if demanding what her loyalties are.

He peers from his box, taking off his hat and rubbing his forehead with the back of his hand. Can't make out the numbers with his eyesight. Is it odds on the right, is it? Hates it when the punters don't know where they're going, though for a continental she's very exact. Finally, he sees the number in the fanlight.

'Number 13,' he calls, and hops down to open the door. She steps out and he begins, 'That'll be …'

She holds up her hand to stop him, the little frothy umbrella swinging from her wrist, the pearly gloves still on. God, she's spotless, not a hair astray. Her other hand is lightly holding her hat.

'Please wait.'

That's him in his box. He climbs back onto the cab, glad to get the weight off. She makes for the front steps of number 13. There's just two of them up from the street, shallow, soft-lipped. She heads for the front door and stands beside the foot-scraper, but she doesn't lift the knocker. Instead, she leans over the railings around the area and peers in directly into the reception room front. Bold as brass. There's a blind pulled down halfway but that doesn't deter her. She winds her neck around to have a good old snoop. Merciful hour, she'll get arrested carrying on like that. If there are fearful tenants inside and they've spotted her, they'll be thinking her to be a bailiff's agent. But don't you have to serve an eviction notice in person, put it into the poor unfortunate's hand? And if she's not with the bailiff or the housing department, she'll be reported for suspicious behaviour carrying on like that. Talk about curiosity killed the …

A tabby prowls past, insinuating itself up against the railings while Herself lightly strokes the arrowheads. Is she counting the spears? None of his business. But he can't help himself. Maybe she'll explain when she climbs back in. Hardly, Teddy boy, doesn't look the type for small talk. Anyway, she's foreign so he'll not get much change out of her.

Finally, she turns around. Nipping lightly behind the cab, she scurries over to the other side of the street, looking up at the house opposite, then to the street lamp and then back again. Then from her purse she fetches a little notebook and a tiny pencil, like a tradesman would wear behind his ear, and she starts taking notes. She surveys the street, then the house behind her, then number 13 again. Is she taking measurements or what?

Slowly she saunters back towards the cab, standing for a minute in the middle of the street and wheeling slowly around. The sky overhead is watery looking, rain on the wind, he can sense it.

'Very well,' she says looking up at him, shading her eyes against the grey glare. 'Let us advance.'

She points to the end of the street where a stolid red-brick house stands on its own.

'Onward,' she commands.

'It's a dead end, Miss,' the cabman says.

And suddenly she understands.

'Araby' was the first story of his she read, haltingly, slowly, out loud. It was how G had taught her. Back when he was just Professor Zois to her. He had long since dispensed with the *Schlüssel's Englisch Grammatik* he'd used when she took classes with Emma Cuzzi and Olivia Hannapel. They used to gather in the old nursery in the Cuzzis' house. Trouble was Emma and Olivia were half in love with him. Not so surprising, really. Aren't you supposed to be in love with your English teacher? Everything about the *professore* whispered neglect. His clothes spoke of thinness, worn to an inch of their lives, frayed cuffs, sheeny trousers. Rarely a full suit, but unmatched halves. A centaur in sheep's clothing. But poor as they were he always wore them with a puckish air, a jaunty bow tie or a raffish pocket square, or the gay boater which he wore in all seasons even when the bora blew. And those ridiculous tennis shoes! He had a long stride. Sometimes she wondered was he trying to save his soles with those giant steps. And when he sat, he folded his legs around the furniture with a languid tort, like he was a barley twist himself. She liked his hair, the foppish fall of it. And those eyes, who could not be mesmerized?

Emma had been the ringleader of the in-loveness, loudest in her protestations. She – or her mama – was a font of knowledge about the *professore irlandese*. His wife had abandoned him the day he arrived in Trieste, ran off with a Hungarian peddler, she'd heard. Left him at the station, if you please!

Well, *my* mama, Olivia piped up, says they were not even married! And she was in the family way!

As Emma and Olivia skitted over Professor Zois, Amalia bided her time.

One Friday afternoon Olivia came agog with fresh gossip which made Amalia's heart sink. The *professore* had already proposed to one of his students, had kissed her – and not on the hand – and then popped the question, bold as you like. The girl's father was apoplectic. A pecunious English teacher, the audacity of it! The impropriety! The father had wanted Professor Zois to be drummed out of the country. Did some investigating. Apparently, he'd been teaching at the naval college in Fiume before coming to Trieste. Had a reputation as a lady-killer, they said.

'And when was this?' she asked Emma. Carefully.

'Oh way back, years ago.'

Oh well, then.

There was more scandalous excitement when Emma had been struck down with a burst appendix. She'd nearly died, the surgeon said. She was in the hospital for weeks. When she came back, she was pale and wintry looking.

'Guess what!' she said, her eyes popping behind her owlish spectacles.

'What?' she and Olivia cried in unison.

'The *professore* came to visit me in the hospital. He brought grapes.'

Amalia pretended indifference.

'Imagine – I nearly died!'

Emma was still under the influence of morphine, and afterwards she'd had the most delicious dream in which the *professore* had whisked her off on a train journey through fields of corn waving like brushed gold, and leaning up close to her in the carriage he'd whispered in her ear, *May I, May I ...*

'And what did you say?' Olivia asked.

'I woke up before I could say yes.'

Emma was a weaver of fantasies, Amalia knew, but she'd been excited by Emma's dream. The scenario of helplessness appealed, a white room, a mortal illness which only his presence can cure. And Mother pleading with Papa, 'Poldy, Poldy let him stay', and Papa, firm and rejecting, says 'Letizia, for pity's sake, he's the English teacher, not a healing monk', but in her daydream Mother wins the day, his hand in hers on the white sheet, his voice close to her ear, rousing her from sleep's seduction and she comes back to ...

'Amalia, Amalia!' Emma's flirtatious voice. 'You were miles away!'

The *professore* is calling for her to decline the verb 'withhold'. She has to check herself. She looks down. Her appendix in its place, no sickle-shaped scar that Emma has told her about but didn't show. That will be for my husband's eyes only, Emma had said saucily and laughed, twisting around in the seat to wink at Amalia, eyes wicked with knowledge as if she'd guessed Amalia's secret.

That was when she decided.

She inveigled Papa into paying for private tuition. Wheedled for months: *The others are distracting, they are not serious students, I really need individual attention.* (Not anyone's individual attention, his alone.) *If I am ever to get into the University ...* She did not mention the *professore*'s unusual teaching methods – songs from Shakespeare, or a paper fortune he'd bought from a beggar on the street. Or the way once he'd slid down the bannisters in the Cuzzis', his long legs akimbo, or had the girls do ballerina high kicks while he played the nursery piano. Even then, his showman side was evident. He did these things to entertain Emma and Olivia; they loved it.

But not Amalia.

She's had an epiphany! Nothing can curb her sense of victory. Not even the cabman's lurch as he drives the poor nag to the end of the street and turns violently. She has to grab the strap over the door to steady herself. Is he angry with her, but for what? Won't he get a fat fare at the end of this? Anyway, she doesn't care. Being here has made it all clear to her. North Richmond Street being blind has two meanings. It's a dead end!

Finally, Papa had agreed on the condition that her sister, Lisetta, take the classes too. But Lisetta was easily bribed and Papa was never in the house when the lessons took place. She only hoped he wouldn't discover that the *professore* was claiming fees for two pupils when only one turned up on a regular basis.

Oh, the relief of being free of Emma and Olivia. The *professore* was pleased too for Papa had offered a much better rate than the Berlitz. For her first class, she dressed carefully and made sure that he would arrive and be shown into Papa's study before she would appear. It was she who'd decided the class would be held there, being a manly and studious place. This was serious business she was engaged in.

The hall maid came to the drawing room to announce him, after being told to leave the study door ajar so that the *professore* could hear her being summoned. She wanted to give the impression of a life so busy that the appointment might well have slipped her mind. He would never know that she'd been pacing the floor for over an hour before the class was due to start. Checking the pier glass one more time, she deliberately delayed a few minutes more, before clacking noisily down the chequered hallway on newly minted heels – the shoes chosen so that he would hear her before he saw her, and to remind him that although she was still at the Liceo, she was no giddy schoolgirl.

So important was this, that she went against her nature when that first class was drawing to a close by berating him. He was gathering up his Berlitz *First Book Grammar* (she was a bit offended by this; shouldn't she be on to book two?) as a prelude to leaving when she noticed by Papa's mantel clock that it was still ten minutes to the hour.

'If I were a patient in a doctor's rooms,' she began.

'Ah, well done, Miss Popper,' he interrupted, 'the subjunctive.'

'I would feel cheated if he cut short my visit before the time was full.'

His face fell but he gallantly subsided into Papa's leather chair. He couldn't have known then the depth of feeling that had prompted her remonstration. She couldn't bear the dousing disappointment when he withdrew his presence, especially when it came early.

'Up,' he said.

'I beg your pardon?'

'The correct usage, Miss Popper, is before the time is up.'

Afterwards, when they were trading sweet, retrospective confessions, he told her that while he was used to being treated like a servant, that did not mean he had to like it.

'So I decided I'd get my own back,' he said. A phrase he had to explain to her.

'How?' she asked.

'I was deliberately late for the next three classes,' he said.

Stepping into the landscape of G's boyhood, so unknowable up to this, she sees other things clearly too. How pressing his desire must have been to rise above the musty suffocation of such hemmed-in streets. And this, G had informed her, was one of their better addresses. Which can't be said for the house the Joyces live in now. She shudders at the memory of last evening in the tiny, cramped hovel tumbling directly out onto a street of slimed cobble. She was shocked, she can't pretend otherwise.

'Be prepared,' is all G had said, 'don't come over all Lady of the Manor.'

What's he talking about, she thought to herself, they were all perfectly respectable. Their hats at the station had fooled her.

But at home, somehow, it was different. There they all were, the haunt-eyed sisters, the gadabout brother, his neglected little wife with scrabbling children crawling over her. Pappie all bluff with bonhomie blissfully unaware of the little house's impoverishment and the dumbshow the girls were putting on to hide the holes in their threadbare existence.

'Come in, come in and welcome, my daughter,' Pappie expostulated at the door. No dumbshow there. (He had given up on pronouncing her name.) He crushed her in a muffling embrace, a peck on each cheek then. 'The Eyetalian way, aha!'

She and G stepped into a dingy hallway then immediately left into the good room, as it was called, claret red walls, a fire burning in the grate – at least that, though who would have thought it necessary coming up to midsummer's eve? Without the distractions of hats, Eva and Eileen were reduced to scuttling maids at his beck and call. They disappeared almost immediately and she could hear the clatter of plates from somewhere further back in the dim house.

Everything was cloudy. The light, such as it was, was obscured by a thickly patterned lace curtain so they were sunk into a kind of sepulchral gloom though it was still early afternoon. Charlie, Mary and the children were squashed together on the beaten sofa, draped with a kind of shroud the colour of cold tea, while she and G perched on a stiff, scarlet chaise longue. Obviously, the best seat in the house. Pappie lorded it over them, standing at the mantel.

'Aha,' he said and lit up a pipe.

The sweet male perfume of it was welcome. It wasn't that the house smelled exactly, and it was clean (the sisters had probably been up scrubbing till midnight for there was no sign of a servant.) But there was an undertow of dampness, the fungal fumes of sunless rooms and unaired clothes. Remember, at home, how Bertha would still the sheets billowing on the lines with her palm and gather them in, crisply dry. The Joyces' laundry had clearly never known such freedom. Where would they dry anything here – if there was an outside, it could be no more than a sooty yard. This, she thought, must be the smell of poverty.

'You'll have a drop?' Pappie said to G. 'Sherry?'

G nodded.

'Eva?' Pappie roared, and the nominated sister bustled in. 'Drinks, for our guests.'

She returned with a clink of unmatched glasses, two with stems, and a pair of tumblers. They raised a toast on Pappie's urgings. 'Good luck to ye now, a match made in heaven.'

Hardly, she thought.

She recalled the struggle she'd had to convince Papa about the suitability of the penniless Irish *professore* she wished to marry. *If he saw this ...* she stopped. She looked around the dim inward-looking house that would comfortably fit into the boot room of the Villa Alice and she wanted to bolt. She could stand up as if in search of the sanitary facilities – *though in this house what kind would they be, O Dio!* – and make instead for the front door, out onto the ramshackle street and be gone. *Calma*, she told herself. You haven't married *them*. And Papa will never see this and when the ordeal is over, you can wipe it from your memory. Unknow it. It was G's interior world she wanted to know, not these ragged circumstances over which he had no control and which can no longer touch him – though, of course, they still did. There were constant pleas from the sisters to save them from the bailiffs; she'd seen the begging letters. Think of G, just G, she urged herself, and how he took possession of you, and smarting half-delightedly at the memory, she breathed a little easier.

She noticed the upright piano in a corner of the room with candle sconces and a scrolled music holder. Could this be his mother's, saved despite their downward drift? Could anything of value have survived the pawnbroker's grasp? She speculated meanly to herself as Pappie expounded on the war – *damnedest business* – and then moved on to the girls' general uselessness: Eva couldn't hold a job, Eileen was a confounded idiot. There was no sign of Florrie, either in person or in Pappie's complaints. The house was so full Amalia wondered if they could only inhabit it in shifts.

As if in sympathy with Pappie's disenchantment, Charlie's children set up a lament. As the children's cries grew more insistent G took one of them, a little boy, and settled him on his lap. (Were the others boys or girls, she couldn't figure, for they were all in smocks and so close in looks – pallid with runny noses – and age, like steps of stairs.)

'Georgie, make nice to your uncle now,' Charlie said, as G made clopping sounds. For a moment, Georgie halted mid-bawl, as G played horsey-horsey with him, jigging him up and down. The boy watched him wide-eyed, his hands reaching for the stem of G's spectacles. Amalia watched, charmed; it was a good sign, was it not, his ease with children? But after the first fright of being taken in hand by this new strange uncle, the child started grizzling again prompting the others to join in.

'Stop it now, Georgie,' Charlie warned and raised his fist.

'He's only making strange,' Mary ventured, the first words Amalia had heard her speak.

'Oh for heaven's sake, take them away,' Charlie ordered, 'if they can't behave themselves in company!'

Georgie slithered down from G's lap as Mary marshalled the babies. All Amalia could see were too many clutching hands for one small woman to hold as Mary led the snivelling tribe from the room.

Relieved of his avuncular duties, G stood and stretched. He moved towards the piano, lifted the lid and began to vamp. Soon all of them joined in. They worked best as a family when they sang, she thought. She didn't recognize the songs. They must be old familiars because the sisters knew the choruses and the men took the verses.

The singing was followed by tea in the back parlour around a scratched table, covered hurriedly with a linen cloth newly starched and an incomplete china set, relics of their mother's ancient domesticity. (The rest of it must have been pawned, G joked in her ear.) The tea was tarry and she dared not ask for a slice of lemon. The sweet cake was a rough, fruit-laden relation to bread rather than anything that resembled patisserie.

As the clock struck five, she made desperate eye signals to G.

Basta cosi.

He must have been keen to leave as well for he took up her meaning immediately.

On their way back to the Gresham, G said nothing in the carriage, just stared out the window. The city was at its best at this hour, bleached and pearly. She was glad of the silence after the hectic sociability. Anyway, what could she have said that would sound even halfway truthful? What an honour to meet his father, how sweet his sisters. No, she wasn't a complete hypocrite. And he wasn't a fool; he'd pick up on her reserve and then charge her with snobbery.

Let this be over soon, she prayed to herself, as she glanced at G's profile and felt that vertiginous chasm opening up between them that made her see all the difficulties of her situation – an uncertain exile with a foreign husband away from all that was familiar. She could feel herself quail. In such a weighty silence, betrayal can sprout. The sooner they were away from here the better. But there was still this awful concert to face tomorrow. As

they sat steeped in this morose mood, she wished muti-
nously for the concert to be a flop.

§

*'For sheer pleasure, simple beauty and all the things that make
life worth living, there is nothing to compare with a concert of
Signor Joyce.' – THE IRISH TENOR John McCormack*

GIACOMO JOYCE,
Renowned Irish-Italian Tenor
Antient Concert Rooms,
Great Brunswick Street,
Dublin
(Accompanist: Miss Kathleen Kearney, R.I.A.M.)

Thursday, June 16, 1915

§

He'd moved heaven and earth to have that date. Wrote
letters to Signor Boylan, the impresario, insisting. An
omen too good to pass up on, he said. If it's June, it has to
be the 16th for *Il ritorno d'Ulisse in patria.*

Why, Amalia wondered, but she didn't ask. G had so
many superstitions, it was pointless trying to trace the
source of all of them. The thunderstorms, the dogs, the
propitious dates. There was invariably history attached to
them, a history she didn't want to know about because it
pertained to Nora, she was sure. She suspected it was his
way of keeping her memory alive.

On the journey here, she'd expressly forbidden him to
seek Nora out. He'd heard on the grapevine – a curious

phrase – that Nora had returned to Dublino some years ago. Despite the solemn promise he'd given her, Amalia wasn't sure if he'd be able to resist the temptation to put his finger in the wound. Every time he stepped out on an errand she'd wonder where he was off to. Today, for example, was he really seeing Dottor Gogarty? And later, when he says there will be a dress rehearsal at the Concert Rooms with Miss Kearney. Is that where he's really going?

Just this morning, as if sensing her suspicions, he'd said, speaking of his accompanist, 'Don't you worry your head about Miss Kearney, she's probably a right old battleaxe.' He doesn't understand that it's not the obvious betrayals she worries about, it's the unstated one. But look who's preaching from the pulpit. Where exactly is she supposed to be this morning? Taking a nap at the hotel, isn't that what she has told him?

The cabman has picked up speed now. She thinks of G's jigging knees with Georgie aboard. They are ploughing down a wide boulevard, if you could use such a term here, for even the widest streets seemed huddled. Plane trees shiver on either side and Amalia suspects she'll need her umbrella at the next stop. Isn't it strange, she thinks, she grew to love G through how he wrote about Dublino. But being here has not bolstered her understanding of him one whit.

Comprehension, G used to say when he was Professor Zois, is half the battle, as if learning English was gladiatorial combat. Unseen texts, he decreed, not mentioning at first he was using his own work. The paper on which 'Araby' was written had been folded over several times and had lived in his breast pocket, like a love letter, a little too long. Grime lodged in the folds like the rings she was later to notice on his overworn shirt collars. She had great difficulty with his handwriting, and there was so much crossing out, arrows shooting off into the margins – she thought of Cupid – but she persisted with it while he sat, his spectacles pushed up on his forehead, one hand clutching his brow, shielding his naked eyes.

He would sigh – or sometimes harrumph – as she lurched from one word to the next. Was it her English he was noting, or his own? She didn't know until she finished.

'Now, tell me what the story is about.'

'It is about love.'

'I know, I know, but what kind of love?'

'Unrequited love.' The foolishness of it. The impossibility of loving him, the absolute guarantee of disappointment.

He mused on her response.

'You are quite the lady of letters, Miss Popper,' he said.

But is she, really? Can she really do this? It all seemed possible in Trieste … But, no, she can't think of Trieste now, else she'll tear up. Banished from it, it's as if the city doesn't exist anymore. Which would be worse? That it be razed to the ground, destroyed by this awful war, ravaged by the enemy – or that it go on as before, but without her? Trieste is the city of their love. What will happen to their sacred landmarks if she's not there to acknowledge them? Will they fade, lose their power, if she can no longer see them?

There's that spot on the Piazza Grande, close to the arches, when she first realized she was not imagining what she felt for the *professore*. That day she was just sixteen. It was a moment, nothing more. They'd met by chance, outside, when usually they were cloistered inside. A windswept day on the piazza, peelings from the fruit and vegetable stalls whipped up in a flurry of green and rot by the bora, the white-topped waves bucking and neighing in the harbour and there he was, Professor Zois, tipping his silly hat grandly at her. She saw him before Mother did. They were both engaged in the tussle with the wind. Mother, bonnet clutched in place by both hands, was fiercely charging ahead, while she had retrieved her hand from her muff, the pale grey rabbit one, to clear a piece of grit the spiteful wind had lodged in her eye. He intercepted her with some stammered excuse – changing the time of their class on account of ... she can't recall. It was his habit with pupils to speak in English, or his habit with her, at any rate. Then with one eye over his shoulder on Mother, he had lightly laid his hand on her blue-veined wrist, then placed it on his breast, and said – '*Lei capisce?*'

The effect was a kind of sizzle. The removed muff, her defenceless wrist, Mother some way ahead unaware of this scandalous advance. She knew he could feel it too and even though she was only a girl, she came into her womanly majority that day, recognizing the effect she could have. How to use it only came later. They parted on the speckled piazza, both of them understanding the moment.

They are hurtling now around a heavily sooted church sitting in the middle of the street, the cabbie yells something about the devil? *Diavolo*? She has given up trying to understand him. They turn right onto a long, busily poor street, a shabby muddle of mean shops selling ironware and badly plucked chickens. They pass a grey church built like a fortress. She loves the city of G's stories, the sweet, remembered melancholy of it, but the bricks and mortar of it is harder to love. But isn't it just such transformation that makes him an artist? She feels her voice rising in her head in protest. It is an oft-rehearsed argument she has with herself because she cannot have it with him.

Why, oh why? Why has he abandoned his calling as the greatest writer the world has ever known – *no, I do not exaggerate* – to tread the boards, as he calls it. She plays the devil's *avocato* in a court of her imagination.

Yes, of course, she concedes, *his voice is good, your honour. Rich and pure.*

Pure, a strange word to use in relation to the accused, the judge replies.

'I have the same quality as McCormack,' he's told her, 'O'Brien has always said so.' O'Brien was his first teacher in Dublin, who'd also trained McCormack. McCormack – she is weary of the eternal comparison; it's worse than the rivalry of Mozart and Salieri.

But Illustrissimo Signor Giudice, she argues, *there are many good singers in the world, but how many great writers are there?*

Quite so. The judge peers over his spectacles. *But how can we persuade the man in the dock to see the error of his ways?*

She has no answer.

You live in Trieste, do you not? the judge queries, as if that's reason enough.

She understands what he is suggesting – hers is a city where there is no shortage of would-be singers. They crowd the *loggione* of the Teatro Verdi, standing room only, scores in hands, mouthing the words. She's never been to the upper reaches of the Verdi, but G has described them to her – and the bodily fumes of the clientele – in forensic detail. Once he used to mock them, but now he takes himself too seriously.

But the crowning reason why he should not follow this disastrous course, your honour, is that it is not a free decision on behalf of my client. There is an unseen other who has manipulated his affections. None other than the siren Signorina Nora Barnacle. She is the creator of this folly. She it is who should be in the dock for planting this ruinous idea in his head.

How many times has Amalia heard G quote her? 'Wouldn't you be better off altogether with the singing than bothering with that old writing business?'

Well then, before I can rule, this Barnacle woman should be brought before the court.

Yes, Amalia thinks fiercely, yes, she should!

Henrietta Street is their next stop, right in front of the arch. Thinking her business legal, the only part of the expedition the cabbie understands, he hops down and opens the door for her. Amalia is suddenly afraid – his fears for her, contagious. *Sometimes, however, he courted the causes of his fear.* That's what G wrote. The words give her courage as she steps onto the cobble. The day has brightened, the sky flowery with cloud, yet the street seems dark, overhanging, the houses seeming to shoulder out the sun.

'Please wait,' she tells the cabman who's standing, cap in hand, a kind of indignation in his aspect. *Aspetta.*

Imagine! Little Chandler, the sorry clerk, must have stood just here. On her left is a building several storeys high with the shut-in look of a convent. Somewhere within, a bell clanks twice. The street dips down in front of her, and there huddled in a doorway just feet away are the children, the same grimy ones who appear in 'A Little Cloud', she'd swear to it. Two little girls in ragged pinafores stand peering gummy-eyed at her, while a huddle of barefoot boys squat at marbles. A third girl with a sty in her eye whips a hoop. Amalia looks up at the gaunt mansions, yes, just as G described, their windows like ramshackle spectacles. A little further down, a cart lumbers to a halt and the figure of a man jumps off and heaves a bag of coal from the back. The horse drops its weary head.

The man opens an iron porthole in the street and begins to tip the contents in. At the cascading rattle, the marble players leap up abandoning their game. They run towards the cart, scrabbling to catch the leavings, loading their pockets with lumps of coal. Even at a distance, she feels a minute dusting on her skin. She breathes it in even though it irritates her throat.

'Are you not going in, Miss?' the cabbie asks, jerking his head at the arc.

She shakes her head and then he shakes his. At last, they're in unison, though hers is firm and his is baffled.

The girl drops her hoop and approaches her, stick still in one hand, while she stretches out the other.

The cabbie swats at her. 'Don't be annoying the lady.'

Amalia climbs back into the cab and shuts the door leaving the beggar girl, fringe licking a pair of green eyes, standing mouthing *please Miss*. She goes through her purse and throws a couple of coppers out. She doesn't understand the money here. The child drops on all fours grabbing at the spiralling pennies.

'Don't be encouraging them, Miss,' the cab driver says as he heaves himself up to the box.

But she wants to do something. The poverty here frightens her. She expected it on the street, but the genteel dilapidation of G's family is more troubling and immediate. What to do with the knowledge of it?

'Next?' the cabbie shouts.

Look at the list, she wants to shout. But there's no point in antagonizing him. She tries a different tack.

'What is your name, Signore?' she asks. He's now consulting her list, she sees, as if he has heard her internal rebuke.

'My name?' he repeats, looking around as if there is a crowd behind him to whom she's addressing the question.

Why in the name of all that's good and holy does she want to know that? Better play nice all the same or she'll report him to the beadle at the Gresham and he'll lose his place on the rank. He has a missus and five children, the younger ones only half-grown.

'Teddy Coombs, Miss, at your service.' He bows and thrashes the air around his thighs with his hat.

'And I am Signora Joyce.' She has learned how to pronounce it properly, particularly here.

She sees his brow furrowing.

'Mrs Joyce,' she says.

Joyce, a country name, is it Galway? Must be married to one of us. That's how she'd have the English. But where is Mister Joyce and why does he let her out and about like this, gallivanting about on her own on some kind of wild-goose chase. Unless ...

'You are most kind, Signor Coomsah,' she says and smiles at him sweetly, deliberately.

'So where are we off to now, Missus?'

She dreads another debate with him so she points to the list.

'Are you sure now?' he asks.

'Yes, thank you.'

Maybe it was a mistake getting too familiar with him. He sighs and climbs aboard after settling her in. They lurch back down Henrietta Street, past the gaping children and the blackened coal haulier with his broken-down horse. Is everything in this city broken down, the houses, the people? Now, stop it, Amalia, she chastises, even the humblest places can have significance. Even these cross-eyed streets, the slovenly houses. Isn't this what your pilgrimage is all about?

She remembers the humble green at the Südbahnhof. She smiles to herself. That was special, wasn't it? Imbued. A site of *their* love, hers and G's. They used to snatch time there before she departed for Firenze at the start of each university term. It became a little ritual of theirs. While Fabrizio fetched down her luggage and supervised a porter to wheel it onto the platform, they would stroll across and sit on one of the benches, hold hands, utter sweet vows away from chaperoning eyes.

He wouldn't say farewell on the platform. Bad luck, he said. She suspected he didn't want to be seen, in the hindsight view of the moving away train, alone, bereft. Or was it because it was at this very station that Nora Barnacle had deserted him? That much she did know. (*How is it that woman manages to crop up everywhere? Here, there, in my lady's chamber.*) G would kiss her in the park and walk her across to the turning circle at the station, where Fabrizio would be waiting to escort her inside. By the time she got to the station doors and turned around, G would already be a distant figure, striding away, without a backward glance.

She checks her breast watch – *O Dio*, it's already noon, and she has at least three more locations to get to. The cab picks up speed as if Signor Coomsah has been privy to her inward panic. The horse is bolting now as they rattle down one leg of a green square, the liverish brick and the squinting windoes of the houses blurring in the corner of her eye and then they are back where they started, whizzing past the Gresham – does the beadle recognize her and wonder if she's been abducted? Hardly. They're travelling at such a lick he has probably not even seen her. Nelson looms. G has threatened to take her up to the top of the Pillar.

We'll buy a punnet of plums and make a day of it with the one-handed adulterer. He laughed; not for the first time she didn't get the joke.

She doesn't want to go up the inside of a dark column – if he's superstitious about thunderstorms and dogs and railway platforms, then she has a secret fear of her own. The furry inside of a dark confined space and a hundred and sixty-six steps to climb before reaching daylight. Makes her breath go fast even thinking about it, especially now, in her condition.

The General Post Office sails by. The way Signor Coomsah is driving you'd think he was chasing a fire. Other cabs thunder past them, as if they're involved in a race. Are the Irish lawless, by nature? They draw level with the blackened hulk of the Liberator and his bare-breasted angels. Look at him, G had said, standing with his arse to the street.

Over the Liffey they go – the cabbie identifies it with a hurl of his hand. She'd have guessed it on her own from the smell. The river's dank reek and the singed hum of the brewery join in an unholy marriage. One sharp, the other strangely homely, like chicory. Only the gulls are familiar from Trieste, though here their braying seems more harshly forlorn as if their cries are scratching against the sky. She keeps an eye out for a white horse. Another of G's superstitions – they say you never cross O'Connell Bridge without seeing a white horse. But though she scours the thoroughfare she doesn't see one. Oh dear, will that doom her expedition?

Oh Mali, hark at you, you don't believe in all that nonsense!

Signor Coomsah halts, two streets facing them, falling away like the legs of a scissors, a squat castellation keeping them apart. Which one, she wonders idly, but the cabbie takes neither, but lurches left down the quays. This is the part of the journey Signor Coomsah objected to most vociferously outside the Gresham. She is trying to follow the jagged route of hostelries and public houses that Farrington, the beleaguered clerk in 'Counterparts' takes, his *via dolorosa*, as G called it. She wants to get a sense of its distance, the mood of the streets, though she's completing it in broad daylight and not on a foggy winter's night.

Never mind. Wasn't this how she kept the idea of G alive for three years while she was in Firenze? She made him catalogue all his favourite haunts, some of them places she'd never been in her own city – the Ristorante Bonavia, the Trattoria Viola, the Osteria alla citta di Parenzo on Via del Ponte, or the Andemo de Pepi. He'd probably left out a few places of ill repute, like Il Metro Cubo or La Chiave d'Oro. She might have been sheltered but she had brothers; she'd heard them talk of such places. Her innocence allowed for the fact that she couldn't know everything about G. And might never.

During the long winter terms and the humid mosquito-ridden springs in Firenze, she would imagine him drinking Opollo in the Andemo de Pepi, sitting on the upturned wine casks and trading triestino with the sailors and porters and the other low company he favoured. Mapping out his territory in her mind like this kept him close to her heart.

Originally they had planned to go to Firenze together; he would teach classes there while she studied. That was the plan.

She was secretly relieved that it hadn't come to pass. She'd learned about Nora by then – Nora as G's concubine, that is – and she feared that once they were together in Firenze, he might expect the same of her. She'd already had to win her Papa around on so much. That her English *professore* wanted to marry her, for one, that he was a penniless writer, and a foreigner with irredentist leanings. That was quite enough to be going on with.

If Papa had known they had plotted to live in the same city, he might well have vetoed the match altogether. Which he nearly had after the burning of the manuscript business.

'Is he *pazzo*?' Papa had demanded.

It had taken all her powers of honeyed persuasion to assuage his fears. As it had when she had to break the news to G that he wouldn't be coming to Firenze with her, after all.

'I am young, we can wait,' she placated.

'You mean, I can wait,' G said. He was sour.

'Well … if you love me.'

He didn't hold with much love talk. Innuendo, strange oathy imprecations in rough triestino, lustful whisperings in her ear, yes. But not declarations.

'Haven't I waited long enough?'

That was true. He'd waited for her to reach her legal majority.

'How long is too long?' she asked.

'My empress,' he breathed and she put her fingers to his lips. Her elevation to a person of title embarrassed her. It made him seem servile. If she was his empress, what did that make him?

'Let us make a bargain,' she said. 'While I am away, you must write a new masterpiece, so that by the time I wear my laureate's wreath, you will be ready to conquer the world.'

She had kept her part of the bargain, but G had not.

*

'The Scotch House, Mulligan's, O'Neill's, Davy Byrne's?'
Signor Coomsah is apoplectic at the next four destinations
on her list. His face purples. 'No place for a lady.'

How can she explain to him that she just wants to view
these establishments, see what Farrington saw, though
as G explained to her, Farrington is half-cut so doesn't
see much clearly. But that's precisely why she must go,
to know what he cannot describe. She needs to see these
places for herself. She doesn't admit that she also has a
sneaking curiosity to view their interiors, where smoke
hangs and beer is drunk and where G must have spent his
youth.

'Signor Coomsah,' she begins, 'I wish only to stop outside, not to go in.'

'All the same, Missus,' he says huffily.

Now the cab is veering right and she sees it: The Scotch
House. Coomsah soothes the horse to a stop but doesn't
climb down. Part of his protest, she guesses. The building rears up several stories, turning the corner of the street
into a serpentine round. A brewery float is parked by the
kerb. The pub is open even at this hour of the morning,
but there are no match-sellers by the door as on the night
Farrington was here. In fact, the place looks deserted. But
she daren't alight. Coomsah might drive off in a temper.
She peers out and suddenly there is thunder. She looks
up expecting the sky to have darkened, but it's not the
weather. It is the thunder of the beer barrels being rolled
along the street. An iron grating is open on the pavement
like a portal to the underworld and they drop the barrels
down, one by one, as if into a bottomless pit. But it's not
bottomless. Below, G has explained, the barrels make a
soft landing on the cushioned pillow of a sandbag. She

thinks of the coal merchant she saw earlier and wonders –
in Dublino does everything happen underground? Is that
where the real life of the city is lived?

'Next,' Coomsah calls impatiently and without waiting
for an answer he sets the cab in motion.

They move at a stately pace and take the first left down
a narrower, darker street away from the open vista of the
river. A little further on, they stop in front of Mulligan's.
It's a low-slung place, crouched on the street. Again Coomsah lingers but makes no move. This time she feels bolder.
She pushes open the door of the cab and steps down onto
the street.

'Missus!' Coomsah cries out aggrieved.

'Signor Coomsah,' she soothes.

Now that she's at street level, she can't resist the urge.
She tiptoes towards the door. Hastily, she dips in through
the double doors. She can hear Coomsah at her back scrabbling to get down from the cab and muttering under his
breath. She presses on. It's like a wine-coloured cave inside,
a hunched-down feel as if the ceiling is only just above
her head. There are a couple of men sitting up at the bar
on her right with their backs turned. The barkeep setting
down a brown bottle on the counter gawps as she sweeps
past them. Show no uncertainty, she tells herself. Above
is a large beam with John Mulligan inscribed largely on
it as if the place had been turned inside out. Behind her,
she can hear Coomsah labouring through the door but she
strides on. She's looking for the parlour at the back where
Farrington went. She veers right and pushes one side of
a narrow set of doors. She hears the bar-keep protesting,
something about ladies, and Coomsah muttering something at him. The doorway is so constricted that she has to
bundle her skirts up to squeeze through. There is nobody

in here. An empty fireplace sits ashenly. She inhales a smell she has come to associate with G. Stale smoke. Coomsah barrels in behind her, huffing and puffing.

'That's enough, now, Missy,' he says and marches her back the way she's come. The drinkers at the bar gape at them as they go past, the cabbie and the lady. What are they thinking, she wonders, that this man is her father, or her husband, taking control of a wilful woman? He disengages from her when they re-enter the glare of the street. Outside, even in its misty dullness, seems starkly bright.

'No more of this now, Missus,' he says.

He opens the door of the cab.

Civility returns. She feels like telling him not to worry, but she doesn't. He's discommoded, she can tell, and she realizes she's broken his trust. She sits chastened in the cab while Coomsah heaves himself up heavily.

'Usher's Island,' he calls out and she realizes there will be no more public houses.

The Ballast Office whizzes by; she recognizes it from yesterday when they walked across the bridge. A tram gong sounds. The quays are livelier with people than yesterday. Now they're passing small knots of soldiers in khaki and puttees, the only sign of the war here. Being in Dublino is like travelling back to a time when the war has not yet started. As if the Irish haven't quite caught up with events, as if the *Lusitania* hasn't foundered, or the Somme isn't being bloodily fought over. The war is still a debate here, while she and G are already on the run from it. There are recruiting posters plastered on doors and shop windows full of plaintive questions – *Will you make a fourth? When are the other boys coming? Will you go or must I?* As if the war was still something to choose, or not.

She sees the spindly arch of the Halfpenny Bridge, its curlicued railings like writing scrawled on air. Her spirits begin to sink. Despite her list, she is travelling blind. There's so much she doesn't know of G's secret history. Just now she might be passing places of significance, without realizing it. Places that Nora knew, knew *with* G, their version of the Piazza Grande, *their* obelisk park, and she has no way of knowing. When she read his stories first, this was what she was looking for. To find clues. About him, about them. Together.

G had often listed the sites of Nora's betrayal and told her about them. Even after years they are still fresh in his grudgeful memory. In Londra where she was not in the mood, or the Hotel Corneille in Parigi where she spurned him because the magnificent marquis was visiting. (Oh yes, Amalia was not spared any detail of Nora's intimate history.) And then in Zurigo, at the Hoffnung guest house, *elle etait touchée*. G boasted of it in a note to Stanino, imagine! The Lord knows what he has written to Stanino about her, though hopefully the prison censor at the Schloss Kirchberg will strike his red pen through the most florid passages. But of his and Nora's time together in Dublino, G is strangely silent. It's not just the ghost of Nora that's here, it's her all too fleshy flesh.

She should never have agreed to come. The concert, the secret translation, the meeting with the family, all seem part of the one terrible miscalculation. Does she know where G is, at this precise moment? Still with his friend Gogarty? He has consulting rooms on Ely Place and gave G an appointment slot at a quarter past eleven. Should she have gone with him? She has need of a doctor's opinion, but she'll wait now till Zurigo. The *medicos* here are all quacks, G says, and anyway, Dottor Gogarty is in the wrong department. He's ear, nose and throat. And that's not what's wrong with her, Amalia knows that much.

She has been rehearsing how she will announce it for days. *It is my belief that I may be with child.* Even saying it to herself sounds momentous for it is only an instinct, a female intuition, and when has she ever called on that before? But since her marriage she feels a new familiarity with blood and innards, their pulses and surges, and afterwards, their withdrawals. It is not an altogether bad feeling. It has awoken in her a new sense of herself as biological. Which is why these past few days she can't rid herself of the sensation that a seed has been planted. She doesn't like to think of it as a seed, so she imagines time speeded up – not so difficult with Signor Coomsah as driver – to when she has a baby in her arms. He will be Leopold, after her father. Little Poldy! Won't Papa be pleased?

She prefers to foresee the joyful birth than remember the act itself. G's taste in *amore* runs to a certain candour she was not prepared for. The tender touching of her wrist on the Piazza Grande or the chaste hand-holding in the obelisk park were but tentative preliminaries. At first, she thought she'd enraged him somehow, when he moved into the vigorous engagement of his married appetite. There were – *come si dice* – demands, that could only have originated from two sources: women of the night, or Nora. After all he *was* practically married to Nora; she had made a man of him, isn't that what he said? But perhaps all Irishmen liked their love to be so, so urgent.

There was no one to ask. Not Mother, who has surely never been required to submit to what G has suggested. It is not just the acts but the words that go with them. When she demurred because her English wasn't ... he said, 'No, Mali, let me hear it in Italian, English is for the classroom.' He breathed a language all mixed up, *let down your cocon, che mona bella*, as he laboured down below. Words she'd never heard.

'I've a good ear,' he said proudly.

And what girl could broach such a thing with her father? He might have sired four children but he can't have wanted his wife on all fours, approached in the rear of the premises ... she stops this line of thought.

Has G done that to her? Coarsened her?

Signor Coomsah has produced a whip and sets spittle flying, his own and the poor horse's, as he urges it on, go on now, go on, go on.

As she must.

'Whoa, whoa,' the cabbie calls, as if their sudden spurt of speed was the horse's idea, and they come to a halt in front of a large red-bricked house, its windows diminishing as she looks up.

'Number 15, Usher's Island,' Coomsah shouts out and doesn't even bother to dismount. He's still annoyed with her, so she alights, unaided. The house of 'The Dead'. It towers above her and its companions and glares across the river to grim neighbours on the far side. G's great-aunts used to live here, ran a little music school from the upper floors when he was a child. So the music was there from the start, as was the impulse to perform. She looks up and thinks of Gabriel Conroy who came to this very house in G's story. A man jealous of his wife's dead lover. A disappointed man.

Is G disappointed in her?

Or after Nora Barnacle, is he permanently disappointed?

Is she paying for Nora's sin?

Will the debt ever be paid off?

Is he waiting for her to do the same?

The horse shifts from one hoof to the other. It's started to spit rain so she reaches back into the cab and fetches her umbrella. She unfurls it. The rain in fine drops makes a skittering sound on the dome, the lace trim shivers. She looks up at the house. It's substantial, four storeys rise red-brickly above her. But there are signs of neglect. Weeds are sprouting between the steps leading to the front door. The fanlight is smashed, the brasses not polished.

'Am I to wait?' Coomsah asks.

But she doesn't answer.

What in God's name is Missus Joyce's business, Teddy Coombs is thinking, *nothing official about it and that's for certain, acting more like a jilted wife trying to find her hubby around the joy spots of Dublin. Won't get him this way*, he thinks. *No one welcomes a prying wife, sticking her nose in.* Missus Joyce mounts the shallow steps carefully, the umbrella resting on her shoulder, grazing the brim of her hat. As she stands there, indecisive, the front door opens. Teddy Coombs leans over speculatively. *Oh maybe, at last she's expected here.* A messenger boy streaks by her, message held high like proof of his importance. Quick as you like, she puts her dainty foot on the footleaf halting the door's weighted spring, and disappears inside.

Not expected, so.

She finds herself in a dun-coloured hall and what little light comes through the shattered fanlight is begrimed, degraded. There is some sort of covering on the floor that has a spongy feel underfoot. She can see from the large brass plate on what must be the front reception room that these are offices, on the ground floor anyway. As they were when 'The Dead' was written. A corn-factor wasn't it? Although Amalia didn't rightly know what a corn-factor did. She'd have to find the Italian equivalent, the better to understand.

Comprehension is half the battle.

She glances up the stairs. She almost expects to see Gretta Conroy standing there, transfixed, and the strains of ghostly music coming down from above. 'The Lass of Aughrim', wasn't that the name of the song? She had such trouble saying it when she read it aloud in class – Ocha-creema, was that it?

'I love all of your Italian elaborations,' G would say, 'everything so expressive, the moue of your mouth, your hands like puppeteer's.'

But you, Amalia thought, *are pulling the strings.*

When she looks up the stairs again, she realizes, stupidly, that Gretta is Nora. Of course! Another epiphany, this one unwanted.

Gretta has Nora's erect bearing, her soft accent, the same intensity of feeling that G used to praise her for. As if she were the only woman in the world capable of it. Nora was fiery, he would say, a creature of impulse, like coming away with me, she made that decision in an instant. He snapped his fingers. And did she decide to leave you in an instant too, Amalia wonders.

As time went by, he told her the whole story. If it was the whole story. Where Nora was concerned, Amalia was never quite sure. He'd left Nora guarding the suitcases at the station to go and find the Berlitz school and maybe book some accommodation to tide them over for their first couple of nights in Trieste. But in the Piazze Grande he'd come upon a couple of English sailors, engaged in a shouting match with a third party. G, having both languages, stepped in to make the peace. But he had no sooner started his intercession than the police came in a whistle-blowing fury and he was led off and slung into a police cell for breach of the peace. As the hours went by, he was frantic thinking of Nora sitting at the station, but he was confident, he said, that she would wait. She'd always waited before – in London, in Zurich, in Paris. The British consul was called but he didn't even talk to G. All his admonitions were for the sailors who were wearing a uniform of the Crown and making a show of themselves and the Empire on foreign soil. G was released as unceremoniously as he'd been detained, no charges preferred. He rushed back to the spot where Nora had been since early morning. But by then it was dark and Nora and the luggage were gone.

It is, paradoxically, the only time Amalia feels sorry for Nora. G always paints himself as the one who was abandoned. But hadn't he abandoned Nora first? Amalia shakes away the fellow feeling for Nora. She can't afford it. She thinks of the unfinished manuscript in G's luggage that Nora took with her. Or left behind? Those pages he spent years laboriously recreating from memory, only to have Roberts reject them, and then the final indignity, being thrown on the fire by their author. Was there ever a manuscript so imperilled?

No, she reminds herself, Nora is her enemy. G's first wife who is not a wife but who holds the same rank as one, who wasn't a wife long enough to disappoint, who remains, despite their squalid intimacy, a mystery. What torments her is the thought that G still longs for Nora, despite her betrayal. Or because of it. Is there something forever unfinished between them? That's what Amalia fears most.

*

She climbs the stairs. Little rolls of fluff gather in the corners of the risers and she can see the faint mark of footprints in the dust. It is quiet except for the clacking of a typewriter from further up the house. She imagines a woman, hair in coils, pecking at the keys, a sharp crease of concentration between her brows. Transcribing a legal document, *the party of the first part*. She pauses in the sallow light on the return, not daring to go any further for fear of being challenged. Suddenly, there is a thumping sound from above, the hurried approach of heavy footsteps. Hobnail boots. A figure in a cap and a rough-hewn jacket pounds down the unadorned stairs. Amalia backs into the corner to avoid him, but her movement brings him to an untidy, threatening halt. He's breathing heavily. She cowers in the shadows willing him to go on. But she has arrested his attention now.

'Mary ...?'

His eyes are bleary, a bruise has flowered on his cheekbone. A smell of drink comes off him in sour fumes. She catches it when he opens his mouth again.

'I've just been above with that jumped-up boss of yours who says ...'

'Sign –' she interrupts but he lunges at her, pressing himself against her, so that she's trapped in his spreadeagled prison. He has hold of her wrist with one of his hands, his other arm is splayed against the wall at her temple.

'Mary,' he mutters, 'who have you been with?'

His breath is hot against her ear, her hat knocked sideways. She turns her head to one side to escape the fumes and the scald of his rough chin. He's tieless and his collar is none too clean. She tries to wriggle out under his arm but she is firmly manacled. She can't breathe, her nostrils crushed up against his clothy shoulder. A door opens above on the next landing and daylight floods in.

'Miss Driscoll, is that you?'

Distracted, her attacker turns and twists his gaze upwards. It gives her enough air to call out. '*Aiutami!*'

'Miss Driscoll,' the voice above says. 'I've just had your young man here very much the worse for wear. We, all of us, feared for our safety.'

'*Aiutami!*' she cries again but her voice is so weak it could be a mewling cat.

And then, somehow, Coomsah appears. He yanks the young man away from her with a beefy arm, sending him sprawling.

'You blackguard!' he roars. 'What did you do to this lady?'

As the assailant struggles to get up, Amalia sees that he's only a boy, really. And she sees the realization of his mistake dawning on his face.

'Missus Joyce,' Coomsah asks, turning to her, 'are you all right? Has he laid a hand on you?'

She shakes her head. Apart from the imprint on her wrist, the worst he has pressed up against her is his breath.

'Good grief,' the voice upstairs says, 'what's going on down there?'

The assailant is upright now. Coomsah catches him by the lapels, bunching his coat in a flower in his fist, and lifts him off his feet. 'How dare you importune this lady!' he snarls, 'I've a good mind to take you to the barracks.'

'No,' Amalia says weakly – where has her voice gone? She can see three moves ahead – G summoned to the *questura*, Coomsah explaining the context, and G recognizing from the destinations on her list what she has been doing. No, no, she can't have that.

Coomsah sets the boy down. He sways on his feet or is it she who's about to swoon? No, no, not here, not now.

'What is going on down there?' the querulous voice above inquires.

'Missus, he could have done you untold harm,' Coomsah says.

And she thinks of the baby then. For the first time.

The boy looks from one to the other. Coomsah still has a hold of his arm.

'Release him,' Amalia says, 'he mistakes me for someone else.'

If she had been Miss Driscoll, she thinks, what would he have done to her? And does *she* not have the bearing of a wife, a mother? Clearly not. She is still someone who can be mistaken for a girl.

'Is he down there with you now?' the voice upstairs continues. 'First I had to give Miss Crosby the Bodley and Kirway contract to type and now I find you canoodling on the stairs ...'

Amalia lifts her head and sees the black shiny tops of the voice's boots sticking out through the bars of the bannisters. Then a face peers over, quivering jowls, a bulging eye clamped around a monocle, grainy upswept eyebrows.

'Oh, I beg your pardon,' he says when he sees her face. Coomsah and the assailant are out of his line of vision. 'I thought ... I thought you were ...'

'Scram,' Coomsah says to Miss Driscoll's young man. 'Go on, before I change my mind and have you arrested.'

He takes off, clattering down the stairs, hauls open the front door and lets it slam behind him. The whole house shakes. From above in response there's the sound of hesitant steps on the stair, the tread of an old man. He appears, spindly, gripping the bannister with a bony hand.

'May I help you, Madame?' he asks, giving Coomsah a disparaging look. 'Have you business here?'

She has no business here, that's a fact. But she has no voice either now, not even the kitten's yowl.

'Missus?' Coomsah says to her.

She feels like one of the small, foolish characters in one of G's stories. And Miss Driscoll's young man seems like another. Even dear dependable Coomsah could have come from G's fervid imagination. She has finally entered *Dubliners*. Isn't that what she wanted? And now her instinct is to escape.

She leans on Coomsah's arm and they make a stately retreat, leaving Mary Driscoll's doddery boss standing perplexed on the stair. She can feel fright setting in now, and tears are threatening. What on earth was she thinking?

Coomsah opens the front door and they step outside. He hurries to open the door of the cab. She sinks gratefully into the cab's upholstery, her breath coming in quick spurts. She can still smell the man off her. Rank as the river.

Coomsah moves out of sight and she can hear him sweet-talking to the horse.

He'll let her recover but he's in a right temper now. It's not his job to be rescuing his fares from altercation, more than his job's worth. He could have told her she was courting danger, whatever the blazes she was up to. The way she bowled into Mulligan's ... doesn't know what's good for her. Now, she's got her comeuppance. But all the same, Teddy can't help feeling sorry for her.

The rain has stopped and the eggshell sky has cleared. Sun is breaking through the heavy cloud. After a few minutes, when her breathing has returned to regulation, Teddy leans in, about to lay down the law. He will have no hand, act or part of this escapade any longer.

But she gets there first.

'Take me home,' she says.

She's had enough. Enough of this unlovely, uncherished city. Enough of the past and its ghosts, enough of the dead, and the not-so-dead. She shakes her head.

Coomsah looks at her pityingly; she can't bear it.

'The Gresham, if you please.'

Let him not be there. That's what she prays as Coomsah drives her back to the hotel. Imagine, wishing away her beloved husband! But her prayers go unanswered. When they arrive at the Gresham, G *is* there. Waiting for her. Although you couldn't describe what he was doing as waiting, for that would suggest a passive occupation. What G was doing was prowling, up and down the pavement outside the hotel, gesticulating with the *portiere*, finger-wagging, spectacles probably misting with indignation. Unlike earlier, there is a row of cabs stationed directly outside the hotel, so Coomsah draws into the island in the middle of the street. She wants nothing more than to rap on the roof of the cab and command Coomsah to drive on. But she knows she has to face the music.

She sees G halt in his pantomime and peer short-sightedly as Coomsah opens the door of the cab for her. She steps down, her furled umbrella hooked over her arm. Be composed, she tells herself. A tram trundles by and obliterates her view of G standing on the pavement opposite. She rummages through her velvet wrist purse but the wretched umbrella impedes her, and she has only managed to get the drawstrings open by the time the tram has passed and G is upon her.

'What are you doing?' he says.

Foostering, he calls this; he is full of such strange words.

'How much?' he barks at Coomsah.

When Coomsah states the fare, he says, incredulous: 'How much?'

Coomsah is frowning at Amalia as if she has accused him of cheating. She tries to say with her features – for how could she begin to articulate this in English? – that she is sorry for this scene, that it is not his fault, but the fault of an impatient husband who is angry with her, and with the world. But her face is not agile enough and Coomsah grumbles to himself as G counts out the shillings from his own pocket and thrusts the money bad-temperedly into his hand.

'Now, scram!' he says.

Scram? This man has defended her honour. But, of course, G doesn't know that, does he? And how could she explain?

Impossible.

Coomsah heaves himself aboard heavily and clucks at the horse. Amalia feels her only ally deserting her. She has this odd sensation, as if she's been away on a very long journey to a far-off place with Coomsah. His bulky fortitude seems more familiar to her now, more beloved almost, than her new husband, so long fought for. *Stay,* she wants to say to Coomsah, *be a witness, an umpire, defend me again.*

But she has exhausted the poor man's patience with her strange requests, her refusal to take his fatherly advice, her encounter in Usher's Island. An irate husband is the final straw.

He is pulling away and leaving her.

She is on her own.

G steers her roughly from the island, back across the street holding up his hand to the traffic as they scurry raggedly, coming to a halt under the hotel's portico. The *portiere* is standing there, eyes averted. He doesn't want to get involved and who would blame him? G has clearly been berating him – another person, like Coomsah, bearing the brunt of Amalia's transgression.

'Where the hell have you been?' G snarls at her.

There is no hint of concern, no worry – G's gone past that. His eyes are popping behind his spectacles, accusing, old betrayal reflected in them.

She feels her face flush.

Caught! And she has nothing prepared, no story for him.

'The maid told me you went out hours ago,' he says.

'Jasmine?' She sees in her mind's eye the stout, fair girl feeding the fire.

'What?'

'Jasmine, the maid,' she says. 'She told me that was her name.'

'For pity's sake, Mali, don't be ridiculous,' he says, 'no maid in this country is called Jasmine.'

She feels the loss of the name; in her mind, the girl will forever be Jasmine.

'Shall we go inside?' she says, eyeing the *portiere*.

The street is busier than earlier and if there's to be a marital argument, she'd prefer for it not to happen here with an audience. G catches her arm and pulls her into the dangerous swirl of the revolving door.

Careful, she wants to say, *I am with* …

'I asked her her name and she told me it was Jasmine,' she says as they are delivered into the hotel's lobby. Why is she even bothering with this?

'Oh Mali,' he says, softening and she thinks maybe she has diverted his anger. 'She was saying "Yes Ma'am".'

Yessum. Jasmine.

O Dio! It's always the same. When she doesn't pick up every word in English, her imagination supplies her with the most poetic alternative. If things were different, G would turn this into a mocking joke at her expense. But he's not in the mood for humour now.

'Where the blazes have you been?' he hisses at her, eyes narrowing, and she thinks of Miss Driscoll's young man and his rage and what he might have done to her had Coomsah not intervened. But no, she cannot tell G; she won't. But she has to offer him something.

'I have been to see a doctor,' she says.

The words were not planned, they just came out.

They stop him in his tracks. She knows how dangerous this game is. And how it's bad luck to speak a baby into being before you're sure. But these are just silly superstitions she doesn't believe in. And if she doesn't believe in them, how can they hurt her? Anyway, if she's to keep her secret safe, she must resort to guile.

'Are you sick?' he asks.

Worry is back now, a thin covering on his irritation.

'What's wrong with you? You never said anything this morning, did it come upon you sudden?'

He doesn't believe her, she thinks, suspects it as a ruse. And it is, but true as well. How can it be both? But it is.

'I have news ...' she begins.

'What?' Irritation is back.

They are standing in the middle of the echoey, palmy lobby. A pair of elderly ladies with black hats, the nets like spiders' webs on their faces, sit at a low occasional table nearby, sipping tea.

'You know,' she says, 'news.'

He's told her himself that this is how pregnancy is announced when discretion is called for. But maybe she has not remembered the expression correctly.

'What is it, spit it out,' he says.

'I am expecting …'

'Expecting what?'

O Dio, this is too much.

'I am waiting, no, *aspetto* …'

'Waiting for what?'

'*Aspetto un bambino*,' she says baldly.

Still he looks at her blankly. Has his Italian suddenly deserted him?

'Expecting,' she says. 'Pregnant.' The ugly word seems to bounce off the walls. The two old ladies lean in, she swears they do.

'What?' he demands.

O Dio, how many ways are there to say this?

'I am with the child,' she says.

He has been bending over her like a chastising father and now he steps back.

'And this is how you tell me,' he says, raising his voice, 'shouting it out in the middle of a hotel vestibule for all the world to hear?'

It is her turn to be enraged. What is wrong with him?

'I was trying to be discreet. It was you who made me shout …'

He moves in close again and grips her by the waist this time and pilots her towards the stairs, out of earshot of the elderly listeners.

'Aren't you pleased?' she asks.

He steps away as if she has some infectious disease.

'And what are we going to do now?' he asks. 'How are we going to manage? Exiles in Zurich with a baby on the way and no money coming in … and the world …' He throws up his hands.

She understands! He is talking as a poor man. As if he is still with Nora Barnacle with only his teaching lessons

288

to support them both. At least with Nora, he once said approvingly, there were no babies. She was adept, he told Amalia. Nora had womanly tricks to avoid just this situation. Did he expect the same of her? Is that what's wrong? Has she failed him again?

'But it's a joyous thing, is it not?'

'It's a burden,' he says.

'A burden?'

'We can't afford it. You'll end up having it in the pauper's ward.'

Has he forgotten her father? Papa will join them in Zurigo as soon as he has wound up his business affairs in Trieste and Mother has packed up the Villa Alice. Her precious Papa who will never see his darling daughter in distress. She has never had cause to doubt *him*.

'We will have a midwife and a doctor at home,' she says firmly, and the image that comes to her is her bedroom on Via Alice. 'In our home in Zurigo. We will not be living on the side of the street.'

Papa will see to that, she wants to say, but doesn't. She knows that will only enrage him further. She thinks of Mary Driscoll's young man – the same fury. Are all Irishmen in the grip of such choler? She has seen more raw and angry life in a week in Dublino than in her entire experience up to this and she finds she doesn't like it. She wants calm. But will there ever be calm with G?

'You are a renowned tenor,' she says, 'we will have no need of charity.'

When he was a writer, he was proud of his capacity to scrounge, to beg and borrow, but now he wants to be independently wealthy. *I want to make pot-loads, like McCormack*, he's told her. *To show everyone*. As if that was his *raison d'etre*. To show them, whoever *they* are. It's never her, never Amalia he's trying to impress. It is as if he has nothing to show her.

'Let's go to our room,' she implores.

She wants to make it up to him. She longs to take off her boots; her arches are aching as if she has walked for several miles.

'You go,' he says, surly now. 'I have a dress rehearsal in the Concert Rooms, I'm already late as it is.'

'Aren't you happy?' she says, but he doesn't answer. Instead he strides off across the lobby towards the street. The revolving door embraces him, leaving her bereft.

The scene in the Piazza Grande comes back to her again, the start of all this. His fingers on her pulse, her hand on his heart, his words.

You understand. That's what he said.

But was it a statement or a question?

Either way Amalia doesn't understand, and she doubts that she ever will.

Encore

The end when it comes, comes down the stairs of the Concert Rooms in the shape of a lady bearing a huge bouquet
of flowers, red roses and that delicate flower with the
gypsy name she can never remember. Behind her there
are two gents. All three pause at the foot of the stairs and
wait. One of the men is plump and balding with a stately
paunch and a pair of whiskers that'd take your eye out.
The other, an elderly gent in a mustardy suit, holds his
hat in front of his privates. The next thing she sees is the
golden dazzle of the dying sun outside flashing on a pair
of spectacles. She doesn't actually see their owner, but she
knows it's him, no mistaking.

Aha, says the man in the mustardy suit, as the vision
becomes a man in swallowtails, making his way lightly
down the stairs. When he reaches the bottom he leans in
towards the lady and whispers something in her ear, so
Norah cannot rightly see his face, but she doesn't need to.
She knows the set of him; oh she knows that.

He hasn't seen her. Not yet. It's the lady, suited in midnight blue with a peacock-blue hat swathed in chiffon,
who's the first to notice her. She gently tugs his sleeve with

291

her free hand. Finally, he turns to face Norah. She's right in his line of vision, his poor afflicted vision. But he's too far away to see her properly, she knows that much.

Jim, she calls out.

How long is it since she's uttered his name aloud?

He may not be able to make out her face, but he hears her. He immediately unlinks the peacock-hatted woman. Behind them, the hubbub of chat between the other two – something about tickets and dinner – peters out. He's peering at her now.

Nora? he says eventually.

The lady, who's really no more than a girl, is looking at her with serious intent. Looking at her like a wife, Norah thinks.

Nora? The way he says it she knows he doesn't see the haitch at the end. Never did.

He moves away from the party and into the centre of the foyer. She takes him in. He's filled out, not as lanky as he used to be. She notes the watered-silk facings of his jacket, the white dicky bow, the sprig of woodbine in his buttonhole. She checks his footwear – black dress shoes, thank God. And are they mother-of-pearl cufflinks? In one hand he brandishes a cane. *Holy God, is his sight gone that bad?* But no, he's not holding it like a blind man would; that's just for show. Over his other arm, a brown mac falls in a dead faint. Must be expecting rain.

Is it really you?

He steps closer to her. Gingerly. Spectacle-enlarged eyes, still bluest of blue, with the far off look.

Who else? she says.

Now that I hear your voice, he says, I know it is.

She goes to stand, forgetting for a moment that she needs the ruddy stick to be upright, and she has to reverse.

What are you doing here? he demands.

She bridles.

I'm waiting for you.

He can scarcely believe it. Nora Barnacle, sitting right here in front of him. True, he'd gone looking for her, but he never believed he'd actually find her. Or she him. Running Finn's, he'd heard, though he didn't believe that either. As he'd stood at the reception desk and pipped the bell, he knew it must be a false rumour; sure Nora couldn't abide the place. By the time the little lame maid arrived and eyed him doubtfully, he thought no, no this isn't where Nora is and even if it was, he couldn't face her just now, not with all his other troubles. On the spur of the moment he made up that ridiculous request about viewing the maids' quarters, anything to buy him time. That sent the maid into a terrible skitter. As soon as she'd hobbled off, he'd left the card and turned tail. But he had left the card.

Behind him, his party is still stalled. The foyer is deserted. Good. He'd waited in the green room purposely until even the stragglers would be gone, so that he wouldn't be accosted. He won't be able to relax properly till he sees the Saturday pink. He remembers, with a pang, that awful wobble on the Alfredo.

Nora, he repeats. Like a new word in a foreign language.

How strange to utter her name again, though he'd spent years with it on the tip of his tongue. In the early days in Fiume, he'd follow women on the street whenever he saw a battered hat, or a certain kind of stride, thinking, *finally she's here*, and not caring about the hows and whys of it, only to discover … no, he was mistaken. It happened so often, it made him think she must be dead, the way his mind was intent on conjuring her up, as if she'd become a shade. Used to happen shortly after his mother had died; he'd get visions of her in every harried woman he saw.

But he's not mistaken now.

Jim, she says.

She looks prosperous, almost well-heeled. A far cry from the bedraggled creature he left behind at the Süd-bahnhof, wearing his gaberdine coat. He didn't need it then, but by God, that winter in Fiume he fairly froze without it. A shiver runs through him at the memory. She's wearing a suit of some grey material, with a lilac blouse showing underneath; he always loved that colour on her. Her hair seems tamer than he remembers, held down by a matching hat. Something about her looks different. What is it? She's older, well aren't we all, he thinks. Older than Mali, is that it? But there's something else. Some rounded motherly look, and her free hand, the ungloved one, is leaning on a stick. What's the stick all about?

What happened to you?

I fell, she begins.

No, I mean ...

Oh, she sees. He's not talking about now.

Time seems to shimmer and falter. She's back on the park bench outside the station and he's stepped out of some leafy dream. As if on cue, a train in Westland Row lets out a tromboney burp. Fingers of wan, sun-deserted light edge in through the high-built windows. Nearly the longest day of the year.

What happened to *you*? You didn't come back.

But, he says all reasonable-like, you didn't wait.

I waited, she says evenly.

Is that all you can say, she berates herself, you're like a cringey dog tied to a post. How many times had she rehearsed this moment? In her version, she did all the talking. *How could you have abandoned me where I didn't know a soul, left me to fend for myself, penniless, if you'd wanted to ditch me couldn't you have just said it, instead of traipsing half-way across the world and then doing it? And after you'd had your way, you selfish article!*

You did *not* wait, Nora.

She feels a tide of fury rising. She wants to tell him to stop using her name like that. It belongs to her now. Nora with a haitch. But instead, all his other names for her come back to her in a rush: his empress, his queen of the night, his love. And saltier ones, his cunty Kate.

You did not wait, he says again.

They're like a pair of squabbling children. *I did, you didn't.*

What was I supposed to do? Wait forever?

The hurt and aggrievement of years bubbles to the surface. She's reduced to being that useless twenty-year-old girl, heart in her mouth. But she is no longer that girl, thanks to him.

He pounces. So you admit you didn't wait.

What is this, the ruddy High Court?

The point is, where did *you* go?

He sighs deeply and she thinks, *oh am I wearying you, is it too much of an effort to explain.*

I got way-laid.

The drunkard's excuse.

What do you mean, way-laid?

His party has moved from the foot of the stairs, creep-ing silently in behind him. The willowy girl with her Roman nose, her thin serious face now quizzical, the two gents flanking her either side, and the bouquet.

Jim slides a finger between neck and collar. *Barb itch, is it? Or is he getting hot and bothered? Too good for him!*

I was in the Piazza Grande on my way to the Berlitz and there were these three sailors, Navy fellas, having a row with a ...

He stops and looks around to see if his wife is listening.

Are you joking me? She's hanging on every word.

With a ...

A hoor, I suppose. Holy God could you not come up with something better than that?

He's hoping Mali hasn't heard that; he's never mentioned that detail.

Well, yes ... he says, squeamish all of a sudden.

The little wife looks a bit taken aback – news to her, I suppose.

And I stepped in ...

The two gents behind Jim exchange looks.

And then the police came along and we were all marched off to the *questura* where they thought I was a deserter.

Well you were, weren't you?

No, Nora, an *army* deserter, he says, mock-patient.

She remembers this. Oh yes. All hoity-toity, full of himself.

Did you not tell them about me?

I tried, but they wouldn't hear a bar of it. They put me in the cells, thought I was involved in some way when I was only trying to be the good Samaritan.

And when you were let out, you thought you'd just walk away, is that it? Glad to be shut of this nuisance girl you wouldn't marry?

No, *never*! He says it so vehemently she almost believes him. In all these years, I've never ...

Never what?

And what about all *my* years, she wants to say. The panic at the railway station, the mortification of how

Hector had found her, accused of being a criminal on the run, the awful unmooring of those first few nights in Trieste when she still believed he might return for her, and the long dark months of servitude when she was relegated to being a skivvy again

You seem to have landed on your feet, she says.

Jim suddenly becomes aware of the audience. He turns towards the peering trio behind him.

This is my wife, he says, and the peacock girl nods stiffly.

Norah feels a douse of desolation, her suspicions confirmed.

Why? she asks and it comes out plaintive.

Why did I marry?

No! *Though it's a good question, when I had to depend on a curtain ring.* Why didn't you come back for me?

I did come back. But it was nearly midnight. I was frantic when you weren't there. So I waited for you all night. Slept on that bench until dawn when the station opened.

Amalia feels a sickening smart of recognition. Is that *our* park he's talking about?

The station master told me that yes, there had been a mishap involving a woman, but that she'd been taken away by a gentleman who had got on a train …

No, Norah says.

What do you mean no?

A gentleman who came *off* a train. I got on no train.

Amalia thinks, I owe my marriage to the difference between *prendere* and *scendere*.

But you're not denying there was a gentleman …

He's getting riled now and she wants her turn.

So *you* just gave up? she counters

What else could I do? I couldn't go back to the police, hadn't I only been let out of custody? They were already suspicious of me. And what would they make of me if I went back and told them my wife had just deserted me, gone off on a train ...

The girl shoots him a glance that reads *I am your wife.*

I did not go off on any train, Norah says between gritted teeth.

Anyway, he says, why would I go looking for someone who'd deserted me?

And what about me? – it comes out as a wail – I could have ended up on the streets.

But you didn't, obviously.

No obvious about it.

Did you not see the ad in the paper?

What ad?

And Norah can't say for she never saw it either, even after all those sessions with Mister Precious.

Did you not go to the Berlitz school? If you had, you'd have known that I went looking for you there.

He shook his head, side to side.

I hadn't the heart after ...

So what did you do?

I went to Santa Maria Maggiore ... He laughs to himself.

What?

The Jesuit church in Trieste. I knocked on their door and threw myself on their mercy ...

You? The man who's allergic to nuns?

Despite herself, she feels all the old easy familiarities return.

I know, but once a Jesuit boy ... He smiles ruefully.

Any port in a storm, I suppose.

She remembers this about him, his knack of getting out of a fix, particularly where money was concerned.

They set me up with a job teaching in the naval academy in Fiume.

Fuming? *Is this the place Gogarty talked about?*

An hour or two south, he explains.

While I waited in Trieste. Waited and waited …

But I didn't know that, did I?

His eyes narrow behind his glasses. Anyway, *you* went off with a man. Even if you didn't get on a train.

He folds his arms like a constable.

Was that a prior arrangement? Or did you just let him pick you up?

How dare you!

She'd give him a slap on the kisser for that, if she were standing up. She remembers their courtship when their fights would turn from fists to lovey-dovey palms on cheeks. The strangeness of him stays her hand, but the familiar of him nearly chokes her. Those hands, those eyes, his slender hips and the sit of his hair, the angry flare of his spectacles. She feels herself weakening.

The plump bald man steps forward but Jim swats him away. She tries to raise herself up but she can't, so she's stuck looking up at him.

So where did you go? he asks.

Oh, so now you care? A kind man, a proper good Samaritan, took me in.

Where? In Trieste?

Yes, I was there for a year and a half and there was still no sign of you. I used to go back to that little park by the station as well. Juicy took me.

Juicy?

My friend. She falters on the word.

Your gentleman friend, is it?

No, Juicy was like a sister to me when I had nobody …

Nora, he says and hunkers down like a man making a proposal. He stretches out his hand but she waves it away. What would a touch do to her, turn her to jelly, no thank you very much. And yet, she longs to reach out and touch him. To stroke his cheek or push back that stray lock of his hair. If she touched him, all the difficulty would melt away. Every row they ever had ended in touching, the other sort. Reach out, she urges herself, but she can't and the moment's gone. A touch can't dispense with a wife, can it?

He gets the message. He straightens and slides his hand back in his pocket.

So this is her, Amalia thinks, the great Nora Barnacle. A woman on a stick.

What can I say? he says, and Norah knows then there's nothing to be said but she cannot let it go.

Say nothing, Amalia urges silently. *How could G have loved this, a plain-looking creature, dumpy, provincial.*

And who have we here? It's the elderly gent with a twinkly eye and drink on his breath, who steps up to stand with Jim. Must be stone deaf for he doesn't seem to have been following what's going on.

A deorum to celebrate? Aha! He pumps Jim on the arm.

Pappie, Jim begins.

So this is the old man! Beery old face on him, big red nose.

But the old man doesn't wait for an answer.

What do you say, Amelia? he says turning to the girl-wife. Told you it'd be a triumph!

The bouquet in her arms rustles and some petals fall to the floor.

Were you at the concert, Madame, he says to Norah, mistaking her for a signature hunter.

No, she says.

You missed a treat, so, he says.

Oh please, just go!

Andy-amo, Wifey says.

Oh, so she's Italian!

Pappie's hopping from foot to foot as if he needs to go. Then rubbing his hands together as if he's clinched a deal. Aha!

But Jim's looking at her, and he's wanting rid of them. This she knows. She can read him, even after all these years.

Pappie, he says, take Mali and I'll follow you. I'll be with you when I've dealt with this.

Deal is it, like I'm a hand of poker?

No, Wifey says.

Now there's two of us saying no.

Nora, he pleads. What on earth does he expect her to do?

This is Nora? Pappie says, incredulous, squinting at her.

Oh God, how many more people are going to stick their oar in? All she wants is a minute alone with him. Is that too much to ask?

And now here comes the commissioner, rattling his bangle of keys.

Time please now, ladies and gents. Mister Boylan, Sir, we really do have to lock up now. Can you get your artist to ...

What happened to the writing? she asks suddenly, so suddenly it's a surprise to herself.

What? Jim's brow clouds behind the specs.

The writing, she repeats. *Your* writing.

He shakes his head dejectedly.

Oh love, what's happened to you? Abandoning what's most precious to you.

Why did you give up?

Excuse me, Madame, Signor Joyce is a renowned tenor and opera singer, Wifey pipes up.

Who stepped on her hem?

Look Missus, she wants to say, the singing was my idea. But he wouldn't do it for me. Like he wouldn't marry me neither.

Yes, gave it up, he says, and he unhooks his spectacles and takes a hanky from his breast pocket and wipes the lenses.

That's a shame, she says, and in that moment she means it, even if she never understood a word he wrote. Is it this highfalutin girl who's responsible for that? Did *she* make him give it up? No money in it and that's for sure.

Giacomo, Wifey tries again and catches Jim's arm.

Oh really, stop all that nonsense, his name is Jim!

But the foreign name seems to hold him under a spell. Norah feels him slipping away from her now and it can't end like this, not for a second time with so much left to be said. She feels an old panic rising, of being left once more.

Madame! she says to the little wife. It comes out shrill, the voice she uses in Finn's. Please leave us be.

Pappie, Boylan and Wifey each take a step back. The commissioner who has retreated to his position by the door jangles his keys again.

Come on now, folks, Mister Boylan says, else we'll be locked in.

Giacomo, Wifey calls sweetly.

He's mine, Amalia wants to shout at Nora, *I stayed faithful to him. For three whole years in Firenze. Even when Michele Risolo was pursuing me and I was trying to fend him off, even though I was sorely tempted ... Another thing G doesn't know.*

It's as if G is in a trance. The pair of them caught in some kind of eye-lock. Well, she won't stand and watch.

Pappie, she says brightly, falsely, the first time she has called Signor Joyce such and it nearly sticks in her throat but he's the closest on hand to a Papa. She lands the bouquet in Signor Boylan's arms, then links Pappie's arm. She steers him towards the exit. He keeps on twisting around to peer at Nora, as if he really wants to stay. Boylan beetles after them, hat in hand, a flower bed on legs. Jim turns to look after them.

She can see that he is caught, the guilty way he looks at the girl. But she's not having any of it.

Oh that's right, don't mind me ...

He turns back to her.

Give me your time, she says, you owe me that.

I owe *you*?

You left me with nothing.

You had your fancy man, he sneers.

He was not my fancy man! *Not then anyway.*

Jim's party has reached the doors now, Wifey still calling softly but hesitantly: Giacomo, Giacomo, like the bloody Pied Piper.

I waited for you.

For the first time he looks at her squarely. Sees her.

And I stayed true to you, he says.

Something hard inside her collapses and swims up into her gullet.

Will you sit beside me?

He hoiks up his tails and complies. He places the mac on the other side of him and props his cane up against the pew.

Look at us, he says. The blind and the halt.

He smiles. Like the sun coming up, that smile. She'd forgotten about it.

He grasps her hand which is lost in the wrinkles of her dress and looks to check on Wifey but her back is turned and the party is too far away to see. She and Jim sit, side by side, staring ahead, like strangers waiting for a train.

This is like something from one of your stories, she says.

You never read my stories.

But you talked about them, all those unhappy people who couldn't be plain with one another.

He looks at her sidelong, a stricken look on his face. What has she said?

I lost my writing too.

The bag with his papers, the one she left out on the street, with all the writing inside. *Oh Sweet Divine, is that why he gave up?*

I'm sorry, but I was that mad with you.

I had to start all over again, he says.

Is she to blame for that as well? So did I, she wants to say, but he's talking about his precious writing not his life.

So what happened?

It all went up in flames, he says, and she knows by the downward set of his mouth that he'll be saying no more about that.

So not her fault then. She changes tack. She no longer wants explanations for they solve nothing. She wants times and dates.

And how long were you in Fuming?

Stuck it for three years, he says.

At least, we weren't in the one place and still missing one another.

I couldn't have stayed in Trieste without you. All our plans ... he says.

Our, first time he's uttered it. *Our.*

But you came back, didn't you?

He colours, she swears it, he blushes.

How did you know?

Your card, she says.

He smiles at her, his heartbreaking smile, then looks shamefaced. As if he's been caught out in a lie.

For the girl, was it?

He doesn't answer.

It's not too late, Jim, for us. She's pleading now, something she swore she wouldn't do.

I have a wife, in case you haven't noticed. A new wife. We're on our honeymoon, as a matter of fact.

And what about your old wife?

We never ...

If she still had the curtain ring, she'd flourish it in front of him. But one of her first purchases when she returned to Dublin was a proper gold wedding band to make Hector official. The sharp-eyed would spot the ridge of it under her glove.

I have as much a claim on you as the blushing bride.

How many pieces would you like to carve me up in?

If it were up to me, I wouldn't settle for just a portion of you.

They can both see the commissioner holding the door for the Joyce party, his arm like a wedding arch while Wifey, Pappie, the impresario and the bunch of flowers pass underneath it. The faint hum of a summer's night drifts in. The door closes.

Is that right, now? he says, a bitter smirk on his face.

She can hear it in his voice, the sleeve of his interest unravelling and the draw of the other who has replaced her.

It's impossible, Nora.

In his mouth, she sounds like her old self.

What's impossible about it? You came looking for me. Why did you do that? Unless you wanted something …

I, he begins. I …

He thinks of the baby, a thorn in his side. And Amalia and Zurich and the singing, the architecture of his life all changed since he last saw Nora.

It isn't that simple.

Isn't it?

Ah grow up, Nora, we've missed the boat.

Grow up, is it? Grow up? *I have grown up, isn't that the problem?*

She drops his hand. Time has turned malignant between them.

She should go. She looks toward the doors and sees Mister Coombs, as if on command, standing by the main door. She hadn't told him to wait but he must have all the same. He's a downright gent, there's no doubt about it, and here he is, come to get her, his greatcoat stretched across his barrel chest.

He sidles up, inserting himself into the company. He's delicate on his feet for such a big man.

Mrs Smith? He bends down to help her up.

Mrs Smith? Jim repeats as he also rises.

Yes, she says, Mrs Smith. *Two can play at that game.*

Is that your knight in shining armour?

Yes, she says simply.

You married him?

Did you expect me to wait forever, is that it?

Oh, no, he says, not you. I expected nothing from you but what I got. Betrayal.

Now, Sir, Mister Coombs begins. *Well, look at who we have here! How many women is this fella stringing along?* He's

306

just seen the foreign lady from yesterday outside on the steps. And now here's her blackguard husband. Yer man doesn't recognize him, that type never do. Just as well. Coombs wants no further truck with him. A scoundrel, no better than the ruffian who assaulted his wife on Ussher's Quay. The sooner he gets poor Mrs Smith away from him, the better. He leans over and, catching Norah's free elbow, raises her up to standing.

Rich coming from you, Norah says, as she grips Coombs's arm. For the second time in the encounter, she's on the same level with him. His eyes are mean behind glass.

Come, Mrs Smith, Coombs says.

They begin their hobbled passage. She can feel Jim's eyes boring into her back.

Mrs Smith, is it, he calls after her. Really?

She halts, places a staying hand on Coombs's arm and turns.

Mrs Hector Smith, if you must know, who is twice the man you'll ever be!

Produce him, so!

Has she to prove everything to him? And even so, he would not believe.

I thought as much, Jim calls after her. Made him up, I'd say.

Isn't that more your department? she says. Come on, Mister Coombs, get me out of here.

Or have you killed him off, like the others?

The memory of Sonny Bodkin pierces her heart.

She tries to halt and turn but her eyes are awash and her bottom lip won't stop jibbering.

Mrs Smith, Coombs repeats. He places a large hand on the small of her back, squiring her expertly, not letting her turn around. Used to unruly mares she thinks, but no, aren't all those cab horses castrated? Nevertheless, she leans. The acreage of floor to the door seems to yawn. She can't remember it taking so long when she came in and she has help now. She and Coombs, like father and daughter. Just like her Pappie would do if he were here. Who am I codding? If Pappie were here, he'd have given Jim a dig in the snitch.

The commissioner hurries after them. Coombs helps her outside and she labours down the short flight of steps to the street. A little further on is Jim's party, huddled by the railings, like witnesses to a street accident, Wifey eclipsed by an enormous flourish of roses. Just like when she and Jim left on the mail boat all those years ago, a crowd for him, no one for her.

All over now, she wants to shout at them. Nothing to see.

Coombs sprints ahead to open the door of the cab. The horse harrumphs, strikes its hoof on the ground, like the *thwock* of a judge's gavel.

Is it really all over? Is that it? If she could only run back inside. Tell him the truth of the matter, her truth of *them* apart, the long hard grief of it. The not knowing of it. But she can't run anywhere with this blinking foot which throbs worse than an aching heart.

Anyway, what would be the use? There's no cure for the silliness of what broke them apart, is there? A row on the street with a hoor. The difference between getting on and getting off a train. Stupid words. They'd been separated for nothing. And when they had a chance to make amends, they'd wasted their time spitting at one another like fishwives. He, at least, got to parade his new young wife. A wife in the flesh speaks volumes. But she never got the chance to tell him about her Georgie, who's with his aunt Nellie tonight. George Italo Smith. From the night of the fire when she threw caution and the dodge to the winds.

Mrs Smith? Coombs is back.

She squares up.

I can do this alone, thank you, Mister Coombs.

Because this time she's the one going. She makes for the coffiny opening of the cab door. She knows Jim is still watching.

What's he waiting for? To see her go, to see the back of her.

Very well so, if you're sure, Ma'am.

Yes, she says, though Coombs can't hear her. I am, yes.

He stands, scalding with shame, at the top of the steps, the doors clattering shut behind him and watches as she clambers painstakingly into the back of the cab and settles herself. Coombs whooshes himself up and gets the nag going. Slowly, at funeral pace, her face passes in front of him. He can't see the details of it, his wretched eyesight, but he doesn't need to. That face is enshrined – an icon, the face of Veronica – there's no removing it. Nor the boulder in his throat.

He can't let her go like this. He'll chase after the carriage on foot, he'll call after her, Nora, Nora, Nora.

Giacomo! Amalia waves at him, her voice carrying on the street while his own stutters into silence. It's a kind of answer. He has two more days in Dublin, two days before he can leave this desolate city and never return. There's nothing here but the ruins of love. He trains his eyes on Norah and follows her all the way down the street until the cab swerves right onto Westland Row.

As she passes, Norah recognizes the hopelessness in Jim's blind, bleating gaze. But she refuses to look back. She can feel the thin thread of longing unspool between them. As if they had never met, as if they have yet to meet, as if the next time it will be different. All the bad luck and bad-mouthing in the world can't undo it, neither new wives nor darling sons. In spite of all that, it'll just run and run. Nothing can break it now.

Acknowledgements

Although this is a speculative work, I did a great deal of research about the real lives of Nora Barnacle, James Joyce and their circle, in order to depart from them. I am indebted to the scholarship of the following books.

- *Nora: A Biography of Nora Joyce* by Brenda Maddox
- *Nora Barnacle Joyce: A Portrait* by Padraic O Laoi
- *James Joyce* by Richard Ellmann
- *The Years of Bloom: James Joyce in Trieste 1904-1920* by John McCourt
- *Memoir of Italo Svevo* by Livia Veneziani Svevo (translated from the Italian by Isabel Quigly)
- *James Joyce and Italo Svevo: The Story of a Friendship* by Stanley Price
- *Italo Svevo: A Double Life* by John Gatt-Rutter
- *This England is So Different: Italo Svevo's London Writings* edited, translated and interpreted by John Gatt-Rutter and Brian Moloney

To my first readers – Colbert Kearney, Joanne Carroll, Valerie Coogan, Tadhg Coakley, Margaret Mulvihill, Loredana Salis, Terence Killeen, Orla Murphy and Douglas Kinch – a big thank you. And, finally, much gratitude to Eimear Ryan and Laura Cassidy of Banshee Press, for taking this book to their hearts and giving it its day in the sun.

BANSHEE
PRESS

Banshee Press was founded by writers Laura Cassidy,
Claire Hennessy and Eimear Ryan. Since 2015, *Banshee*
literary journal has published twice a year. The Banshee
Press publishing imprint launched in 2019. Titles include
Paris Syndrome by Lucy Sweeney Byrne, *Gold Light Shining*
by Bebe Ashley, *I Want to Know That I Will Be Okay* by Deir-
dre Sullivan, *In Her Jaws* by Rosamund Taylor, *Pacemaker*
by David Toms and *Let the Dead* by Dylan Brennan.

WWW.BANSHEELIT.COM